Skyscraper of a Man

A Novel

Michael Bowe

Villa Campanile Press
Vashon, WA

for Myrna, my brightest moment

4 | Michael Bowe

1.

Before skyscrapers, only gods and angels inhabited the limitless sky, wayfarers of the heavenly plain, lingering on soft, fluffy clouds, enjoying unrivaled views of earth. Who could resist such nobility for neighbors?

Few can truly relate, but most would judge my circumstances at college and the decade that followed as quite fortunate. I know I do. While some accomplish great things, others like myself, simply manage to be in the right place at the right time as momentous events occur, members of a fellowship that I call The Coattails Club. It is, after all, an inevitable aspect of human history—a talented, inspired few will live noteworthy lives while a fortunate few will bear witness. And for any writer, again like myself, there is no role more fortuitous than that of witness.

Consider the cases of Tom Williams and Glen Foster, card-carrying club members and grand monarchs of their local chapters. In 1927 and 1928, Tom was a batboy for the New York Yankees; two stellar seasons that featured the legendary play of Gehrig and Ruth and culminated with World Series wins. From the top step of the dugout, young Tom watched the great ones at the plate, patiently wait for their pitch, mercilessly drive it over the outfield wall, and triumphantly trot the bases while Yankee fans cheered. Tom could relate.

In the early sixties, Glen was a secret service agent assigned to President Kennedy. From his position in the wings, Glen watched as the president challenged his countrymen to reaffirm their heritage by supporting civil rights and committing to space travel. Inspired by his youthful energy and eloquence, Americans experienced a rebirth of their optimism, wholeheartedly believing blacks would ride alongside whites on buses in The South, and that we, as a nation, could ride to the moon. Then sadly, Glen walked beside white horses, a caisson, and a flag covered casket as a devastated nation buried its fallen leader. Glen could also relate.

Membership in The Coattails Club was achieved whenever an average person secured an onlooker's role in a world-class production in some theater of human endeavor. In my case, my membership was secured via my association with my longtime friend and business partner, Benjamin Matthews. From the moment we met, I knew Ben was the most exceptional person I'd ever encounter; someone destined for a remarkable life, one of productivity, contribution, and renown. Ben would make his mark, no doubt about it. He would have a building or a bridge dedicated in his honor and his death would be noted in the Milestones section of *Time* magazine. I was as certain of that as I was certain I was average. I'd been bred for it.

I was born Peter David Dalton in 1958 and I grew up in suburban Delaware in the 1960s and 1970s, perfect conditioning for an insignificant life. True suburbanites worried about keeping up and fitting in but never about succeeding. Every family on our block had four or five children, a station wagon, a medium-size dog, a trampled lawn, and a house built to one of three models available, easy marks for contractors adding fireplaces and decks. Typically, when siding salesmen knocked on our front door in the spring of 1968, my father wrapped our house in aluminum—not to better protect the wood or insulate the walls—but simply because it was the thing to do.

On a warm April evening in our living room over pound cake and coffee, two salesmen from the Omega Siding & Gutter Company gave my parents a presentation about aluminum siding. On an easel beside the coffee table, the salesmen placed a large spiral booklet with humorous illustrations on each page. Taking turns, the two men talked about the benefits of siding: how it extended the life of wood, how it never required painting, and how its ease of maintenance simplified a man's life. They talked for almost an hour, but, in actuality, all they had to do to close the deal was read the list of our neighbors who were already under contract.

"Many of your neighbors have purchased complete installa-tions at our discounted spring rates," the portly, Oliver Hardy-like salesman told my father.

Unlike the muddling comedian, this guy knew how to sell. He understood his prospects; he knew suburbanites. This fast-talker knew how to quickly secure that all-important signature on the bottom line of the sales contract.

"Work will commence within the next thirty days at the Wilson's, the Reed's, the Campbell's, the Clark's, the Steins', and the Jenson's," he stated confidently, almost smugly, like he knew his work was done.

As the salesman recited the list, my father's eyes widened with each successive surname. Previously, he'd only nodded and added an occasional "hmmm," but Oliver Hardy had his attention now. My father would never allow our home to appear grimy or weathered or faded while other homes glistened. The thought of our neighbors washing their siding with sudsy water and a garden hose while we repainted every five to seven years was unacceptable. Sitting in quiet reflection, my father's face revealed serious contemplation and even quiet calculation. This was life-changing technology all right and, more importantly, suburban status changing technology.

"Where do I sign?" my father asked, apparently convinced by our neighbors, and not the salesmen, that aluminum siding was a necessity of suburban life.

Over the years, I noticed that families in each of the three styles of homes in our neighborhood shared common traits, almost as if the style of home was assigned, rather than chosen. The families in the "colonial" homes were the aristocrats of the neighborhood with substantial incomes, late model, luxury automobiles like Buicks and Oldsmobile, enviable vacations, and children in private schools. The families in the "ranch" homes were folks with modest wants and means, reliable during an emergency or snowstorm, made of sturdy stock like mid-westerners, and children who excelled in high school sports. The families in the "split-level" homes labored in the middle between the ranches and the colonials, quietly dysfunctional but noticeably muddled, with patchy, overgrown, dandelion-speckled yards and busted lawnmowers, old Chevrolets in the driveway, and children as riven as their homes with some reserved, some excelling, and some troublesome.

My family lived in a split-level home.

September 1991

Relaxed at his desk, his feet propped up, Ben Matthews stared out of the sliding glass doors that stretched the length of his office and opened to a balcony. Though small and modest relative to Ben's position and prominence in the community, what the office lacked in dimensions it made up for in presentation. The desk and credenza were a rich cherry wood that matched the built-in bookcase opposite the sliding doors. A black leather sofa, two matching chairs, and a cherry wood coffee table formed a small conversation area directly in front of the desk.

Upon entering the publisher's office, the first thing most visitors noticed were three framed, black and white *Cavanaugh Weekly* covers displayed behind Ben's desk. In the center was the premiere issue from May 1980. Flanking it, the November 1980 issue, which proposed an integrated light-rail and bus concept for Cavanaugh Public Transit, and the January 1984 issue, which proclaimed that Cavanaugh was "The City of the Future" and advocated a twenty-year horizon for city planning. Ben's contributions to those early issues served as the blueprint for city council policies throughout the 1980s and resulted in national acclaim.

When I entered, I found Ben staring out the windows.

"Do you ever do any work?" I jabbed. "It's amazing we've stayed in business all these years with this kind of leadership."

"Listen to you," Ben scoffed, "next, you'll be telling me how you've been carrying me all these years."

I sat in one of the black leather chairs before Ben's desk and braced for confrontation. In our decade plus of publishing, only a handful of controversial articles and one specific topic had produced heated disagreement between publisher and editor. When I told Ben that the topic was advertising space, his demeanor changed instantly to match mine.

Sounding fair warning, Ben declared, "You know my feelings on this topic, Pete. Do you really want to talk about ad space?"

I wasn't deterred.

"The sales guys tell me we can add seven to ten additional pages of ads to our next issue of *Cavanaugh Weekly*," I advised him. "They're having no difficulty attracting top quality ad clientele. Our sales manager told me, 'we've got heat.'"

That line of reasoning would go nowhere with Ben and I should have known better. In Ben's mind, hot trends and fashion, in general, are for people with inadequate self-images who are incapable of forming their own thoughts. Ben was absolutely unimpressed with the fact that *Cavanaugh Weekly* was hot and vehemently stated his position.

"I don't want *Cavanaugh Weekly* to become another fashion plate on the magazine rack—all style and no substance, like a swank, nouveau meal at a fad restaurant. There are plenty of magazines on the racks for people who just want to look at the advertisements. That's not the *CW* market and as far as I'm concerned *Cavanaugh Monthly* has already slid way too far into that genre. The *Weekly* is not going that same way, not on my watch. We've already expanded *CW's* ad pages well beyond my standard, and I've done that as a concession to you."

Ben loved *Cavanaugh Weekly*. The newspaper was the social tool he envisioned, the realization of his entrepreneurial dream, and the embodiment of his belief system. It was a publication that fostered community and facilitated the exchange of information and ideas. Aside from a significantly larger circulation, *The Weekly* had changed little since its premiere issue landed on the newsstands more than a decade ago. It was still a black and white newspaper, 100 or so pages, folded magazine style, focused on local issues, read mostly for its calendar section, edgy, slightly anti-establishment, and free. *The Weekly* had heart and soul, even attitude.

Conversely, Ben despised *Cavanaugh Monthly*. Though its creator and publisher also, *Cavanaugh Monthly* was seldom present on the coffee table in Ben's office. The *Monthly* represented everything Ben didn't want the *Weekly* to become: glossy, full of color pictures, focused on fashion and style, lacking substance and insightful articles, infused with models and celebrities, crammed with full-page ads, and tremendously profitable. Ben commented privately that the readership wasn't readers at all but gawkers who flipped through its flashy pages seeking escape from their problems. The *Monthly* presented a world where appearance, possessions, and lifestyle were highly valued, and image truly mattered. It was superficial, mindless, and trendy. Ben didn't have the time or patience for shallowness.

Ben rose from his desk.

At six foot four, Ben towered over most people. Height aside, he still towered over most. He had more intelligence, confidence, and charisma than any thirty-three year old ought and, strangely enough, he'd always had it. He was as impressive when we first met fourteen years ago in college. He had a medium build, wavy black hair, and working class good looks. Never overlooked, Ben had a presence that commanded attention.

Ben moved to the sofa and continued. "Ad revenues are not the measure of a great magazine."

"Agreed," I said, nodding, though I'd no intent of conceding anything, "but they're not inconsequential to a magazine business either. And, like it or not, Utopia Publishing is a business."

I paused, regrouped, and looked for another tact.

"Ben, these additional advertising dollars flow right through to the bottom line. The additional cost to a production run our size is a pittance, totally insignificant. We are looking at an easy ten to twenty grand of additional profit per issue. We can use that money for more computers. They're really making a difference in our productivity."

I appealed to his business sense. Our company was still struggling to fund its internal push toward automation that began in late 1988. Computers, printers, and graphics software were not cheap.

Ben leaned his head back onto the sofa and addressed the heavens as if he was exasperated with his earthly company.

"This isn't about profits or computer equipment," Ben said in an exasperated tone. "This is about integrity."

But I wasn't offended, not in the least. I knew Ben had a tendency toward the theatric, like his entire life was being played out on a grand stage in front of a large audience, which was often the case.

Then, Ben returned to earth and looked my way. "Maybe you ought to ask yourself what's really important here, what's really at stake? You can't put a price on things that you believe in."

Appearing content that the conversation was going his way, Ben eased even further into the sofa. After all, Ben wore his integrity on his sleeve as comfortably as the Brooks Brothers blazer, white cotton shirt, and faded blue jeans that were common to his daily attire. Ben readily dismissed fashion, but he exuded style and integrity.

Slapped by the firm backhand of his strong sense of integrity, I was getting a little pissed off.

"Oh, I get it, Mr. Self-Fucking-Righteous," I returned. "I am greedy and unprincipled. I worship at the altar of capitalism. Is that what you think?"

Ben smiled as if in agreement.

I continued. "If I thought we would compromise the quality or integrity of *The Weekly* with these additional ad pages, I wouldn't be sitting here."

"Alright then," Ben said. "What do you believe in? What's more important to you than making a buck?"

"What do I believe in?" I echoed thoughtfully. "I'll tell you what I believe in. I believe in thoroughbreds that switch leads during the final-stretch run. I believe in freshly cut lawns and pressed cotton shirts with sharp creases."

I paused, relishing the challenge Ben had laid before me. Two positive clauses of the unwritten covenant of our friendship have always been that we never hesitated to challenge one another or to lighten a tense moment. We both understood that good friends know when to push harder, when to back off, and which lines not to cross.

I looked Ben directly in the eyes and continued. "I believe in pizza night every Monday. I believe Joe Golden deserved a Pulitzer Prize and I believe that rock and roll is long passed its prime. I believe in fast food, slow kisses, frosty mugs, lacy red teddies, and fireworks on the Fourth of July. Finally, and most importantly, I believe in the wisdom of the heart and the power of love because when it's right you know it, and when it's right—it's magic."

I paused again, this time satisfied I'd met the challenge.

"No beliefs. How are those for no beliefs?" I demanded.

Ben released the tight smile he'd restrained since I started my speech and erupted in boisterous laughter. He had a laugh that felt like warm praise to those around him.

"I've got one thing to say about that ridiculous dissertation," he offered as a pseudo critique, "and that is I am sure glad you edit my publications because you're good."

Next, Ben commented on how little our friendship had changed, how similar my response was to what it would've been during college, and the fact that together we've shared great successes and only a few disappointments.

I rose from the chair saying, "Well, I take it I've lost my plea for additional ad pages, huh?" suspecting I hadn't.

"I'll tell you what," Ben said. "I don't want to pass on an opportunity so I'll agree to seven additional ad pages, but only if you agree that this issue is closed indefinitely!"

"That's a deal," I said as I reached the door.

Ben was right behind me. Our meeting wasn't over. Stan Tilden, who shared the title of co-editor with me, arrived at the door just as I did, coming from the opposite direction.

"You wanted to see me, Ben?" he asked.

"Yes I do," Ben returned, "both of you. Close the door."

Stan and I sat on the sofa. Ben sat facing us.

"I'm going to run for the office of mayor in the next election," Ben informed his co-editors, as casually as he'd suggest a restaurant for lunch.

It was a topic we'd considered privately but never discussed. Whether Ben would pursue political office had long been the subject of earnest speculation by both the local and national media. Ben was a rising star in both venues. Neither Stan nor I responded, but our physical responses revealed trepidation. Ben sensed our unease and tried to calm our fears.

"Nothing will change around here," Ben reassured us. "I'll continue to provide direction and occasional articles but, let's face it, you guys manage the newspaper, both magazines, and the business already."

"What if you're elected?" Stan asked.

Ben's election to office was the least of my concerns. While Ben told Stan that he'd distance himself from Utopia Publishing if elected to protect our company from conflicts of interest, I was more concerned about the road to City Hall. The incumbent, Mayor Dale Greenwood, won his first mayoral election by using two repugnant political strategies: slandering his opponent and buying the support of the powerful dockworkers union. At the time, there were whispers of voter intimidation and ballot box manipulation by the union in support of the mayor but nothing came of it. In my personal experience, what was whispered was often far more telling than what was spoken or shouted. Most telling was the belligerent nature of the tactics as the mayor had often been described by colorful adjectives, but subtle had never been among them. Mayor Greenwood was the type of man who used a sledgehammer to drive a thumbtack in.

At this stage, it would've been unwise to underestimate either the mayor's political machine or the tactics they'd use to ensure his reelection, and the more formidable the opponent, the more despicable the tactics would be. Ben would be a formidable opponent but no certain winner. In my estimation, this political campaign would be a classic, almost biblical, clash of good against evil, and I wasn't so sure that good would win out. In the Bible, good and evil are usually quite evident and the lessons are clear-cut. Good is rewarded and evil is punished. In the world of politics, it's often hard to distinguish good from evil because blurring the line that separates them is evil's first offensive. Life isn't fair and politics even less so.

"Do you know what you're getting into, Ben?" I asked. "This won't be a political campaign, it will be a bloody street fight."

"I realize that, and I appreciate your concern, but our city is approaching an important crossroad. In the coming years, Cavanaugh will design and build a mass transportation system that will determine its future. Entrusted to Mayor Greenwood, we can only be certain that the mayor and his cronies will benefit. We can't be confident that the best interests of the city will be first and foremost. Cavanaugh is currently one of the best cities in the entire country to live and work, and its citizens deserve honest leadership. I know what I'm up against and that is precisely why I've got to do it."

Unfortunately, Ben's point only added emphasis to mine. Development of the light rail system would place more than a billion dollars onto the political playing field and that enormous bounty would make the mayor that much more determined to win reelection. He would do anything to win. In my mind, I believed I had legitimate concerns for both the physical safety and emotional well being of my friend. Though Ben tried to ease our minds, I grew more concerned.

On the other hand, I also had to concede that Ben had gone further on charisma and good intentions than most would've thought possible a decade ago. And, better than most, I knew not to doubt Ben once he set his sights on something. I'd never known him to fail at anything. I also knew that when all was said and done, I'd be a reluctant supporter but a committed supporter nonetheless.

"If that's your decision," I told my longtime friend, "you can count on my support."

Over the years, he'd more than earned my support, but I believed in Ben right from the start.

August 1977

Feeling as uncertain as a puppy in a new home, I arrived at Stanton University three days before the start of classes to attend freshman orientation. Immediately, the orientation period seemed woefully inadequate. In canine terms, I needed a month to get over my litter stress—the anxiety felt by young mammals when removed from their birth litter—and at least two additional weeks before I could function as a college student. I needed to sniff every inch of my new surroundings and identify the proper places to eat, sleep, and pee. I also needed to determine which of the other puppies were friends and which were foes, which ones would share their chew toys and which would bury mine. All this anxiety, believe it or not, despite the university's best efforts to welcome me.

Two weeks earlier, an envelope from Campus Housing had arrived at my home so I'd have advance knowledge of my dormitory assignment and the layout of the campus. I was assigned to Room 315 in Yarborough Hall and my roommate was a fellow freshman named Daniel Patrick Grainger. Also included in the envelope was a photo of the dormitory, a detailed map of the campus, Yarborough Hall rules, an orientation schedule, and other general information.

When the cab driver dropped me at the curb, I stood, my bags and chin at my feet, staring at Yarborough Hall and the large banner that spanned the front door and read "Welcome Class of 1981." It was just before 2pm so the front steps bustled with students, a few nodded or smiled while others simply rushed passed with backpacks in tow. From out of nowhere, an older student with a clipboard appeared.

"Let me give you a hand," he suggested.

Before I could get an admonition out, the student grabbed one of my bags from the curb and started toward the entrance.

Panic filled my mind. Prior to boarding the aircraft, my father warned me never to let my bags out of my sight, adding, "There are hooligans everywhere," in a fatherly tone. Fearing a fatherly "I told you so," I grabbed my other bag and chased after the student. He was ten-steps ahead as I passed the elevator and bound down the hallway toward the rear doors. I felt relief when he turned into an office with the faintly stenciled insignia of Hall Manager above the doorway.

"My name is Martin Reynolds," he said as he tossed my bag beside a gray, metal desk, circa World War II, and sat behind it. "I am a junior at this institution, a psychology major, and lord of this manor. Did you get a copy of the rules with your room assignment package?"

"Right here," I said, removing an envelope from inside my coat pocket.

"Good, memorize them tonight so there will be no confusion. I get a small weekly stipend and an oversized room for watching you little weasels. It isn't all that much so I have no intention of working hard or suffering any aggravation. Understood?"

Martin, wearing a loose-fitting shirt that hung like draperies over the top of his pants, didn't give me a chance to reply, but simply moved on and asked, "Your name?"

After I told him, Martin produced some paper work from the drawer and a freshly cut key, "315" chiseled in its shiny base. Then, while I signed repeatedly wherever he pointed, Martin described some of the basics of dormitory life. His tone was brash to the point of rude, but I figured it was all part of the initiation. While taking Psychology 101, Martin probably learned that conditioning during stress was more likely to modify behavior than when a subject was relaxed. Adapted to the vocation of hall manager, this meant intimidate the hell out of them on the first day, and the rest of the year will be uneventful.

"Finally," he said, "when in the presence of upper classmen always remember that freshmen, like snotty-nosed children, are better seen and not heard. Any questions?"

"I blink, therefore I am," I said, acknowledging his major, his advice, and my non-participatory role in this exchange.

"You've got it," he declared, chuckling at my observation.

When I opened the door at Room 315, it was painfully obvious that Daniel Patrick Grainger had moved in. His bed was disheveled, chair piled high with winter coats, and the top of his dresser crammed with football trophies. Pizza boxes, fast food wrappers, and beer bottles were scattered about the east side of the room, and since fall semester students were only allowed access to the hall four days ago, Danny should be commended for the speed at which he so thoroughly trashed our room. But, in his defense, the mess was mostly contained to his side of the room, leaving the two halves resembling before and after photos of a fraternity party.

Dorm rooms were symmetrical; each side contained a dresser, nightstand, bed, bookcase, desk, desk lamp, and chair. Viewed from the door, my side was stark and monochrome compared to his side, plastered with posters. Farrah Fawcett, Terry Bradshaw, Fleetwood Mac, The Eagles, and Easy Rider were a few of the images on the twenty or so posters that covered almost every inch of wall space. Though I'd never met or set my eyes upon him, one thing was clear to me right from the start: Danny Grainger was born to be a college student. He was in his element and that might be really good for me. Clearly, I was not.

I was busily placing white Fruit of the Loom underwear in the second drawer of the dresser when the door suddenly flung wide open and in walked Danny Grainger, a six foot two inch, athletically built sort with short blonde hair, blue eyes, and a few faint freckles near his nose. He had an all-American boy quality to him that overshadowed his sloppiness and he looked like he'd been at the malt shop. He also had a big, welcoming smile on his face, as if roommates were instantly and automatically best friends in his mind.

"Martin told me you arrived," Danny announced. "I was in the lounge watching the Pirates lose another game."

As I put my clothes away, Danny picked up a few sandwich wrappers and beer bottles from the floor, and we swapped background information. Danny grew up in western Pennsylvania, near Steel City, which accounted for his love/hate relationship with the Pittsburgh Pirates. He was the oldest of three children, with two younger sisters, and a child of blue-collar parents; his father worked at a foundry and his mother worked the makeup counter at the local drugstore. Danny was the type of kid everyone liked: adults—because he was respectful and well mannered, girls—because he was entertaining, confident, and a little mischievous, and guys—because he was an athlete and girls liked him. Though a bit of a free spirit, I was relieved when he told me he got mostly As in high school; otherwise, a roommate with little concern about grades would surely impact my own.

In Pennsylvania, Danny was a three time all-state quarterback with invitations to play at top ranked college football programs like Purdue, Notre Dame, Michigan, Alabama, USC, and UCLA until he tore the ligaments in his left knee during the homecoming game last October. Almost simultaneous with the tearing of his knee, the same college recruiters who'd so aggressively pursued him quickly tore up their scholarship offers and moved on. With one iniquitous bend of his knee, Danny went from someone with unlimited invitations to someone with nowhere to go. But, seemingly undaunted by his costly mishap, Danny rolled up his soiled corduroy pant leg to reveal two long thick scars that formed a mountainous topography across his knee cap not unlike the Smoky Mountains of eastern Tennessee.

"Picture this," he offered, grinning like a first-time father with an ultrasound of his handiwork. "My high school football career had clearly ended. I was carried off the field on a stretcher and rushed in an ambulance to the emergency room at Mercy Hospital. After hours of prodding and X-rays, I had finally made it home and propped my leg up in a recliner. Just when I was sure things couldn't get any worse, my girlfriend, Terri, stopped by to check on my condition. As soon she got her cute little ass parked along side me in the La-Z-Boy, she asked if we're still going to the dance."

Later that night, Danny showed me a photo that caused me to set aside all my stereotypes about high school athletes. The photo brought tears to my eyes, something I never expected from my new ex-jock roommate. Danny's little sisters, Kate and Christi, ages seven and nine in his sophomore year, attended his football games and always brought their neighbor along, a mentally challenged nine-year-old boy named Howie. During the games, the three youngsters sat near the cheerleaders and often mimicked the routines of the squad. And, every time Danny completed a pass, his little fans jumped up and down and shrieked with elation; touchdown passes produced even more jubilant celebrations.

One Saturday afternoon, Howie's father, the owner of a local silkscreen company, outfitted the three little fans in royal blue and white sweatshirts with "Grainger's Rangers" on the front and Danny's number "15" on the back. It was quite a sight, and the idea caught on quickly. Over the course of Danny's three seasons as quarterback, more and more kids joined Grainger's Rangers until there were almost fifty kids in royal blue sweatshirts behind the goalposts cheering for Danny. The kids' ages ranged from seven to thirteen and about one-third had some sort of special need like Howie. Though a nationally ranked high school football program in its own right, the kids behind the end zone garnered almost as much attention each game day as the action on the field.

In the photograph, Danny stood beneath the goalpost of his high school football field, his uniform damp with sweat and stained by grass, smiling the full face smile of a lottery winner, while surrounded by thirty kids in Grainger's Rangers sweatshirts who seemed to be enjoying the biggest moment of their young lives. Danny told me that many of the kids had special needs that always made them feel different, not normal, unlike the other kids. Though some didn't even understand the game of football, those kids were Grainger's Rangers because they simply loved being part of something. For a few hours on Saturday afternoon, they felt like the other kids and part of the crowd.

"We won the state championship in my sophomore and junior years," Danny remarked, sweetly reminiscing, "but when I look back, those kids were the best part of my high school football career."

* * *

On my second day, I walked the campus during the morning hours while the air was still moist and cool against my skin and lightly scented by pine trees. I was eager to view the sights I'd only seen in brochures, and I knew my afternoon would be occupied with freshman orientation. As I strolled, the cobblestone pathways meandered along rolling hillsides, through thinly forested tracts, passed university buildings, and across stone bridges built at the turn of the century. It was a truly inspiring campus setting and one suited to photography— as well as reflection, contemplative thought, and university studies.

Stanton University was thirty-five miles north of downtown Cavanaugh in an area of rolling hills sheltered by maple and pine trees. Though the university marked the northern boundary of a major metropolis, the stress and agitation of the city didn't intrude upon the campus grounds, unable to survive in this peaceful setting. University buildings consisted of three different architectural styles, with each style delineating a period of expansion. The four original buildings— grand gothic structures with magnificent front steps, tall arched doors and windows, and towering spires—were constructed in the early 1880s of granite and flagstone. A surge in enrollment after World War II resulted in the construction of seven red, brick buildings ranging from four to eight floors in height and each fulfilling functions ranging from dormitories to classrooms to an athletic center. With enrollment climbing once again in the 1960s, the university broke ground once more, using modern steel and glass construction and the natural designs of famed architect J. Bennett Wainwright to construct the final four buildings.

Returned from my walk, I found Danny lacing his "Chucks" before departing for pick-up basketball games at the courts next to the dormitory. At that time of the morning, Danny said there were usually fifteen to twenty players, and the games were not overly competitive. He emphasized the words "strictly for fun" in an obvious attempt at coaxing me into playing.

"You'll meet some of the other Yarbies," Danny added as a clincher, the first time I'd heard that campus nickname for residents of Yarborough Hall.

Despite my walk, I was still brimming with nervous energy.

"Are slam dunks allowed?" I asked.

"Yeah, but no hanging on the rim," Danny answered, knowing I couldn't dunk a basketball unless I used a stepladder.

We arrived before of the morning crowd. Having played the past two days, Danny introduced me to the players as they trickled in, sometimes coining nicknames based on playing styles, until we finally had enough for a game. One of the players suggested Ben and Rick—or Swish and Elbows as Danny referred to them—do the choosing, so the team captains moved to the free throw line, and the other players drifted into the lane.

"Shoot for first pick," Danny said as he tossed a ball to Ben, waiting at the top of the arch, as was standard before pick-up games.

Ben took two short, quick dribbles, lofted a high arching shot toward the basket, stepped backwards, and watched its flight. The ball swished through the basket. It hadn't bounced twice before Ben made his selection.

"I've got Pete," he said, pointing in my direction.

I almost passed out.

I'd never been picked first. Hell, I'd never been selected during the first half of the picking process. What was he thinking? I almost disrupted the process by blurting, "Why," but I took my place behind Ben instead, customary when choosing sides.

In life, some things defy explanation: the circular patterns that appeared overnight in barley fields in England, the weeping statue of the Virgin Mother in Brazil, and Ben's logic for selecting teammates. But then, compounding my confusion, Ben selected Danny next, a strong candidate for first draft pick, not me.

Obviously, Ben and Danny played a lot of basketball growing up and accounted for most of our team's scoring as we won the first game 15-11 and lost the second 16-14. Just as Danny had promised, the games were pleasant in character as all participants seemed more interested in a workout than in winning, and egos and testosterone levels were kept in check. Games were played to fifteen with a win by two points qualifier, sending some games, like our second one, into overtime.

With the tally split at one game apiece and the start of orientation still two hours off, we went ahead with the rubber game, court lingo for a tiebreaker. Our two star players continued to gel, becoming more accustomed to each other's playing style and more anticipatory of each other's next move. We jumped out to a 7-2 lead as Danny and Ben both forced the defense to overplay them and then passed the ball at just the right moment to the other for an open shot. Unfortunately, we relied on Ben and Danny too much during those three close contests and both were exhausted in the late stages of the final game.

Our opponents cleared an errant shot for a fast-break bucket to tie the game at 14. Then, both teams traded baskets for the next five minutes until finally, with the score favoring us at 20-19, Danny grabbed a rebound of their failed shot attempt and, suddenly, we had a chance to win the game. He walked the ball up court slowly. During this temporary break in the action, several players wearily hung their heads in exhaustion and yanked their shirts skyward to wipe the sweat from their eyes.

"I'm dying," my defender mumbled, bent over before me. His lumpy profile matched mine, and I had a feeling his stories from high school gym class would also.

When Danny finally arrived at the top of the key, he passed the ball to Ben and then set a pick to free Ben for a chance to drive down the lane. As Ben dribbled across the foul line and turned sharply toward the hoop, my defender left our spot in the corner and stepped into the lane to obstruct Ben's pathway. Ben continued onward, but stopped just short of the defender and bounce-passed the ball to me shouting, "End it," as he released it.

I caught the ball cleanly and turned quickly to square with the basket. Though wide open, I rushed the fifteen-foot shot, choosing to ignore form and fundamentals and rely on dumb luck. My shot arched in perfect line with the basket and clanked against each side of the rim several times on arrival, like a pinball between the rubber flippers, before dropping through the net. It was only my second basket of the day, but for one brief shining moment, I felt like a number one pick.

As was customary at a game's conclusion, the other players shook hands while I absorbed the moment: my only athletic triumph, ever. None of the other players would've given that final bucket a second thought, but it was noteworthy for me. Unprecedented in my young life, I'd sunk a game-winning shot.

Two things were evident that day: I shouldn't let my game-winning basket dupe me into trying out for the university's basketball team and the three of us would be good friends at college, Ben and I most particularly. Our camaraderie continued throughout the day as we sat together at lunch and at orientation.

* * *

Later that evening, Ben and I retreated to the quiet of his dorm room and talked for several hours, until midnight, about: college, family, high school, girls, careers, journalism, and hobbies—basically anything that popped into our young inquisitive minds. In all my life, I'd never talked with anyone so extensively, so candidly, never family members or even high school friends. Ben Matthews was like no one I'd ever met before.

Ben had a single room on the fifth floor of Yarborough Hall but not for the usual reason students roomed alone: wealthy parents. Ben was an insomniac and regularly slept only a few hours at night. Lacking a medical explanation, Ben believed his insomnia was somehow related to his mother's death from heart failure when he was only four years old, leaving Ben to be raised as an only child by his father, a printer who owned and operated a small printing business in South Cavanaugh.

Growing up, Ben spent many hours at the print shop and that time had a real impact on him. Fascinated, young Ben watched as blank sheets of paper were fed into the massive printing presses, stamped with words and images, and then neatly stacked in bins at the opposite end of the shop. Even the metallic clanking and clattering of the elaborate machinery added a musical element to the movement that enthralled the young boy.

"It seemed magical," Ben said, his eyes lit. "One moment the page was blank, and the next moment it was imprinted. As I got older, I realized the real magic was the power of published ideas."

Most impressive, Ben had mapped out his course in life while other kids our age were directionless. He had a timeline that was so brimming with objectives that he didn't plan to graduate from college. Instead, Ben enrolled at SU to expand his personal network, to meet the movers and shakers of the future, the like-minded individuals of his generation. Ben knew the usefulness such a network could bring to the table and how much they could accomplish together. He would graduate someday, but it wasn't his priority for now.

In a year or two, Ben planned to leave college early and start a weekly newspaper aimed at restoring a sense of community to urban life. Central to its appeal, the paper would contain a city calendar section that featured events, activities, and entertainment—everything from nightclub performances to art shows to craft fairs to athletic events. But most importantly, the paper would also feature articles about community affairs, small businesses, council policies, political issues, and significant people and thereby provide service to the community as a forum for information and debate. His intent was that his paper would establish a more connected, more communicative community.

Typical of Ben, he had the big picture in mind. Ben believed the pitiful state of most U.S. cities was the result of what he called "apathetic democracies," where citizens elected their city government officials and then disconnected from the process. Issues were left solely to the command of elected officials—people with the time and money to run for office but not necessarily the best ideas or solutions.

"Even the best of the lot can't be proficient on all subjects that come before a city council," Ben said.

In Ben's mind, the limited discussion and debate of issues that occurred in most cities limited the broader range of ideas and solutions that could come from the entire community, the greatest benefit of "government by the people." Ben believed his city, while still a young metropolis, could develop a strong sense of community, encourage the freer flow of ideas, and create greater participation in its government. The result would be more thoughtfully managed growth and an overall better quality of life.

"For me, it all comes down to three simple words, 'We, the people,'" Ben said as an attempt to abridge his belief system. "Those words placed an extraordinary measure of faith and trust in the people because our Founding Fathers believed that only the people could best decide their own course and destiny. To live up to their vision, we must forever strive to be the best 'We, the people' possible. It's our obligation as citizens. It's our mission for all humanity. Whether or not our system of government works depends largely on whether our citizens actively participate."

Ben believed his weekly newspaper would be the heart and soul of the city. He believed it could make a difference; he believed he could make a difference. He talked as if the first issue was clear in his mind, from the front page with the large *CW* insignia for *Cavanaugh Weekly* to the layout of the calendar section to the first articles he wanted to include. I listened intently as Ben described his plans for the next five years in a level of detail that suggested more than a little consideration. He wasn't winging it. And, as he spoke, with such passion and purpose, the answer to the question that had gnawed at my mind since earlier that morning was suddenly clear to me.

Why had Ben picked me first?

Ben hadn't misjudged my athletic abilities, nor did he believe my short, pudgy physique and lack of jumping ability would translate into basketball greatness. In fact, his selection had nothing to do with the game we were about to play. Ben sensed a connection between us, a kinship. It was as simple as that. He picked me first so we'd have the opportunity to develop that connection. Typical of him, Ben was focused on the big picture.

Over time, I'd come to learn that Ben had some kind of sixth sense, an intuitive gift that provided him insight on the inner workings of people. As easily as others read the pages of a newspaper, Ben read people, instantly and thoroughly, at a core level, easily determining their strengths, weaknesses, motivations, and fears. He perceived their true self, their perspective on life, and what made them tick. I have no idea how it worked; I just know he had it.

Did Ben also know the nature of our connection and where it would lead? I didn't know that either. But, our connection was real just the same. He was absolutely right about that. After all these hours together, I sensed it, too.

When I returned to my dorm room late that night, I sat at my desk, turned my desk lamp on its low setting, opened one of the ten spiral notebooks I'd purchased at the bookstore that morning, and began keeping a journal for the first time in my life. Though I'd been a college student for a mere thirty-four hours, I sensed a real change happening in my life, a rapid acceleration forward. Deep in my being, I knew that meeting Ben Matthews would be a significant milestone and that, from that point forward, my life would forever be divided into the period before our meeting and the period after our meeting. From that day forward, my life experiences would transition from mundane to noteworthy, and my nascent journalistic instincts shouted two words over and over, loud and clear: start writing.

Danny stirred briefly, groggy and a little concerned at the sight of me writing late at night. "That's not a suicide note, is it?" he asked, his eyes barely open.

"No," I replied, "just a request for a new roommate."

"Well, okay then," he muttered, and he rolled over and went back to sleep.

2.

Built in 1885 to the towering height of just nine stories, the Home Insurance Building was regarded by many as the first skyscraper. Though twentieth century structures climbed ten times higher than its once remarkable height, in its day, the Chicago landmark soared.

A spectacular display of turning foliage occurred in October of my freshman year. Resplendent shades of crimson, gold, bronze, and orange stippled the trees and matted the earth as I'd only witnessed previously during a family vacation in the woods of New Hampshire. Whenever a wind gust unsettled the tree branches, leaves fluttered to the ground and painted the damp cobblestones like gold plating on a medallion. Cloaked in Mother Nature's handiwork, the campus transformed into a natural marquee that enthusiastically announced the arrival of autumn, the season of transition. Its effects were evident in the trees, temperatures, and students, most subtly in the students.

Each fall semester on college campuses, students struggle with the biggest transition of their young lives—from nurtured, protected child to independent adult. They struggle with the freedoms and responsibilities that come with maturing. In Yarborough Hall, at any hour of the day or night, students could be found studying textbooks or popping flip tops, and in some instances, both. Ben, Danny, and I made the adjustment to college life with relative ease, all possessing the discipline to attend classes, study two to three hours each day, and limit our partying to the weekends. For others, enticed by free flowing alcohol and late night festivities until horrific exam results served the wake-up call, the transition was more difficult.

Adding layers as the days demanded, I continued my morning walks across the campus, with most of each excursion focused on trying to come up with an idea for an article to submit to the school newspaper, *The Stanton University Signal*. During a visit to the newspaper's office where we were abruptly rebuffed, Ben and I learned that freshmen weren't allowed to join its prestigious staff. Staff positions were posts that had to be earned. New staff writers were selected at the start of sophomore year from a list of nominees compiled by English and Journalism professors, based on freshman compositions and class work, or through automatic nomination, which came with a published freshman article. The latter, though, was extremely rare. *The Signal* had published only eleven articles penned by freshmen writers during its illustrious eighty-one year history.

Each morning while I walked, Danny jogged three miles and then proceeded to the athletic center to lift weights. Sometimes from the cobblestone pathways that ambled across the rolling hillside above the football practice field, I noticed Danny atop the bleachers in the end zone watching the team scrimmage. His face revealed more than an average spectator's interest, a much deeper passion forged from participation and a true love of the sport. It had been a whole year since "Black Saturday," Danny's name for the star-crossed afternoon he injured his knee, and it was obvious to me that he missed football. His world was out of balance and incomplete; he should be otherwise occupied this time of year. As his roommate, I worried he might get depressed as football season progressed, but with the Grizzlies four games into a lackluster 1-3 season, Danny was as affable as ever.

One morning in mid-October, I climbed into the bleachers to watch the Grizzlies workout alongside Danny. Difficult for him to simply watch, he painstakingly analyzed each play and, true to his quarterback instincts, focused on the offensive side of the field. During each play, Danny would point out our team's weaknesses: the line didn't create enough forward momentum, the quarterback's drop and release were slow, or the running back missed the hole. Several times, immediately after the play concluded, the coach stormed onto the field shouting the same criticisms. Danny knew football and, though I'd never seen him play, I sensed from his accolades and quiet confidence that he was quite the field general in high school.

Previously, I'd never been interested in sports. Growing up, my home state of Delaware didn't even have a professional sports franchise. For me, sports were the shows that flashed on the screen while I searched the channels for something to watch. But, I learned a lot about football from Danny. Mostly, I learned how seriously the sport was regarded in Pittsburgh Steelers' country where he was born and raised. Football wasn't a game in western Pennsylvania—it was sport, it was business, it was communal, it was religion, and it was a way of life, but it was not a game. Games were inconsequential and played by young children. Football mattered.

"In the early sixties, Joe Namath was the quarterback of my high school's team," Danny told me—vividly illustrating the gridiron tradition he grew up with.

Even I knew about Joe Namath. In the late 1960s, "Broadway Joe" was a sensation both on and off the field. He was an American icon. When Danny mentioned him, I remembered seeing him shave his legs on television during a shaving cream advertisement.

"Like any kid from the Beaver Falls area," Danny continued, "I idolized him. I wanted to follow in his footsteps."

But, even before his scrambled knee, Danny never expected to be the next Broadway Joe. That was too big a dream for this humble, small town kid. In Danny's hometown, the legend of Broadway Joe was as miraculous as biblical stories and just as worshipped. Getting out of small towns was a difficult enough task and success of that measure much harder. Danny's dream was to play college football and earn a backup spot on a professional squad.

"Thirteen months ago, I was sure I'd make it," he remarked somewhat sadly.

As we walked up the steep hillside toward our dormitory, I realized why Danny ran like a marathoner and worked so hard in the weight room each morning. It was all part of his rehabilitation program so he could return to the game of football and quarterback again. He'd already completed ten months of hard work and his knee was approaching its old form.

"Are you going to play again?" I asked.

"I haven't even told my parents yet, but yeah, I am. It's why I came to SU. I couldn't get consideration at a major program anymore, but I can play here."

"Next year?"

"Yeah."

"Why?" I asked, knowing another hard crumpling of his knee could be crippling.

"It's always been my goal. It's a part of me. I can't move on with my life until I play college football."

* * *

Ben and I had the only common class amongst the three of us, Professor Kimmel's English 101 at 11am in Heard Hall, which setup a short walk from the class to the cafeteria where we met Danny at noon for lunch each day. He was never late. He was always famished by 11am. Danny burned a lot of energy during his morning workouts so he was always waiting for us when we arrived, without exception, grumbling about feeling starved and weak and pacing back and forth impatiently like his food was getting cold. Worse still, if there was a line in the serving aisle, Danny was unbearable. In a very concerned manner, he'd lean against the stainless steel counters and gaze forward at the offerings to determine whether any of his favorite items were depleting. Heaven help us if the mashed potatoes were getting low.

"Don't worry, they're not going to run out of food," I would tell him almost every day.

One Friday, as we arrived at the front door of the cafeteria, Ben suggested we drive into Cavanaugh to his father's print shop so he could take his father to lunch for his fifty-fourth birthday.

"Tyler already said she wanted to go along," Ben said. "What do you say? Do you want to come meet my old man?"

Meeting Kirk Matthews and seeing the print shop I'd heard so much about were two things I'd been looking forward to, so I eagerly accepted. Danny declined because he said he had an exam in Art History that afternoon, but I wondered if he simply couldn't postpone his lunch for forty minutes while we drove to South Cavanaugh. I also knew we'd all be better off if he didn't.

Tyler met us at Ben's car, a 69 Pontiac Lemans, so we could ride together to South Cavanaugh. I pushed the bucket seat forward and climbed into the cramped confines of the backseat, leaving the front seat for Tyler. In their company, I felt frayed and frumpy, like well-worn luggage stowed for an extended journey. It wasn't anything Ben or Tyler said or did, it was just that they were polished, stylish, confident people—and I wasn't. It also wasn't a question of jealousy or envy. Ben was my best friend, and I was happy for the two of them. Ben and Tyler looked great together.

We first met Tyler Danzig, a sophomore, journalism major, and recently appointed *Signal* staff writer, several weeks earlier during our visit to *The Signal*. She was the child of a Philippine mother and French father; a unique mating that produced an exotic racial blending of cocoa brown skin, prominent check bones, striking azure blue eyes, and long brown hair that reached into the small of her back. She was also a child of affluence and privilege who had attended the best preparatory schools in the east and put forth a comfortable deportment that added warmth and intelligence to her almost overwhelming beauty. As we left *The Signal* that day, there was a smitten look on Ben's face and it was duplicated on mine. Neither of us had encountered someone like Tyler Danzig in the neighborhoods of our youths.

"She is really something," Ben remarked.

In the few weeks since their first meeting, Ben and Tyler had formed a close but still platonic friendship, though something grander and physical seemed inevitable, even unavoidable. While I've never placed much credence in fate, the fact that those two perfect people found one another could certainly be construed as evidence that it existed. Their children would be magnificent and formidable.

As we drove the back streets of Cavanaugh, Ben described his father as warm, gregarious, feisty, and an avid Revolutionary War buff, which accounted for Ben's middle name, Franklin.

"As a printer, my father feels an affinity to Ben Franklin," Ben stated. "And, considering his fascination with the Revolutionary War, it could've been worse for me. If he'd named me Benedict Arnold Matthews, I would've spent my adolescence in therapy."

Ben's father had owned The Common Sense Print Shop on Gaines Avenue in South Cavanaugh for over thirty years, causing Ben to question whether his father had red blood or black ink coursing through his veins.

"My Dad is truly one of the lucky ones," Ben remarked just before we arrived. "He really loves what he does and he's taught me the importance of that."

When we reached the industrial south side of the city with its factory smokestacks and battered warehouses, Ben turned onto a dead-end street and pointed to his father's shop on the corner, a simple building with an antique wood-burned sign out front, The Common Sense Print Shop scripted in black. Inside, there were two large printing presses churning away, a backroom area for shooting film, developing negatives, and producing plates, and a smaller office area with a desk and three file cabinets. Tacked up randomly throughout the shop on every inch of wall space were menus, posters, road maps, pamphlets, promotional items, magazine covers, lithographs, and book jackets, samples from thousands of jobs. Also present throughout the shop was the strong stench of ink and solvents.

"Wow!" Tyler exclaimed, twirling 360 degrees as she entered, astonished by the wall hangings. "This shop is basically a museum."

On entry, Ben waved his hand to attract his father's attention. Kirk Matthews, a short, stocky man with a graying black beard and mostly bald head, was on the other side of the grand presses and didn't notice our arrival, drowned out by the constant clanking noises of the machinery. He was busy moving a cart of finished posters away from the printing area.

Though Ben never mentioned his plans to his father, Kirk wasn't surprised to see his son when he finally spotted us. He knew Ben would remember his birthday. It was just the two of them and they were close. Kirk wore a dark-blue, SU tee shirt and white, ink-stained overalls with most of the logo concealed.

"Happy Birthday!" Ben declared, embracing his father as he finally reached us. "I came to take you to lunch."

"Why didn't you tell me you were coming?" Kirk asked.

"Because," Ben replied sternly, "you would've said you were too busy for lunch. Now, you have no choice."

Ben introduced us to his father, noting that he'd brought us as an insurance policy, knowing Kirk wouldn't turn us away.

"He's right about that," Kirk said. "I might have sent Ben right back to school, but I'm glad to meet you."

"This is quite a shop, Mr. Matthews," Tyler told him. "If you ever get tired of the printing business, you can turn this place into a museum and give tours. What a historic collection you've got here."

"Some of these items are thirty years old," Ben said. "Why don't you show them some of the more interesting ones, and I'll go say hi to Carl. Where is he?"

"Out back at the dumpster."

Ben exited the steel back door. Without any hesitation, like a tour guide with a practiced oratory, Kirk pointed to items and told us stories about each. On one nail hung thirty menus from Dusenberg's, one of the city's most acclaimed restaurants. Kirk said there was a copy of every menu ever placed before patrons, dating back to around 1962 or 1963 when the restaurant first opened.

"I love that place," Tyler said as she thumbed through the crinkled yellowed parchment. Then, noticing the prices on the older menus she added, "These prices wouldn't cover the tip there today."

Carl, wearing a short sleeve, gold Ban-Lon shirt that revealed several faded tattoos on his forearms, souvenirs from his years in the Army, was breaking down cardboard boxes when Ben emerged from the back of the shop and greeted him. For sixteen years, he'd been Kirk's assistant and friend, though personality-wise they were exact opposites. Kirk was boisterous and outgoing while Carl was quiet and reserved. Since Kirk's wife passed fourteen years ago and Carl had never married, the two relied on one another. Carl resided in a small building behind the print shop, remodeled years ago so that a third was a storage area and the remaining was Carl's apartment.

After visiting briefly with Carl and failing to convince him to join our outing, Ben interrupted the tour so that the four of us could make the drive to The Frothy Tankard Pub, Kirk's favorite watering hole. With a closed door muffling the noise from the print shop, Carl told Kirk that he could finish the couple of short runs they had left to accomplish that afternoon, so there was no reason for Kirk to return. Kirk nodded.

At least three stars short of four-star status, the pub was dark and cool with a comfortable ambiance most enjoyed after hard work. Its bill of fare was burgers, sandwiches, and beer by the pitcher, and its clientele was warehouse and factory workers from nearby facilities. We sat in a booth crafted of high-back medieval style, wood benches that were padded with black, leather cushions for comfort. Two hours and three pitchers of beer later, the remnants of our sandwiches before us, the conversation drifted from small talk and family memories into more cerebral territory.

"I can't lunch with young journalists," Kirk began, sounding both preachy and slightly inebriated, "who will shape the minds of the future, without telling you why I named my shop The Common Sense Print Shop."

"I'd be interested to know," I said.

Tyler nodded in agreement.

"It's a reference to the pamphlet that Thomas Paine published in January of 1776, the first essay about the colonies that addressed the significance of their predicament. In Common Sense, Paine wrote, 'if now, while their society was still uncorrupt, natural, and democratic, these colonies should free themselves from a vicious Monarch, they could alter human destiny by their example.' Paine understood what America's real mission for all of humanity was."

"What was that?" Tyler asked.

"To show that people can live freely and democratically, and that, in and of itself, is a basic human right. Paine believed that government only existed to ensure individuals that portion of their natural rights that unaided they couldn't secure themselves. It was a brilliant and inspiring publication. In only forty-seven pages, Paine moved the colonies to revolution and changed the world. I don't know of a single greater accomplishment by a writer, do you?"

"I don't," Tyler replied. "My curiosity is piqued," she added, smiling at Ben, "and I will definitely make a point of reading Common Sense, the first chance I get."

"Ah," Kirk returned, obviously enjoying the exchange, due to the subject matter and the interest on Tyler's face. "My point doesn't reside in Paine's words so much as the state of journalism then and now."

"You've lost me."

"What I want to impress upon you is this," Kirk stated. "Paine was a precocious man and a wanderer in his early years. There was quite a story in young Tom Paine, some real *National Enquirer* fodder, if you know what I mean. But, the power of journalism isn't found in reporting on people and events, but rather in the conveying of ideas. If Paine had written Common Sense today, modern journalists would have dismissed his ideas and focused on the man."

"I can see where Ben gets his integrity," Tyler said.

"Not to mention his good looks, right?" Kirk chided Tyler.

"Right," she answered, winking at Kirk.

* * *

Sometimes even the extraordinary begins ordinarily. Around dinner, the evening of November 8th seemed like any other, but that would change by midnight.

Ben and Tyler finished an early dinner at the cafeteria and then rushed across the campus to make it to the university bookstore before it closed at 6pm. Tyler wanted to purchase a SU sweatshirt as a gift for her father who was coming for a visit that weekend, a detour at the end of a business trip. They made the ten-minute walk from the cafeteria to the bookstore and arrived with just five minutes to spare.

Hurriedly, Tyler chose a traditional gray sweatshirt with bold, blue block lettering across the front. She grabbed a size "L" from the back of the rack and jokingly warned Ben that her father was a large man who considered his only daughter his most prized possession.

"Don't get on his bad side," she cautioned him.

Tyler's father, Jonathan Danzig, was the President of Danzig Capital Management, a venture capital company that provided start-up funding for small companies with the goal of turning them into large companies. In his stable of successful ventures were several fast-food chains, a brewery, two major retailers, a stock brokerage, and a potato chip company. Jonathan Danzig was a millionaire many times over and piloted his own Gulfstream jet whenever he traveled.

Next, after deciding to grab some munchies for a late night study session, they walked fifteen minutes across campus again to the basement of the Walton Building where the student store was located. Together they filled a hand-carried basket with two six-packs of soda, orange juice, bananas, granola bars, cheese, potato chips, and four green apples.

With bagged groceries in hand, they then set off across the campus one last time, passing the circular driveway and the statue of Ulysses P. Stanton at the center of the campus for the fourth time that evening, walking in the direction of Springer Hall, Tyler's dormitory. As they walked, Tyler did all the talking, mostly about her father's visit and her upcoming midterms. Ben was deep in thought and never acknowledged a single word.

"Are you listening?" she asked.

Twenty minutes later, at Tyler's room, Ben was sprawled out across Tyler's bed, his economics book open, munching an occasional potato chip and staring blankly while giving the subject matter before him minimal attention. Tyler sat at her desk actually studying her textbook.

"You haven't turned a page in ten minutes," Tyler pointed out.

Once again, he was unresponsive.

After a moment of silence, Ben asked, "Who was the last freshman published in *The Signal*?"

"I don't think that's going to be on any of your midterms."

"Seriously, who was it?"

"That sixties writer, Joe Golden," Tyler replied. "Why?"

"No reason," Ben answered while gathering his textbooks and loading them into his backpack. "I'll see you tomorrow."

* * *

Ben was breathless but excited when he arrived at my door that night, just before 9pm. "Twelve and thirteen," he whispered like a government spy coyly uttering the secret password required for entry. "We're going to be twelve and thirteen," he repeated.

When he finally caught his breath, Ben explained that he'd spent the evening walking the campus with Tyler, and he'd thought of an idea for an article for *The Signal*. With that added clarification, his numerical references were now clear to me. In Ben's estimation, we'd be the twelfth and thirteenth freshmen published in the paper. His statement was awfully presumptuous, but my morning walks hadn't produced anything to write about, so I was anxious to hear his idea. I was also flattered that he wanted me to co-author the article, whatever the topic.

Finally, as if he needed something more to get my attention, Ben added, "We're not just going to get published, we're going to reinvent this campus."

While repeatedly crossing the campus, Ben concluded that the university needed a student center to serve as a central location for after class activities and social interaction. The current layout of the campus limited student interaction after classes to their dorm mates because most students spent their free time in their dorm rooms.

"Imagine," Ben said, "one central facility with a bookstore, cafeteria, student store, two or three fast food restaurants, student government office, newspaper office, student activities center, intramural office, student lounges, and study rooms. Students would congregate at the facility, and the result would be a more connected and unified student body."

It was already late, and I was already tired. Still, we talked for an hour, each proposing different ideas for the article. Eventually, my creative juices started flowing once again and Ben, the chronic insomniac, was always churning late at night.

Ben suggested we explore two possibilities: construction of a new student center—most probably on the undeveloped parcel of land between Yarborough Hall and the main library—and a reallocation of existing facility space so as to create a new student center. I suggested we include campus impact material concerning student centers at other universities. Ben suggested that we recruit an architecture student to draft a design for the center or, even better, sponsor a contest amongst architecture students and publish some of the better submissions. The more we talked, the more I thought Ben might really have something, and I realized I'd never get any sleep that night. Though we believed the idea had a lot of potential, we also acknowledged that the hard work was still ahead, success or failure would be determined by the execution. To get published as freshmen, the article must be flawless: thoroughly researched, thoughtfully organized, and meticulously written. If there were any deficiencies or room for criticism, the editor would never print it. After all, *The Signal* had a long and storied tradition that didn't allow for compromise.

"I wish I'd brought those potato chips from Tyler's room," Ben said as he picked up a package of stale Saltine crackers from the bookcase, sampled its aged contents, and added, "I'm hungry."

"When was number eleven?" I asked.

"Some guy named Joe Golden."

"Joe Golden," I exclaimed, reaching for the novel *The Torn Tuxedo* from the bookshelf, just inches from where the crackers had been stored. "He was a freshman at Stanton in 1957. I've read this book at least ten times. It's one of my favorites. Joe Golden is the reason I came to Stanton University."

"You're going to be number twelve, buddy," Ben assured me. "Believe it."

* * *

Among the "stacks,"—the rows of bookshelves that lined the upper floors of the main library—were small worktables and desks, piled high with books and positioned wherever a nook accommodated quiet study. For more than a month, Ben and I met nightly at a table on the fourth floor where the surrounding subject matter, Ancient Civilizations, produced little foot traffic that would distract us while we organized our project. Rarely did any students pass by our work area. Deep in the stacks, we glimpsed one secretive couple fondling one another but no one doing actual research.

Each evening, we allocated our first two hours to the article, gathering information and reference materials and then divvying up sections of the article for each of us to draft. Once we made headway on the article, we shifted gears and focused on our own individual class assignments and study requirements. It was a very intense period for both of us with our nightly work efforts easily exceeding our daily class time, sometimes making me wish I were an insomniac, too. Ben was more accustomed to nights with little sleep, and I noticed that he looked more alert each morning. I looked like someone coming off a four day, non-stop, sleepless bender in Las Vegas.

From the time we started the article, we hoped to submit it to the editor of *The Signal* before the winter holiday break began on

December 16th. On the 13th, as I lay sleeping on the bed in Ben's dorm room, Ben pecked out the final version of the article on the Corona typewriter we borrowed from his father's print shop. The clanking of the keys hadn't disturbed my slumber, but I awoke when Ben yanked the final page from the roller because it made a sound like something charging at me.

"What?" I cried, shaking my head.

"Finished," he declared.

While still groggy, Ben told me he had lunch the previous week with Tyler, Stewart Yost, and Stan Tilden, a senior writer and the editor of *The Signal,* respectively. Tyler and Ben choreographed the whole affair, so it seemed like a chance meeting and not the pre-planned introduction it was in actuality.

"You told them about the article?" I asked, assuming that was the purpose of the meeting.

"Never mentioned it."

Ben hadn't arranged the meeting to discuss our article or even alert the *Signal* staffers about our plan to submit one. He arranged it because he felt the editor would give an article more consideration if he knew the submitters than if he didn't. Ben believed in the power of contacts and connections.

"I wanted Stan Tilden to have a face to associate with the text. If my plan works," Ben said, "he'll start reading our article with me in mind, and by the time he finishes, he'll want to meet you."

Ben's lunch with the *Signal* staffers also produced one very important piece of information. When Tyler asked Stan whether her article would be in the next issue, Stan responded by saying that they had a lot of material for this next issue and they were still weeding through it all.

"If your article doesn't make these next few issues, it'll run in late March," he told her. "During February each year, material starts to thin and we scramble to find publishable articles, so keep writing."

With Stan's words in mind, Ben proceeded from lunch to the archive section of the library to search through dusty, yellowed *Signal* issues to find out when previous freshmen articles had been published. In all, it took two hours—starting with May of 1958 and regressing to April of 1946—to find the last three articles published by freshmen. As Ben expected, each of the articles was published late in the school year, two in late March and one in April.

It made perfect sense. It was just as Stan had unknowingly suggested. *The Signal* was flush with material during the first three-quarters of the school year and it was during the last quarter when material started to dwindle that the staff was more likely to publish a freshman article. All those freshman articles submitted in the first three months of the current year were probably tucked away in a box in a corner of the paper's office, never read and forgotten. Ben and I would wait. Together, we decided to submit in mid-February when the crunch for publishable material was starting and timing would work to our advantage.

Ben reached for an automobile calendar from his desktop, a freebie from a Common Sense Printers' job, and flipped to the month of February, a picture of a baby blue Corvette with a split rear window above the monthly grid. With a red marker, Ben circled February 15th and wrote "Submit Article to *The Signal*" within it.

Then, Ben reached back to the desk, returned the calendar to its spot in the clutter, fumbled through an unruly stack of papers, and casually handed me two photocopied sheets, pages three and four of *The Signal* dated March 24, 1958. Once I saw the date at the top of the page, I instantly understood the legacy it held. It was something I'd planned to retrieve, but I just hadn't gotten around to it. My eyes quickly canvassed page three, searching the bylines until I found the one that read Joseph J. Golden, Class of 1961, beneath the bold three quarter-inch headline "The Weight of Expectations."

"I thought you might be interested in that."

That was all that Ben said and in a surprisingly nonchalant tone, though he knew my curiosity and interest far surpassed normal reading. For a minute or two, I stared in silence at the headline and byline, careful not to peek into the article itself until I could savor the reading of each word, and then I rose to leave the room.

"Thanks," I said, opening the door. "I'm going back to my dorm room."

* * *

The article wasn't what I expected. *The Torn Tuxedo* was an autobiographical tale of an impassioned liberal columnist working for a conservative newspaper in Washington, D.C. during the tumultuous summer of 1969. It was a classic tale of one man's struggle against the entrenched, political machinery of the time, sort of "Mister Non-Conformist Goes to Washington." "The Weight of Expectations" was also autobiographical, but this time around, Joe Golden was recounting his final days at Holy Sacrament High School in Philadelphia during the spring of 1957. I greatly admired and respected the author of *The Torn Tuxedo*. Suddenly now, I could relate to him, too.

In the spring of 1957, the U.S. was in the midst of a warm and fuzzy, bobbysoxer kind of era when Slinkys and hula hoops reigned, and Joe Golden was an honor student in his senior year of high school trying to earn a scholarship to SU. Joe's best friend in high school was a scrawny, Italian kid named Jack Delgato, or simply Gator to his friends. Joe described Gator as the perfect friend: trustworthy, quick with assistance or a consolatory pat on the back, constantly laughing and joking, and just plain fun to hang around. But despite his good nature, Gator was sent to detention often and was unexceptional in both academics and sports. He put his heart and soul into everything he did, but nothing came easily or naturally, except being a friend.

One late April afternoon, Joe and Gator were seated beside one another in Room 251 working on a mid-semester Chemistry exam, one of the more difficult exams of senior year and one that vaporized scholarship hopes like forgotten liquids on a Bunsen burner. Midway through the test, Joe noticed that Gator was anxious, perspiring, and visibly uncomfortable. With ten minutes to go, Gator began carefully glimpsing the markings on Joe's exam paper, quickly copying answers whenever the teacher looked the other way. Despite the school's honor code, Joe didn't conceal his work and even positioned his right arm, so it wouldn't obstruct Gator's view.

A month later, and just a week before graduation, Brother Bonaventure, the school's principal, called the two boys to his office to talk about their upcoming graduation and their future plans as well. Brother Bonaventure told them they were two of his favorite students, and he wanted them to do well. In a slightly preachy mode that came naturally to a man in a long black robe, he also told them that they were the recipients of a first-rate education and they should work hard and do good things with it.

"I'm going to be a writer," Joe told the brother proudly.

When Brother Bonaventure prodded Gator for his intentions, he reluctantly said, "I'm not really sure, Brother, but my parents want me to be a doctor."

Brother Bonaventure concluded the conference by telling them to always remember these words, "To whom much is given, much is expected."

"Gator didn't leave a note before he did it, so my words are mere speculation," Joe Golden wrote, "but I believe the weight of expectations was more than my young friend could carry."

I read the article five times. Though I found it both passionate and poignant, two adjectives I'd also use to describe *The Torn Tuxedo*, it was hard to believe the works shared a common author. I guessed that there was probably ten years of time separating the essay and the novel, and I wondered if we all changed so significantly with the passage of time. Is it more pronounced in our twenties, or was Joe Golden an exception?

The naive boy who penned the essay was very different from the determined man who wrote the book. The innocence was gone, a toughened worldliness in its place. Would I change as dramatically? Now, it seemed my journal would serve a greater purpose than simply recording my thoughts and activities as originally intended. Years from now, it will remind me of the young boy I was so that I can better evaluate the man I become. It will be my reference point.

Finally, before I set the article aside, I wondered how Joe Golden remembered the young Joe Golden, Gator, and Brother Bonaventure: fondly or sadly? Had he been able to comfortably shoulder the weight of expectations?

* * *

A lot happened while Ben and I waited to submit our article to *The Signal*. I traveled home for the holidays, my first time back since I departed for college. As the first Dalton to venture outside our home state to attend college, I was welcomed with open arms and great enthusiasm. My mother prepared all my favorite meals, and my family actually toasted my return when we gathered for dinner on Christmas Eve, a twenty-pound turkey with crispy, golden-brown skin in the center of the table before us, ready for the carving knife.

Far and away, that Christmas was the best holiday season I'd experienced until then because it was the first time I was in a position to miss my family and truly appreciate how important they were to me. Originally, I was scheduled to return to Cavanaugh on December 30th to celebrate New Years, but I changed my flight at the last moment so I could remain in Delaware until the day before classes resumed on January 9th. Even then, it was difficult to board that westbound plane.

Ben and Tyler embraced the New Year by embracing one another. On the night of the 31st, when the countdown to midnight ended, Ben kissed Tyler, expecting nothing more than a holiday kiss in return. While other partygoers blasted noisemakers and sang Auld Lang Syne, Tyler's kiss deepened. She pressed her fingers against his back, squared her bosom to his chest, and pulled their bodies firmly together. Ben sensed need and urgency and searched her eyes for confirmation. When Tyler returned his passionate glare, Ben knew their kiss would celebrate the start of something new, something more significant than the turning of the calendar, even in a young life, especially in a young life.

"I sometimes felt out of synch with the other girls because I was a virgin," Tyler said as the morning light appeared. "Now, I know I was waiting for you."

During lunch in mid-February, Danny informed Ben, Tyler, and me that he planned to introduce himself to the SU football coach and make his intentions known. Once more, the Grizzlies had ended their season without any invitations for postseason play and a typically lackluster 3-7 record. After his morning workout the next day, Danny stopped by the coach's office.

It was only 9:30am and forty degrees. In the basement of the athletics center, Coach Wilson, a balding, ex-jock in his late thirties, wearing SU sweats and Nike running shoes, was huddled in his office over a hot cup of coffee. Excepting the desk, the room looked more like a sporting goods store than an office at an institute of higher learning, as promotional posters from athletic shoe companies and an assortment of athletic gear provided its only decor.

"Got a minute, Coach?" Danny asked as he entered, removed a couple of softball gloves from a chair, tossed them onto the cold concrete ground, and sat in their place.

All things considered, Coach Wilson was a frustrated man. Four years ago, he coached a team to the state championship at the high school level in Kansas but had yet to post a winning record in three seasons at SU. On far too many days, the coach wondered if his coaching career had already seen its best days, already peaked. When Danny told the coach about his high school football career, his offers from Division 1 schools, his knee injury, his rehabilitation, and his plan to try out for the team, Coach Wilson received his declaration apathetically. While Danny talked, the coach never even looked up from his steaming coffee. He held the cup three inches above the desk, turned his wrists slowly in a circular motion, and watched in a trance-like state as the black liquid swirled about the rim.

"You're welcome to come to camp and show us what you've got," the coach replied in a gruff morning voice. "But, I'll warn you right up front, son, Randy Porter played some good football this year, and he'll only be a junior next season. Unless somebody shows me something really special, Randy is my starting quarterback."

Danny was as unmoved by the coach's words of caution as the coach had been by Danny's words of introduction.

"Anything else?" Coach Wilson mumbled.

"Yeah," Danny said, rising to leave. "Get ready for a show."

* * *

Ben and I felt confident as we arrived at the Walton Building for the appointment Ben had scheduled with the newspaper's editor, Stan Tilden. *The Signal's* office was located on the second floor, directly above the student store, surrounded by the faculty offices of mostly English and journalism professors. It was the size of a small SU classroom, about forty by seventy feet, crowded with desks, file cabinets, and work stations, and reduced in floor space by three makeshift offices in the rear, housing the editor's office, a copier area, and a darkroom for photography. The staff of the paper consisted of the editor, eighteen writers, five photographers, and two graphic artists, but only five or six people milled about when we arrived.

Stan Tilden was short and thin with uncombed black hair, wearing a wrinkled white shirt with a button-down collar, corduroy pants, and black-rimmed glasses—all in all, an unimpressive but collegiate and studious appearance. Though clearly lacking adequate newspaper instincts during his first year in the job, Stan was in the homestretch of his second year as editor of *The Signal* and a seasoned newspaperman at this point. As we entered, he was reading *New West Magazine* and only begrudgingly lowered it to the desk.

"Serves us right for putting a peanut farmer in The White House," he said with a disgusted look on his face. "What did you want to see me about, Ben?"

Ben introduced me. Stan and I shook hands. Ben talked briefly about our subject matter, and then I gave him the large, white envelope that contained our work. In turn, Stan politely accepted the envelope and told us he looked forward to reading it.

All in all, Ben and I were in and out of that office in less than ten minutes. As we exited, I glanced back over my shoulder, watched Stan place our envelope on top of a foot-tall pile of papers, and return to his spot in the magazine. It hadn't gone as I'd hoped.

That evening, the hot dinner choices at the cafeteria were pot roast, halibut, or spaghetti. We sat at our usual table, but I did not feel like my usual self. Ben and Danny devoured their pot roast, mashed potatoes, and rolls while I picked over my halibut. Feeling distracted and without appetite, I didn't eat much because I was busy digesting the events of the last few days, wondering why I was the only one at the table who was concerned. I simply couldn't muster my appetite for a second rate plate of halibut while my most significant freshman effort was sitting atop a humongous pile of submissions on the *Signal* editor's desk, unread and unconsidered.

"How was your workout this morning?" I asked Danny. Then later, "Do you think Stan will read the article?" I asked Ben.

Both responded casually, in a matter-of-fact manner, as if they expected success regardless of any obstacles or deterrents. They were completely unfazed by the negative signals and forewarnings we had received, almost as if their ears could only receive the positive. At that moment, I realized I worried more when given positive feedback and encouragement than either of them when challenged and discouraged. They lived in a blissful state of blind faith. Everything would work out for them. Nothing would go wrong.

Why did I have to be born into the real world? I thought. *Why couldn't I have been born into their perfect world, the one without any failures or heartaches or disappointments?*

But, it wasn't so bad. Danny's fragile knee would be spared a crippling re-injury, and Ben and I still had the traditional nomination process for *Signal* staff positions.

"Don't you feel well?" Danny asked, noticing my uneaten fish and potatoes.

"I'm alright."

"You going back for more?" Ben asked Danny.

"Is a football made of pigskin?"

"And laces made of the finest virgin wool," Ben added.

"Let's go."

3.

Without safe hydraulic elevators, skyscrapers would never have been built because stairs that climbed more than three flights were impractical. In this context, "Going up?" the question often asked beside elevator doors has a grander meaning than originally intended.

Three weeks passed while Ben and I waited for a verdict from Stan Tilden and *The Signal*, a frustrating stretch for two reasons: We yearned for feedback and our freshman year was waning. It was late March and we both felt the end of the school year looming, the same way the late-day sun loomed on the horizon until it slipped beneath it. With those same feelings of finality and inevitability, time was running out. In no time at all, we would cram for final exams and then leave for summer. In our minds, the ticking clock of our freshman year sounded like a big bass drum and we couldn't look forward to the close of the year without a *Signal* byline. It had become essential, the all or nothing gage of success or failure on our freshman experience. Good grades were no longer sufficient.

Ben and Tyler monitored the activity at the *Signal* office for news. Always conscious of his outsider status at the paper, Ben was careful never to appear to be spying or campaigning. And still, there was never any mention, never any word. Successive *Signal* issues were compiled and released, one after another, after another, and still no news.

Our frustration increased.

* * *

On the last Monday in March, Ben, Danny, and I staked out a prime position in one of the student lounges to watch the final game of the NCAA Basketball Tournament between Kentucky and Duke. We knew it would be standing room only by tip-off so we arrived about an hour early to secure a sofa location in front of the TV. Having left to retrieve three beers, Danny and Ben were taking sides when I returned.

"I've got to go with the more experienced Kentucky squad," Danny said. "I played in the state championship game twice, and I can tell you firsthand—experience wins the big ones."

"Never underestimate the young and determined," Ben returned defiantly. "Duke's starting line-up is mostly underclassmen, but it's a talented team. Youth will be served tonight, my friend, and I've got five bucks that says Duke wins."

"Make it ten."

"You're on."

Making it official, they shook hands and then continued debating the finer points of the game as tip-off approached.

My own experience with team sports was limited to two unremarkable seasons of little league baseball while in elementary school, but I understood the positive impact it had on kids, teaching them the value of cooperation and accomplishment. On the playing field, the life lesson learned is that we're all better off when we cooperate and rise to meet a common challenge. Unfortunately, some people never learn that lesson and, instead, function in a manner basically the opposite of teamwork, belittling others to feel superior. Seated beside our sofa on a folding chair was one such person.

Nick Sweeney, a *Signal* writer in his senior year at SU, was a brash, blowhard from Hoboken, N.J. without a personal filter for his comments and whose very presence on the *Signal* staff could only be explained as providing another viewpoint. He had glimpsed our article earlier that afternoon and couldn't restrain himself from dispensing his hostile review of our material. His folding chair beside our sofa was not coincidental.

"We all had a good laugh at the *Signal* today," he told Ben who was seated nearest his chair beside the sofa. "Your proposal for a new student center is hilarious. Personally, I can't wait to hold hands and sing campfire songs at the student center."

He was talking to Ben, but all in the vicinity heard him.

"Sweeney," Ben returned unruffled. "I've only known you for about three months, but you sure talk a lot of nonsense. Whenever you open your mouth, you're always sucking out loud."

Ben's use of the term "sucking out loud," which basically means brashly spouting stupid stuff, confounded Sweeney but amused the other students listening to the exchange.

Ruffled by chuckling students around him, Sweeney blasted back, "Do you know what your problem is, Ben? You don't think big enough. You've got to think bigger. You should propose that a one hundred-story skyscraper be constructed right smack in the middle of campus. Then, all university students could live together above the student center. Wouldn't that be cozy?"

"I think our proposal is quite large enough," Ben replied in a dismissive tone. "But, thank you for your input."

"Don't you realize that it's been twenty years since a freshman article was published in *The Signal*?" Sweeney countered, unwilling to concede the last word. "You've absolutely no chance of getting published as freshmen!"

"It had been twenty-five years between Triple Crown winners, but that didn't stop Secretariat."

"What's that got to do with anything?"

"In all likelihood, a surly horse in Secretariat's stable said it couldn't be done also."

"What do you think about Sweeney's remarks?" I asked Ben a few minutes later after the game commenced.

"I don't," Ben replied, never taking his eyes off the action.

"What do you mean?"

"Do you value Sweeney's opinion?"

"Not really."

"Exactly," Ben returned. "The only opinion that matters at this moment is Stan Tilden, and I have a lot more respect for his depth and intelligence than Sweeney. Don't let Sweeney taunt you."

"What if others at *The Signal* were laughing at our article?"

"Pete," Ben said, finally looking away from the game. "If you're going to accomplish anything in this world, you have to learn to ignore the naysayers like Sweeney. They are everywhere and all they bring to the table is negativity and deterrence."

Sporting event socials or "keggers," as they were called on campus, were held six or seven times a school year, whenever a major championship like the World Series or the Super Bowl rolled around. It was customary for hall residents to donate a few dollars to a fund earmarked for refreshments. Refreshment tables, located in the hall-way, always groaned beneath the weight of beer kegs, soda cans, and pretzel and potato chip drums. Whenever the contest was lopsided, the assemblage became more party-like with attendees talking, dancing, and basically ignoring the game. But, if the score was close and the outcome in question, like that night, the gathering would be blaring and spirited, as the crowd voiced approval and anguish at the outcome of every play.

Duke fans and Kentucky fans were indistinguishable from one another as all dressed in blue and white colors common to both universities and all shouted loudly at every basket attempted, made or missed. With five minutes left in the game, I noticed Tyler in the midst of the congestion that blocked the door. Bouncing up and down like a Radio City Rockette, she was ecstatic, waving her hands wildly to lure us into the hallway. That wouldn't be possible until after the final buzzer sounded, so I waved acknowledgement and signaled to her that we couldn't make it to the door.

The game ended with Kentucky securing the title. Making good on his wager, Ben reached deep into his pocket and begrudgingly presented ten crumpled dollar bills to Danny, a payment consistent with his broke student circumstance. While the payoff happened, Tyler squeezed between students departing the lounge and made her way to us. Brimming with enthusiasm, she practically burst on arrival and shouted, "Stan wants to meet with you tomorrow."

Ben and Tyler embraced. Danny and I jumped up and down and slapped high fives. To the other students still milling about the lounge, we must have looked like extremely happy Wildcat fans.

"Did he say anything more?" I asked.

"No, we've got a staff meeting tomorrow at five o'clock and Stan told me to ask the two of you to come."

"That's got to mean we're in, doesn't it?"

"I don't know," Ben answered, "but it has been five weeks since we submitted the article, so any news is good news."

* * *

The Signal was published every other Monday throughout the school year, and staff meetings were held every two weeks, on the day after publication. The newspaper's cluttered quarters were too small for the meetings so the staff gathered in the faculty conference room just two doors down. Stan Tilden chaired the meeting. His usual format consisted of reviews and comments concerning the newly published issue and then ideas and assignments for the next one. Sometimes the newspaper's faculty advisor, Sheila Lambert, attended, other times not. On that afternoon, she was seated beside Stan at the head of the conference table. Ben and I sat to the left of Stan, several seats removed.

As the meeting progressed, we both wondered when our article would be introduced. Finally, after more than an hour, Stan looked our way.

"I've asked Ben Matthews and Pete Dalton to join us today because I want to address an article that the two of them submitted to *The Signal*," Stan began. "As you all know, rarely does *The Signal* publish freshman articles, it has only happened eleven times—eleven extraordinary efforts that are a proud part of *Signal* history. When I read their article about Stanton University's need for a student center, I believed that I'd been presented with the latest rare exception. In my estimation, this article represents an opportunity for the paper to participate in shaping the future of our university. Its publication might be a milestone for both the university and *The Signal*."

As Stan introduced our article, Professor Lambert glanced approvingly toward Ben and me, several times, the same way my mother looked at me whenever I did something inconsistent with my age, a look that conveyed both surprise and enjoyment. The professor was in her early fifties and scholarly and refined in appearance, with meticulously groomed gray hair, tailored clothing, and expensive accessories. We'd made direct eye contact several times since Stan began, and I interpreted that as a good sign.

Stan continued. "It has been almost twenty years since a freshman article was published and the historical significance of such an event should not be discounted. So, I sought the counsel of Professor Lambert and the six senior writers on the paper. I gave each a copy of the article and asked them to respond, yea or nay, to one simple question: All things considered, should *The Signal* publish the article?"

At that point, Stan suggested Professor Lambert take over. She smiled and said, "Thank you, Stanley," as if this was a Hollywood awards ceremony and she'd been handed the microphone. Since Stan was clearly acting in the role of emcee, her role must be that of celebrity presenter. With so much on the line, Ben and I would've gladly skipped the formalities and simply ripped the envelope open, but Professor Lambert continued from where Stan left off.

"When Stan asked me to review the article, I commended him on his discretion and prudence. Before we publish a freshman article, we must be certain it's worthy of the honor. This would be an historic event, indeed. I also concur with Stan's instinct that this decision is not solely the editor's, and I thought that his impromptu committee was an excellent idea. I further suggested that each of the votes of the senior writers would count as one vote, and Stan's vote and mine would count as two. Thus making the total of the tally ten, and we would require seven affirmative votes to publish."

The staff meeting was abruptly halted when a teaching aide leaned into the conference room and told the professor she had an urgent phone call.

The professor rose from the table. "I'll be right back."

Just like that, Ben and I were suddenly in awards ceremony hell. Waiting for the professor to return, we were basically smiling and clapping through category after category, nervously waiting on our moment, except that there weren't other nominees to contend with. Four little "nays" would defeat us.

Ben turned to me and whispered, "You realize it all hinges on Lambert, don't you? We know we have Stan's two votes and I'm certain we can muster three votes amongst the six seniors. It'll be Lambert's two votes that make the difference."

"Then, we are in," I said.

A few of the other staff members extended wishes of good luck during this unscheduled intermission. One of the voting seniors from across the table leaned in and said, "Either way, it's a good effort and you should both be proud."

From his statement, I couldn't deduce whether he'd voted yea or nay, but I thought his sentiment sincere.

Tyler sat against the wall with the other underclassmen since seating at the conference table was usually limited to seniors. Ben and I had been treated like visiting dignitaries that day and seated at the table. She held her hands in front of her face so we could see her index and middle fingers crossed in support. Though it seemed longer, only ten minutes passed before Professor Lambert reappeared.

"I'm sorry for the delay," she reiterated as she took her chair. "Now, where was I?"

"You were about to announce the results," Stan said.

Professor Lambert opened the brown, leather bound journal before her and flipped through a few pages until she found the notation she sought.

"I am very proud to inform all of you that the results of the voting was nine affirmative and one nay," she announced. "The article is hereby approved for publication in *The Stanton University Signal*. Details concerning publication are left to the sole discretion of the editor, Stan Tilden. My sincere congratulations to Mr. Matthews and Mr. Dalton."

Oh my God, we won! What did I do with my acceptance speech? I could only imagine what it felt like to take home the big prize at an actual awards ceremony, like Best Picture or Best Actor, or for that matter, what it felt like to take home the lead actress. Those feelings would surely be amazing, but this feeling was right up there. On this day, we were taking home the big prize. Just as Ben predicted a semester ago, we were, indeed, twelve and thirteen.

Instantly, I felt overwhelmed by emotion. Though I wanted it badly, I'd cautiously readied myself for disappointment, for rejection. I shook hands, nodded, but never uttered a word. Publication was more than extraordinary. Ben smiled and good-naturedly grasped the hands extended in his direction. I'm quite sure he expected it and was prepared for the moment. With a very content look on his face, Stan eased back in his chair. He'd recommended the article so the vote was validation of his judgment. Further, Stan knew the results in advance and had already decided his course of action. He waited quietly until the festivities subsided and then asked everyone to "settle down."

"We still have business to conduct," Stan shouted.

Stan envisioned further redemption. As a junior, many had doubted his selection as editor. For twenty months, Stan had worked hard to prove his worthiness and earn the respect of the student body, the newspaper's staff, and the faculty. And still, there were doubters. Stan believed this article and issue would establish his legacy. He, too, would have his place in *Signal* history.

"This article will be our cover story for the April 10th issue," Stan said, causing a collective gasp from the staff. "I will hear ideas for related stories through next Tuesday, so get busy, be creative, and give me your best work. This will be something special, I promise you."

The room emptied. When we reached the staircase and other students proceeded down, Ben suddenly grabbed my shirt at the collar and dragged me up the stairs.

"Where are we going?" I asked as Ben accelerated our ascent and we started running up the stairs. We climbed three flights to the top floor and then raced the length of the hallway to the opposite end, all the while I kept inquiring, "Where are we going?"

The Walton Building was one of the older buildings on the campus with Gothic styling and an iron fire escape attached to the stone on the outside of the building. Ben opened the window and crawled onto the platform beneath it, staying clear of the opening and descending ladder. There were three more platforms and ladders below this one that forged an iron pathway to safety, in case this place of higher learning ever became a blazing inferno. As soon as Ben was seated on the platform, I followed him out the window.

Above us was a breathtakingly beautiful night—a sky as black as freshly poured pavement and dashed by a billion twinkling, white stars. Below us, the university after dark—a trickling of students passed beneath lampposts on the sparsely lit walkways of the campus. We were breathless and panting.

"This building has an elevator, you know," I managed to voice between my gasps for oxygen.

I felt like I would burst from excitement, but I didn't say anything more as my breathing normalized. I sensed a reflective mood in Ben and waited on his words instead.

"I come here a lot," Ben finally offered. "Sometimes when I can't sleep, I walk over from Yarborough Hall and climb to this perch. I sit in awe of the magnificence of the world, and I pledge to myself that I will live a life worthy of this backdrop. I will make a difference, I tell myself."

"Ben," I said, exasperated, "we're on the cover of *The Signal*. No freshman article has ever been the cover story. This is more historic than I ever imagined or hoped. It's incredible."

I grinned from ear to ear. Ben continued.

"I'm happy," Ben replied. "It's historic alright. You're a great writer and you sure did some great work on this article. You should be very proud."

With that said, Ben pointed to the dark area between Yarborough Hall and the main library, lit slightly by spillage from the tall windows of the buildings flanking it.

"When that darkened hillside is the site of the new SU student center," Ben offered as an explanation for his casual disposition, "we will have done something more significant than simply put words on paper. We'll have made a real difference. That is my yardstick, my friend."

After a short silence, I observed, "The vote was nine to one. Who do you think voted against us?"

Both sure of the nay vote, Ben and I looked at one another, smiled and simultaneously declared, "Sweeney," before breaking into gut-busting laughter.

* * *

For the next ten days, Stan Tilden was relentless. He drove the production of this *Signal* issue like none previous. He pressured the writers for better ideas and articles and summoned Ben and me to his office on a daily basis. The three of us worked nonstop on the issue, with graphic artists arranging layouts and font styles, with photographers selecting images, and with writers sharpening their ideas and crafting articles. It was a production pace not seen in this country since the construction of the Empire State Building in the 1930s.

Previously, we'd never worked with Stan. We didn't fully understand his motivations, but we sensed this issue had a very special significance to him. We believed Tyler when she told us he was a different person, much more passionate in his normally perfectionist ways. And, though Stan pushed us even harder than even his staff, Ben and I never complained—it would've seemed ungrateful. Along with the cover article and the freshman bylines, we figured we were getting a crash course on the job of editor as well. One quirk I learned about Stan was that whenever he had a dilemma, he'd snare a red rubber ball from his top right drawer and play a game of one-man catch against the wall.

"I think better this way," he would say.

Tyler submitted an article depicting a couple of SU students during a typical evening at the student center. The students wander about the facility doing somewhat trivial activities: purchasing books and supplies at the bookstore; grabbing snacks at the student store; attending a student government meeting; checking intramural scores and schedules; meeting friends to exchange class notes; and enjoying a meal at a restaurant. Two of the highlights of the article were new features that Tyler added to the proposed student center that we had not included: a gallery for student art works and a small amphitheater for student performances. These additional features expanded on a key theme from the cover article that the university was largely young, maturing adults, and it was just as important to encourage growth and expression, as it was education.

A last minute submission, Stan and I read the article in Stan's office around 8pm on Wednesday evening, just twelve hours before the issue would be turned over to the printer.

"I think it's too trivial," Stan said bluntly while reaching into the drawer for the red rubber ball. As he tossed it repeatedly against the wall, I sensed that he wanted a second opinion. Personally, I thought the article had a place in the issue, and I knew Stan had to decide right now. The ball was out, so he wasn't sure.

"I think its triviality is its heart and why it will work so well in the issue," I argued as the ball thumped against the concrete wall.

I continued. "The article adds a real human feel to all the fancy talk about community, and it demonstrates how the center will impact students' daily lives. When you finish this article you really understand that the student center will play as important a role in students' days as their dorm room, maybe more so. Just as important, I think the article will provide a nice balance to the cover article. It's only nine hundred words, let's squeeze it in."

"You're right," he returned. "I got the same feeling from the article that you did. I just didn't want to admit it because it means we have to reorganize the issue again. Let's see what we can do."

I didn't like Stan Tilden at first. He wasn't warm, engaging, or funny, and he barely acknowledged Ben and I that first day in his office. But after working side by side with him for ten long days, I realized Stan was the first real journalist I'd met. What separated him from the others at the newspaper? The duties and responsibilities of a journalist mattered to him. In his time as editor, Stan never deluded himself into thinking that *The Signal* was more than a small college newspaper or that its content was changing the world. And still, Stan understood the traditions that true journalists honor. Journalists have died for the right to publish, and readers place their trust in those pages every day. For real journalists, there are standards, traditions, and heritage they honor regardless of the circulation of the newspaper or the significance of the assignment. Stan felt that, he lived it, and so did I.

* * *

You carry some moments with you all your life. They are permanently etched on your soul, and they define the person that you are. This was definitely one of those moments.

I was stretched out and asleep on the couch in the lounge at about 6pm on Friday evening when Stan nudged my shoulder.

"I've been looking all over for you," he said. "I thought you'd want to see this early copy of the paper."

Fresh from the printers, Stan handed me a copy of the next edition of *The Signal*, dated for distribution that following Monday, April 10th. Extending both hands, I accepted the paper like I was being handed a newborn child in its birth blanket. Slowly, I raised it to eye level until I saw the bold headline and the smaller byline beneath it.

The Grizzly Den, An SU Student Center
Benjamin Matthews and Peter Dalton
Class of 1981

Staring at the beautiful simplicity of black ink on white paper, my eyes brimmed with tears and the headline blurred before me. I swallowed hard and struggled to keep my composure.

"Can I have this copy?" I asked.

"Sure you can."

I didn't say anything more. I couldn't. I knew I'd never forget this moment, but I had nothing to add to it either. Stan extended his hand and said, "Congratulations, Pete, I'm honored to publish it."

That week, Stan had earned the designation of journalist in my mind. That byline, on the front page of that small college newspaper, was confirmation for me too, that I was, indeed, a journalist.

"I'm thinking of framing it," he told me, smiling from ear to ear. "I know you will."

* * *

Maybe I hadn't noticed before—my name had never been on the front page of a college newspaper—but on Monday and Tuesday, people were reading *The Stanton University Signal* at every turn. I saw students and faculty members with the newspaper open before them in classrooms, in hallways, on campus benches, in lounges, in the cafeteria, in the library, in the bleachers, and just about everywhere. And, not just reading it, everyone was talking about it. As I crossed the campus, students I'd never met before stopped me and told me how much they enjoyed the article. Many asked if there'd been any communication with the administration and some even asked when the groundbreaking would happen. It was all very satisfying, but also a harbinger of events to follow.

Ben and I arrived at the cafeteria at our usual time Tuesday, just a little after noon. Danny met us on the front lawn. We checked the lunch specials and entrée choices as we entered the building and then proceeded to the hot meal line, all in accordance with our usual routine. Then, as Ben and I emerged from the stainless steel dessert gallery, the last stop on the serving line, and headed toward our regular table, a slow deliberate clapping began at our right where a group of *Signal* staffers were seated.

At first, Ben and I chuckled, amused by the impromptu and seemingly glib tribute. But, as we walked, the applause spread a little farther with each step, as more students joined in, until finally, when we reached our table, more than half of the students in the cafeteria were clapping. Unsure of how to react, I placed my meal tray on the table and sat conspicuously behind it. Ben smiled easily, nodded his head, and waved his hand in acknowledgement, an early indication of his political instincts and inclination.

Danny arrived at the table. "Can I sit here or is this table reserved for famous writers?"

"Do you know this guy?" I asked Ben.

"Fame sure brings out the riff-raff," he answered.

Tyler and Stan, who were seated at the table with the *Signal* staffers, scooted in our direction and brought their trays with their half-eaten lunches to our table.

"You're celebrities," Tyler exclaimed. "The whole campus is buzzing about *The Signal*."

Then, she looked across the table at Stan and encouraged him to take over.

"Tell them about Lambert," she said.

"Professor Lambert stopped by my office last night around 5pm," Stan informed us, perplexed by the unscheduled visit. "She has never come to my office before. She always calls me on the telephone and makes me walk to her office."

Stan had resumed eating, so his words were intermittent between chews.

"She held the new issue in her hand, waved it emphatically, and said it was the best issue of *The Signal* she'd ever seen. She also said she'd received a lot of positive feedback from other faculty members, too."

"That's incredible," I declared.

"Wait, there's more," Tyler interjected, so Stan could continue the recounting of his time spent with the professor.

"Professor Lambert told me to tell you both that this article has secured two of next year's six sophomore positions at *The Signal* for you. As far as she is concerned, there will be only four positions available to this year's nominees. You're in!"

"And rightly so," Tyler added.

I left the cafeteria that afternoon to retreat to the peaceful sanctuary of my dorm room. Even more noteworthy, I skipped my first class since arriving at college, Philosophy 101 at 1:40pm. I was worn out. As inconspicuously as possible, I entered Yarborough Hall through the glass doors at the rear, but as I passed the hall manager's office, I heard my name called from within. Cautiously, I peeked my head around the corner.

It was Martin. He was seated behind the desk, in his usual position, with his feet propped up and *The Signal* in his hands.

"I thought we had an understanding, Pete," he said, shaking his head in mock disappointment. "Freshmen should be seen and not heard. Remember?"

"Whoops," I returned, not knowing what else to say.

"Way to go," he said. "It's a hell of a good article."

I enjoyed my newfound fame, but I also knew that fifteen minutes, as the saying goes, would be plenty for me. Sure, the positive reaction to our work and the positions at *The Signal* were gratifying, but the acclaim was both overwhelming and exhausting. As expected, Ben was thriving in the limelight, and I figured that he would somehow find a way to parlay it into something bigger and that would be positive, too. But, in my case, I just wanted to withdraw from the hoopla and fuss, and quietly savor the moment in my own way.

Just before 2pm, I arrived at my dorm room and collapsed onto the unmade sheets, closing my eyes to the midday glare and, finally content with the waning days of freshman year, I drifted off.

* * *

"Pete, Pete."

Like a cruel curse, someone was always waking me.

"Wake up, Pete."

As I struggled for orientation, Danny—just a fuzzy gray figure hunched over me—nudged my shoulder a final time, told me it was 6:30pm, and asked if I was going to dinner. The cafeteria closed promptly at 7pm, so Danny warned me that I might inadvertently sleep through mealtime—an action consistent with good roommate etiquette but frustrating nonetheless.

In absolute disbelief, I confirmed the time on the clock radio beside me. I had slept four hours and felt just as worn out as when I first laid down, maybe more so. I needed a break—some kind of vacation—even if it was just for a day. I'd earned it.

"Let's take tomorrow off," I suggested to Danny as my mind cleared. "We'll drive to the coast and hang out at Driftwood Bay. No books, no papers, no classes."

Among his many talents, Danny was a great accomplice. He loved road trips, group adventures, and well-planned conspiracies, and required little persuasion to ditch classes. But, as I proposed my plan, I sensed conflict in him. In the past, Danny had suggested similar escapes and I'd rebuffed him, so he found himself both pleasantly surprised and compromised. He knew that flight was my motivation and didn't fully approve—he wasn't the type to run from anything. Danny did things on his own terms, always strutting like a henhouse rooster and never even glancing back as he walked away.

And still, first and foremost, Danny was a good friend so he didn't question a friend in need.

"Sounds great to me," he finally responded.

* * *

Whenever I rode in Danny's car, a Chevrolet Monte Carlo with engine knocks and rusted side panels, I always wondered how that heap of scrap metal made the two thousand mile journey from Pittsburgh to Cavanaugh. It never should've made it passed Nebraska or over the Continental Divide. Whenever pressed, Danny would begrudgingly concede that "Monte," as he referred to it, wouldn't make the return trip, but he also insisted it would carry him around Cavanaugh for four years. I added his prediction to my list of things that I'd only believe if I'd seen it with my own eyes. After breakfast and a quick prayer by the open car door, Danny and I set off for the bay, leaving the rigors of campus life behind.

Driftwood Bay was one hundred thirty-five miles west of Stanton University. The northern section of the bay was home to fishing villages and tourist towns and the southern section was the site of Cavanaugh's thriving seaport. One of our favorite destinations for weekend road trips was the small fishing village of Condor with its salty shops, seafood restaurants, greasy eateries, and picturesque waterfront, where small fishing boats rocked alongside weathered docks in the town's marina. Danny favored Condor for the public park near the marina, where older residents played chess and recounted stories of fishing and the sea.

It was about 10am when we arrived. Instantly, I felt revived by the moist ocean air as it slapped my face like a white cotton sail gliding across the frigid waters of the bay. The air temperature was considerably cooler than the inland locale we departed that morning, probably low fifties at most, so Danny and I both put on sweatshirts we'd stowed in the backseat. We parked on the main street in front of some shops that overlooked the park and marina below. One shop, The Ink Stain Tattoo Parlor, had an assortment of colorful designs in the window that caused Danny to remark that we should get medieval dragons tattooed on our chests, fire-breathing optional.

"Next trip," I told him.

In the marina, several tugboat-like vessels had already returned from their morning outing, and we could see the fishermen unloading their catch onto the dock, some still flopping and fighting. From our elevated viewpoint, I could also see two games of chess in progress at the concrete tables in the park, so I knew Danny would wander that way. I quickly scanned the tattoo designs, considered how angry my mother would be if I painted my torso, then followed Danny as he crossed the grassy lawn.

As we approached the small gathering, a heavyset man in his fifties with a shaved head and ruddy complexion, looked up from his chessboard and called out to Danny, "Hey QB, how have you been?"

"Coop," Danny responded, "I was hoping you'd be here."

Coop was Robert Cooper, and he owned two local businesses: The Bayside Motel, a weathered, low-rent, flophouse near the water, and The Rusty Anchor, a seafood restaurant and bar. Coop was wearing a gray pullover, blue pants, and a captain's hat, and looked like he spent more time swabbing decks than tabulating sales. He was already well versed on Danny's plan to play football at SU, so he often addressed him as QB or Quarterback and the first question he asked, once we were seated at his table, concerned the status of his knee.

"Are you going to be ready for camp?" Coop queried.

"I am ready," Danny answered.

"That's great. I can't wait to see you play."

When he trapped his opponent's king in a checkmated position in a corner of the board using his queen and red bishop, Coop won his game.

"Coop is a real schemer," Danny advised me. "I think that's why he's so good at chess."

Two hours later at The Bayside Motel, I learned the meaning of Danny's comment when Coop asked us if we'd unload some boxes for him. In the alley behind the motel, Coop raised the sliding rear door of a white-panel truck and revealed fifty large boxes of cigarettes, each containing eighty cartons. The boxes filled about half of the truck's large cargo box and probably represented an hour of work for the two of us.

"I'll take you guys to Maria's for some Mexican food and cold beers, if you'll carry those boxes to the storage room for me."

"That's the best Mexican food I've ever had," Danny added as an inducement.

"Alright," I said, "let's do it."

As we carried the boxes to the storage room, Danny gained momentum with each box, and I struggled to keep up with him. When we returned from our tenth circuit, Danny bounded into the truck and I slowly pulled myself up. I was winded and sweating profusely. Which one of us was the writer and which one of us was the athlete was quite evident.

"Why don't you take a break?" Danny suggested. "You look like you're going to have a stroke or something."

"I'm fine," I said, lying. "I walk every morning?"

"Take a break," he insisted. "I want to go to lunch, not the emergency room."

Taking his advice, I sat on the rear of the truck as Danny set off with another box.

"Coop must sell an awful lot of cigarettes at the motel and restaurant," I observed when he returned.

"Are you kidding me?" Danny replied. "He couldn't sell this many cigarettes in twenty years. These cigarettes are hot."

"Stolen?"

"Of course."

"We're unloading stolen cigarettes?"

"Well, I'm unloading stolen cigarettes. At the moment, you're recovering from nearly having a heart attack."

"We're involved in a felony?"

"Again, I'm the one doing the unloading."

"I'm not carrying any more boxes."

"Relax, I've got them."

While I remained behind and reassessed my first impression of Coop, Danny set off with more cigarettes.

Coop was a guy who never fully exhaled. He tried to appear easygoing and affable, but he wasn't. Instead, he had a deep-seated tenseness about him that made me uneasy. In two hours, I'd heard him tell many stories, but I could never figure out how much was truth and how much was fiction. For instance, Coop told us he served in the Navy, but I doubted it; service and the military seemed like things he'd avoid. Initially, he seemed like a good guy, but, after some time with him, I came to the conclusion that Coop was a small-time thug who'd mastered the art of appearing legitimate. Apparently, the motel and restaurant were simply fronts for his more lucrative side businesses. As Danny's friend, it concerned me that he seemed drawn to Coop.

What kind of journalist am I going to be, I asked myself, *when I let this thug dupe me into participating in grand larceny with him?*

"We should get out of here," I told Danny on his return. "I don't trust this guy."

"Don't worry, Pete. Coop is harmless. I come from a blue-collar town that is full of Bob Coopers. I know how to handle him."

"If we get caught unloading these stolen cigarettes, you won't play football at SU next year."

"We don't actually know that they're stolen. We're not in on the deal. We're just unloading some boxes for a friend."

Three hundred feet away, a police cruiser turned into the alley and slowly crept our way. Never cool under pressure, my sweating and heartbeat accelerated while the cruiser continued its approach in an evaluating manner. Scared and ready to run the other way, I looked at Danny, but he seemed unconcerned. In my mind, the image of prison cells and the sound of slamming doors alarmed me. As the cruiser neared us, I saw the face of the officer through the windshield, and he didn't look much older than Danny and me, but his youthful appearance wasn't a comfort to me. I knew his handcuffs were just as steely as any veteran on the force. A minute later, when he emerged from the cruiser, I expected the man in blue to shout, "Freeze," but he addressed Danny instead.

"Hey Danny, have you seen Coop?"

"He's in the office."

"Thanks."

* * *

I visited *The Signal* when I heard that Professor Lambert had posted the names of the six new writers. As promised, Ben's name and mine headed the list, so we were officially *Signal* staff writers when the fall semester started. It was customary for the faculty advisor to also appoint a new editor, if a senior vacated the spot, but there wasn't any mention of Stan's replacement, and this produced a firestorm of speculation amongst the staffers.

"She's considering you and Ben for the position of editor," another student commented as we stood before the list. I didn't take the notion seriously and neither did Ben when I informed him of the omission.

American literature was my final exam, and I couldn't wait to be done with it. Danny and I planned to spend our last night as freshmen at the Matthews' home because we had early flights and their house was only twenty minutes from the airport. Kirk promised to make his homemade lasagna, and we all agreed it would be an enjoyable way to spend our last evening before summer break.

Italian scents, tomato, oregano, basil, and garlic, filled the air when we arrived at their home, located fifteen minutes walking distance from the print shop. It was a small and simple craftsman-style home with two bedrooms and two baths in a traditionally blue-collar neighborhood and, aside from a portrait of Ben's mother on a living room wall, all traces of his mother had long since faded from the decor. Miraculously, Danny's car had, once again, conveyed us to another destination, but there wouldn't be a return trip, as it would remain parked in the Matthews' driveway for the summer. Ben would start the engine periodically until Danny returned for football camp in early August.

It felt so good to have our exams behind us, and everyone was in high spirits that evening. Occupied instead by a last minute review of my American lit notes, I didn't have time for lunch that afternoon so my mouth watered when I glimpsed the Italian bread and tossed green salad on the dining room table. With a bottle of red in each hand, Ben filled the wineglasses at each place setting as we all took our seats at the table. Kirk placed the second of two large tins of lasagna on the table, and we all marveled at the bubbling cheese and tomato masterpieces before us. On a celebratory occasion like that evening, it was easy to note how significant a role good food and good friends played in a full life.

There was little talk of school, classes, the print shop, or even *The Signal* that night. Everyone's thoughts were closer to home—food, family, and friends. Kirk spoke of his wife Constance with a warm reverence that made it seem as if she had died months ago and not fourteen years ago.

"Connie and I married when she was just nineteen and I was twenty five," Kirk told us, fondly reminiscing. "We wanted children but, when ten years passed, we reluctantly accepted that it simply wasn't meant to be. Then, one evening, I came home from work and found Connie beaming, absolutely lit up from within. She was the picture of joy and I knew right away. She didn't have to say a word. 'You're pregnant,' I said, and she just nodded. I've never seen anyone happier. Ben was a miracle for us."

"I remember when my little sister, Christi, was born," Danny shared next. "I was eight years old at the time and I was absolutely fascinated by her. For hours on end, I sat beside her crib, reaching between the bars to touch her little fingers so she would wrap her whole hand around my one finger and squeeze as tightly as she could. I thought she was amazing."

"I'll bet she adores her big brother," Kirk responded.

"Both of them," Danny answered. "I've got two little sisters and we couldn't be any closer. My parents worked so much that I usually cared for them. Their school was right down the street from my high school so we traveled to and from school together everyday. I dropped them off each morning and picked them up each afternoon and, if I had football practice, they would come to the practice field and watch from the sidelines."

We sipped red wine, nibbled on crusty chunks of Italian bread, and swapped sentimental stories while waiting for the lasagna to cool and Carl to arrive. Though the lasagna was still in a state similar to molten lava, Kirk, on hearing the front door open, called to Carl from the dining room, "Where you been, Carl? Dinner is getting cold."

"Cleaning up your mess," Carl returned as he entered the dining room. "Whose pile of junk is that parked out front?"

"Mine," Danny said, "if you are referring to that classic Monte Carlo in front of the house."

"It runs?"

"Of course it runs!" Danny replied. "It's got one hundred and twenty-two thousand miles on it and plenty more to go."

"I wouldn't count on that," Carl countered.

After dinner, I noticed a videocassette tape on the living room bookcase beside the television labeled, "Ben's Revolutionary Events." Curious, I inserted the tape into the nearby player and, much to my surprise, Ben appeared on the screen in a gray colonial-era coat and white powdered wig, apparently on the set of a local television station during the evening news broadcast. He looked a bit younger but not by much.

"What's this all about?" I asked, turning to Ben.

In May and June of 1976, Ben appeared weekly on a local television news program for eight, three-minute segments in which he recounted stories about our Founding Fathers and our unformed nation's road to revolution. In each segment, Ben dressed in attire consistent with the colonial period and described historical events involving John Adams, George Washington, Ben Franklin, Samuel Adams, Thomas Jefferson, John Hancock, and others. It was all part of an informational series he'd pitched to the station manager as a lead-up to the bicentennial celebration that Fourth of July.

"Immediately, the station manager liked the idea of a high school student doing educational segments as part of the bicentennial celebration," Ben explained, downplaying his early media experience. "It wasn't a hard sell at all."

Ben was a natural for the assignment. As a child, Kirk read colonial and Revolutionary War stories to Ben in the same manner most parents read children's books. He was a colorful storyteller, and he so loved that period in American history that he vividly brought the characters and events to life for Ben. Instead of *The Cat in the Hat*, Ben listened intently while his father recounted the famous midnight ride of Paul Revere. Rather than *Make Way for Ducklings*, Ben listened to tales about the historic challenges and accomplishments of the First Continental Congress. Unflinching character, pure ideals, grandiose plans, and courageous actions were the hallmarks of the era and the foundation for those heroic tales. Young Ben idolized Revere, Washington, Hancock, and Franklin in the same way other young boys idolized Flash Gordon, Captain Marvel, and Superman.

In the television studio while taping his segments for the bicentennial, Ben replayed for the television audience the astonishing narratives that Kirk had told him as a youth.

It was 11pm when Carl tired and asked Ben for a ride around the corner, and midnight before Kirk turned in. Ben, Danny, and I sat up until 3am, for no other reason than we knew we wouldn't see one another for three months. To succeed at college, you have to master the routine, and we were all very comfortable with our routines and one another. But now, it was all about to change; our routines would be interrupted, at least temporarily. The mood was bittersweet by 2am. For me, Ben and Danny represented one greatly exceeded expectation, as I never would've dared to hope for such good friends in college. I'd never had such good friendships in high school.

There was so much to be positive about: finishing exams, summer break, sophomore status, and returning home, but our minds inevitably kept finding their way back to the sad facts: parting, separation, and distance. Ben summed up our collective sadness when he dropped us at the airport. With our baggage piled at the curbside, we all stared at one another blankly, not really sure of what to say.

"Growing up, I never looked forward to the start of another school year," Ben observed, "but I will this summer."

4.

In New York City, at the onset of the twentieth century, skyscrapers reached ever higher. The Singer Tower was 612 feet tall and the Met Life Building was 700 feet tall when completed in 1908 and 1909 respectively, each World's Tallest for a brief time. For a young, ambitious nation in the midst of an industrial revolution, no height seemed unreachable.

I received the biggest shock of my young life when I returned to campus in late August. A note left at the hall manager's office requested my presence at Professor Lambert's office at 3pm, so I waited outside her locked door. I wasn't concerned by her absence because I assumed she'd been detained by a staff meeting or freshman orientation and was running a little late. So I waited. Standing alone in the hallway, I heard the sound of footsteps echoing in an adjacent hallway, coming closer. Expecting to see the professor emerge, I watched the spot where the two hallways connected and, instead, Stan Tilden turned the corner. His feet shuffled quickly and purposefully as he walked, hustling toward me like a man with dirty money in his pockets.

"What are you doing here?" I asked, befuddled.

"Your meeting is with me, not the professor."

In his hand, Stan held an antique key. He opened the grand, wooden door, and we entered the dignified office. A floor-to-ceiling bookcase dominated the wall behind her desk with pictures of the professor and her family scattered amongst the books. One shelf, above a collection of leather-bound *Signal* issues covering the six years Professor Lambert had been faculty advisor, had four framed photographs in a row across it, each a picture of Professor Lambert with a *Signal* editor in cap and gown on graduation day. The newest addition to this gallery was a photo of the professor and Stan on what appeared to be a brilliant Cavanaugh afternoon.

"I shocked the old broad when I recommended you as my successor," Stan said. "She hadn't considered a sophomore."

"I never considered it either."

"I told Professor Lambert that I worked very closely with you on the student center issue and I was impressed. I also told her there might be a short learning curve, God knows I had mine, but I really believe you are the right person for the job."

The professor asked Stan to take some time away from his new position as a staff writer at *The Cavanaugh Dispatch* to talk to me about the editor's position. She told him that if he and I concluded that I should accept the position, she would honor our decision. Her apparent confidence in Stan's judgment was the obvious rationale for this arrangement, as she hardly knew me.

"You're going to be a great journalist, Pete. It's in your heart. This job will be a lot of hard work, I'm not going to kid you about that, but you are head and shoulders above the rest. You're clearly the right choice for the position."

"What about Ben?" I asked, thinking him a more probable and deserving selection.

Similar to choosing sides on a playground or gym class, it was always hard for me to view myself as the first choice. My suburban upbringing had conditioned me to feel more comfortable in the crowd, not out front leading it. Blending in came naturally.

"Ben is a talented guy," Stan returned, "but I don't think Ben is focused on writing or journalism. It is a means to an end for him. It's everything to you."

Stan was right, at least about Ben, and though I knew my workload would be horrendous, I believed I could do it. I looked at the photos of the editors along the bookshelf and tried to imagine my picture at the end, next to Stan. Funny thing was, I didn't see anything so exceptional about the editors as graduates that would exclude me from this prestigious club. I would probably regret this decision later when my class obligations and *Signal* responsibilities conflicted, but I was gradually convincing myself to take the position.

"This is a great opportunity, Pete. I think you ought to do it."

"I will."

When I left that office, I felt euphoric. I'd never considered the possibility of the position of editor, not for a minute. It was a very talented group at the paper, plenty of worthy candidates, so when Professor Lambert didn't name a new editor last spring I thought it was simply a decision she was deferring until the fall. As I descended the grand stairs in front of the Walton Building, my euphoria changed to apprehension as I wondered whether this appointment would impact my friendship with Ben.

At first, I thought I'd withdraw my acceptance if it had an adverse affect on Ben and me. Our friendship meant that much to me. But then, I questioned the quality of our friendship, if that was the end result. In the end, I didn't know what I'd do, but I knew I had to find him and tell him myself.

* * *

When I arrived at his dorm, Ben and Tyler were alone in the dark with the curtains closed and the overhead lights off. Entering, I felt like I might've interrupted an impending tryst—causing zippers to retrace their tracks and buttons to re-find their holes—but I couldn't come back later. I needed to talk with Ben right now. As bad as I felt for my interruption, I felt even worse when I asked Tyler if I could talk with Ben alone. I knew Ben would be straightforward with me if no one else were involved, if it was just he and I.

Fortunately, Tyler wasn't offended. Without so much as a grimace, she stood to leave and offered to bring back sodas or snacks from the vending machine. We declined.

"What is it?" he asked, immediately sensing something afoul.

"I've been offered the position of editor at *The Signal*," I said. "Can you believe that?" I added, laughing nervously.

"That's incredible," Ben stated without hesitation.

"Really?"

"What do you mean—really? That is incredible," he repeated.

"You're not disappointed you didn't get the job."

"What makes you think I want the job?"

"I don't know. I just figured…"

Ben interrupted.

"Well, you figured wrong. I'm not an editor, but you most definitely are. You're a natural. You'll be the best editor *The Signal's* ever had. I have no doubt. I couldn't be happier."

"That means a lot to me."

"This is great news for me, too."

"How so?"

"Someday in the not too distant future, I want you to be the editor of my newspaper, *Cavanaugh Weekly*, once I get it started. Now, I know you'll be ready."

We sat in silence as I absorbed the moment, one that felt very similar to the publication of our freshman article. I remembered Stan handing me that advance copy of *The Signal* in the lounge. I will never forget this moment either. Tears began welling in my eyes, as I knew this would never have happened without Ben. I wanted to thank him, I needed to thank him, and I tried, but I couldn't speak. Ben noticed my emotion, sensed my inability to speak, smiled and nodded, and I knew he understood.

"I can't believe it," I remarked, finally managing to rejoin the conversation a few minutes later. "I never imagined this happening."

"You deserve it."

"What do you call it when your dreams come true before you even have the chance to dream them?" I asked.

"Providence," he answered definitively.

Equally enthusiastic, Tyler hugged me when I told her the news and exclaimed, "I can't think of a better choice."

Concerned my youth might be a source of animosity I asked her whether she thought the juniors and seniors at *The Signal* would be okay working for a sophomore editor.

"They'll be fine," she said, "but they'll expect you to show your abilities and worthiness quickly. I would guess you've got a two-issue grace period."

"One month," I replied with a slightly concerned look.

"You're not alone. Ben and I will help you."

It was almost 6pm when I left that evening, after declining their invitation to go to dinner.

"I've got something to do," I said. "Maybe I'll see you there."

* * *

I went to the *Signal* office and found it dark and unoccupied as I expected. I flipped the light switch on and paused in the doorframe, imagining the room buzzing with energy as a Wednesday evening deadline rapidly approached. I walked to the small office in the rear with Editor stenciled on the door, mentally acknowledging the paper's staff members as I passed their desks, and sat in the chair that Stan had occupied for the last two years. It felt surprisingly comfortable.

I worked with Stan on one of the best issues ever published.

I can do this, I thought.

It had become my mantra since I first heard the news. If I can duplicate the passion and the sense of purpose that Stan brought to this job, I can do this. I looked into the drawers to survey the assortment of bent paper clips, gnawed pens, and loose staples Stan had left behind, and there, in the top right drawer, was Stan's red rubber ball. I couldn't believe he'd left it behind until I saw his note scribbled on a napkin beside it and realized it was intentional.

"Pete," the note began, "I've never reached one hundred tosses before the answer was revealed to me. In your case, I doubt it will take fifty. Good luck, Stan."

I turned to my right and tossed the ball, it produced a loud thump when it struck the gray concrete wall, and I caught it in midair on its return flight.

I can do this.

*   *   *

When I returned to my dorm room that evening, Danny was incensed, sitting at his desk with a textbook open before him, but he wasn't reading. His chin was propped up on his hands, his teeth were clenched, and he was glaring at the wall before him. Previously, I'd never seen Danny angry, but he was that night, no mistaking it. I knew it wasn't the right time to tell him about my new position at *The Signal,* so I simply grabbed a bag of potato chips from the bookcase and started my economics reading assignment.

I'd only read five pages of chapter six, "Economies of Scale," when Danny blurted out, "That son of a bitch, Wilson, won't give me a chance. I spent the whole practice watching Randy Porter from the sidelines. He's got the weakest arm I've ever seen on a quarterback."

Danny made the football team. His efforts at summer camp and the following tryout had been impressive enough to earn a spot on the squad, but Danny was relegated to the role of backup quarterback and he wasn't content with a second string position. No one who went from All-State to backup would be content with that outcome.

"I want to play, goddamn it," Danny shouted. "I didn't work this hard to watch the games from the sidelines. If all I'm going to do is watch the games, I can purchase a ticket and sit in the stands. Four dollars is a fair price for a spectator's view, not fourteen months of hard work."

Whenever Danny reverted to quiet seething, I offered words of encouragement, telling him that his talent would win out in time, but Danny wasn't looking for consolation. An intense competitor, he'd never quit, and his tirade would only serve as a means to channel his anger so that he could use it, harness the force of it. His outbursts would only increase his resolve. Danny ranted sporadically until we turned off the lights at midnight, but he was his usual affable self in the morning.

"I'm sorry I disturbed your studying," he said as he pulled a Steelers T-shirt over his head.

* * *

Most teens learn the unfortunate after-effects of alcohol during high school by consuming more than prudent one night and waking up with a blotchy memory the next day. Others wait until freshman year at college to learn the lesson, waking up to the same pounding head and foggy regrets. In my case, it wasn't until my sophomore year that I had my first regret-laced overindulgence—a night that seriously jeopardized all the good things I had going on at college, a night that could've cost me my newly appointed position as editor of *The Signal* before ink had been pressed to paper for my first edition.

It all started innocently enough, as was often the case. It was a mild Friday evening as I strolled toward my dormitory after dinner, feeling ecstatic about my accomplishments at college. In truth, my college experience was markedly better than I ever dreamed while in high school. Back then, I basically feared college and now it felt like I had somehow mastered it. Barely into my sophomore year, I had great friends, respectable grades, a historic freshman article, and the post of editor of the newspaper. How could things get any better?

In retrospect, I was a little full of myself that evening. Pride cometh before the fall, and the fall often cometh after alcohol.

As I strolled along the walkway, euphoric and carefree, I noticed Tyler crossing an old stone bridge ahead of me and I called out to her. She was unmistakable, even at two hundred yards, even at night. We met beneath a large maple tree midway between us, talked for about five minutes about our mutual lack of plans for the evening, and then decided to go off campus to a biker bar called The Kickstand for a drink or two. It was about a quarter mile from where we stood so just a casual, ten-minute walk.

Lifetimes are the product of a million little decisions. Made well, the life will be one of character and productivity and substance. Made poorly, the life will be one of excuses and trailer parks and probationary periods. Thinking them inconsequential, most people underestimate the impact of little decisions on the overall quality of their life, but that is painfully incorrect. In this one evening, I would make five very bad decisions, the kind of decisions and outcomes that would leaden my spirit for months to come.

My first bad decision that evening was drinking to excess with the girlfriend of my best friend.

"One more round," I told the waitress, though I'd already had four beers, my usual intake on most partaking evenings.

"Let's call it a night," Tyler protested. "It's getting late."

"One more," I said.

It was a little after 10pm and far too early in any night to be as inebriated as I was. Drunks never realize that time is not on their side. My mind was getting fuzzy at the edges and I should've realized it was time to stop. My thoughts were like none I'd ever had before. As Tyler rambled on about her fall classes, I wondered what it would be like to kiss her. Her lips were so red, pouty, moist, and full. Of course I'd noticed previously, but the fact that she was Ben's girlfriend had always been clearer in my mind. All I had to do was lean forward and press my lips against hers. It would be delicious. I was sure of that. I wanted to kiss her, but, thankfully, I didn't get the chance.

"I'm going back to my dorm," she told me.

"I'm going to stick around for awhile," I said.

Starting to leave, Tyler hesitated beside the table. Her face expressed concern about leaving alone and disappointment in her escort, and still she turned and walked toward the door. None of it registered with me.

My second bad decision was sending one of my best female friends out into the night air to make her way home alone, something I never would've done five beers ago. After all, my mother would be quick to remind me that I was raised better.

"Always accompany a girl to her door and make sure she gets inside safely," she had told me as a youngster.

The truth was I did know better. Manners were the bedrock of a suburban upbringing.

My third bad decision was continuing to order pint after pint as my thoughts moved from kissing Tyler, to dating Tyler, to making love with Tyler, to marrying Tyler, to growing old with Tyler. In actuality, I didn't know if I wanted Tyler, my best friends' girlfriend, or someone like her. She was, after all, a walking ideal.

So much was unclear. As the night progressed, I believed the answers to my questions were in my next pint of beer, so I continued, ordering, searching. Drunks often think they're on the verge of an epiphany. One more will do it.

My fourth bad decision came around midnight when I started tossing back Tequila shots with total strangers, a couple of really big dudes and a bristly woman at the pool table. I'd never done Tequila shots. When I staggered out of the bar at closing time, my vision was blurry, my speech slurred, and my wallet empty—it seemed I was buying. In the days that followed, I couldn't recall any portion of my conversation with the three strangers, only splotchy flashes of black leather, colorful tattoos, and motorcycle helmets, which made me all the more curious about our conversation.

But, my worst decision of the night was still to come. Even worse, I remembered little about it, again all I had in my mind were splotchy flashes.

Around 7:30am, I woke abruptly when I heard Ben and Martin talking in his doorway. With little recollection of how I got there, I found myself stretched out on Ben's sofa with a large SU blanket covering me, and, to my astonishment, my clothes were soaking wet beneath it. Martin's tone was loud and annoyed, so much so that even I couldn't sleep through it.

"Someone broke the water pipe in the second floor bathroom," Martin said. "Water is everywhere. It could be thousands of dollars in damages. Did you see anything suspicious last night?"

Ben hesitated but only momentarily. Presented with this new information, Ben and I simultaneously pieced together the goings-on of the previous night, or more correctly, the early morning hours of that day. Before I arrived at Ben's dorm room, I vaguely remembered stopping in the bathroom to pee and possibly swinging from a copper pipe in the ceiling when I was done. I also remembered crashing down hard and water spraying furiously at my face like an opened fire hydrant. Beneath the blanket, I laid quiet and lifeless, knowing that my wet clothes and bloodshot eyes would answer Martin's questions.

"No," Ben answered. "I didn't."

"Did you leave the room after midnight?"

"Not at all. Pete and I were here all night," Ben responded in a hushed manner this time, motioning toward me, supposedly sleeping on the sofa, introducing a late wrinkle into his story.

"Maybe Pete saw something," Martin queried as he stepped through the door, attempting to circumvent Ben.

Uh oh, I thought.

"No, he didn't either!" Ben responded, casually blocking his advance. "We were working on a new article and Pete is extremely focused when he's writing. Nothing distracts him."

Whew, I thought, *that was close*.

"Well, tell him to come see me if he has any information."

Oh shit, I thought.

"I will," Ben assured him.

Hung over and soaked, I had cover for the moment, but like the throbbing in my head, I knew this incident wouldn't pass that easily.

* * *

We published the first two issues of *The Signal* for the 1978/79 school year on September 11th and September 25th. Ben was vigilant in his quest to keep the topic of the student center in front of students, faculty, and administration so the second issue included a follow-up article penned solely by Ben about student centers at other universities. It was a very visual edition with fifteen photographs and elaborate graphics, and the final result was a well-received issue. The issue also included a data box, researched and compiled by Tyler, which illustrated the need and benefit of constructing the center. On one side, there was a graph depicting the ever-increasing number of applications received at SU, rising 7 percent or more each year in the 1970s. On the other side, there was a table that listed vacant floor space estimations and benefiting departments if the student center was built and the affected student services were relocated.

In some ways, I thought Tyler provided a more convincing argument for the construction of a student center in her small data box than Ben and I had in our wordy article the prior spring. The numbers were convincing. Personally, I felt I hit my stride with the second issue and demonstrated that I could handle the job of editor—with a little help from my friends, of course.

For the second issue, I wrote a four-paragraph article about the damaged plumbing in Yarborough Hall and buried it near the back without any credit to the author. Under normal circumstances, the incident was clearly an item for page 2 or 3 with at least twice the column space allotted. In my article, I was apparently preparing my defense strategy when I wrote, "Staffers at the Campus Housing Office are conducting a thorough investigation to determine who caused the damage and whether the late night incident was a vindictive act, a malicious prank, or simply a drunken accident." To date, no witnesses to the 2am antics had come forward, but I lived with daily fear that I'd be found out and guilt over my own stupidity. As editor, my first two *Signal* issues were strong, but they also contained what I could only hope would be the least professional act of my publishing career.

* * *

One evening after dinner, I spotted Ben seated on the fire escape on the Walton Building. With only psychology and economics assignments ahead, I wasn't in a hurry to return to my dorm so I took the elevator to the top floor. On arrival, I popped my head through the window sash and said, "Hey."

Ben lurched. He hadn't seen my approach on the path beneath him, but his start quickly eased and he invited me to join him.

"I've got big news," Ben said. "It's been an interesting day."

Invited by President Stewart, Ben had spent the afternoon in a planning meeting of the University's Board of Directors. As it turned out, the board had been quietly considering expansion plans since January 1977 because three thousand students were turned away the previous year. Several plans were being considered: a conservative one that called for construction of a new classroom and laboratory complex and more aggressive versions that also included one or two new dormitories. Budget amounts ranged from $200 to $500 million.

Our articles resulted in a modification of the existing plans so that a new student center would replace the proposed classroom and laboratory complex. These revised plans, as our article demonstrated, would produce the equivalent increases in educational space while also reorganizing the campus into a more student services-friendly layout.

"Stanton University is deeply indebted to *The Signal* for the initiative it provided," the president told Ben.

"So," Ben concluded, "we've got demographics on our side. It seems the university will expand and I'd say the chance that it will include a new student center is better than 90 percent."

"That's great," I observed. "Why aren't you happy?"

"I am happy. I'm just thinking ahead, that's all."

"You know, Ben," I said. "I've known plenty of people who celebrated minor victories indefinitely. They'd party if they got a good haircut, wouldn't stop until it was time for the next one. You, on the other hand, pull off the impossible and then move right passed it. This is phenomenal. Can't you just enjoy it for a moment?"

"Timing is everything. I need to start raising money. It'll be time to leave school and start *Cavanaugh Weekly* shortly, maybe as soon as the end of this school year, and I figure I'm going to need $100,000 to get the newspaper up and going.

"That's one large stack of dead presidents," I declared, flabbergasted by the number, six figures. "Where are you going to get that kind of money?"

"I don't know just yet, but I will find a way."

"Let's find Danny and grab a couple of beers to celebrate?"

"Nah, I'm going to stay here for a while. I do know one place I can get the money, but it would be at least 5 percent interest."

"Five percent interest would be great. You'll never do better than that."

"Five percent per week that is."

* * *

With kegs of beer and a rock band, the annual Halloween costume party was scheduled for Saturday, October 28th, the same day the Grizzlies were scheduled to play their rival, the University of Central Washington Eagles. The Halloween party was the best social function of the year with an enormous turnout, always spilling out of its cafeteria venue onto the front lawn of the university, and everyone in attendance dressed in elaborate and outrageous costumes. The addition of the UCW game only served to heighten anticipation as the weekend approached.

The Grizzlies had posted a very bear-like 3-3 record thus far, while the conference leading Eagles' record stood at 6-0. UCW was favored to win by fourteen points, but the betting line would've been much more if the game wasn't being played on the Grizzlies' home turf. Danny, who hadn't seen any action in the first six games, was excited about the game but for all the wrong reasons. At dinner on Wednesday night, he told me that he expected the Eagles to be ahead by at least three touchdowns by halftime.

"It's going to be a blowout and Coach Wilson will have to put me in," Danny told me.

"Do you think you can make a difference?" I asked.

"Absolutely not. There is no way we can beat UCW, but I'll finally get a chance to show what I can do."

Ben, Tyler, and I arrived at the stadium about a half-hour before the 1pm kick-off. So far, it had been a particularly unsatisfying season for the Grizzly faithful because the team had accomplished the unusual feat of losing all its home games and winning all of its road games. For the three of us, it had been particularly frustrating. We hadn't seen the team win or Danny in action. At the conclusion of each of the previous games, I felt as though I should stop at the ticket office and demand my money back. I wasn't getting what I wanted from my price of admission.

The stadium was about half full, meaning somewhere around ten thousand spectators on-hand, most wearing the crimson and gold colors of Stanton University. Small patches of blue and gold dotted the south end of the stadium, and the sound of an occasional Eagle cheer could be heard originating from there. We always sat in the cheap seats, the student seating sections in the north end zone, just above the pep band. On this crisp, sunny afternoon, the band was as loud as I'd ever heard them; their blaring horns and booming drums blasted fight song after fight song to energize their team and rouse their supporters. And, though their musical efforts hadn't produced any positive results yet, Grizzly supporters weren't discouraged by the team's mediocre record to date. Chants and cheers were as constant and energetic as the season opener.

"SU Grizzlies, SU Grizzlies," Ben jumped to his feet and yelled, joining the chant started by the cheerleading squad.

Tyler leaned behind Ben.

"I was a cheerleader for one day in high school," she said.

"One day?" I asked, intrigued by her short tenure.

"When I was a sophomore, I tried out for the cheerleading squad and I made it. But, when I told my father he said he would never permit me to be on the sidelines of anything, cheering for others. He said women were too often relegated to the sidelines and he'd never allow that to happen to his only daughter. It was contrary to everything he had planned for me. The next day, I told the captain of the cheerleaders that I couldn't be on the squad."

"That's sad, but I don't picture you as a cheerleader anyway."

"Yeah, maybe not, but it still looks like a lot of fun to me."

We sat quietly for a moment.

"We don't have a chance in hell, do we?" she asked.

"No."

The Grizzlies had their one highlight-film moment on the first play of the game when our returner weaved and sprinted to the Eagles' nine-yard line. Their kicker, the last remaining defender between our returner and the end zone, lunged and managed to wrap one hand around his ankle, causing him to stumble and fall. Otherwise, the Grizzlies would have scored the first touchdown, something no one expected. Grizzly fans erupted for five minutes but were silenced three plays later when Randy Porter dropped back into the pocket, lobbed a pass into the corner of the end zone that was intercepted by a UCW defensive back who then streaked the length of the field for the first UCW touchdown. True to the sport's metaphor, the Grizzlies had snatched defeat from the jaws of victory.

"If that play doesn't cause Coach Wilson to go to his backup quarterback," Ben complained, "nothing will."

"We want Grainger," Tyler chanted. Ben and I joined in.

It was an exciting opening series, but it was all UCW Eagles from that point forward. They dominated our Grizzlies. When the gun sounded ending the first half, the band rushed onto the field and Ben and I rushed toward the refreshment stand. Just as Danny had predicted, the score was 28-0 at halftime, and it was painfully obvious the Grizzlies didn't have any chance to win this game. In the first half, Randy Porter was intercepted three times, the Grizzlies had just two first downs to their credit, and their total offensive production was only twenty-six yards. Both the scoreboard and the statistics displayed a lopsided contest.

Tenth from the front when we arrived, we waited in the beer line and overheard disgruntled fans on all sides of us.

"I've heard that a lot of the players want Danny Grainger at quarterback," one older gentleman commented on the quarterback situation. "They say he's got quite an arm."

Ben and I smiled, delighted to hear the endorsement, but then the older gentleman's companion responded with a dose of reality.

"They need a lot more than a quarterback, Ernie. If this team was a racehorse, they'd take it out back and shoot it."

It was comforting to learn that we weren't the only ones in a stadium of ten thousand hoping to see Danny play that afternoon. My belief in him was based on our friendship and had nothing to do with his ability to throw a football. I'd never seen him in action on the playing field. The fact that he had the support of other spectators and some players was reassuring. Given the chance, I somehow knew Danny would accomplish great things.

We continued our periodic chanting of "We want Grainger" throughout the second half, usually whenever the SU offense left the field and after UCW scores.

For two reasons, it was obvious that the Eagles were playing their second team in the second half. First, we scored a field goal late in the fourth quarter and, second, their rate of scoring slowed as the game progressed. I don't know how many second team players our Grizzlies had on the field late in the game, but I do know we never saw Danny. Number 15 never parted company with the clipboard he carried up and down the sidelines and he never grabbed his helmet to enter the game. When the final gun sounded, our team had endured a humiliating 45-3 trouncing by our rival.

We thought we had heard a lot of dispirited grumbling in the beer line, but we heard even harsher remarks as we exited the stadium.

"What's your costume for tonight?" Tyler asked me.

"I borrowed surgical scrubs, gloves, a mask, and stethoscope from a medical student, so I'm going as a surgeon."

"That sounds great," she said.

"What happened to the funny hat and press pass?" Ben asked referring to the last-minute garb I assembled last year.

"I'm putting a little more effort into it this year," I told him.

"If you had nothing more than a scalpel in your hand, you'd outdo last year's costume," Ben returned.

"What are you two dressing as?" I asked, ignoring Ben's jab.

"We're borrowing some Revolutionary War attire from Kirk," Tyler said. "I haven't even seen it yet, so I'm trusting Ben."

"We'll see you at the party around nine or so," Ben said as he and Tyler diverted towards the parking lot. "You should probably avoid Danny for a while."

Ben's prudent advice echoed in my head so I called back to them over the cars that now separated us.

"Hey, wait for me, I'll go with you."

* * *

The Grizzly locker room was silent and still. With their heads hung low, players sat in quiet humiliation on aluminum benches before their lockers. Equally deflated, the coaching staff stood in the aisle before them. "Grizzly Pride," in gold letters on a red banner, mocked their downtrodden egos and, even their team mascot, the grizzly bear, was suddenly a misnomer; a cuddly bear cub seemed more appropriate because there was nothing powerful or fierce about their performance. Sadness was etched on their weary faces in measures more consistent with a funeral parlor than a locker room.

The team's record was only a mediocre 3-3 going into this game, but the previous games had been close contests. This loss was clearly different and bordering on demeaning. On this day, the Grizzlies were overmatched and outplayed by a far superior football team. Sure, they'd made mistakes that added to the severity of the loss, but they knew, deep in their guts, they couldn't beat the bigger, faster, more talented Eagle squad on their best day. After their three prior victories, the Grizzlies hooted and hollered and proclaimed their superiority over their foes. Now, they struggled to accept painfully obvious limitations.

Shattering the still, Danny rose from the bench, lifted his head defiantly, walked the sullen aisle past a graveyard of discarded helmets and shoulder pads, and approached Coach Wilson.

"Can I have a word with you, Coach?" Danny asked.

Acting inconvenienced, Coach Wilson shrugged his shoulders and followed Danny into a row of lockers where they were out of view but still within earshot of the rest of the players. Immediately, Danny confronted him.

"I want to know why you didn't put me in," Danny demanded in a tone that discarded their player-coach relationship.

"I play the lineup I think will help us win football games and I don't answer to you."

"Any coach worth a shit gives the second team a shot when games are out of reach like today. They do it so they can bring the backup players along and see what they've got. I work my ass off every day at practice and I've earned a shot. I think this is personal on your part."

"You'll play when I tell you to play and not a moment sooner. If you don't like it, quit."

Danny was fuming already, but the word "quit" irritated him. Quit was a vulgar, stomach-churning word to Danny, one that suggested a cowardly act that he'd never considered, not even on his worst day.

"I'm no quitter," Danny blasted.

"You better watch your words or you won't have to quit. I'll kick your ass off this team."

"You know," Danny said, "like any kid playing high school football, I wondered if I was good enough to play at the college level. But now that I'm here, I know I am. I never thought my coach might not be good enough for this level."

Coach Wilson's next words would surely have ended Danny's football career at SU, but like a referee separating two boxers, Coach Kolar interceded.

"It's been a tough day," Coach Kolar observed as he stepped between them. "Danny, get a shower and go home."

* * *

With a large wooden false front attached and a realistic gray stone appearance, the main cafeteria had the look of a timeworn English castle during the Renaissance period, the handiwork of set designers from the Drama Department. At a quick glance, one could easily imagine Henry the Eighth or William Shakespeare roaming the cold, damp hallways lit by burning candles and blazing torches. A small card table was set up beside the entrance where admissions were collected in accordance with a sign that read "$2 Admission, $5 with Beer Pass." Two massive Grizzly football players, wearing shoulder pads and Frankenstein masks, were positioned as bouncers on each side of the entrance. I paid the witch, literally, with a five-dollar bill and she stamped BEER in orange ink on the backside of my hand.

"You may walk amongst the undead," she instructed me, her voice quivering.

"Undead and soon to be comatose," I told her, recalling the drunken stupor in which most attendees left the event last year.

Upon entering, a small stage with a dungeon-like backdrop was at the far end of the hall where band members fumbled with their instruments, finishing sound checks. As I waited in the beer line, I overheard a conversation between a hooker and an Army soldier, just in front of me, as he tried to convince her that it would be criminal for her to charge a veteran. A policeman in the same line turned around and vouched for the soldier.

"It would be a crime," the cop told the hooker, "and I'd have to arrest you."

Most students were immature and unconfident so Halloween was the perfect opportunity to create a new identity and, for once in their young lives, be the person they imagined themselves to be. Whether monster, superhero, or tramp, the real transformation came from leaving their insecurities behind. On past Halloweens, I noticed that a lot of the shier, more reserved students, bolstered by cakey makeup or plastic masks, shed their insecurities and did things they normally wouldn't. On any other night of the year, that pimply soldier would've been speechless in the presence of that attractive hooker. But, on this magical night, fantasy reigned and everyone forgot real-life limitations. After all, who couldn't come up with an opening line on Halloween?

As soon as I got my beer and left the line, a junior writer at *The Signal*, dressed in cowgirl attire with a white cowgirl hat and matching boots, corralled me to find out what my thoughts were about the big showdown after the game.

"Danny and Coach Wilson went at it," she said when she realized I hadn't heard about the incident. "Coach Kolar stopped them just as they were about to exchange punches."

Over her right shoulder, I caught a glimpse of Danny entering the cafeteria wearing a Navy pea coat and white sailor hat. Intrigued, I excused myself from Miss Kitty so I could hear about the skirmish firsthand. The band launched into its first song of the night as I made my way through the dense crowd and, when I finally reached Danny, I had to shout above the music to be heard. I told him about the rumor and he was quite amused.

"Punches," Danny shouted, laughing at the thought. "I wish. All I did was tell him off."

"Was that wise?"

"That son of a bitch was never going to play me anyway."

"They were awfully good, huh?" I said referring to UCW.

"The best we've played, but that's not saying all that much."

Shortly thereafter, Tyler and Ben arrived, dressed head to toe in Revolutionary War garb and carrying long muskets. Ben wore a bluish-gray coat with crossing white sashes, typical of the Colonial Army, and Tyler wore the famed redcoat of the British Army. A slight betrayal of the period, both wore black jeans tucked into tall black boots. A gray tricorn hat and white wig completed Ben's outfit, giving him the dashing appearance of a young Samuel Adams. Tyler's hair hung straight and unfettered against the bold red of her coat, and she didn't look like any soldier who'd ever fought for the crown.

"Well done," Danny said. "Those are the best costumes I've seen tonight. You might win the costume competition."

"I heard you kicked Wilson's ass today," Ben said.

"It gets a little more exaggerated with each hour that passes," Danny answered, again laughing. "Let's just say we disagreed about his coaching methods."

"Good for you," Ben returned. "You deserve a shot."

"Can we have fun tonight?" Danny asked in an exasperated tone. "I'm sick of hearing about football."

Though I'd seen several genies that night, Danny's wish wouldn't be granted. Just as the words left his mouth, the band announced a break, a DJ dressed in Wolfman-Jack-attire took over, and an inebriated Randy Porter, accompanied by two Grizzly linemen, passed before us. Randy and Danny generally got along on the practice field, but the scene in the locker room and Randy's blood alcohol level would make for an unpredictable encounter. Randy, a husky, six-foot-three-inch physical education major from Houston, stopped short when he saw Danny and more than half of his beer spilled over the side of his cup onto the floor.

"Fumble," one of the linemen yelled.

"What have we got here?" Randy said. "It's an enormous ego dressed in Navy clothes."

Randy looked Danny up and down. "You really think you can do better than me, Grainger?"

As he spoke, Randy stepped toward Danny so they were face-to-face, two feet apart, spitting distance. The crowd watched as the quarterbacks squared off, sensing a fistfight might breakout. At college parties, fistfights were simply unscheduled entertainment.

"Step back, Randy. Get out of my face. We'll talk about it tomorrow when you are sober," Danny insisted.

Angered by his tone, Randy pushed Danny hard in the chest, but Danny barely flinched.

"I don't usually beat up drunks," Danny said, "but I will make an exception if you don't back off right now."

Ignoring the warning and further taunting his rival, Randy stepped even closer until two were chest-to-chest and nose-to-nose. Angered, Danny grabbed Randy by the biceps and threw him, flailing and stumbling backward into the arms of the two linemen. Randy managed to stay upright, but wisely decided not to reengage, realizing from his lack of coordination that he wasn't in any condition for a fight. Also, Danny's steely glare made it clear to Randy that his restraint wasn't going to last much longer. If Randy had pushed him any further, I sensed that Danny would have released the months of frustration built up while watching his less talented rival on the playing field in his stead, frustration more appropriately aimed at Coach Wilson than Randy, but that detail wouldn't have stopped him.

"You just don't get it," Randy said, slurring every word. "We suck. We lost 45-3. You couldn't change that if you were Roger Staubach. And, you ain't Roger Staubach. You're just the second-string quarterback of the University of Stinkin Grizzlies."

One of the linemen was bothered by the comment about the Grizzlies and mumbled beneath his breath, "No one trashes my team, not even the damn quarterback."

Then, the lineman grabbed Randy by his collar and dragged him like a child's rag doll with its puffy arms and legs flailing wildly in the direction of the front door. Rather than being bowled over by the fast moving pair, the crowd parted, creating an unobstructed pathway from the site of the confrontation to the front door.

Ben, Tyler, and I breathed a collective sigh of relief as the crowd filled in behind them and they quickly disappeared from our view. Danny was unaffected by the encounter.

"He's just drunk," he said in a matter-of-fact manner, turning back to the three of us, expecting the conversation to pick up from where we left off.

* * *

By 12:30am, attendance had easily surpassed previous years, and the crowd overflowed the front lawn onto the university driveway. It was getting uncomfortably cramped inside the cafeteria so Ben and Tyler went to the dance floor for one final dance. None of us wanted the evening to end, but it was so hot in the cafeteria that the spilled beer on the floor was creating a steamy, sauna-like atmosphere. As I watched Tyler and Ben dancing, I noticed Danny, who'd wandered off a few minutes earlier, also on the dance floor with the hooker from the beer line.

She must have a thing for men in uniform, I thought.

Following his lead, I searched the crowd for a woman with a fondness for doctors. For our last song of the night, I asked a black cat if she would dance with me.

"Are you a veterinarian?" she asked.

"Heart surgeon," I answered, and she extended her paw.

The black cat was a sophomore business major that resided on the fourth floor of Springer Hall, the same dormitory Tyler lived in.

Her cat suit consisted of a flattering black body stocking that revealed a curvaceous figure, complimented by cat ears and paws and mascara whiskers. Up until that moment, I'd always considered myself a dog person, but that was a preference I suddenly found myself questioning.

When the song finished, the six of us found a place to sit on the front lawn. Coincidentally, the hooker and the black cat lived just three doors apart in the dormitory and were friends, but they'd only seen Tyler about the hall and didn't know her. Still, everyone seemed comfortable until the hooker caught us off guard.

"Small details are the difference between average Halloween costumes and the truly great ones," the hooker said.

With that said, she showed each of us the homemade sign dangling on her necklace like a miniature sandwich board. It read:

Price List
Hand Job $15
Oral Sex $25
Fuck $40

Tyler and the black cat blushed when they read its contents. Ben and I were surprised, but we tried not to show our embarrassment. Not having noticed the sign while dancing, but amused by its boldness, Danny laughed loudly.

"I've only got one thing to say," he declared, "I can't afford you. Do you offer any discounts or payment plans?"

In the center of the circular driveway, east of the grassy lawn where we sat, stood an eighteen-foot-tall statue of Ulysses P. Stanton, the founder of the university. The base of the statue was six feet tall and the statue itself reached another twelve feet into the dark, October night sky. True to the late 1890s, Ulysses was sculpted wearing a stiff, bowler-style hat, a long topcoat, muttonchops, and high boots while holding a closed book in his hand. His appearance was indicative of prominence and affluence in his day. Blocked from our view by a patch of birch trees, we couldn't see the statue, but we could hear the raucous crowd at the circle getting louder and rowdier.

Placing underwear or lacy red panties atop old Ulysses' head was a traditional prank at the university, so we all figured that was the cause of the merriment. But, when an ambulance with its red light pulsing brightly and siren shrieking intermittently, pulled slowly into the crowded driveway, we got curious, abandoned our grassy location, and walked toward the statue. As the six of us strolled and chatted, the number of onlookers swelled beyond any reasonable capacity for the area, so we were quickly thwarted in our attempt to get any closer. It was shoulder-to-shoulder, ten students deep, and we couldn't see the paramedics or the reason they were called.

"What happened?" the hooker asked the policeman from the beer line as he passed, walking in the other direction.

"Randy Porter fell off the statue," he said with amusement in his voice. "I think he broke his leg or ankle or something. It was a really nasty fall. The guy is very wasted."

"Well now," I observed, directed at Danny, "that is certainly an interesting turn of events."

"It's a good thing there were two hundred witnesses and you've got an airtight alibi," Ben added as he slapped Danny on the back.

"I'd feel sorry for him," Danny responded, "but I don't think he's feeling any pain."

5.

During the first half of the twentieth century, industrial and societal conditions were quite suited to skyscrapers. Automobiles and railroads were still in their infancies so condensed cities made for a better quality of life. It was much easier for city dwellers to ride an elevator to the fiftieth floor than travel twenty miles from their homes.

Coach Wilson didn't take the news of Randy Porter's injury well. "Goddamn it," he yelled as he slammed his fist against the desk. "What was he doing on the damn statue in the first place?"

In the coach's mind, things couldn't get worse. His team was en route to another disappointing season and his starting quarterback was out for the remainder of the season with a broken leg. On top of that, the coach was midway through the fourth year of his five-year contract and it looked like a fourth lackluster season in a row. He knew that unless the program showed marked improvement soon, he wouldn't be returning to SU when his contract expired. To add insult to injury, literally, the coach would have to choose between two unpleasant options: starting Danny at quarterback, despite his outburst after the last game, or starting his less talented third string quarterback.

"We're so screwed," Coach Wilson yelled as he banged his fist against the desk again.

But, Coach Kolar didn't commiserate with the head coach. During practices, he'd spent a lot of time working with the three quarterbacks, and he thought highly of Danny. All along, he believed Danny should start, that he was clearly the most talented of the three.

Several times during the season, Coach Kolar suggested that Danny be put into the game, but his recommendations were never heeded. He was waiting for Danny by the door to the locker room when he arrived for practice that Monday afternoon. As he approached, Danny walked the bouncy, light-heeled walk of someone walking towards the Promised Land.

"You're getting the start," the coach said.

Danny smiled. Coach Kolar patted him on the back, and they walked down the hallway to Coach Wilson's office.

"When I was a young boy," Coach Wilson began when player and coach arrived, "my mother told me to be careful what I wished for because I just might get it. Danny, I hope you're as good as you think because you're going to start against Ridgely this Saturday. You're getting your wish and now we'll see what you can do with it."

Enthused, Danny smiled at Coach Kolar, knowing he'd played a significant role in this outcome, and then he responded.

"When I was a young boy," Danny said echoing the coach's childhood tale, "my mother told me I could do anything I set my mind to and I believed her. By Saturday night, you're going to wish you'd given me a shot a lot sooner."

* * *

In the cheap seats as usual, we were all there on Saturday afternoon. Earlier that morning, Ben drove into South Cavanaugh to pick up Kirk and Carl, all in accordance with Kirk's instructions on Tuesday when he told Ben, "No way I'm going to miss Danny's first start at quarterback." I didn't see him in the crowd, but Danny told me that Coop made the two-hour drive from Condor and brought the whole chess contingent with him. For a guy who hadn't thrown a pass in a college football game, Danny had a lot of people rooting for him. The truth was, there was something about Danny that made everyone root for him.

Tyler, Ben, and I had been to all four home games that season, but we felt very different this time around. Usually, we arrived at the stadium with no expectation of victory and only a faint glimmer of hope that we might see Danny enter the game. On this day, our hopes and expectations were soaring. We had real interest in both Danny's performance and the outcome of the game. I guess you could say that, for the first time, we were true Grizzly fans and not just spectators as in the past.

After Danny told me what the coach had said, "Be careful what you wish for," I wished only for good weather. After all, it wouldn't have seemed fair if Danny finally got his shot and had to throw the football in rain on a muddy field. He'd worked so hard and overcome so much for this opportunity that it should be authentic, a real chance to showcase his abilities. So, I wished for good weather and left the rest to Danny. When we arrived at the stadium, the sky was a beautiful blue, the sunshine bright and warming, and the wind as still as the statue in the university's driveway, perfect conditions for any sporting event. I interpreted the beautiful weather as a sign that this day would indeed be one when wishes came true.

The Grizzlies returned the opening kickoff to their own twenty-four yard line so Danny and the SU offense took over at that hash mark. Danny trotted onto the field, scanned the entire stadium, quietly acknowledged the personal significance of the moment, and then joined his teammates in the huddle. His first play served as a prelude for the afternoon, the rest of the season, and the start of a new era.

Danny took the snap from the center, dropped back behind his line, and spotted an open Grizzly receiver streaking across the middle of the field near the thirty-five yard line. With a quick flick of his right arm, Danny delivered the ball in perfect stride for a gain of twenty-seven yards. Most of the crowd, maybe eight thousand people at most, rose to their feet and cheered loudly. Our miniature cheering section was probably as loud as the other seven thousand nine hundred and ninety-five combined.

Kirk was quickest to his feet shouting, "Way to go, Danny!" Ben, Tyler, and I joined in, screaming, "Danny, Danny, Danny," as loudly as we could. His usual quiet self, Carl remained seated, but he smiled and nodded.

On that drive, Danny was every bit the field general I expected. He led the Grizzlies on a nine-play, seventy-six yard effort that was topped off by a fifteen-yard pass for the touchdown. Better than anyone, I knew how hard Danny had worked for that moment. After completing his first touchdown pass in a college football game, I watched as he trotted off the field, and I'd never been happier for anyone in my life. It was perhaps the most earned and just moment I'd witnessed in my short twenty years.

When the gun sounded ending the game, Danny had posted impressive statistics for the afternoon. He had completed twenty-six of thirty-five passes for a total of three hundred ninety yards with four touchdowns and no interceptions. Beyond his personal performance, it was obvious that the Grizzlies were a different team with Danny at quarterback, a much better team. It has been said that the great ones make everyone around them better, and it sure seemed like Danny had that effect on his teammates. Every position, not just quarterback, seemed improved during that game. And, as a total unit, they seemed more in synch. The Grizzlies easily won their first home game of the season by the score of 35-14.

As we left the stadium, I thought about the editorial balancing act I'd have to perform when covering SU football games. As editor of the school newspaper with the newly christened star quarterback as my roommate, I had to make certain that *The Signal's* coverage of the games was appropriate. If *The Signal* placed too much emphasis on football games or gave Danny too much individual credit, it would be interpreted as editorial bias. If the coverage was minimal and Danny's contribution downplayed, then we'd short-change our readers, football fans, and Danny as well. Fortunately for me, our next issue, scheduled for distribution in two days, was already back from the printers, giving me two weeks and one more game to determine an appropriate column space and perspective for Danny's remarkable debut, a little breathing room at least. It would be a challenge, sure enough, but one I was ecstatic to be facing.

Danny celebrated with his Grizzly teammates that night and then stayed over at the Matthews' home, so I didn't see him until noon on Sunday. He was a collection of contrasting emotional states; his eyes had large, dark bags beneath them, his body was weary and sore, but his face and smile were alert and bright. Danny placed a container of orange juice on the table and joined me on the sofa in the lounge.

"I feel great," he said, as if I didn't already know.

"It was a great game," I returned in a raspy, depleted voice, almost hoarse from all my screaming. "You should've seen Kirk. You wouldn't have believed it."

"I saw him last night. He still hadn't calmed down."

"What did Coach Wilson say?"

"He just said, 'Good game, Danny,' nothing more. But I have a feeling those were the three hardest words he has spoken in a long time, and that's good enough for me."

Danny laughed. So did I.

He continued. "We're never going to get along, you know, him and me. It's personal, no doubt, and I don't know why. But, after yesterday, he's stuck with me."

"It doesn't matter. You did it."

"I know. But, you know something else?"

"What's that?"

"It's kind of ironic, but it's all the sweeter because of that son of a bitch. He tested me. He wouldn't give me a chance. But I hung in there, I didn't doubt myself, and now I'm doing it. I'm playing college football."

"I know it's asking a lot," I said, "but wins in the final two games would make the team 6-4 for the year—the best Grizzly record of the 1970s."

"Believe me," Danny responded, "I've thought of that."

*   *   *

Ben always knew the right people. He had a connection for everything. In this instance, Ben enlisted the help of a third-year business major to help him compile a business plan for his newspaper. On a nightly basis, this junior consultant brought the necessary materials to Ben's dorm room—things like graph paper, calculators, ledgers, spreadsheets—and provided financial expertise and legitimacy to the project, despite the fact that their agreement called for payment for his services in college currency: cases of beer.

After four long nights of effort, the resulting business plan was completed, a five-year projection of revenues and costs in standard income statement and balance sheet format. Also included was a cash flows statement—all-important for any small, start-up business—that showed the company turning cash positive in twenty-seven months, meaning it would no longer need the owners to fund its operations. Detailed subsidiary schedules included projections of advertising revenues, salary costs, overhead costs, and printing costs. For about thirty dollars of sudsy expense, Ben had gotten his money's worth; the financial section of the business plan was comprehensive and well presented.

Ben also enlisted the services of a graphic artist at *The Signal* to design the logo for *Cavanaugh Weekly*, which consisted of a prominent *CW* with the newspaper's name alongside. For further polish, Ben drafted a narrative section that served as an introduction by describing the newspaper's mission, target market, and business plan. When I flipped through the eleven pages of the finished plan, I believed Ben and his team had compiled an impressive package. Reviewers would surely believe that financial professionals had put it together. Ben had a short list of five investors in mind to approach for investment capital, and he planned to spend the rest of 1978 visiting them.

Ben's first appointment was scheduled for November 8th, with J. William Benton, President of Cornerstone Management. Ben first learned of the company when he heard they provided the start-up capital for Red Potatoes, a cafeteria-style restaurant that frequented The Common Sense Print Shop for printing services. Ben asked Red Potatoes President, Ted Weston, to arrange the meeting. Ben always said it was better to be introduced than to walk in off the street because a man's contacts were a sign of his initiative.

* * *

On the morning of the 8th, Ben waited in Cornerstone's lobby, decorated with Italian marble, leather seating, original artwork, and the words "Where There Is No Vision, The People Perish" etched in fine glass above the door. Ben looked around at his surroundings, guessed that the cost of the lobby was considerably more than the start-up capital he wanted, and gradually convinced himself that an investment in *Cavanaugh Weekly* would be an easy decision for a successful firm like this one. As he waited, Ben gripped three bound copies of the business plan in his left hand, emblazoned with the *CW* insignia on the front cover.

Bill Benton, looking casual but polished, finally appeared at the tall, glass doors behind the receptionist and summoned Ben to his office, overlooking most of western Cavanaugh and Driftwood Bay.

"Ted speaks highly of you," the venture capitalist stated as he motioned for Ben to take a seat at the small conference table by the window. "He told me he was doing me a big favor by making this introduction."

As Bill's assistant placed a pitcher of water and glasses in the center of the table, Ben presented Bill with a copy of the business plan and proceeded to walk him through it one page at a time. First, Ben described the newspaper's concept and format, its uniqueness on the newsstand, and its impact on the community. Then, Ben talked about the financial statements, emphasizing their projection of a positive cash flow just two years after inception and their goal to be debt free by the seven-year mark, meaning Cornerstone would be paid back by then, having made a comfortable return on their investment.

Bill wore wire rim glasses that he put on and took off many times during their time together, wearing them to view the statements and taking them off for reflection. During their hour together, Bill asked several probing questions aimed at determining whether the projections were realistic or a best case scenario, and he seemed quite satisfied by Ben's answers. His extensive experience with small, start-up companies was evident in his questions.

"I've tried to include everything, even small contingencies as a cushion," Ben said. "Most start-up businesses fail because they're undercapitalized. I've been complete in my planning to ensure that *Cavanaugh Weekly* doesn't suffer such a fate."

"It's a sound proposal," Bill said. "I would like to hold onto it, study it further, and have some of my colleagues analyze it also. I should warn you though; our business is about more than ideas and money. At Cornerstone, we look for strong management teams with proven track records. Your friend Ted, for instance, had ten years in the restaurant business and it was his experience that gave us the confidence to invest in Red Potatoes. Without Ted, it would've been just another restaurant concept."

"I know I'm inexperienced, but I'm savvy enough to bring in the right people. I..."

Bill interrupted. "We'll consider your plan. I'm not turning you down. I'm just saying that the difference between funding or not could be a few years of real-world experience, some time spent working at a magazine or the local newspaper."

*   *   *

The meeting at Cornerstone was indicative of things to come. Each of the following meetings proceeded in much the same manner: interest in the newspaper's concept, kudos for the comprehensive business plan, and, finally, deal breaking concerns about Ben's lack of publishing or business experience. After all, $100,000 was a lot of money. Investors had tough requirements when they put that kind of money on the line and, perhaps most importantly, they wanted managers with more on their resume than a youth spent in a print shop and two years of college.

"I'd rather you get your seasoning on someone else's nickel, and then come to me when you're ready to make money," Ben was told by one of the more candid investors.

*   *   *

Old Cavanaugh was three miles of scenic waterfront where the town was founded in the 1870s. Some of the buildings dated back to the founding, but most were three-story, red brick buildings built between the turn of the century and the Great Depression. In the late 1970s, Old Cavanaugh was a popular tourist destination with bars, restaurants, arcades, souvenir shops, and other small businesses. In spite of a few crumbling relics, the area maintained a quaint, tree-lined ambience, reminiscent of colonial Boston after a few British cannon blasts, that attracted tourists during the day and a restaurant, bar, and nightclub crowd after dark. Its place in the rapidly changing landscape of the larger metropolitan area was a regular topic of debate amongst the mayor and city council members.

In the spring of 1977, Crestfield Development Company, one of the largest construction companies on the west coast, arrived in the city with grand plans to demolish Old Cavanaugh and replace it with condominiums, restaurants, retail, a multiplex-theater complex, and a waterfront walk. The entire project, beginning with demolition and ending with the grand opening of two, thirty-seven story towers with 955 units, would take three years and $550 million to complete. The towers and surrounding infrastructure were proposed under the designation of Cavanaugh Waterfront Towers, or CWT as it came to be abbreviated in the media. If approved, CWT would be the largest development project in the history of Cavanaugh. To promote its grand project, Crestfield Development established a visitor center in a building in Old Cavanaugh with billboards flanking it that showed the project as it would look upon completion.

The Matthews' residence and The Common Sense Print Shop were both less than a mile from Old Cavanaugh, so the CWT project would have a positive impact on the value of both properties. Despite the opportunity for personal gain, Ben believed that Old Cavanaugh was an unpolished asset, a quaint, historic part of the larger Cavanaugh that would nicely complement the growth occurring in the business district, an area that should be restored, not demolished. The main section of Old Cavanaugh, with the original courthouse, City Hall, mercantile, hotel, post office, pharmacy, and five grain storage silos, was particularly important as it harkened back to the founding of Cavanaugh. If demolished, those structures and their historic value would be gone forever. In Ben's opinion, the city council needed to adopt a longer horizon, bigger-picture approach to city planning in order to understand the value of Old Cavanaugh. Concerned by what he'd heard on the radio and read in *The Cavanaugh Dispatch*, Ben decided to talk with his councilman.

Councilman Dale Greenwood, a bulky forty year old with a pock-marked face, curly black hair, and an uncomfortable smile, represented the 9th district of the city, which included Old Cavanaugh and South Cavanaugh where the Matthews' home and the print shop was located. During his bid for reelection to the city council two years earlier, *The Dispatch* endorsed his opponent and referred to the councilman as an "eye-poker and shin kicker." Despite this negative portrayal by the city's largest newspaper, the councilman was well connected elsewhere, won reelection easily, and was on the cusp of announcing his bid for the mayor's office.

Coincidentally, Councilman Greenwood maintained an office in Old Cavanaugh in the Madigan Building; a building that, thirty years ago, served as the post office but was modified in the 1960s for use as professional offices. When Ben called the councilman's office for an appointment on Monday, the only time available was 3pm on Thursday afternoon, which meant that Ben would have to skip his economics class. Ben thought the meeting was important enough that he accepted the time.

"I have friends at SU that speak highly of you," Councilman Greenwood said. "They tell me that your *Signal* article about a new student center has become an integral part of the larger conversation about an expansion plan."

For almost an hour, Ben and the councilman talked about their personal journeys, each providing background information they hoped would be the foundation for a long-term relationship. Both men knew the value of connections. Both men sought alliances. Ben elaborated on the concept of a student center for the campus and the councilman talked about his road to the city council as well as his three years serving on it. It wasn't until the two men felt comfortable with each other that they moved on to the true reason for the meeting.

"I requested this time today," Ben said, "because I want to talk with you about the proposal by Crestfield Development. Though their plan is impressive, I don't believe the demolition of Old Cavanaugh is in the best interest of the city."

"I haven't made up my mind yet," the councilman responded, "but I will say that tax revenues from the project would be substantial and beneficial to the city going forward. It could be a very significant milestone in the city's development."

"I want to encourage the city council to take a longer view when it comes to development," Ben offered. "Imagine Cavanaugh years from now as a beautiful metropolis that includes a restored and revitalized Old Cavanaugh carrying on as the heart and soul of the community as it did in the 1900s. The city doesn't lose anything by keeping Old Cavanaugh, but it loses a lot by leveling it. Certainly, Crestfield Development can find another location for their project."

"We are both advocates of community involvement," the councilman said, "so my suggestion is that you organize a rally in Old Cavanaugh so that its restoration is considered alongside the Crestfield Development proposal by the city council. It's never good when only one side of an issue has a voice."

"That's a good suggestion," Ben observed, feeling elated, as he'd just interjected himself into the midst of another project. "I'm really glad we had this time together."

"You and me both, Ben," the councilman added, flashing his uncomfortable smile.

* * *

The Grizzlies took the field twice more that season but their quest for a winning season was denied, splitting the games by posting a victory over Harcourt College 28-10 and losing a tough one to UWS 45-42. Their final tally was 5 wins and 5 losses for the season, typical of past Grizzly records. Danny, however, continued to play brilliantly, throwing for nine touchdowns with no interceptions in the final two games, giving Grizzly faithful hope that the following year might be a standout season. After the loss to UWS in the final game of the season, Danny, his knee sore from a hard hit delivered in the third quarter, spent three hours in the training room, applying ice first, then the soothing heat of the hot tub. By more than an hour, he was the last player to depart the locker room at almost 7pm that evening.

As Danny walked the dark underground hallway of the stadium, his hair still wet and gym bag in hand, he noticed light emanating from the coach's office at the end of the hall. Twenty feet from the large window at the coach's office, Danny stopped and stood motionless against the block wall, concealed by a veil of darkness, watching Coach Wilson and Randy Porter from a distance. Randy was seated in the coach's chair, his right leg in a hard, white plaster cast, propped up on the desktop, two crutches behind him against the file cabinet, and the coach standing before him.

Why are they still here? Danny wondered.

The game had ended three hours ago. While soaking in the hot tub, Danny assumed he was the only one left in the building. Then, Danny noticed tears on Randy's cheeks that caused him to linger longer than otherwise. His former rival was obviously upset. Danny couldn't hear the conversation, but Coach Wilson, with his arms crossed in front of him, was doing most of the talking. Were they talking about next season? Surely Danny had staked his claim to the starting position and that wasn't the issue. Was Randy simply upset over losing the starting position?

As Danny speculated, Coach Wilson reached forward and caressed his injured quarterback with both hands, running his fingers through the young man's shaggy blonde locks and wiping the tears from his cheeks. When Randy sighed, the coach lowered his gaze until the two men were staring into one another's eyes, in an unmistakable lover's gaze, a clearly intimate moment that had nothing to do with the game of football. Then, the coach placed one finger on his companion's lips in a hushing manner, as if to signal that the time for words had passed. Randy acknowledged the coach's intention by gently kissing his finger.

Still in the shadows, Danny was dumbfounded. He couldn't believe the scene he was witnessing. On so many levels, this was just wrong.

That son of a bitch, Danny thought, *it was even more personal than I ever imagined.*

Cringing but still as a statue, Danny watched as the coach leaned forward and kissed Randy on top of his head, several times, a little more caressing each time, then lower onto his forehead until Randy's neck bent and their mouths met for a deep, passionate kiss.

The kiss caused Danny's legs to lock. He'd never seen two men kiss and the shock of this unlikely couple immobilized him, paralyzing him in much the same way as that halting fear that makes people unable to scream during a nightmare. As much as he wanted to get out of there, to be anywhere but there, he simply couldn't move. He couldn't command his legs. He noticed the light switch on the wall beside him and, for a brief moment, considered flipping it and illuminating the bright florescent lights of the hallway, but even he, the victimized one, didn't want to shine a light on this scandalous affair. Although shocked, Danny also recognized the importance of this revelation because he now had confirmation of what he suspected all along: The coach had an ulterior motive for not playing him. Coach

Wilson kept Danny on the sidelines all season, despite his superior abilities, and played his lover instead. At least now, Danny knew the truth.

Inside the coach's office, Randy's hands were underneath the coach's baggy sweatshirt, and their kissing was even more passionate than before. Both emotions and actions were starting to escalate and disrobing seemed the natural progression. Danny's original shock was quickly transforming into an intense anger, but he was certain of only one thing at the moment: He didn't want to see any more. Disgusted by the scene and the revelation, he turned away, walked the shadows of the hallway to the exit, and departed the stadium.

*   *   *

"Tough loss," I remarked when Danny arrived. "Let's find Ben and Tyler, and we'll get a beer."

Danny didn't acknowledge my invitation. He had a pale, glazed look on his face like someone about to vomit. I wanted to ask if someone had died, but the suggestion was too ominous. Danny threw his gym bag on his bed and sat, with his head in his hands, on the edge in silence.

"What's wrong?" I asked.

"I saw Randy Porter and Coach Wilson kiss one another."

"What?"

"You heard me."

Danny looked up for the first time.

"Fucking perverts," he added, shaking his head in disgust. "What am I going to do?"

"You've got to report him," I said. "The fact that they're both men is irrelevant; it's unethical for the coach to have a relationship with any student."

"They'll only deny their affair and it will look pretty suspect coming from me. No one will believe me, and I'll be the joke of the campus. Anyway, I'm really not concerned about their affair."

"You're not?"

"I care about playing football, and I don't see how I can play for Coach Wilson anymore. He's screwed me for a second time."

"You can't quit, Danny, things are going so well."

"I can't turn him in and I can't keep playing for him. I don't know what the hell I'm going to do."

* * *

Ben was fortunate that his fondness for large projects and noble causes was complemented by unlimited access to free posters and printed materials. With just a phone call to The Common Sense Print Shop, Ben had one hundred color posters in the works, heralding the "Restore Old Cavanaugh Rally." Prior to the phone call, Ben secured a permit from the parks department for a community gathering to be conducted in Old Cavanaugh in two weeks time. Ben also convinced five of his Yarborough Hall dorm mates, who played in a popular college band called "Lost at Sea," to provide entertainment that evening and recruited four civics club volunteers to distribute posters around campus and throughout Cavanaugh. With key details for the rally coming together, Ben placed three more phone calls to the local news programs to ensure media coverage at the event, and each news director assured him that a reporter and camera crew would attend the rally. Finally, focusing on his own role as newly appointed spokesman for the cause, Ben rented a stage, podium, and loudspeaker system, and then began crafting his speech for the evening. His speech would be a call to action to save an important part of the city's heritage, a historic location that, coincidentally, was part of the neighborhood Ben grew up in, so he was already brimming with ideas and catch phrases.

* * *

"Thank you all for coming on this beautiful Old Cavanaugh evening," Ben told the crowd of more than seven hundred on the night of the rally.

Earlier that day, police cruisers blocked select intersections, and police officers rerouted traffic as four blocks at the center of Old Cavanaugh were designated as "pedestrian only" to accommodate the rally. In the rally zone, the mood and environment was similar to a street festival as attendees were treated to a concert by the soft rock band Ben recruited and many local craft vendors had set up booths and small tents to sell their wares. Aromas from popcorn, freshly baked breads, fried delicacies, and grilled fare floated on the air. Consistent with Ben's overall plan, it was the kind of event and evening that showed a scenic, tourist area like Old Cavanaugh in its best light.

Ben continued. "When I look at that skyline in the distance, I am excited about the growth and development that is occurring. Our business district is becoming the most important financial center on the west coast. Many great companies have located their headquarters in our city, including 17 of the Fortune 500. Additionally, technology companies in our city are changing the way the world communicates and conducts business."

At that moment, Ben was interrupted by polite applause. It was evident from the turnout and enthusiastic response to his speech that citizens were passionate about saving Old Cavanaugh; Ben had tapped into an authentic sentiment. Before he could continue, the chant, "Restore Old Cavanaugh," started in the back, spread forward quickly, until it was joined by all present.

"Restore Old Cavanaugh. Restore Old Cavanaugh."

"The future of our city is bright," Ben continued when there was finally a lull in the chant. "In twenty years, I imagine that our skyline will rival the other great skylines of the world, even New York City. But, as we rush toward the future, we must be careful to not simply push aside the past, for it is the past that reminds us of who we are and where we came from. As we moved forward, Old Cavanaugh must remain an asset for our community, not something to be leveled and forgotten. We can have that amazing skyline and a restored and revitalized Old Cavanaugh, too. One does not preclude the other, but rather, I would suggest, the two areas complement one another and our city will be better if we have both."

When Ben concluded his speech, the crowd returned to its enthusiastic chant of "Restore Old Cavanaugh" and continued for a full five minutes. Eventually, the chanting waned and the attendees slowly dispersed, but many remained in Old Cavanaugh as the restaurants and bars were starting to rouse.

* * *

Around 3am, long after the bars and restaurants had emptied, two hulking men in hooded sweatshirts crept outside the Cavanaugh Waterfront Towers Visitor Center scribbling the words, "Stop the CWT" and "Save Old Cavanaugh," repeatedly in black spray paint. The men continued to spray additional graffiti markings across the large billboards that showed the images of the condominiums. Done with the spray paint cans, they dropped them into the trashcans and poured gasoline in. Then finally, in a flurry of destructive activity, the men hurled stones through the windows, set fire to the trashcans, and dashed from the visitor center to a waiting car. In less than seven minutes, the shiny presentation at the visitor center had been damaged and marred.

The next day, the local news programs gave equal time to both the Restore Old Cavanaugh Rally and the subsequent attack on the visitor center, reporting on the two events in a back-to-back manner. Unfortunately, this combination caused many in the community to associate Old Cavanaugh with rowdy, late night partying and mayhem. All three programs showed snippets of Ben addressing the rally crowd and firemen with hoses putting out the fires in front of the visitor center. Visually, the image of the emergency response, with flashing lights, rushing water, and firemen in protective gear, was far more compelling than Ben at the podium, but worse still, the two images created an unsavory cause-and-effect impression. For months, the damaged visitor center remained in the collective memory and tainted the perception of Old Cavanaugh, gradually moving public support from the restoration of Old Cavanaugh to the Cavanaugh Waterfront Towers project, an outcome exactly opposite of the rally's intent.

* * *

By December, Ben's newspaper venture was still unfunded. Despite his efforts, he'd exhausted his best possibilities and would have to resort to Plan B, which didn't exist. Three venture capital companies and two wealthy individuals had rejected his request for start-up capital. Most voiced concerns about his inexperience and some cited a difficult economic environment for start-up businesses.

In mid-December, Ben and I paused in the cafeteria entryway, zipped our topcoats closed to protect us from the frigid night air, then stepped out of the cafeteria for our walk back to Yarborough Hall. Throughout our meal, Ben had been unusually quiet and we'd hardly spoken at all. I knew he had something on his mind, but, with Ben, it was usually best to let him arrive at the point where he wanted another opinion. As we passed the statue, Ben finally let it out.

"Should I pitch Mr. Danzig for the start-up capital for the newspaper? Tyler thinks I should."

"He's got it. That's for sure," I replied.

It wasn't much of an answer, but I'd been caught off-guard by the question.

"Yeah, but my girlfriend's father. It doesn't feel right."

Though I hadn't given it much thought, I sensed that Ben had already made up his mind and was actually looking for a push rather than a second opinion.

"Don't pitch him as your girlfriend's father, pitch him as President of Danzig Capital Management. It's his business, Ben."

"Then you think I should?"

"I do. I know how much this means to you."

"He's flying in to pick up Tyler on the 20th. She wants me to have dinner with him."

"Have dinner with him, show him the business plan, and see how it feels," I suggested. "If he offers you the money and it doesn't feel right, you can always decline."

With that said, we walked almost a quarter mile in silence again, our breathing visible in the cold air like smoke puffs from a chugging locomotive, and I sensed that Ben was not satisfied with my suggestion. Instead, he seemed perplexed by the fact that he hadn't found the funding yet. In his mind, he was falling behind schedule. All along, I think Ben thought it would be much easier.

"I've got to find a way to get the money. I am running out of options. It's just too important to this city for me to fail."

"You've just got to be more patient," I counseled him. "It will happen. I know it. You'll find the funding. Give it time."

"I've never subscribed to the "wait and hope" strategy when it comes to challenges in my life," Ben said. "One way or another, I will fund my newspaper. I'm simply going to have to get more creative and more aggressive in my efforts."

* * *

Tyler made a reservation for three at 8pm at Dusenberg's, one of the city's finest steak and seafood restaurants. Ben had first met Mr. Danzig more than a year ago, but only long enough to shake his hand and exchange pleasantries, five minutes at most. Since Tyler and Ben were not seriously involved when he last visited, Ben stayed out of the way so Tyler could enjoy some quality time with her father. It seemed like the proper thing to do at the time. In light of recent developments, Ben now wished he'd spent a little more time with the venture capitalist and knew him better.

Piloting his Gulfstream jet, Mr. Danzig arrived at County Municipal Airport at 7pm. In thin fog and drizzle, Ben and Tyler waited on the tarmac as the aircraft taxied from the runway to the business aviation terminal. Only moments after the aircraft's wheels stopped, the side door opened, and Mr. Danzig, dressed in a topcoat, silk shirt, and Italian loafers, appeared at the jet's doorway and called to his daughter, "Sweetheart."

"Daddy," Tyler cried.

As the two embraced, a long, black limousine crept slowly into position alongside the aircraft. Parked at the tip of the wing, the driver scooted around the automobile and opened the back door.

"Good evening, Mr. Danzig," he said.

"Daddy, we've got Ben's car," Tyler informed her father."

"My office didn't know. We'll drop Ben at his car after dinner."

When they were seated at their table in Dusenberg's, Mr. Danzig suggested they order a round of drinks and take a look at Ben's proposal.

"We'll get business out of the way early so we can all spend some time together," he said. "Let me see your business plan, Ben. Tyler tells me you want to start a newspaper."

Ben handed the booklet across the table to Mr. Danzig and began, what was by then, a well-rehearsed presentation. He was a little nervous this time, more so than the other five meetings, because Tyler was at his side and he was presenting to his girlfriend's father. In his heart, he still didn't believe this was a good idea, but he was desperate for the funding. He started talking about the newspaper's concept, citing its uniqueness on the newsstand, and the fact that it didn't exist in any market in the country.

"Once *CW* is a success in Cavanaugh, there will be copycat publications in every major city in the country," Ben stated nervously. "It's that good of a concept."

"Ben," a heavy-set gentleman called out as he walked toward their table. It was Luther Trask, the owner of the restaurant and long-time friend of Ben and his father. "I didn't know you were coming tonight. Was the reservation under Matthews?"

"No, Danzig," Ben explained, and then he introduced Tyler and her father.

"This is the wonderful benefit of owning a restaurant," Luther said. "Every night, I'm surrounded by friends. And, they introduce me to their friends. I'm a lucky man. How is your father? Is Kirk coming?"

"No, not tonight."

Luther's arrival at their table was unplanned but quite timely and fortunate for Ben. He was a large, jovial man who, during the course of his many years as a successful restaurateur, had mastered the art of hosting and the duty of making his guests comfortable. He had a large, resounding laugh, a smile as warm as the bread on the table, and many humorous anecdotes from his years in the business. He was as comfortable beside the tables in his restaurant as he was on the sofa in the living room of his home. Everyone was relaxed and comfortable when Luther departed the table, and Ben resumed his presentation with his normal confidence.

For almost an hour, Mr. Danzig listened intently, diverting his attention only once to signal the waiter for a second round of drinks. Apparently influenced by his dinner companions, two college students, he focused on the business plan, like there would be an exam on the material following the meal. At almost 9pm, Ben finished his lengthy presentation of the financial statements and asked Mr. Danzig if he had any questions.

"Ben," Mr. Danzig said, "you've been thorough and given a solid presentation. But, I want you to know that I'm going to treat your proposal like any other at DCM. It won't receive any special consideration because you're dating my daughter."

"I wouldn't want that, sir."

"At DCM, our entire team works together and selects the companies that we want to be involved with. I'll show your proposal to the team and we'll see what comes of it. You can expect feedback from us in late January. Now, let's take a look at the menu. After flying for three hours, I am very hungry."

* * *

Charles House, the rustic residence of university presidents, was located on the northern boundary of the campus at the end of a cobblestone pathway that connected the home to the main campus near the Walton Building. Originally built for logging baron Rutherford Charles and his family in 1904, the residence consisted of twenty-three rooms and seven bathrooms and blended harmoniously with the dark forest that surrounded it. In 1921, the house was purchased by Stanton University to serve as classrooms until the late 1930s, when it was converted back to a residence. Undeniably, Charles House was a place of significance—notable for its grand structure, prestigious residents, and the conversations and ceremonies conducted within its walls.

Three U.S. Presidents had been the guests of honor at dinners hosted in its large, cathedral-like dining room.

Since appointed president of the university in 1971, Alan Stewart, his wife Colleen, and their two daughters had lived at the home. Central to its function, the house included a large dining and entertaining area with dinner seating for fifty-five and a massive stone fireplace. Select board meetings, fundraisers, awards dinners, and political events were held there. Regularly, *The Cavanaugh Dispatch* featured events held at the home in its style section.

Each year in mid-January, it was customary for the president to host an annual dinner for the University's Board at Charles House. It was also customary for the president to invite students to represent the undergraduate community, usually ten or so, and Ben and I were among the eight selected to attend on Wednesday, January 24, 1979. Ben received his invitation with his usual nonchalance while I looked forward to the event with great anticipation.

* * *

At 6:30pm on the 24th, Ben and I braved the thirty-degree evening and walked from Yarborough Hall to Charles House, the chilly wind in our face every step of the way. My hands and face were crimson when we arrived at the home, with a front porch that spanned the length of the structure, reminding me of a lakeside resort where my family once vacationed in upstate New York. Inside, the great room beckoned, gently warmed and softly lit by a flourishing blaze in the fireplace, its flames reaching four feet skyward toward the granite chimney that occupied most of the west wall.

Most of the other guests had arrived so the room was near capacity. Board members, invited guests, and students stood in clusters of four and five, and a low murmur filled the air. I spotted Professor Lambert talking to two gentlemen next to the fireplace and, since my fingers were still numb and ready to snap off, I figured that was the right place for me. I walked toward the glowing warmth. Ben strolled in the opposite direction toward the dining room.

"I really enjoyed *The Signal* this week," Professor Lambert commented as I joined the group, while also informing the others that I was editor. "I'm looking forward to next issue."

"Thank you," I said, though puzzled by her second remark.

"I wrote for *The Signal* in the 60s," Steve Todd, a corporate lawyer, stated. "I've heard very good things about the paper these days. I hear you're doing a great job. I'm sure the high standards set by the journalists who preceded you are in good hands."

I was taken back by his familiarity and complimented, too. But, I couldn't help but focus on his years at *The Signal*.

"Did you know Joe Golden?" I asked.

Steve smiled nostalgically. "Joe was a good friend of mine."

His smile deepened, and he seemed to leave the group for a brief moment, privately reminiscing.

"He was a character alright," he added, "funny, mischievous, and full of pranks. But, I haven't heard from him in a decade, and I doubt I will."

"Why would you say that?"

"I don't know exactly, just a feeling that started when I read *The Torn Tuxedo*. He wasn't the same guy anymore. I knew Joe wasn't coming back. I just sensed it."

President Stewart stood at the entrance to the dining room and requested everyone's attention. When all heads turned in his direction he announced, "Dinner is about to be served. Please join my family at the table."

I followed Steve to the dining room, but I was thwarted in my effort to hear more about Joe Golden by white placards at each place setting, indicating seating. Steve was on the same side of the table as me, but five places removed. I was seated between Ben and Professor Lambert, ten place settings from the head of the table.

As President Stewart passed behind us, en route to the head of the table, he placed his hands on Ben's shoulder and mine and whispered softly.

"I'd like to meet with the two of you privately at the end of the evening," he informed us, "so please don't run off."

Ben and I looked at one another, perplexed.

About midway through dinner, the conversation in my section of the table shifted to Grizzly football. A surgeon in his late fifties voiced concern over Coach Wilson's ability to manage the football program saying, "I can't believe Coach Wilson had that Grainger kid on the bench all season long and never played him. He made a big difference in those last three games."

"Grainger's going to be one of the best our school's ever had," a student to my left added. "Next year will be very interesting if the Grizzlies can improve their defense."

The surgeon inquired of the president, "How much longer does Wilson have on his contract, Al?"

"One more year, I believe."

"Well, as far as I'm concerned, he had best produce a winning season next year and show us he's capable of coaching, or else we should look for another coach," the surgeon stated.

"Let's not form a mob," the president said. "We'll address the coaching situation when the time is right. The program isn't any better or any worse since Coach Wilson took over."

"That's a fact," the surgeon returned, "but it's not an excuse."

At the table, I was the only one who knew the truth about Coach Wilson, about his salacious indiscretions and inappropriate conduct. As I listened, I realized that I'd never thought about the coach's actions from a journalist's perspective; I'd always considered his actions from the viewpoint of Danny's friend. For the first time, it occurred to me that the coach's actions weren't just inappropriate, my initial reaction, but they had clearly affected his job performance also. His personal feelings had negatively impacted the performance of his duties and his responsibilities to the team. It wasn't just my opinion—it was obvious to anyone who watched the Grizzlies last season. Many speculated that the team's performance and final record would have been markedly better if Danny had been at quarterback from the start of the season.

What kind of journalist am I if I sit on this story? I thought. *What kind of friend am I if I don't?*

By 10pm, the dessert table was ravaged. Baked goods suitable for display in a museum only an hour ago were reduced to crumbling fractions of the original masterpieces. Pies, cakes, and pastries with buttery crusts, delicate layers, and creamy frosting were an especially welcome treat for the students in attendance because the cafeteria never served anything as tasty. Ben and I waited a courteous interval before returning to the table for seconds. With an ivory cake server in hand, I had just placed a thick wedge of gooey fudge cake on my plate when President Stewart approached.

"Why don't we take dessert to my study where we can talk?" he suggested, scanning the baked goods. Then, President Stewart, making his selection, placed a slice of Boston cream pie on a plate and remarked, "My mother made the most delicious cream pies when I was young. Though it never compares, I can't pass it up whenever it's offered—the memory is so delicious."

We left the dining area with plates in hand and walked down the main hallway to a stately library where President Stewart worked when in the residence. The president sat behind the large oak desk in the center of the room, and Ben and I sat in red leather reading chairs before him. He placed his pie on the corner of the desk, dismissing it after just one bite, and reached into a drawer to his right and retrieved three stapled pieces of university stationery.

"I have something for you," he said, handing the materials across the desk to me. In bold letters across the top it read, University Press Release, directed to *The Stanton University Signal* with a second release to the general media on February 7th.

"I'm pleased to inform you," the president said with a broad smile, "that the University's Board of Directors have approved an expansion plan that includes construction of a student center and two dormitories. Groundbreaking will take place in the spring of 1980 with completion by the close of the summer of 1981."

"That's great news," Ben declared.

"Please note that this press release is provided to *The Signal* only until February 7. I think it's appropriate for *The Signal* to be the first media outlet to announce the expansion plan."

"On behalf of our staff, I thank you for the consideration," I said. "*The Signal* is honored to announce the plan."

"The next issue of *The Signal* is due February 5th, right?" the president asked.

"That's correct," I answered, "and I can see the front page already, University Announces Expansion - Student Center Included."

Ben and I left Charles House and walked to our dormitory. It was five hours later and ten degrees colder, but I didn't notice the bitter cold this time. Even the slapping of the wind didn't remove the smile from my face. We were both elated and already looking forward to the reaction when the next issue was published.

"I feel like a junkie," I confessed. "I can't wait to get this issue out and feel that buzz on campus again. I feel good when I know an issue is quality work, but every once in a while it feels great to create a genuine buzz."

"We've only got seven days until the deadline," Ben said, "so we'll have to work quickly."

"It's best this way," I suggested. "Any more time and word would leak out."

"You're right."

* * *

When Ben and I arrived at our dormitory, we proceeded to the fifth floor to hang out in Ben's room. "I'll catch up," Ben said as he tossed his keys my way. "I have to take a piss."

I entered his dorm room, turned on the overhead light, and sat at Ben's cluttered desk. There, amongst the loose papers, I noticed the return corner of a white-linen envelope, embossed with a scripted DCM insignia, Danzig Capital Management. My curiosity roused, I reached into the mess and removed the envelope from its partially concealed location. The envelope, postmarked January 8th, was torn open and its contents were limited to one solitary page. From the postmark, I assumed the letter arrived last week, and, since Ben never mentioned it, wasn't good news. I slipped the letter out of the envelope, unfolded the document so that only the top third was visible, and read the first line.

"I am sorry to inform you that our DCM review team has reviewed your proposal and must decline your funding request for the start-up of *Cavanaugh Weekly* newspaper."

I didn't read any further. I returned the letter to its envelope and the envelope to its place in the clutter. I knew polite reasons and kind words of encouragement followed, but I wasn't interested in reading on, and I doubted Ben had either.

I wished I hadn't read that letter. It totally erased the euphoria I'd felt since departing Charles House with the press release in hand. I felt sorry for Ben, but mostly I felt guilty and ashamed. In truth, I'd secretly hoped Ben wouldn't secure the funding so he'd start the newspaper after we graduated and I wouldn't have to make that difficult choice, newspaper or college. I hated myself for rooting against his efforts, but if Ben secured the funding, dropped out of SU, and started the newspaper, I couldn't turn down his offer to be editor. I'd have to accept the position and that would mean the end of my college days. I knew it was selfish, but I simply wasn't ready yet. Worse still, I couldn't imagine telling my parents I was dropping out. I could still hear my father warning me that college would be a long journey that required unyielding commitment. I was a selfish chicken shit, plain and simple.

"I'm a little tired," I said when Ben arrived. "How about we hit it fresh tomorrow?"

"Sounds good," he replied, and I left for my room.

6.

Ego was a driving force behind skyscrapers. Due to an office glut in 1910, bankers wouldn't fund the plans to build the massive Woolworth Tower. Frank Woolworth, the five and dime magnate, was determined his tower would be built so he put up the money for construction.

At 2am, three cranes were shrouded in light mist and fog as dockworkers abandoned their posts at the Port of Cavanaugh for their meal break. The continual back and forth movement of containers between ships and docks ceased for an hour each night as workers turned to brown bags, the only option available as little was open in the immediate vicinity. Walking south from one of the cranes, his steel-toed boots creating small splashes in the puddles, a stocky fifty-five-year-old dockworker passed through light then shadows then light then shadows, over and over, as he strode beneath the lights on his way to the employee parking lot. For a man who answered to punches on a timecard, he walked at an unusually unhurried pace until he reached a Chevrolet Impala with large splotches of gray primer on the exterior. Once in the driver's seat, he cranked the engine several times until it started and then he drove toward the empty road.

Less than a mile from the crane, a normally busy liquor store was dark and unoccupied at that late hour, its neon "Open" sign unlit. Near the corner of the block, the stocky dockworker stopped his car and walked in his typically unhurried manner toward the front door of the store, one hand plunged deep into his pant pocket. As he extracted a crumpled sheet of paper and coins from his baggy work pants, the stocky man stopped beside the pay phone. After cautiously glancing around, he wrapped a white T-shirt around the mouthpiece, dropped two coins into the slot, waited for the dial tone, and then methodically pressed the seven digits noted on the crumpled sheet. Waiting for an answer, the man removed a second, folded sheet of white paper from the breast pocket of his work coat.

In Yarborough Hall, Ben Matthews' dormitory was the only window lit at that late hour of the night, not unusual for the insomniac. Ben sat at his desk in a studious posture with an American History textbook open before him, a course Ben could just as easily have taught as attended. On the left page of the textbook, an illustration depicted the seizure of Fort Ticonderoga by Ethan Allen and the Green Mountain Boys. Ben knew all this history from his childhood but simply loved reading about it time and time again. While examining the colorful depiction, he was startled when his phone rang.

"Hello," he said apprehensively due to the late hour.

"Is this Ben Matthews?" the caller asked in a muffled voice.

"Yes," Ben responded, confused.

"I have a written statement to read to you. Don't talk or ask any questions as I do."

"Okay," Ben replied, even more confused.

"Councilman Dale Greenwood," the caller began, clearly reading as he spoke, "has long been a supporter of both the Cavanaugh Waterfront Towers project and the Port of Cavanaugh expansion project, and both projects have been before the city council for more than a year. Additionally, Councilman Greenwood has a longstanding relationship with the dockworkers union, a relationship that has included financial support and mutual favors. In appreciation of the councilman's support of the expansion project and at the request of the councilman, the dockworkers union sent three men to graffiti and damage the visitor center in Old Cavanaugh so the participants at your rally would be blamed. The intent was to make Old Cavanaugh appear to be a problem area that would be improved by new condominiums. I'm telling you this because I've known your father for twenty years and I don't want to see you or your father harmed. These are bad people, Ben. Don't mess with them."

With that final admonition, the caller abruptly hung up, leaving Ben thunderstruck, angered by the councilman who, at almost twice his age, had taken advantage of his youth and inexperience. Based on the call, he manipulated Ben to advance his own political agenda as a supporter of Cavanaugh Waterfront Towers. In essence, the councilman provided advice to Ben that magically transformed into a crane and wrecking ball that would demolish Old Cavanaugh. As this reality settled in, Ben felt the embarrassment and shame of a prostitute after her first trick, suddenly recognizing the inequity of the transaction, a large piece of her soul for a small bit of currency. Like the naive whore, Ben had been used.

"That son of a bitch," Ben mumbled under his breath, fuming.

* * *

Before the fall semester of 1979, Randy Porter left SU and transferred to Harcourt College. Unfortunately, his departure didn't remedy the animosity and tension between Danny and the coach. How could it? It didn't change the encounter Danny witnessed or the injustice he had endured the previous season. Throughout the summer workouts, Danny took snaps, threw passes, and listened to instructions but never spoke to Coach Wilson, not so much as a word. He focused on his conditioning and fundamentals and didn't allow himself to be distracted by the past. But inside, at his core, Danny seethed.

Football was sacred to Danny, full of rituals and elements he revered: the coin toss, the kickoff, the huddle, a tight spiral, a hard hit, a clean block, a precise lateral, a fingertip catch, a gutsy punt return, all of it. Where Danny came from, churches, cemeteries, and football fields were sacred ground, holy cathedrals all. In Danny's mind, his coach had disgraced the game of football and dishonored himself. How could he play for a coach that would have a sexual relationship with his quarterback? It wasn't just ethically wrong—it was sacrilege. Danny might be able to overlook the homosexual relationship, even the student-teacher relationship, but the coach-quarterback relationship was an offense to the game, and he couldn't overlook that.

One afternoon after practice, Danny lingered in the Jacuzzi, simmering like the hot water that bubbled around him. He knew he couldn't contain his growing resentment much longer; he'd explode. Somehow, he needed to get control of the pressure building within him, so he decided during his soak that a managed detonation was better than an uncontrolled explosion. He needed to resolve this problem on his own timeframe and terms. Impatiently, Danny waited until his teammates had showered and departed and then, once again, he walked the darkened hallway to the coach's office. He found the coach making notes in the margin of a spiral-bound playbook but the coach didn't notice Danny as he entered the office in front of him. He was startled by Danny's voice.

"I saw you with Randy Porter," Danny declared, scowling.

Coach Wilson looked up from the playbook.

Danny continued.

"I left the facility late after the UWS game last year and I saw you kiss him. I know why Randy didn't return this year. I know why you didn't play me last season."

At that point, Coach Wilson looked down at the desk, both ashamed and terrified and unable to make eye contact with his accuser. He struggled to find the right words of denial. He knew he had to be careful not to say the wrong thing as so much rode on his response: his job, his career, his reputation, and even his marriage. His grip on the yellow pencil unwittingly tightened until it suddenly snapped, as if the pressure in Danny had been transferred to the coach.

"I don't know what you're talking about, Grainger," he finally stammered, a generic denial and all he could come up with under such pressure.

"I saw you kiss him so don't deny it."

At that moment, every trace of composure and refutation drained from the coach's face as he recognized his denial was futile. Just like the pencil in his hands, the coach broke.

"I'll be ruined," the coach pleaded. "I was wrong and it's over. Please forgive me."

"I'm not going to tell anyone," Danny said, as he noticed the twitching of the two pencil halves in his trembling hands, "but we are going to come to terms right now—my terms. I can't play for you. I detest you."

"You're quitting?"

As soon as the words left Coach Wilson's mouth, he realized how foolish the query was, but he wasn't thinking clearly.

"No fucking way," Danny returned, even angrier now as the coach had used the word "quit" again.

"You want me to resign?"

The coach was thinking more rationally now.

"From now on," Danny instructed him, "Coach Kolar handles the quarterbacks exclusively; we are no longer your concern."

Solemnly and slowly, the coach nodded, his honor and pride lost but his job and all else spared.

"No one needs to know about our agreement," Danny said. "You just stay the fuck away from me."

* * *

Ben and Danny were closer during our junior year. They hadn't hung out together our first two years, not without me, but several times in early fall, when I went upstairs to Ben's room I found them together, usually talking football. I was glad to see it. Ben was my friend and Danny was my friend, but in the past, I usually brought them together. They hadn't hung out without me. Now, it seemed that our friendships were a complete triangle and, I thought, better that way.

Despite impressive performances by Danny in both contests, the Grizzlies were 1-1 in the first week of October and were preparing for UWS. Last year's game, an aerial duel won by UWS, was decided by a field goal with only eighteen seconds remaining so Grizzly fans eagerly awaited the rematch. On campus, there was more interest in the football team this season because, win or lose, it was an exciting team to watch. The Grizzly offense was wide open, passing on more than half its downs, and the team's defense was improved though still not unyielding. The odds makers offset UWS' home field advantage with Danny's conference leading statistics and called the game even.

On Wednesday evening before the game, Danny was in Ben's dorm room when I arrived, stretched out on the sofa while Ben studied a textbook beneath his desk lamp. I sat on the bed, leaned against the wall, and picked up *The Cavanaugh Dispatch* sports section from the blanket beside me, already open to the college page. As I spoke, I glanced at the preview of the SU game.

"Everybody's talking about the game," I observed. "There are even banners hanging from dorm windows all over campus. It's so different from our first two years when so many people ignored the football team."

"It's football deprivation," Ben theorized. "SU hasn't fielded a respectable team in years, so when one comes along, the fans go crazy. Hell, they don't even care about winning and losing, it's just nice to see the game played properly once again."

"Not to mention Golden Boy here," I chided Danny. "We've got the best quarterback in the conference."

"And beyond," Ben said.

"Is the team ready, Danny?" I asked.

Danny didn't respond. He had closed his eyes since I'd arrived, but I was sure he wasn't asleep.

"Let Golden Boy rest," Ben advised.

"The game is being billed as a big showdown between Danny and UWS quarterback, Dale Raymond," I continued, paraphrasing the article before me. "The ball will be in the air all game long according to *The Dispatch*."

"When did you start reading the sports page, Pete?" Danny demanded, his eyes now opened and narrowed.

"Hey, I have been rooting for you from day one, back when you were still sitting on the bench," I said. "What's with you?"

"It's just a football game, goddamn it," Danny said, speaking words I never thought I'd hear from him.

"Just a football game?"

Danny rose from the sofa and headed toward the door saying, "Stanton University is small-time college football. It's not the NFL or even Collegiate Division I, it's basically a sandlot pick-up game. No one really cares about these games. Don't make a goddamn fuss."

He slammed the door as he left.

"What's with him?" I asked.

"Must be nerves."

* * *

The game was broadcast on Saturday by one of the local stations, so Ben suggested we watch it at The Frothy Tankard. It was a 4pm kickoff so Tyler and I left the university in her BMW around 3pm. Ben had spent Friday night at the family home. When we arrived at the pub, Kirk was in our usual booth, Ben was at the bar talking to the bartender, and the crowd, a mix of regulars and SU supporters, was the largest I had seen in the place, probably seventy or eighty people. Kirk greeted us with his usual enthusiasm, rising from the booth to hug us. He beamed like a proud father as he declared, "Have you been reading *The Dispatch* this week? Our Danny is the talk of the town."

"It's going to be a great game," Tyler said as Ben joined us at the booth.

"Yeah," Kirk added. "I'm tempted to place a little wager on the Grizzlies, maybe twenty."

"No, Dad, let's just watch the game. I don't think Danny would want you to bet on it."

"That's probably true," I said. "He's under enough pressure already. He's been kind of agitated these days."

The game was an offensive battle from the start. On the fourth play of the game, the UWS quarterback connected with his wide receiver beyond the Grizzly defense for a fifty-two yard touchdown. But, Danny brought his team right back, orchestrating an eleven play, eighty-yard-scoring drive, capped by a fifteen yard touchdown pass to his tight end. It was the first of several successive tied scores. The scoring continued at a frenzied pace until halftime when the two teams left the field with the Grizzlies trailing 28-24.

On their opening possession of the second half, the Grizzlies progressed to the UWS twenty-five yard line. On second and three, Danny underthrew a Grizzly receiver, breaking toward the far sideline, allowing the defender to intercept the pass and race the length of the field for a touchdown. On television, the partisan crowd roared with approval. At The Frothy Tankard, the crowd moaned. On the verge of scoring, SU gave up a touchdown instead and suddenly trailed 35-24. It was Danny's first interception at SU, and it was a game turner. The Grizzlies fought back, extending their already wide-open offense even further, but they couldn't catch up, losing 49-45.

The UWS game was typical of the Grizzly season. Win or lose, they played exciting, competitive football, a real change for fans from past seasons. Most felt the team was better than the 6-4 record, insisting the team could have been 7-3 or even 8-2 if a couple close games had gone their way. When the record books were closed on the 1979 season, Danny's conference leading statistics for completed passes and total yards ranked among the best that ever played at SU despite the team's barely better than breakeven results. As a postscript to Danny's first full season, a sports columnist at *The Dispatch* wrote, "Forget the mediocre record, this Grizzly team, led by quarterback Danny Grainger, is very talented and will compete for the conference title next year. Grainger may be the best quarterback in the school's history and one of the best in conference history as well."

Despite the respect and accolades, Danny wasn't the same guy anymore; once easygoing, he'd become someone with a big chip on his shoulder. On some nights, he was withdrawn and quiet and other nights, bitter and angry. At first, I thought his moods were attributable to pressure and nerves, but after some thought, I realized that wasn't it. He oozed self-confidence; that hadn't changed. After a couple of beers one night, I confronted Danny about the change, but he shut me out, gave me nonsensical answers.

"Life doesn't always work out like we hope," he said. "It gets more complicated with every candle on the cake. We forget about the simple joys of youth, the beauty of innocent motivations. As we grow older, we make compromises, we make the best of bad situations."

"What didn't work out?" I asked, confused by his rant. "You belong at a major college? You're better than SU?"

"When I was a boy, I used to throw passes at an old tire we'd hung on a rope in our backyard. I'd take an imaginary snap from center, back peddle four or five paces, and then throw that football in a perfect spiral through the center of that tire. Nothing I do at SU will ever compete with that feeling. It was pure joy."

"You don't get that feeling when you connect with one of your receivers for a touchdown?"

"It's different now, more complicated. Back then there were no coaches, no alumni, no fans, no statistics, no records, no rankings, no rivalries, and no line. I threw that football because I loved to, no other reason, no great implications."

"You don't love it anymore?"

"That's just it, I don't. I'm glad the season is over. I'm tired. In our backyard, I turned our porch light on so I could see at night. My mom would flash the light as a signal for me to come in, but I wouldn't stop, I was having too much fun. Finally, she would open the back door and make me come in. Otherwise, I'd have thrown that football all night. For the first time in my life, I was glad to see the porch light flash."

* * *

To those things we dread in life, we provide certainty. In spite of my prayers and denials, one Saturday in early December brought the question I dreaded. On the pretense of helping Kirk at the print shop, Ben and I drove to South Cavanaugh, but Ben turned the car in the opposite direction away from the print shop when we arrived at Gaines Avenue.

"Where are we going?" I asked as Ben diverted.

"I've got something to show you," he said.

We drove six blocks to a row of run-down warehouses near the train station; three of the warehouses were occupied, the sites of a transmission shop, a welding shop, and a glass company; the fourth was unoccupied, its signage removed and several windows broken. We parked beside three black trash drums at the unoccupied ware-house and Ben led me to its steel front door, weathered by years of dirt, grime, and soot, and discolored where the previous tenant's sign had hung. Ben had the key, so we entered the drafty building.

"Welcome to the future home of *Cavanaugh Weekly*," he said as we entered the three thousand square foot space with a small wooden loft area overhanging for storage. "I've got the money to start the business, not the whole $100,000 I planned but $83,000. We will watch our expenses closely and ramp up advertising revenues quicker than planned. We'll make it work."

"Where did you get all that money?"

"An investment," Ben answered. "It has come in piecemeal throughout the fall."

"What kind of investment?"

"That's not important. I've got the money. The newspaper is going to be a reality."

"When will you start?"

"In the new year," he stated. "I'm going to finish exams next week and start working here in January. I want you to come with me as editor. What do you say?"

"This place is going to need a lot of work."

"I've taken that into account. I figure it's four months before we publish the first issue. We will refurbish in January, hire and train in February, focus on promotion and sales in March, and publish in April. It's going to be a lot of hard work, but it's also a one-of-a-kind opportunity.

"I know," I said, still working through the shock of it all.

"We'll only pay ourselves seven hundred fifty dollars a month as starting salaries, but you'll be a 50 percent partner in the business, also," Ben elaborated.

"Fifty percent partner? You're putting up the money."

"You bring a lot more to this venture than you realize. I want you in, Pete. Together, it's a sure thing."

Overwhelmed, I told Ben I'd give him an answer when I returned from the Christmas holidays at home.

"I have to talk with my parents before I drop out of SU," I advised him. "They were so supportive of my decision to enroll."

* * *

In many ways, my parents, Thomas and Angela Dalton, were indistinguishable from the other parents on our block. My dad, like the other dads, shaved and showered, donned a blue or gray two-piece suit and tie, and walked down our driveway at 7:10am to meet his carpool. My mom, like the other moms, stayed behind, cared for the children, cleaned, shopped, cooked, and, finally, waited patiently for my dad to be dropped off. At 5:40pm, my dad returned, exhausted, tie loosened, collar unbuttoned, walking up the driveway with the toll of another workday chiseled in his brow. Equally worn, my mom greeted him at our front door. It was a routine repeated daily in every home in suburbia.

In our home, dinner always included meat, potatoes, a green vegetable or salad, and milk and was served promptly at 6:30pm. During dinner, my dad watched the evening news and commented on world events while mom and us kids vied for his attention.

"Keep it down, I can't hear Walter Cronkite," he would shout at least twice each meal whenever we overwhelmed the daily recap.

It was during dinner each evening, with a grainy, black and white television broadcast in the background, that I got my first small glimpses of the world that existed beyond suburbia. Blacks marched, students protested, women rallied, and musicians rocked. None of this activity ever affected my world directly, but the rest of the world was changing profoundly. In July of 1969, I watched a man in a space suit bounce playfully across the surface of the moon, an accomplishment unthinkable just a generation ago and one that surely marked the start of a new era, one where anything was possible. Again, none of this affected me directly, but it was a time of possibility.

Through good news and bad, the times when we were all gathered together as a family always passed too quickly and usually ended with me being sent off to bed. Tomorrow was another day and yet, in many ways, tomorrow was the same day. Sure, I would grow a little or add a few pounds as the months and years progressed, but my life always felt safe, secure, and monotonous. Living in our home was a lot like living in a cloistered monastery—conversations were limited, meals were hearty and timely, and all issues of significance were left to higher powers.

I was the fourth of five children. Lynn, the oldest, attended a junior college about ten miles from our home and earned her degree in history. My older brothers, Doug and Russell, second and third born respectively, were so different it was hard to believe they shared common parentage. Doug was an honors student, a star athlete, and outgoing and popular at school. Russell existed along the fringes throughout his adolescence, never cared much about school or other activities, and always traveled in the company of outcasts. Whenever recognition beckoned, Doug got handed a trophy at a team banquet and Russell got a reprimand in the principal's office. Finally, there was my little sister, Stephanie, a surprise birth that happened six years after me. She was everyone's favorite and our focus at family meals and gatherings.

As a child, I never dreamed about great success and that was fortunate because both suburbia and the public school system seemed structured to lower my expectations. Like most children, I spent my early years with my mother in my own world where I was special, the uncontested center of my small universe. But then, it was off to kindergarten where I first learned that there were many more just like me and some better. Then, it was grade school, junior high school, and finally high school, each a larger assemblage where I became increasingly more aware that I was simply one of many.

When I arrived in 1973, Winston Churchill High School had over three thousand students in attendance—an enrollment that suited me because I was perfectly content to blend in with the masses. But, don't get me wrong—I enjoyed school. I just wasn't comfortable with myself, and I didn't fit in with any of the cliques. I wasn't a jock, I didn't know a carburetor from a manifold, I didn't play a musical instrument, I wasn't a tough guy, and I wasn't nearly smart enough to hang out with the brains. Basically, I wandered from class to class without a high school identity. And making matters worse, Doug had been a star athlete at the school four years earlier, still held numerous records, and near-legend status with the jocks.

"You're nothing like your brother," I was told often.

Gym class typified my whole freshman experience. Each class began with stretching, calisthenics, and a warm-up run around the backstops of the baseball fields that formed the perimeter of the athletic field. Without exception, I was part of the athletically-challenged contingent, six or eight kids who walked the second half of the run and finished ten minutes after the rest of the class had started the main activity, flag football, soccer, volleyball, whatever. I might have enjoyed the main activities if I wasn't always a straggler who was substituted into action late. Our school teams were nicknamed "The Bombers" and every time I exited that athletic field, feeling awkward and uncomfortable in my athletic shorts, I gazed upward at that scoreboard and wondered if I was the only one who found irony in that designation.

At the start of sophomore year, I wrote an essay for English class that I titled "The American Nightmare." When the teacher, Mr.

Strickland, returned the graded papers to the rest of the class, he withheld mine, asking me to report to his office after last period. Throughout my remaining classes, I worried that he had misinterpreted my essay, thinking it unpatriotic or radical and planned to suspend me or even kick me out of school. Granted, Russell had been suspended several times, but no member of the Dalton family had ever been accused of being a communist and expelled. It was three periods that dragged on endlessly like an epic, black and white, foreign film with subtitles.

At 3:05pm, seated on a wooden chair before his desk, I waited while Mr. Strickland graded papers. My hands were clammy and knees trembled, and I contemplated how my father would react to my expulsion. Making matters even worse, Mr. Strickland was one of the hipper and popular teachers, making his expulsion more humiliating. In the student culture, expulsion by one of the uncool teachers like "The Fossil," as the students referred to Mr. Fosset, would mean notoriety, but not Mr. Strickland. Mr. Strickland was really cool. He was in his twenties with shoulder-length hair, an MGB sports car, and a little counter-culture when he talked.

When he finished, Mr. Strickland broke the tense air by tossing my essay onto the desk in front of me. Written in red ink, his comments stared up at me.

It read, "A+. One of the best sophomore papers I've read in eight years of teaching."

"I want you to come to work for me at *The Statesman*," he said, shifting from English teacher to his other role as faculty advisor for the school newspaper. "I think this essay shows a lot of rough potential and I've still got three openings for staff writers since last graduation."

Was Mr. Strickland more motivated by my writing abilities or the newspaper's shortage of writers? I didn't know and I didn't care. All I knew was I enjoyed writing and I'd never muster the courage to march into the newspaper's office on my own.

"Sure," I said.

I never wrote a controversial expose or uncovered a scandal, but I contributed some good articles during my time at *The Statesman*. More importantly, and not coincidentally, my work as well as my self-esteem improved with each effort I submitted. Each successive article served as a building block for my previously absent identity until, little by little, I began thinking of myself as a writer, and it felt good. For me, the written word and the act of publication provided a sense of purpose and a connection with the other students. As a writer for *The Statesman*, I wasn't taking up space in the classrooms and hallways anymore—I was contributing to the high school experience.

One of my earliest submissions to *The Statesman* was my favorite high school effort because it taught me about the power of journalism. Catherine Morgan, a junior at our high school in my sophomore year, was one of the really rich kids because her father owned car dealerships. She was attractive, with long blond hair and blue eyes, always impeccably dressed, and considered unapproachable by most kids. Whenever I saw her in the hallways between classes, she was usually alone, never in small groups like many of the other girls. One afternoon after school, I watched her cross the parking lot to a battered, yellow Range Rover, and this was unusual because her brother, Kyle, a senior, always drove brand new Firebirds, Mustangs, and even the occasional Corvette. My journalistic instincts were in a seedling state as I'd only been a writer at *The Statesman* for three weeks, and still I was curious enough to approach her as she placed her textbooks and sweater in the back of the Rover.

"Hi, Catherine," I said, my voice cracking, "I am a writer for *The Statesman* and I'd like to ask you a question if I could."

"Oh, you would?" she replied, chuckling to herself. "What's your question?"

"How come your brother drives all those new sports cars and you drive this old Range Rover?

"Get in, Scoop," she said, "I'll drive you home."

As she drove to my home, Catherine told me about her Aunt Maggie. Maggie was an outgoing, playful woman who loved animals, especially dogs and horses, and was always the center of attention at family gatherings. Holiday celebrations, family dinners, game nights, and birthday parties started when Maggie and her two dogs, golden retrievers named Simon and Garfunkel, arrived. She was the life of the party. In many ways, she was the heart and soul of the family. Maggie took her niece and nephew on regular road trips to beaches and mountains and taught them how to camp, hike, ski, surf, and ride horses. If their parents were out of town, Maggie stayed at their home and looked after them.

"She loved life like no one else I've ever known," Catherine told me. "She was so much fun to be around."

As Catherine spoke, I grew apprehensive because she used the past tense when she talked of her aunt. She glowed as she spoke, but I knew this story wouldn't end well. I readied myself for heartbreak.

After several cherished memories, she told me that her aunt was diagnosed with a brain tumor two years ago and died shortly there-after. She was only forty-three. Her passing was hard on her family and especially hard on her father who held onto his sister's Range Rover and parked it in the back of their garage. Their family was in the automobile business, but her father was not going to let go of that old Range Rover.

"Bring your Mustang to the dealership tomorrow and we'll swap it out for another car," her father told her one Friday evening.

Their family changed cars with the seasons, so this was not an unusual request.

"I'd like to drive Aunt Maggie's Range Rover if that's okay with you, Dad? I have so many great memories of the times I spent with her. It will feel like she is beside me."

Her father smiled. "I think Maggie would like that."

When we arrived at my home, she stopped the Rover beside the curb, moved the shifter to park, reached into the glove box with the sticker of a sunflower on it, and handed me a note card her aunt had left for her before she died.

"To understand how special my Aunt Maggie was," she said, "all you have to do is read that card."

"Cate," the card began in elegant but shaky handwriting, "I am writing this note to express my final wish for you and my final request of you. I hope you'll honor both. My wish for you is that you live a fulfilled life, one where you find people, places, and purpose that touch you deeply and give your life meaning. Always follow your heart, trust your good mind, and never let fear stop you. My request of you is that every blue moon or so, you find a quiet corner and reflect on our times together. When you feel at peace and have a great big smile on your face, you'll know it is time to return to your day. Love, Maggie."

"She seemed like a really great lady," I told Catherine as I returned the card to the glove box.

By that point, I'd heard so much about Maggie that I almost felt like I knew her. She was someone special, indeed, and her journey through this life was thoughtful, generous, and inspiring. My strongest impression was that she had lived more than most people do in full lifetimes. She'd certainly left her mark on the young girl beside me.

"Your stories make me wish I had known her," I added.

As I opened the door, Catherine provided a parting thought.

"Aunt Maggie once told me that the only problem with dogs is they don't live long enough. I guess that was true of my aunt also."

After my article, "The Girl in the Yellow Range Rover," was published in *The Statesman*, Catherine was no longer unapproachable. She was not the rich kid who had everything anymore; she was a girl who had suffered a significant loss at a young age and one who could surely use a friend. Whenever I saw her, Cate was always with a small pack of students, laughing and chatting in a lighthearted manner as the article helped her make a lot of new friends. From that lift home forward, Cate and I stayed friends and she always called me "Scoop" whenever we crossed paths. It was never my nickname at school, just her nickname for me. Walking with Cate in the hallways between classes enhanced my high school identity because she was my only friend that was cool. It didn't make me cool—nothing could do that—but it made me more noticeable, and that was a big improvement.

Almost immediately, the article affected both our lives in very positive ways, and the power of journalism was clear to me.

In December of 1976, I began searching for a college to attend after graduation, the single most important qualifier being a highly respected journalism program. The first round of candidates included some ten or fifteen universities, but I quickly narrowed that field to Maryland, Marquette, and Stanton. Though the first two had more impressive reputations as universities wholly, Stanton University was the standard bearer for journalism schools and considered by many to be the best in the nation. One glance at its alumni listing confirmed it.

Late one night, I noticed one name in particular, Joe Golden, the author of *The Torn Tuxedo*, my favorite novel, amongst the fifty or so in the university's brochure, and his name convinced me to attend SU. After all, Joe Golden was the reason I became a writer. Reading his novel at the impressionable age of thirteen showed me that writing was a virtuous profession, and that stirring the mind and throttling the imagination was a noble act, even beautiful and soulful. His words were passionate, poetic, and lyrical, never resting stark and still on the printed page in black and white but bursting instead into the reader's mind and imagination in full, brilliant color. *The Torn Tuxedo* roused a voice within me that I never knew I had. Walking in his footsteps at SU made a lot of sense.

However, I knew it would take more than a novelists' name on an alumni listing to convince my parents.

Reviewing my case, I had two things working in my favor and one against. First, being the fourth of five children, my parent's child rearing regimen and their earlier requirement for strict oversight had relaxed significantly during Russell's tumultuous teen years. Second, both my parents understood how important writing was to me because they'd witnessed a real metamorphosis over four years. As a high school senior, I had direction and purpose that I didn't as a freshman. But, working against me were the 2,700 miles between our home and the northwestern city of Cavanaugh, the location of SU. My parents wanted me to attend college closer to home.

Finally, one February evening, I waited until Cronkite finished his fabled "And that's the way it is" sign-off, and then I followed my father to his den where he retreated each evening to smoke his pipe. Once he was seated comfortably behind his desk, I told him I wanted to attend Stanton University, as I was convinced it was the best place for me to prepare for a career in journalism, the best place for me to advance my skills as a writer. I never mentioned Joe Golden.

"I also believe that the city of Cavanaugh will be a good place for me," I added, wrapping my practiced oratory. "It's a beautiful city with a population of just over two million people; large enough to provide subject matter for me to write about, but not so large that I'll be overwhelmed by it."

My father, a deliberate and thoughtful man who carefully measured any response, pressed his stubby thumb against the loose tobacco mulch in his pipe, puffed on the stem to relight his smoky cordial, and quietly considered my appeal. His many puffs sent fluffy, white clouds of cherry smoke drifting towards the ceiling. Waiting on his pronouncement, I felt surrounded by silence and cherry smoke, and anxious because I knew his next words would decide the most important decision of my young life. Still, I resisted the urge to add anything more. My father appreciated concise people.

"Four years at Stanton will be a long hard journey," he finally muttered, "one that will test your commitment and reveal the depth of your determination. I want you to consider the entire journey and not just the first steps. If you are sure you're fully committed to the entire journey, I will support your decision to attend Stanton."

When our conversation ended, I rushed to the kitchen to tell my mother the good news. She had a yellow hand towel and a wet dish in her hands. She looked up, noticed my elated expression, and her drying motion ceased. As I informed her about our conversation, her eyes slowly turned sorrowful, moistening with nostalgic tears that overflowed her lids and streaked her pink cheeks.

"My baby is leaving for college," she said, wistfully. "I'm going to miss you so much."

Her sadness wasn't the result of my decision to attend SU but rather her realization that I'd grown up. Still, her tears caused me to refocus. I'd thought so much about where I wanted to go that I hadn't considered what I'd be leaving. The fact that I wouldn't see my mother everyday, like I had on every previous day of my life, moved to the front of my mind. My eyes moistened also. With our time together suddenly limited, I quickly crossed the room and hugged her where she stood, between the gas stove and the sink of drying dishes.

"I'm going to be a writer," I said.

"I know," she whispered, her arms squeezing just a little bit tighter with the acknowledgement.

* * *

Education was always a priority in our home. Flying home, I thought about the emphasis our family had always placed on a college degree. My grandfather wasn't a college graduate, but he insisted the day my father graduated was the proudest day of his life. He spoke of that day often, as well as the sacrifice that went into it. My mother spent most of her evenings at our kitchen table alongside her children doing homework and school projects. In turn, my father told each of his children that we could do whatever we wanted with our lives so long as we went to college first. It was non-negotiable.

"It gives you options," he told us, "something to fall back on."

At the age of eighteen, my brother Russell's relationship with my father was forever tarnished when he rebuffed college saying, "It simply wasn't his thing," in 1960's hippy lingo.

At twenty-eight thousand feet, as I stared out into the black of a winter's night, I realized my parents wouldn't support my decision to leave college. It was contrary to their belief system and it violated our family charter. Nothing I could say would secure their blessing. I needed to brace myself for the worst. I'd wait until the day before my return flight to address the issue. I didn't want to spoil the holiday season for my parents or my siblings, or myself.

As was true of many families, the kitchen was the focal point of our home life. It was the place where meals and mom—the two most important things in a child's life—were found. It was the place where our family congregated, where we spent the most time together, and where the most poignant moments of our lives played out. For more than three decades, our kitchen had witnessed laughter, tears, storytelling, life lessons, disagreements, and reconciliation. It's not an exaggeration to say that the kids in our family grew up in the kitchen.

On the night before my flight, I sat quietly at the large, wood plank table in our kitchen and watched my mother prepare dinner, gracefully twirling like a ballerina between simmering pots on the stove and raw ingredients on the chopping block. It was the same scene I had witnessed as a young boy, and the feeling transcended time. For a brief wonderful moment, my mind lightened and all my weighty career concerns dissipated in the warm, moist air. I was just a boy in my mother's kitchen again. My mother snapped celery stalks in half, chopped cucumbers into slices, peeled yellow potatoes over the sink, and tossed small pinches of leafy spices into the boiling pots on the stove. She handled mixing bowls, frying pans, serving plates, and an assortment of wood spoons and wiry utensils with skill and precision. Watching her work, I welcomed the chance to be young again, finding comfort in the familiarity of the moment. But, all too soon, as was true of my childhood, the steam from the boiling pots, laced with my career concerns, formed condensation on the windows, reminding me of the cold January night outside the pane, and I was grown again.

In our home, good news was announced during dinner and bad news after the meal. It was all part of our unwritten family etiquette. Since my parents would receive my announcement as bad news, I'd save it for after dinner when the dishes had been cleared and the other siblings had departed. We'd talk over coffee.

Until that evening, my relationship with my parents had been a good one as my direction had always been the direction they pointed. In my mind at least, that is how it is intended, the purpose of lineage. Parents provide guidance until the child is ready. At the heart of it all, our disagreement that evening would center on who should make this decision. In my parent's opinion, my decision to leave Stanton would be the defiant act of an ungrateful child, one contrary to the principles they'd instilled in me. From my perspective, it was simply time for me to choose my own direction in life, make my own choices, and live with the results. Only a fool would reject Ben's offer and ownership in the new enterprise. Most people work more than twenty years in their profession waiting and hoping for a comparable one. His offer was, unquestionably, the career opportunity of a lifetime.

My older siblings had come and gone over the holidays, each living away from home but returning regularly for holidays, special occasions, and home cooked meals. It was just the four of us for dinner that cold winter evening: my parents, Stephanie, and me, and still my mother kept seven chairs at the table, her way of signaling that there was always a place for her children in her home and at her table. On special occasions like that evening, my mother delayed dinner until after the evening news, so that we could talk without competition from the television set. It was after 7pm when she called us to dinner.

"Tell Pete about your report card," my father instructed my sister as we sat down.

"All As and one B," Stephanie declared proudly. She was in the eighth grade and would start high school in the fall.

"You're going to have to work harder in your Spanish class, young lady," my father advised her, referring to the solitary B on her report card, "if you're going to get into a good college."

"That's great, Stephanie," I said. "You made the honor roll."

"We already have one vending machine mogul in the family," my father followed-up, referring to Russell who worked for a vending company refilling snack and soda machines and collecting the coin receipts. "We don't want anymore."

My father believed it was better to earn your living using your mind than your hands, brains over brawn, white-collar work instead of blue-collar work. He made no effort to hide his displeasure that one of his sons wore gray overalls and drove a white van for a living. In his mind, Russell was proof of the importance of a college education.

Listening to my father, I knew that talk of Russell that evening wouldn't facilitate my cause.

"I loaned your brother twenty dollars a couple of weeks ago," my father continued, directing his remarks at me. "When he paid me back, he gave me a roll of quarters. Can you believe that?"

"It was twenty dollars, Thomas," my mother protested in her son's defense. "Russell works hard."

"I know he works hard," my father said, "and that's his own fault. He won't be able to do that kind of work when he's fifty. Then, where will he be?"

"Wasn't Billy big?" my mom commented about my nephew, an obvious attempt to change the subject.

But, my father wasn't finished yet.

"Russell isn't going to get rich collecting nickels, dimes, and quarters from candy machines," he added, chuckling. "He'll waste too much time rolling all those coins."

"He has grown a lot since I saw him last," I said, joining my mother's effort to change the subject.

A prolonged conversation about Russell and the virtues of higher education would only make my task more difficult later. For my own sake and the sake of Russell, who was being lambasted like the guest of honor at a celebrity roast, I needed to get the conversation focused on Stephanie.

"Stephanie, too," I added. "You'll be a freshman at Churchill next year, won't you?"

"My baby will start high school soon," my mother wined.

It was a pleasant meal from that point forward. Stephanie was the focal point of the conversation—I made sure of it. She talked about cheerleading, clothes, drama club, girlfriends, driving and, of course, boys. She was thirteen years old, and her world was a frenzied and complex place where even the most trivial detail of her day had to be dissected and analyzed. She found or created significance in every little thing that happened to her. I listened as my little sister rattled on endlessly, and I couldn't help but notice the confident, independent young girl she'd become. She was a great kid, and I regretted not being able to share more of her life.

When our plates were empty, Stephanie assisted my mother as she cleared the dishes from the table and then quickly retreated to her room to chat with friends on the telephone, as she did most evenings.

"Lights out at nine," my mother instructed her.

My parents drank coffee after every meal. The time of day, season of the year, phase of the moon, astrological period, family news, or world events didn't matter; meals ended with coffee, period. At 8pm, my parents had full cups before them with the appropriate measures of sugar and cream stirred in. Patiently, they watched the steam rise so as to gauge the right moment for their first slurp.

"I have something to tell you," I advised them.

"What is it?" my mother asked in a concerned tone. She knew my flight to Cavanaugh was early the next morning so she probably suspected bad news. She knew our family etiquette.

"I've been offered the job of editor for a start-up newspaper named *Cavanaugh Weekly* and I'm going to accept it. I'll also be a 50 percent partner in the business itself."

"What about your schooling?" my father demanded.

"I'll be leaving school, Dad. This is a once-in-a-lifetime opportunity and it won't wait. I can't turn it down."

"You will turn it down," he insisted, his voice raised, his face reddening. "You will finish college first. I won't have it any other way."

"I've already made my decision. I'm taking the job."

"If you leave Stanton University before graduation, you won't get any more assistance from us. You're on your own."

"That seems fair," I told him.

Like a young eagle standing precariously on the edge of the nest, hundreds of feet in the air, waiting for its moment to spread its untested wings and fly off, children too must eventually find their moment and take their leap of faith.

This was my moment.

By dropping out of SU, I was leaving college, my childhood, and all financial dependence behind. From that moment forward, I'd be solely responsible for myself and not depend on my parents any longer. After all, you can't have it both ways—independence and a monthly stipend. That was the life of the uncommitted, those afraid to believe in anything, most particularly themselves. Though young and unsure of so much, I wanted to believe in myself, for whatever that was worth.

My father had cut me off, and I accepted that, but I didn't want our relationship to suffer also. He wasn't an emotional man, but I noticed his fists clenched in anger on his thighs beneath the table, his knuckles white with ire. I'd never seen him so disappointed with me and it was hard for me to watch that. After all, I'd watched while my father's interactions with my brother Russell had steadily tensed until their relationship unraveled. I didn't want to repeat that cycle. It was a state of discord that I never wanted to cause in our family.

Going in, I thought the evening would be difficult, but I held on to an unlikely hope that it might turn positive. I hoped my father would give me some hokey business advice and wish me well on my endeavor. But, that was wishful thinking. My father wasn't going to give up everything he believed in, everything he'd lived his life by, to accommodate my job offer. In my heart of hearts, I knew that.

"A man finishes what he's started," my father shouted as he left for his bedroom, my mother following loyally, trying to calm him. Both cups of coffee remained, abandoned and cooling, still full to the brim.

I couldn't sleep that night.

Normally, whenever I climbed into the warm, comfort of my childhood bed, it felt like I'd returned to the womb. Lying there that night, staring into darkness, I knew it would never feel that way again. This house would always be my home; the place where my childhood memories lingered and the people I loved most resided. And, though nothing would ever change that, I knew I'd never again seek refuge within these walls. From now on, only love would guide me home, never need. I'd return because I wanted to, never because I had to. Often in life, it isn't the words or actions, but the motivation that matters most.

In the middle of the night, my bedroom door opened slowly, creaking as it moved, announcing a visitor. In her white flannel nightgown, it was my mother coming to check on my sleep as she'd done on so many nights in my youth. She peeked her head in.

"Are you awake?" she whispered.

She sat beside me on the bed.

"Don't let your father's anger confuse you," she said in an angelic tone. "He is very proud of you."

"I hoped he would be, Mom, but it didn't sound that way."

"He believes in education and wants you to get your college degree. You know it's important to him. But, he also knows how important writing is to you and, deep in his heart, he admires your courage for pursuing your passion. We didn't have options when we were young. We didn't have the choices that your generation does. It was a different world then. It's hard for him to accept how much the world has changed."

"I will graduate," I said. "I promise you that. But, for now, I have to pursue this opportunity."

"I know."

"Do you understand?" I asked. "It's now or never for this job. I can go back and finish college later."

"I do understand," she responded, "but more importantly, I believe in you. You're at a fork in the road with two roads before you. I know you'll do well regardless of which one you choose."

7.

Advances in construction methods and materials made
skyscrapers a reality. Concrete piers were driven below
street level to solid bedrock for sturdy foundations, steel
beams were molded to create formidable skeletons, and
designs were drafted to withstand the wind. Put another
way, reaching for the stars requires ingenuity.

Is construction the most-noble work? Building something real
and substantial in a location once vacant. The word itself, construct,
means putting powerful verbs into action—to build, to create, to erect,
to form. It is hard work, often backbreaking, and not for the soft or
coddled because construction is arduous. The materials are heavy and
messy, the tools are sharp and powerful, and the skillset is precise and
demanding. In the end, the constructed something is solid and durable, and the workers are better for their effort. It's easy to stand back,
admire a completed project, and marvel at construction. Civilizations—whether ancient Egypt, the Roman Empire, or modern
America—are often defined by their construction: think pyramids, the
Coliseum, and the Empire State Building.

Thus far in life, I'd only worked with words, only crafted
thoughts and ideas, and only produced intangible matter about as apt
to withstand the test of time as a sheet of paper. Previously, my
product had been light as air and cerebral, even invisible, and my
hands had never been callused, only ink stained. But that was about to
change. Just passed my twenty-first birthday, I was about to take on
the art of renovation; the art of taking the weathered, ramshackle, and

dilapidated and making it new again, making it shine again. This work would require me to roll up my sleeves, get down on my knees, and get my hands dirty. This time around, there'd be an end product, something real and substantial that I could gaze upon and touch with my hands. Out of character, I donned a hard hat.

Throughout the month of January, Ben and I spent countless hours restoring the warehouse. It was work neither of us had much experience doing, so we relied heavily upon Kirk, Carl, and Danny, who stopped by in the evenings and on the weekends to provide step-by-step instructions and general guidance. For some of the more complicated and difficult tasks, Ben mined his list of contacts and acquaintances for contractors and handymen to provide expertise and tools at reduced rates.

We worked long, exhausting days, every day, until *Cavanaugh Weekly* was the only building still lit on the south side of town, even outlasting second shifts at nearby factories. We framed seven offices, a conference room, two bathrooms, three common work areas, and a reception area. We laid carpet and tile, replaced windows, piped for plumbing, wired and mounted lighting, hung drywall, and erected a decorative brick wall beside the staircase to the loft. As a final touch, we painted all the walls and ceilings with a fresh coat of white paint and painted the loft and window trim with burgundy paint.

With the work complete and dust settled, I was proud of our new office space. Ours was a noble effort indeed—raising business offices from ash and rubble—and one that I marveled at every time I flipped the light switch. The exterior was still a grimy, old warehouse long passed its prime, but the interior had luster and promise befitting our shiny new enterprise.

On a Saturday morning, Ben and I added the final touch, a metal sign, painted cream and burgundy with a large *CW* insignia and the words *Cavanaugh Weekly* in fancy script. We'd ordered it when we started the project. It measured five-feet-three-inches long by three-feet-nine-inches wide, the precise measurements, allowing a quarter-inch border, of the large window beside the front entrance where we mounted it. It was official that morning; the renovation was complete and we were open for business.

"If we can do this," Ben said, "something we both knew so little about, we can do anything."

"I hope the first issue looks as good as these offices," I added.

"Forget *Cavanaugh Weekly*," Ben replied, "we should open a construction and renovations business."

We both laughed. We walked over to the loft staircase and sat on the top step, a viewing point that allowed us to oversee most of the warehouse. I had never felt more accomplished or tired in my life and, for both reasons, would have sat on that step for the rest of the day.

"I talked to Stan the other day," I said.

"How is he doing?"

"He's not happy at *The Dispatch*. He feels the newspaper is biased in its coverage of the mayor; he has had several articles about City Hall red lined or deleted altogether."

"That doesn't surprise me," Ben replied. "Mayor Greenwood is the most dishonest city official Cavanaugh's ever had. I'm sure he's got paid supporters at *The Dispatch*. Hell, the man didn't even bother to address the issues when he campaigned, he simply made deals with the unions."

"I think we should try to recruit him," I suggested.

"It'd be a coup if we got him," Ben said. "I hadn't considered him available. Would he be okay working for us? It's a reversal of roles from our days at *The Signal*."

"Stan isn't about ego or money. His focus is the work. He'll be fine with it."

"I've been thinking about recruiting lately," Ben advised me. "I think we should each donate 5 percent of our company stock to an employee recruiting fund. That way, we'll each retain 45 percent and we'll put 10 percent of the company's stock into a pool to help us attract good people. We've got two or three key employees to recruit, possibly Stan as one of them, and an ownership stake will help us get and retain good people."

"I think that's a great idea."

* * *

Ben and I were in synch, in a big picture kind of way.

"Ideas are critical," he would say, "but it takes people to make them happen."

"If you want people who'll make things happen," I would say, "hire people who love what they're doing."

I wanted to work with the best because they inspired me, and the final result was better. Ben wanted the best because he knew his ideas far exceeded his own capabilities; no one man could produce on the grand scale Ben envisioned. I sought passionate, talented people who loved what they were doing. Ben sought people who could make things happen. For different reasons, we were both looking for the same people. Together, Ben and I identified our staff requirements as two senior writers, two junior writers, a versatile photographer and graphic artist, an office manager, a runner and delivery person, and an advertising sales person.

We scheduled an advertisement in *The Dispatch* for the last week of January, trying to time the responses with the completion of the renovation, so we'd have time to sift through them. For the ten days after the ad dates, our little black mailbox box overflowed daily, requiring our mailman to ring the warehouse bell and personally hand deliver the excess envelopes. On some days our carrier bound the letters into a block with thick rubber bands, which made the delivery seem more important. Accepting the bundle, I felt like I should sign for them and place them directly into the company safe, except that we didn't have one. We received more than two hundred letters, making Ben and I confident that we would find capable people to fill our eight openings.

* * *

Stan Tilden was our first priority, so we spent the evening of February 13th trying to recruit the former *Signal* editor. When we first greeted him at our door, Stan informed us that he was newly engaged, and I wondered whether this new commitment would preclude him from coming onboard.

"She's a lawyer with a large firm on the seventh floor of the building where I work," Stan told us. "I proposed on Christmas Eve."

We both wholeheartedly congratulated Stan, but I sensed that Ben was equally concerned about the engagement, as he appeared contemplative while he shook Stan's hand. Even with stock options included, we knew ours was a meager offer for someone as talented as Stan, particularly with family obligations now looming. His fiancée worked at Whalen, Simpson, and Stone, one of the more prestigious law firms on the west coast, and she was probably making three or four times our offer, maybe more.

For almost two hours, Ben and I sat opposite Stan at a slightly blemished conference table that had been delivered that morning, describing in elaborate detail our concept for *Cavanaugh Weekly*, our business plan going forward, and the key role we wanted him to play in the formation of the newspaper. We weren't beyond bringing up our past either. Together, the three of us had accomplished great things at SU and we told Stan that we wanted to harness that collective energy once again and use it to drive our new enterprise forward. We believed our opportunity at *Cavanaugh Weekly* to make a valuable contribution to the community was much greater than during our days at *The Signal*. When Ben and I concluded our proposal and formally offered Stan the position, he responded without hesitation.

"Guys, I really appreciate the time and effort you've expended tonight, but I've got to tell you, I knew I wanted the job when Pete phoned on Monday."

"What about *The Dispatch*?" I asked. "Do you have any reservations about leaving?"

"Not one," Stan replied firmly. "I want to work for an entity that has a heart and a soul, one that places journalistic integrity above ad sales and political affiliations. My gut tells me *Cavanaugh Weekly* is going to be a very special publication and one that I'll be proud to be a part of."

"It's not a lot of money," Ben followed up. "Are you okay with that? Will Jennifer be okay with it?"

"Hell, you guys know me well enough to know that it's not about money with me. I want my work to mean something. It doesn't these days. I don't want to spend my life simply filling column space. And, as for Jennifer, she already makes so much more than me now that a little more can't make any difference."

Stan Tilden grew up poor in the panhandle of Florida. His father left two months after his birth and his mother worked long hours as a waitress at a pancake house off the interstate where the tips were usually a "small stack" of coins. They lived in a rented mobile home and bought their groceries with food stamps at the Piggly Wiggly around the corner. He was a scrawny child, with glasses and poorly fitting clothes from the local thrift shop, so he was bullied regularly at school. Growing up, Stan had as few friends as he had pairs of shoes, and neither of those tallies ever exceeded two. Though his childhood was problematic, he was always quick to point out that his mother loved him and always did the best she could for him.

"My mother wasn't blue collar or white collar," Stan once said to me. "She wore an apron and a nameplate, but we were never poor because we had each other."

The saving grace for Stan was the public library. Though the limit was four books per person per visit, the librarians knew Stan well and allowed him to check out as many as ten books at a time. Basically, he was on an "all he could carry" basis. He spent his free time alone reading, everything from biographies to geography to science to astronomy to world history; any books with words that would fill his mind and the solitary hours. He learned at an early age that the world in library books and in his mind far exceeded his real one, so he lived there instead—alone, inside the library or the trailer, with an open book before him and his mind fully engaged. Young Stan was the palest person in Florida, but he was more knowledgeable than most.

"We never owned a television so, each night, I told my mom about whatever books I was reading," Stan said. "She always seemed happiest when I was telling her about what I'd learned."

Growing up poor makes some people crave material goods in an unhealthy manner, the same way a diabetic craves a Hershey bar. They want what they couldn't have in their childhood. Others learn the valuable lesson that many of the best things in life are free and don't feel shortchanged. Stan had little interest in material goods and was clearly in the second group. Even as an adult, the world in his mind was more important to him than the physical world around him.

*   *   *

I thought finding the versatile combination of photographer and graphic artist would be our most difficult staffing issue until Oscar Rhodes ambled through our front door one morning with a scuffed backpack over one shoulder, two cameras over the other, and our classified ad in his hand. He was a black man in his early forties with a short, stocky frame and some graying in his hair at the temples. Like the man, his attire was sturdy and durable, comprised of a weighty blue shirt, a tan vest with pockets bulging with photographic supplies, rugged safari pants, and hiking boots. Oscar looked like he had returned from a long hike in the wilderness.

"I don't have an appointment," Oscar said as he unloaded his cargo onto the conference table, "but I'd sure like to talk to you about the ad in the newspaper for a photographer."

Since Ben wasn't available, I spent an hour with Oscar alone. He was poised and pleasant, with a worldly, self-assurance forged in distant, depressed locations. Oscar had spent the better part of the last twenty years working at small, often underground, newspapers in Europe, Africa, and the Middle East. From his backpack, he produced several examples of his work in the form of wrinkled, yellowed pages from newspapers in Kenya, South Africa, Afghanistan, and Turkey.

There, on those pages, were images of human suffering, captured for all eternity by a single flick of Oscar's shutter, in measures I'd never experienced or even imagined.

"What happened to this boy?" I asked about a boy in one of the photos, his stomach swollen, but his eyes wide and hopeful as he received a bowl at an aid station.

"I don't know," Oscar replied. "Very early in my career and travels, I learned not to get involved or follow-up on the subjects of my photos. More often than not, the outcome wasn't good. I left salvation and reform to those so inclined—my role was that of artist and historian. I had to hope that my images would motivate the good people of the world to work to end the poverty, suffering, and wars."

"Why would you want this job? It's quite a departure from what you've been doing."

"I have a new wife and a six-month-old son, Nahrid. I don't want to drag my family around the third world—that would be a harsh life for them. I grew up in the south bay area, less than fifty miles from here, and it is time for me to come home. I want my family to live in Cavanaugh and my son to grow up here."

Before departing, Oscar produced one final photo from his backpack. As it turned out, Oscar had come to our warehouse the previous Saturday to scout the location. From his car across the street, he watched as Ben and I hung the *Cavanaugh Weekly* sign in the front window and, unbeknownst to either of us, Oscar, with a telephoto lens, snapped a shot of the two of us carrying the sign up the stairs to the front door.

In the photo, the warehouse door was propped wide open; the bright lights and white walls of the offices glowed in the background as we maneuvered the sign, logo side displayed, through the doorway. Our faces bore the hopeful, anticipatory look of young entrepreneurs. When compared to other photos Oscar had shown me that morning, this one paled in significance, and still Oscar had captured the joy of that moment for Ben and me with one simple of click of the shutter, the mark of a great photographer.

"Can I have this?" I asked, amused by the image.

"Of course," Oscar returned. "That's why I brought it."

We hired Oscar that evening.

*   *   *

Ben and I disagreed on our choice for the second senior writer. Ben's choice was another potential defector from *The Dispatch* who requested an interview after he learned that Stan Tilden had signed on. His choice, a twenty-eight-year-old sports columnist, impressed me as someone content to grind out a semi-amusing daily column, "merely filling column space" as Stan had said. Ben liked the idea of raiding *The Dispatch* for a second writer because it sent the message that *Cavanaugh Weekly* was a force to be reckoned with. Personally, I wanted writers who were more passionate about their work and our newspaper.

I was impressed with a forty-two-year-old woman named Laurie Jeffers because I thought she brought a different perspective to our newly forming team. I particularly liked one answer she gave me during her interview. When I asked her if there was one article she'd written that she was particularly proud of, one that she thought really affected people's lives, she answered categorically.

"I'd like to believe every article I've written has touched people and affected their lives," she said. "If not, I wasted my time writing the article, and the newspaper wasted paper and ink printing it. That's why we put the paper in the typewriter, isn't it? That's what we strive for."

Best of all, Laurie said it like she meant it and not like it was simply a practiced answer for an interview question.

It was an arduous, four-week process, interviewing candidates, checking backgrounds, and selecting staff members, but when all was said and done we'd assembled an enthusiastic, and hopefully capable, cast of characters. Ronny Spires, a thirty year old who'd previously sold everything from stereos to automobiles, was selected as our advertising salesman. Cheryl Matlock, a forty-five-year-old housewife returning to the workplace after twenty years spent raising children, became our office manager. Both our junior writers, Fiona Yardley and Matt Derringer, were recent college graduates with degrees in English. Tony Walsh, a nineteen-year-old neighborhood kid who came highly recommended by Kirk, was hired as our errand runner and delivery person. And, when Ben concluded our last discussion about the second senior writer position with, "Pete, you're the editor and ultimately responsible for all staffing decisions," I hired Laurie Jeffers to fill the final position.

* * *

"We've got eight weeks," Ben informed everyone at our first staff meeting, "to design, layout, draft, edit, print, distribute, market, and promote the first edition of *Cavanaugh Weekly*. In other words, we've got a lot of work ahead of us. We'll publish the week of May 5th, so that our premiere issue coincides with the annual Cavanaugh Street Fair. The additional interest and excitement generated by the fair should help us boost ad sales and readership. Currently, we are looking at a first edition pressing of three hundred thousand copies. Needless to say, it has to be a very special first issue."

"How much will the paper sell for?" Tony inquired when Ben paused momentarily.

"It will be free," I said. "Our revenues will come from the advertisements that Ronny sells."

"Do you have a rate sheet for me?" Ronny asked as if he was ready to hit the pavement as soon as the meeting broke up.

"Not yet," Ben said. "What we've got is a long list of things to be done and who will be working on them. At this moment, I want you all to think of *Cavanaugh Weekly* as a blank canvas waiting for a masterpiece."

"Should we be working on articles yet?" Laurie asked.

"Not yet," Ben answered again. "There is a lot of groundwork to be done first, hopefully not more than three weeks worth, and then we'll turn our focus to specific articles, weekly features, and first issue content."

"To meet our deadline," I told the group, "we're going to have focus on the right things at the right time and accomplish a lot in an orderly manner."

"Everyone reports directly to Pete," Ben informed the staff, "except Ronny who reports to me. Pete will meet with everyone and give out assignments. Keep him posted on your progress and give him one hundred and ten percent."

* * *

Quite fortunately, the first issue of *Cavanaugh Weekly* was an enormous success; readership, quality of content, and revenues were outstanding. Our team really nailed it. Advertising sales were almost twice what we planned and Ben, who had many contacts in the local media, called in every favor he had outstanding to ensure blanketed coverage of the newspaper's premiere. He made appearances on every local news program and created so much buzz that tourists probably thought *Cavanaugh Weekly* sponsored the street fair. During the days after the issue's release, Ben was everywhere.

On Saturday afternoon, on a crowded street corner near Fourth and Central Avenues, Ben filmed an interview with Amanda Gregg of Channel 5 News. In his raised hand, Ben waved the first issue of *Cavanaugh Weekly*, a seventy-two-page newspaper, folded magazine style with FREE in a bold letters in the top right corner of the front page, and introduced it to the good people of Cavanaugh like he was talking one-to-one with each viewer in their living room. Ben was amiable and charismatic in person and, for some inexplicable reason, even more so on a television screen.

"*Cavanaugh Weekly* is free because it's not our objective to sell anything," Ben responded to a question about the cover price. "Our objective is to be an integral part of the community and make residents aware of what's going on: socially, culturally, and politically. This city has so much to offer its citizens and its citizens have so much to give back. *Cavanaugh Weekly* will facilitate that exchange and be instrumental in maintaining and improving our high quality of life. It doesn't matter how long you've lived in Cavanaugh; personally, I've lived here my entire life. Pick up a copy of *Cavanaugh Weekly* at your local newsstands or supermarkets and you'll learn things about our city that will surprise you; you'll find events you didn't know about."

* * *

In late September, Ben, Stan, and I were busily assembling our twentieth issue while Danny, in his senior year and Tyler, a first year graduate student, were back at SU attending classes. During that time, it was a little odd whenever we got together because they envied our real world success, and I envied their life as collegians.

One Friday evening, Danny and Tyler came to our warehouse to celebrate the release of the twentieth issue, a milestone that I, personally, was relieved to reach. We were throwing a small party for our staff and about fifty invited guests with catered appetizers and an open bar. The guest list included advertisers, business and community leaders, and local celebrities. Danny, who'd led the Grizzlies to an impressive 3-0 start and was featured regularly on the evening news, was invited as a friend but certainly qualified as a celebrity also.

Despite the presence of outsiders, Ben and I considered the festivities to be a show of appreciation for our *Cavanaugh Weekly* staff and not an event for promotion or schmoozing. Both of us were very happy with the collective works of our team.

On the night of the event, early in the evening, Ben called for everyone to gather in the conference room where we'd removed the large table and ten chairs to allow space for milling and socializing. Before a large burgundy curtain, Ben waited patiently on one side of the room while the group gradually filled the open space before him. Waiting to hear Ben's remarks, Tyler, Danny, and I stood in the open doorway that led to the loading dock and the neatly stacked bundles of our twentieth issue.

Initially, Ben's comments were directed at all our employees, referring to them collectively as a "superbly talented group" and then he introduced each one individually and praised their unique efforts and contribution. His words were heartfelt and even the outsiders in the room sensed the camaraderie amongst our team. In essentially six months, our team had bonded in a way that generally required more time. Intentionally, Ben saved Oscar Rhodes for last and asked him to join him in front of the curtain.

"*Cavanaugh Weekly* is fortunate to have one of the best photographers in the world on staff," Ben said, motioning toward a flushed Oscar. "I cannot tell you all how many times Oscar has brought an image to me and, after Oscar has left the room, I found myself still staring at it, unable to look away. His pictures make us feel and think and, in my mind at least, that is the mark of a great photographer."

Oscar was not aware that he was going to be the subject of a tribute because Ben, Stan, and I had conspired to keep it from him. His face reflected absolute bewilderment as he stood beside Ben in front of the small crowd.

"With Oscar's help," Ben continued, motioning for Oscar to take hold of the other flap of the curtain, "I am very pleased to present our very own Oscar Rhodes Gallery."

Ben slid his flap of the curtain to the left while Oscar moved his flap in the opposite direction, revealing seven framed photos beneath burgundy-stenciled lettering that spelled, Oscar Rhodes. Oscar was surprised, elated, and even teary-eyed.

All in attendance, about seventy, applauded politely.

"I can't believe you did this for me," Oscar whispered to Ben.

"This publication is still in its infancy so we've only selected seven photographs," Ben said when the clapping stopped. "Going forward, we will fill this wall with Oscar's most superlative work."

"That is a really great idea," Tyler said. "And, this is a really cool place to work. Will you hire me?" she asked in jest.

"Sorry," I replied flippantly. "We can't have our staff more educated than management. It simply wouldn't work."

"I've got better opportunities anyway," Tyler responded. "Last Wednesday, I interviewed for an internship at Channel 5."

"That's great," I declared, knowing how much Tyler wanted to work in television news.

Danny chimed in with his own words of encouragement, too. "You'll get it, Tyler," he said. "You're perfect for TV news."

"The news director told me he received eighty applications for the position and he intended to interview the ten best," Tyler informed us, her mood turning serious. "Can you believe that? Eighty!"

Tyler wanted this internship and, though she knew she had a good chance based on her own merits, she didn't want to leave it to chance. She had a plan. Like Ben, she believed wholeheartedly in the value of connections.

"I need your help, Danny," Tyler said.

"Me, what can I do?" Danny asked.

I didn't know what was coming, but I knew it wasn't good. Instantly, Tyler took on the demeanor of someone plotting a crime— she leaned closer to Danny, glanced about the room before she spoke, and lowered her voice to a whisper when she did. While trying to look inconspicuous, Tyler became very conspicuous.

"Call the sports guy at Channel 5. What's his name?"

"Rick Dennis," Danny answered, both skeptical and concerned over whatever request would follow.

"Call Rick," Tyler hesitated, then redirected. "You're on a first name basis with him right?"

"Yeah, I know him."

"Tell Rick that I am a friend of yours and ask him to put in a good word for me with the news director. Tell Rick you'll give him an exclusive when it comes to the interviews you do. You're hot these days, Danny. You're probably the biggest sports celebrity in this city. He'll jump at the chance to have an exclusive arrangement with you."

"I don't believe this," Danny protested. "It's not like I've got any real clout with the news programs anyway. You're supposed to be my friend, Tyler, but you've got an agenda just like everyone else. You're as bad as Ben."

"Calm down," I begged him, trying to restore the peace. "She is your friend. She's just acting like a complete idiot at the moment."

"Get Ben to drive you back to campus," Danny said. "I'm leaving. I've got a game tomorrow."

"I just wanted him to put in a good word for me," Tyler said. "Is that really so bad?"

Just that quickly, in all of two minutes, the whole tenor of the evening changed for me, turning from celebration to calamity. Trying to catch Danny, I walked briskly passed the small group still occupied with Oscar's photography. When I reached the reception area, Steve Todd, the college friend of Joe Golden I had met at Charles House as well as the attorney that handled our incorporation work, grabbed me by the arm and halted my pursuit. I hadn't talked with Steve in three months, since we completed our legal work, but I couldn't ignore his urgency when he tugged my forearm and demanded, "Pete, I need to talk to you."

What now? I thought. *First, Danny and Tyler get into a big brouhaha and now our attorney needs me. This can't be good. We're being sued, evicted, what? Earlier in the evening, I thought this would be an enjoyable party, but now I'm having second thoughts about a fiftieth issue party next spring.*

"I brought Joe with me," Steve said, his voice hushed.

Steve guided me toward a quiet corner while I wriggled within his grasp. As we walked, I glanced over my shoulder trying to find Joe Golden, though there was little chance of that. *The Torn Tuxedo* didn't have a photo of the author, so the only picture I'd ever seen of Joe Golden was his SU yearbook picture, which was taken almost two decades ago. If his legend had even a speck of truth to it, the years had not been kind to Joe and I'm sure he bore little resemblance to that shiny-faced kid anymore.

"He's been in Cavanaugh for a month now," Steve explained. "He's staying at some $400 a month flophouse near the docks."

"Where is he?" I asked, still anxious to get a look at him.

"Will you listen to me? I didn't bring him here so you could meet your idol. I was hoping we could help him."

"How so?"

"He's a bum. He hasn't written a word in ten years. He only came tonight because I described *Cavanaugh Weekly* as a very liberal, somewhat radical newspaper, and because I told him there'd be free food and liquor. With your help, I'm hoping that we can gradually convince him to write again. Maybe, if he has some purpose in his life, he'll climb out of that whiskey bottle he lives in. But just meet him tonight, nothing more."

"Okay."

I'd walked right passed him. Joe Golden, wearing a badly wrinkled, brown corduroy sport coat and dirty blue jeans, was standing with his back to me, viewing the Oscar Rhodes photographs. For the first few minutes, I observed him from a distance as Steve whispered words of admonition in my ear.

"He's not a nice guy anymore. He is mostly bitter and angry. Don't expect a civil greeting."

As I watched him, Joe stared intently at one photograph, a picture of three students standing beside an open locker at St. Mark's High School in downtown Cavanaugh; he never shifted his glance to any of the others on the wall. He repeated three sequences: first, he drank from the cup in his left hand, then he wiped the excess from his lips with his right hand, and finally he combed back his stringy, shoulder-length hair. Watching him, I decided he was either touched by the image or simply staring at the wall in a drunken stupor.

Unfortunately, Steve's admonition hadn't landed. I'd always wanted to meet this guy and, frankly, I didn't care what shape he was in. He was still Joe Golden. He penned *The Torn Tuxedo*, my favorite novel, and he was the main reason I became a writer. He was, in all likelihood, the greatest writer I'd meet during my lifetime. Anyway, it wasn't any different than meeting Willie Mays. He doesn't play centerfield for the Giants anymore, but that doesn't make it any less thrilling to meet him. I'd be honored just to shake Joe's hand. I made my way to the gallery area where Joe now appeared to be staring blankly at the wall in front of him. He'd moved away from the photographs.

"Hi Joe," I said, offering my hand. "I'm Pete Dalton, editor of *Cavanaugh Weekly*. It's an honor to have you visit our newspaper."

"Oh shit," Joe returned, acting as if he was suddenly, rudely nudged and angered by the encounter. His eyes were bloodshot and his complexion ruddy. Alongside his left eye was a two-inch scar that made him look even angrier. Joe didn't look like someone living the soft, affluent life of a successful author; quite to the contrary, he looked like someone that life pummeled on a daily basis.

"Don't tell me, kid," he said. "You read *The Torn Tuxedo* in high school and you think it's one of the best novels ever written."

"Well, that's true, Joe, but…"

"Just for once, I'd like to enjoy a moment in public without someone telling me that I've had a profound impact on their life."

"I didn't mean to intrude, Joe, it's just that…"

"Oh look, my cup is empty," Joe observed, a smirk on his face. "I'm going to the bar for another cup of sweet patience. Yes, patience," he repeated before I could get a word in. "Some others might call it courage, but for me it is truly patience. You see, Pete. That is your name, isn't it?"

I nodded.

"There are legions of people out there, much like yourself, who've read my book and think my tale has some relevance to their lives. It doesn't. Okay?"

I nodded again.

"It was just a fucking book, and it was published more than a decade ago. Okay?"

I nodded a third time. I was speechless and deflated. It's not like I expected a hug or anything, but this was ridiculous. I should've listened to Steve.

"I'd sure appreciate it if you didn't follow me to the bar," he requested as he turned away. Then, turning back he added, "And, if you do, I'll kick your ass. I don't care if you are the president of *Cavanaugh Weekly*."

"Editor," I said as he walked away.

Eager to hear the outcome, Steve approached from across the room as if Joe's departure was his cue to enter.

"Say hey," I offered, my voice dripping with defeat.

"What?" he asked, oblivious to my Willie Mays reference. Willie's nickname while he played baseball was the "Say Hey Kid."

"Nothing."

*　*　*

I was glad to see the crowd clearing out around 9:30pm because I felt like a prizefighter on the punished side of several hard fought rounds. My cheek was red and swollen from the Tyler and Danny incident, and I'd been tagged by several uppercuts during my encounter with Joe Golden. In a flinching state, I was leery that a final knockout punch was looming somewhere. Staggering though sober, I asked the bartender, a gentleman in his fifties wearing a ruffled white shirt and a red silk bowtie, to pour me a strong gin and tonic with lime. Obliging, he set aside the white towel he used to wipe down the bar and began pouring.

During a boxing match, trainers throw a white towel into the ring when a boxer is defeated; it is the boxing equivalent of surrender.

For a brief moment, I considered throwing that white towel high into the air so I could signal my concession. It had been that kind of night. I couldn't take another punch.

"Pour yourself something," I suggested, and he smiled. "You can't expect a man to work in a confectionary all night and not sample the hard candy."

The bartender handed me a cup and hoisted his own, "May you live in interesting times," he stated. "It's a Chinese blessing."

"Have you been to China?"

"No, I haven't," he answered with a smirk, "but I doubt there's a toast, barroom swindle, hard-luck story, or pickup line in this world that I haven't heard."

"Bartender, psychologist, and philosopher, huh?"

"That's the general job description. It all depends on how they're tipping."

Reminded, I reached into my pocket and removed a small wad of folded bills, mostly singles. I peeled off a sawbuck, placed it in his tip jar, and asked, "Why do some people get bitter as they get older?"

"Disappointment," the man in the bowtie answered, without hesitation. "In themselves, their own lives, or others. Disappointment makes them bitter."

"You are wiser than a hundred fortune cookies," I told him and walked away.

Aside from the bartender, there were only a few stragglers still in the building and the caterers who were busy packing their wares. Otherwise, most of the guests had departed and the warehouse was returning to its normal workday occupancy. At that time, there were less than fifteen people.

I joined Ben in his office. He was sitting, his back to the doorway, his feet up on the credenza, and, reading his body language, shoulders hunched and chin down, he didn't look like his evening had been any better than mine. He too, had a cup in his right hand, and I could tell from his slow, short sips that it was something stronger than soda or fruit juice. Ben seldom drank alcohol so I was concerned.

"Where's Tyler?" I asked, standing beside his desk. "You're driving her back to campus. She and Danny had a big fight."

"She called a cab," he said. "Tyler and I had a big fight, too. Our relationship is over."

"Over!" I repeated, shocked. "What about?"

With newfound purpose, Ben took a long sip from his cup, longer than the previous ones.

"She told me about her fight with Danny, and I told her that she was way out of line," he said. "I told her to leave Danny alone."

"She was out of line," I concurred. "I wouldn't have thought Tyler would stoop to that level."

"Tyler will do whatever it takes to succeed, Pete. We are a lot alike, her and me."

They were a lot alike indeed, but I thought that was a good thing. A lot alike, hell, they were both perfect. I'd always thought of them as the perfect couple. Now suddenly, Ben was talking like it was over. It couldn't be. If those two couldn't make it work, what chance did average people have? Plus, they were my friends. If they broke up, I'd see a lot less of Tyler, and that didn't seem right.

There it was, my knockout punch, a combination delivered by my two best friends, Ben and Tyler. I never saw that punch coming, and it landed hard. I knew it because I felt the referee standing over me, looking down at me sprawled out on the floor, beginning his ten count. I was exhausted, down for the count, and I wasn't going to try to get back to my feet and continue. On this night, I had no more fight left in me.

Obviously, Ben was more focused on the newspaper these days than his relationship with Tyler, but I never thought that his distraction would cause a break up. I always assumed they'd marry someday. This was quite a blow.

"It will pass," I said, an attempt at wishful thinking.

"No it won't, Pete. It's time."

Ben was solemn but not sad.

I was amazed by his lack of emotion.

"Love has never come first for either of us," he confided. "We've always been of like minds when it comes to our careers."

Ben leaned forward and retrieved a framed picture from the credenza, a photograph of Tyler, dressed head to toe in Revolutionary War attire, taken at Halloween two years ago. He gazed at it fondly. In the past, I had often kidded him that her revolutionary attire was, for him, the equivalent of lacy lingerie for other men. He always laughed at that comment, but I didn't feel that was the right moment to remind him. I remained silent.

"Career is first for both of us," Ben continued. "Love is a very distant second. We've both known all along that we'd be replaced by each other's careers. It was just a matter of time."

* * *

We went to the SU football game the next afternoon, just Ben and I, the Three Musketeers minus Porthos. I waited quietly while Ben stepped up to the window to purchase our tickets and I remained quiet when he returned with two seats in the opposite end zone, not our usual ones. In their separation agreement, I guess Ben got me and Tyler got our usual seats. I didn't press.

Fortunately for the Grizzlies, Danny was unaffected by the events of the prior evening. On their first offensive sequence, he went right to work, connecting with his wide receiver on their eighth play from scrimmage for a forty-yard touchdown. Ben and I bounded to our feet, extended our arms in celebration, and chanted loudly, "Danny, Danny, Danny."

I stopped a few choruses shy of our usual, as it simply wasn't the same for me without Tyler. In my mind, our chant was hollow and flat. It felt incomplete. True to my suburban upbringing, I'd always been a stickler for tradition and continuity.

Danny played brilliantly that afternoon, completing twenty-eight of thirty-five passes for four hundred nineteen yards and five touchdowns, adding to his already conference-leading statistics. The Grizzlies easily won the game by the score of 42-24 and posted a 4-0 start for the season.

And still, the day was bittersweet for me.

8.

The battle for World's Tallest intensified in the 1920s when two New York projects contended. The architects of 40 Wall Street added a metal lantern atop their plans so their building would rise above the Chrysler Building. But, once 40 Wall Street was completed, the architects of the Chrysler Building unveiled an undisclosed 185-foot spire atop their building, claiming the distinction.

"You want me to what?"

"Hire Joe Golden," Steve Todd repeated during our phone conversation several days after our *Cavanaugh Weekly* party.

Steve had a plan. And, in order for his plan to work, he had to recruit me as his accomplice. Steve asked me to put Joe Golden on our payroll, pay him $100 weekly, and allow him to function as a freelance writer. Steve would provide the weekly stipend regardless of whether Joe wrote anything or not. Joe would choose his own subject matter, work at his own pace, and only be required to come to our office once a week to pick up his paycheck. Even though Joe hadn't written so much as a sentence in more than a decade, Steve hoped that, with time and subtle encouragement, Joe would reclaim the talent he'd forsaken years ago, start writing again, and turn his life around. It was certainly a charitable plan if nothing else.

From what I observed at our party, Joe was in horrible shape. While I don't generally subscribe to the concept of lost causes, Joe was as close to earning that distinction as anyone I'd ever met. He'd digressed from celebrated novelist to drunken ass, opposite ends of the spectrum of success. For me, I took comfort in the fact that Steve's plan couldn't make matters worse. Joe had nowhere to go but up.

All things considered, *Cavanaugh Weekly* had nothing to lose and everything to gain by participating in Steve's arrangement. If Joe didn't write anything, it was Steve's loss entirely, his money wasted on Joe. If Joe wrote again, his new work would be a major news story, a weighty literary event, and generate a lot of attention for our humble, little newspaper. Regardless of what Joe wrote, whether a short story or an entire novel, *Cavanaugh Weekly* would get millions of dollars of free publicity as well as prestigious accolades from the literary world for having resurrected Joe Golden. Steve placed only one condition on our arrangement: Joe couldn't know about Steve's involvement in his pseudo employment. Steve would be my silent, anonymous partner. Without any hesitation whatsoever, I told him I'd do it.

"He's staying at The San Miguel Hotel, and he's registered under the name of Joe Gordon," Steve said before we hung up. "Take a bottle," he added. "It'll get you in the door."

*   *   *

The main entrance to the San Miguel Hotel was at the end of a littered alleyway off Delaney Road, a dark, tunnel-like passageway between two brick walls that created the sense of descending into a seedy underworld; a world where the laws of society were superseded by survival, where fairness and decency yielded to brute strength, and where decency withered. So many in this world relied on drugs and alcohol to make it through their days and, in a twisted way, that made perfect sense because I didn't see anything that would lift the human spirit naturally—not so much as a tree, plant, or flower. Here, even sexual activity was merely sexual commerce, one dose of desperate relief swapped for another with no one better off from the exchange. On the elevator panel for the universe, this alley was a few floors above Hell.

"Got any spare change?" an old panhandler asked me as I walked the alley, making no effort to hide the near empty bottle of Ripple that he wanted to replenish.

If not for the doorframe, it would've been difficult to tell where the alley ended and the hotel lobby began; both were equally filthy. The lobby had a stained couch, overflowing ashtrays, and a rate chart on the wall to differentiate it. The desk clerk, an obese chain-smoker in an unbuttoned Hawaiian shirt who coughed and puffed between every ten words spoken, directed me to Room 319 and pointed toward the elevator when I asked for Joe Gordon. Rather than risk an elevator malfunction that might carry me even deeper into this seedy underworld, I decided to climb the three flights of stairs.

"Got a cigarette I can bum?" he asked as I passed.

"Sorry, I don't smoke."

Around here, everyone looked for a hand out, for their lives were as forsaken as the unfortunate characters in a Steinbeck novel.

"Go away," was Joe's gruff response to my knock at his door, pretty much what I expected. He sounded like I had awakened him. His room was at the end of a hallway that only continued that horrible descent that started in the alley. If I hadn't already arrived in Hell, I was getting awful close.

"It's Pete Dalton, Joe," I called out. "We met the other night at *Cavanaugh Weekly*."

There was no response.

"I brought along a bottle of Jim Beam. I just want to have a drink and talk for a few minutes, fifteen at most. What do you say?"

I heard movement on the other side of the door, rustling that started when I spoke the words, "Jim Beam." After a few minutes, the door opened slowly, only a foot or so, and Joe peered through the gap, asking to see the bottle. I was careful to keep it out of his reach for fear that he might grab the bottle and quickly slam the door in my face. I wasn't stupid. I held it out, label facing him, shoulder height, beside me. The sight awakened him. His face brightened like he spotted an old friend.

"Come in," he said.

As I entered, Joe seized the bottle from my hand and twisted the top immediately, breaking its seal. He angled his head backward and guzzled the golden-brown liquid directly from the bottle. His swig was three or four shots at once. He shook his head from the jolt. Next, he poured a short shot into a murky glass from the dresser top and handed it to me, his hand shaking as he did.

For the first time, I realized what I was dealing with.

The room had a small bed and a dresser and no exterior windows. Though it was daylight outside, all the light in the room came from an overhead, fluorescent light. Joe had removed the blanket and sheets from the bed and thrown them into a large heap in one corner of the room. Apparently, he slept in his sleeping bag on top of the bare mattress, foregoing the discolored bed linens provided by the establishment. A remnant from his old life, he still had some standards. Looking at the murky glass, I presumed the alcohol would kill any germs, so I gulped its contents rather than appear unsociable. For our plan to work, I needed Joe to like me.

He sat at the head of the bed. I sat on the end near the door.

"I've got a proposition," I told him.

He begrudgingly offered me a refill. When I shook my head and declined his offer, he seemed relieved.

"I'm not a writer anymore," Joe reiterated several times as I made the offer.

"One hundred dollars a week for just thinking about writing," I said. "More if you actually write something. I've got your first check right here."

I pulled a *Cavanaugh Weekly* check for $100, payable to Joe Golden, from my sport coat and offered it to Joe.

Joe wasn't reluctant about taking the check, but he sure wasn't appreciative either.

"You're wasting your money, kid," he said as he snared the check from my fingers.

When you lived like Joe, on the fringes of society, you don't turn down freebies, that's rule number one. I understood that Joe's taking the money didn't mean a lot, but it was a start, just the same. If the weekly check did nothing more than establish a connection, then maybe it was money well spent.

As I rose from the bed, Steve Todd's intentions were suddenly clearer to me. Joe wouldn't accept help—most particularly from a college friend—so Steve was simply creating a connection to the real world, a lifeline to help him up. I'd be his link to productive society and hopefully my presence in his life would motivate him to make a change.

"Come to my office every Friday to pick up your check."

* * *

I figured the odds were about fifty-fifty that Joe would show up the following Friday, but he did, and surprisingly enough, the one after that. He never said "Hello" or "How are you doing?" Instead, Joe always greeted me with, "You got the check?" But, I wasn't offended because I knew his mind was focused on the bottle of booze he'd purchase as soon as he dashed with the check. Pleasantries weren't part of his world.

I'd ask Joe if he had any ideas for writing and, generally, do whatever I could to detain him for ten or fifteen minutes so he was forced to have contact with me, whether he liked it or not. Joe always answered my questions with short, curt answers and always fidgeted in his seat the whole time we were together, like he had somewhere else to be. And, I guess he did.

When Steve originally suggested this plan to me, I naively believed we'd induce Joe to write again and that would be a righteous act. We'd restore his God-given gift, he'd write his long anticipated second novel, and reclaim his place of honor in the literary world, not to mention a spot atop the bestseller's list. His first novel meant so much to me and now I had the chance to help him make his comeback. My efforts had a real full-circle quality to them and I felt like I'd be doing the world a great service.

After three frustrating weekly meetings with Joe—encounters that only made me more aware of his disabled condition—my grand objective faded and I began to focus more on the lesser objective of simply helping Joe. During his third visit, I added a new wrinkle to the plan.

"You got the check?" a gruff voice inquired, causing me to look up from my work and see Joe standing in my doorway. He changed his shirt occasionally, but the rest of his daily outfit, soiled jeans and a wrinkled corduroy sport coat, were constant.

"I've got it right here," I answered, waving the check in my right hand to lure him the rest of the way into my office.

Joe sat opposite me. We routinely went through our usual weekly exchange where I tried to get Joe to talk to me about anything and he remained muted about everything. Then, I asked him for a favor.

"What do you want?" he asked.

"Sometime during the coming week, I just want you to read our latest issue of *Cavanaugh Weekly*, that's all," I said, handing him a copy across the desk. "If you have any comments about any aspect of our publication, I'd like to hear what you have to say. If you don't, that's fine also."

"That's it?"

"That's it!"

I thought his feedback might create a conversation between us and improve our communications with one another. Additionally, I was interested to hear his opinion anyway.

"Have a good week, Joe," I shouted as he left my office, issue and check in hand. There was no response from Joe, as usual.

* * *

As *Cavanaugh Weekly's* influence grew, so did Ben's personal profile. With each passing week, Ben was more involved with local charities, business alliances, community leagues, women's groups, and political organizations. When his mail was opened each afternoon, invitations from the groups were abundant, requesting his attendance and, as often as not, a speech. Two or three nights a week, Ben attended a fundraiser or social function and, at least once a week, Ben appeared in my door the next morning with a story from the previous night. Only minutes after Joe departed, Ben walked into my office with a manila folder in his hand and a wide smile on his face.

"I went to the monthly meeting of the Cavanaugh Commerce Board at the Breckenridge Hotel last night," Ben announced as an obvious prelude to a story. "Roast beef or salmon, green beans, and red potatoes," he answered before I could ask my usual first question.

"Make any good contacts?" I asked, skipping ahead to my usual second question.

"You'll never believe it," Ben responded, his glowing face revealing a much bigger story than previously.

"At intermission," Ben began, "I was standing in the aisle chatting with Charlie Rosenburg and I suddenly felt this ominous tapping on my left shoulder, the kind of summons that is usually associated with the Grim Reaper. When I turned around, a big gorilla-like thug in a tight-fitting business suit said to me, 'the mayor would like to have a word with you.'"

"Mayor Greenwood was there?" I asked.

"Yeah," Ben said, "I didn't know he was attending the event either. God, I hate that son a of a bitch."

"I hope there was a referee on hand," I observed.

A former president of the Dockworkers' Union and city councilman, Mayor Dale Greenwood had already assembled a 1940's style political machine during his first six months in office, one that benefitted whenever city contracts were awarded. His inner circle was wealthy and influential and functioned more like co-conspirators than advisors or associates, always concise when it came to explanations or details. At only forty-three years old, many political analysts believed that, barring a scandal or political blunder, Dale Greenwood would be a fixture in City Hall for many years to come. He was well connected. At a large round table with place settings for twelve, the mayor waited alone for Ben to join him.

"It's been a long time, Benjamin," the mayor observed.

"More than two years," Ben said. "If I recall correctly, the last time we crossed paths was at the Restore Old Cavanaugh Rally.

"Oh yes, that was unfortunate, wasn't it? That vandalism sure undermined the cause. Probably college students, don't you think?"

"I don't think so," Ben countered. "I believe it was supporters of the Cavanaugh Waterfront Towers project."

"Interesting," the mayor replied coyly.

He shifted nervously in his seat.

"I hadn't thought of that possibility," he added.

Ben remained silent as he studied the mayor.

"You never mentioned your plan to start a newspaper," the mayor said, changing the subject as he did.

"You never mentioned your support for the Cavanaugh Waterfront Towers project or your plans to run for mayor."

"Well," the mayor replied, "I guess we're all guilty of overlooking things from time to time."

The mayor begrudgingly congratulated Ben on his "apparent" success with *Cavanaugh Weekly,* like the jury was still out in his mind and he wanted to hold onto the faint hope that the publication might be short-lived. The two men, who were featured regularly on the local news programs and who were rapidly becoming political adversaries, were both measured and calculating in their choices of subject matter and words. Still, in the time it took Mayor Greenwood to polish off a snifter of premium brandy, the conversation advanced from cordial to acerbic.

"I've got many friends," the mayor stated as a waiter replaced his empty snifter. "I'm hoping I'll be able to count you among them."

"You can, Dale, as long as your idea of friendship allows for differences of opinion," Ben said half-heartedly, knowing he had little in common with the mayor, personally or politically, and would never be his friend.

"*Cavanaugh Weekly* has political clout in this city," the mayor observed while rolling an unlit stogie between his thumb and index finger. "Maybe Benjamin, my friend, you should consider being less political altogether."

"If you think you can tell me how to run my newspaper, this is going to be the shortest friendship on record."

"You seem intent on telling me how to run my city."

"Your city? You're the mayor, not the king."

Much of the crowd watched the exchange and both men were aware of the eyes on them. Despite their escalating disagreement and resentment, both continued to smile and appear affable throughout the conversation. Onlookers would've thought they were discussing SU football games, the pleasant weather, or the mayor's children—their growing displeasure was well concealed.

"Look at *The Dispatch*," the mayor offered. "They report the news, they don't intercede in political issues or activities at City Hall, and they've been around for almost one hundred years. There might be a lesson in that for you and your publication."

"Look at Charles the First," Ben returned, echoing the mayor's advice. "He put his own interests above those of his people and they cut his head off. There might be a lesson in that for you."

"You little prick," the mayor blurted, still with a smiling, affable appearance. He was angered, but his political instincts always ruled a moment.

Before the mayor finished his angry outburst, Ben stood up. Smiling, he extended his hand so their parting would appear amicable and unprovoked. The mayor, ever the shrewd politician, shook Ben's hand and returned the smile in his typically uncomfortable manner.

"My new column, 'Cavanaugh in the New Millennium,' will premier in our next issue," Ben said, "and I don't think you're going to like it. Why don't you limit your reading to *The Dispatch* that day and save yourself some aggravation?"

With that, Ben dropped the manila folder onto my desk; on its tab in black marker it read "Cavanaugh in the New Millennium."

"My new column," he declared with a defiant twinkle in his eyes. "Plan on including it in the first issue every month."

"Cavanaugh in the New Millennium by Ben Matthews" would prove to be a major milestone in Ben's ever-evolving career in a social and political genre he pioneered and to which the moniker of urban planning, engineering, and activism would later be attached.

His premiere column recommended the development of an integrated light-rail and bus system for the city and examined how existing zoning restrictions would impact its construction when the time came to break ground. At that point in time, Cavanaugh was a city of almost two million people, thirteenth largest in the nation, but not large enough by conventional standards to undertake a project of that magnitude. The proponents of the system that Ben included in the article advocated for advance planning for what they perceived as an inevitable mass transit project.

"We can have the best transportation system in the country if we start planning now," Ben wrote, "or we can cut-and-paste a system together later like most other cities have done."

*   *   *

Ben and I rushed out his front door around 11am, a half hour late. I had overslept. It was a cold and gray November morning, but there wasn't any rain in the forecast and that was fortunate because, rain or shine, we couldn't miss this SU football game. Of all the games we'd attended in the past three years, this was unquestionably "the big one," the most significant in our long series. And, it would be much more enjoyable dry than soggy.

As we drove, we listened to the two sports commentators on WGRZ, the university-owned radio station, as they touted the matchup that afternoon as the most important SU football game in more than twenty years.

"The conference championship will be decided on our field this afternoon and, win or lose, this is clearly the best SU football team since the conference championship team in 1954," one commentator declared as we merged onto the highway traveling north.

"We've got plenty of time," Ben offered as consolation to my obvious anxiety. "We'll get a couple hot dogs and a couple of beers and be in our seats ten minutes before kickoff. Don't worry."

"Just drive," I said. "We can't be late."

"Our 7-0 Grizzlies against the defending conference champion and also 7-0 UCW Eagles," one commentator continued, "in what will surely be the most impressive aerial battle since the allies assault on Germany during WWII. Danny Grainger, the number one rated passer in the conference, will be throwing the football all day long. I look for him to attempt at least forty passes today."

"He's got to," the other commentator added, enthusiastically breaking into the conversation, "UCW has the best defense in the conference against the running game, allowing more than 100 yards rushing only once this season. The Grizzlies are not going to win this game by testing that UCW front line. If Danny Grainger's arm is good and tired at the end of this one, they have a good chance to win it."

"What about Grainger?" the first commentator queried, "do you think he's a potential draft pick for the NFL, Tim?"

"He's got the size and the arm. He could get the nod in the late rounds. I think he'd make a great backup quarterback. I doubt he's a starter. Grainger's got a lot of heart and he loves to throw so he'd be a great addition to the right team. How he performs today in the big one will be a factor in his draft possibilities. You've got to shine in the big ones to get the call to the NFL."

"Okay, time for a trivia question. Grab those phones and get ready to dial. Who was the last Grizzly selected in the NFL draft?"

"Danny playing pro football," I commented, saying each word slowly for emphasis. "Wouldn't that be something?"

* * *

Ben was right. We were in our seats ten minutes before kickoff, hot dogs and beers in hand. The commentators were right, too. It was quite a game; mostly passing plays, plenty of scoring, and very exciting. Only the weatherman was wrong. After the Grizzlies scored a touchdown to take the lead, 31-27, the rain fell hard late in the third quarter. At times, it came down in sheets. And, unfortunately for the SU faithful, the Eagles seemed to adjust better to the sloppy surface than the Grizzlies. The SU defense was slipping and sliding all over the muddy field as the Eagle offense carried out their next offensive possession, trying to reclaim the lead.

Led by their fullback, a sturdy, battering ram of a man wearing number 41, the Eagles ground out an excruciatingly hard to watch, eighteen play, eighty yard drive and regained the lead, 34-31, when number 41 splashed down in the flooded end zone for a touchdown. As their extra point split the uprights, the near capacity crowd was suddenly the quietest it had been all afternoon. The sound of the rain striking umbrellas, rubber slickers, plastic trash bags, and tarps could be heard in our section as there was no other noise to compete with the splatting. But, despite the downpour and go-ahead touchdown, few spectators left. Instead, Grizzly fans slowly and collectively seized on their final hope for a victory: The Eagles had left three minutes and thirty-four seconds on the clock.

"This isn't over yet," I heard one alumnus behind us say.

"The conference championship will be decided on this next possession," his companion added.

But everyone knew, even the most optimistic of Grizzly fans, that it would take a scoring drive of heroic proportions, considering the opponent, the elements, and the condition of the field, for SU to pull this one off. It would take a miracle.

During the Eagles' kick off, I watched Danny on the sidelines, his helmet gripped by the facemask and dangling at his side, his eyes focused intensely on the field. He looked cool and confident, though dripping wet, and he seemed unfazed by a playing surface that was entirely different than when he'd last left the field. The surface had gotten so bad that muddy water splashed around the player's ankles as they ran. Still, Danny looked ready for what would surely be the most important two hundred seconds of football he'd ever played.

As I watched him, I wondered if, somewhere deep in his gut, Danny doubted his ability to meet the enormity of this challenge. He was a gifted athlete, no doubt, but there are limits to human abilities. If the field conditions weren't swamp-like, Danny might command a final drive and win this game, but not today, not on this field. Danny's footing would be unsure, the ball would be slippery, and his receiver's hands would be wet. There are limits, you know.

The crowd expected so much. In essence, these Grizzly fans wanted a miraculous final scoring drive, a game-winning touchdown, and a conference championship delivered from above like the rain that fell all around them. To me, it seemed like mass heartbreak was inevitable; this final drive seemed destined to come up short. How could anyone perform in all that mud?

As Danny jogged onto the playing field, the crowd rose to their feet and cheered enthusiastically, loudly, as if their support could somehow play a role in the final outcome.

"Grizz-lies, Grizz-lies, Grizz-lies," they roared as the offense lined up at the twenty-six yard line.

In succession, Danny completed three quick passes to his wide receivers, each seven or eight yards long, advancing the ball passed their own forty-eight yard line, where it was first and ten with two minutes and twenty seconds left to play. The Grizzlies were operating without the benefit of huddles so each team scrambled back to their side of the line of scrimmage before the start of each new play. As the clock ticked down to two minutes and ten seconds, Danny stepped up to the line once again and rushed his signal calling to start the play before the two-minute warning sounded, a procedural timeout in a football game that wasn't charged to either team.

"Two, twenty-eight, hut, hut," he called rapidly, and then he took the snap from center and dropped back to pass. Danny set his feet where the white chalk for the washed out thirty-five yard line once lay and scanned the middle of field for an open receiver. His primary receiver slipped while cutting toward the middle of the field and fell face down onto the muddy bayou that was, previously, a football field.

Unfortunately, Danny never glimpsed the blitzing, Eagle linebacker, gaining speed with every stride, moving like a freight train down the tracks, coming at him from the left side, his blindside. As he released the football, the linebacker lunged into his back, striking him squarely in the numbers, forcing his right leg to slide out from under him and his left knee to buckle under their combined weight. His pass sailed over the far sidelines and practically disappeared when it landed in a murky puddle of muddy water beside the bleachers. Writhing in pain, Danny rolled out from under his assailant, grabbed his injured left knee, and raised it in the air in the fetal position. Until the team's trainer arrived, he thrashed about in the mud like a deer shot in the hindquarter.

"That's his bad knee," I said to Ben.

"Shit."

The crowd was stunned, standing in concerned silence, even quieter than the moment that followed UCW's go-ahead touchdown. All in attendance sensed the end of a brilliant college football career, and that wasn't the reason they'd purchased their tickets or endured a downpour; they had come to witness a glorious victory and celebrate a conference championship. Once again, the only sounds in our section were the splatting of the rain as it landed on the protective gear of the crowd. On this bleak November afternoon, the football stadium had been mythically and meteorologically transformed into Mudville and there was no joy here either.

Mighty Danny had been struck down.

Sitting atop their interlocked arms, Danny was carried off the field by two offensive linemen, grimacing with pain while straining to support his already swollen knee. This was "Black Saturday" all over again for Danny. I wasn't there for the first one, but I can imagine the sinking feeling was about the same. An ambulance arrived, its red and blue lights flashing, and Danny was loaded into the back for transport to the hospital.

One minute and fifty-three seconds remained on the game clock, but winning was no longer the priority to those wearing crimson and gold, both on the field and in the seats. The Grizzlies backup quarterback was a capable replacement, but when he trotted onto the field amidst a choir of half-hearted cheers, the team's aspirations had already left the stadium in an ambulance. The game, as well as the conference championship, belonged to their opponent.

After the gun sounded, the team's trainer told us that Danny had been taken to Montgomery Hospital so we proceeded directly to the hospital's emergency room to wait amongst the city's injured and ill for word on Danny's condition.

The prognosis was horrible. Danny was out for the remainder of the season, he'd probably played his last football game, and, worse still, he might walk with a limp for the rest of his life.

In the waiting room, I braced myself for Danny's shattered emotional state. But, his knee wasn't my primary concern. What if I couldn't write again? What if I couldn't do what I did? I'd be destroyed, reduced to a husk of my former self with all sense of identity and purpose ripped away. I, too, would limp for the rest of my life. It wouldn't be a noticeable limp; it would be an emotional and spiritual limp but a limp just the same.

"He's in a lot of pain," the doctor told us.

"More than you know," I said to the man in operating room garb. "He's damaged so much more than ligaments and tissue."

*   *   *

As the following weeks progressed, I felt like I should revise my business cards and add a second designation. All of a sudden, I wasn't just a newspaper editor but also a spiritual counselor for the depressed and disillusioned. I'd become a veritable lifeline for two individuals: Danny Grainger and Joe Golden, and the unavoidable irony was that these were two of the most talented people I'd ever met. That circumstance wasn't without its lessons though, and I'd reached one irrefutable conclusion: When people fall from the pinnacle of great success, they get really banged up.

Ambition is a demanding, relentless master. Bold individuals like entrepreneurs, inventors, and artists accept great personal risk as the price of admission, but never realize that success will not lower the risk, as one might expect. In reality, wrong steps and miscalculations are more costly after the initial breakthrough, after the first taste of success, when the stakes are higher, the fall further, and the impact harder. In reality, the price of success is greater than anyone expects.

Unfortunately, these harsh realities were confirmed during my last meeting with Joe Golden.

"You got my check?" Joe asked, appearing once again in my doorway, initiating our weekly ritual. As always, I lifted the envelope into the air so Joe could see it and come into my office.

On this particular occasion, Joe was more wrinkled and soiled than usual and his pathetic condition overwhelmed me. How could someone with so much talent live this way? To me, it was mind-boggling—absolutely nonsensical—and I could no longer avoid the single most glaring question, one that many people had wondered about for years. I didn't know whether Joe would answer it or not, but I couldn't keep myself from asking it any longer.

"I've got to ask you something, Joe. But before I do, I want you to know your answer has nothing to do with your weekly check. It'll be here no matter what you say, even if you don't answer. I'm curious, that's all, and I've got to ask."

"It's your dime, kid," Joe returned, a phrase he used often during our Friday meetings.

"Why did you stop writing?"

His head rocked backward. He was silent and slow to answer. It wasn't hard to gauge the difficulty of the question as it was written all over his face, the only writing Joe had done in the time I knew him. Obviously, it wasn't something that he wanted to talk about, but I also sensed a deep-seated need to unburden his conscience, to confess his failures, and receive some sort of penance. Like his friend Gator, he'd carried this weight for too long. He was conflicted about answering, but he finally did anyway.

"There have been a lot of crackpot theories over the years," Joe said. "If you believe those idiots, I was hushed by either the CIA or the Mafia, disillusioned by government hypocrisy, or turned off by the high cost of young lives in Vietnam. Those theories couldn't have been further from the truth."

"Why did you stop writing, Joe?"

"Some said I burned out," he said in a barely audible mumble. "I guess they were the closest to the truth."

"Why, Joe?"

"After *The Torn Tuxedo* was published, I became a celebrity, my musings at parties were quoted in the newspapers, my travels and whereabouts noted. Hell, I even partied with Elvis and Sinatra. You have to realize, kid, *The Torn Tuxedo* was compared to American classics like *The Great Gatsby* and *Of Mice and Men,* and suddenly my name was included on the lists of great novelists with Fitzgerald and Steinbeck. Everyone was waiting for my next book. 'His greatly anticipated second novel' was always how they referred to it."

Joe was getting a little glassy eyed as he spoke and, for once, it wasn't a hundred-proof sheen. It was a hard truth that had crossed his mind often, but one that he seldom verbalized.

"Whenever I worked on my second novel, my words sounded ridiculous, like crap. I couldn't write anything worthy of a being a follow-up to *The Torn Tuxedo*. It wasn't lack of effort. I just couldn't do it. I threw out my efforts as quickly as I wrote them. I'll bet I wrote ten novels trying to get one good one. In my mind, they all stunk. The problem was that I'd read all the reviews and heard all the accolades and, over time, I came to believe that I couldn't live up to them. Little by little, I drank more than I wrote, until finally, I stopped writing altogether.

* * *

It was the one and only time Joe ever confided in me, and the last time I had any contact with him. Once he finished, he snatched the check and left without saying another word, never to return on any subsequent Fridays. Surprisingly enough, I missed him. A year later, I read that Joe Golden had been found dead beneath cardboard boxes in an alley in Philadelphia. The police report concluded that a garbage truck had accidentally backed over him while emptying a dumpster. Joe was either asleep or passed out at the time. The blurb referred to Joe as a "meteor of a novelist who had produced a brilliant, onetime flash in the night sky of the American literary scene." He had blazed bright, burned out, and faded to black, as meteors do.

I knew that all too well.

I called Steve Todd to see if he'd heard the news.

"Oh, my God," Steve cried and then the phone line fell silent.

I waited for several minutes as I could tell he was unable to speak. Prior to dialing, I hadn't expected the news to have such a debilitating effect on him. Joe and Steve were close friends during college but that was many, many years ago.

"You tried, Steve," I said.

Still, the line was silent.

"He's with Gator now," I added, not sure if he'd understand the long ago reference. But, he did.

"They weren't so different after all," Steve finally managed to say, and then he hung up without saying goodbye.

9.

Ironically, the Empire State Building, a monument to American prosperity and potential, was built after the stock market crash of 1929 and in the midst of the Great Depression. The excavation of its foundation began in January of 1930 and it was completed in April of 1931, a construction pace never equaled since. Often, the most difficult and challenging times produce the greatest triumphs.

Ten years passed, a prosperous decade epitomized by yuppies, BMW convertibles, an obliging stock market, skyrocketing real estate, Rolex watches, designer labels, and rampant consumerism. Grabbing with both hands at the nation's free-flowing supply of money, the city of Cavanaugh participated wholeheartedly. Bulldozers at residential and commercial construction sites broke the reddish, clay-like soil of the region at rates never experienced before. Cranes dotted the skyline as placeholders for towering office buildings and condominiums still in the works. By 1992, Cavanaugh was a magnificent metropolis of skyscrapers and suburban sprawl, a blueprint for modern cities, and a western showplace. On most evenings, the city's skyline glimmered in the golden brilliance of the setting sun like yellow sapphire stones on a precious necklace.

A byproduct of progress, Cavanaugh's population had tripled in the fifteen years I'd walked its streets, with 1990 census estimates placing the populace at just over seven million. Two years into a new decade, the seaport operated at capacity, the business district hummed, the technology corridor rivaled Silicon Valley, and the suburbs continued their expansion. Residents enjoyed a pleasing quality of life as the prosperity produced high paying jobs, safe neighborhoods, solid infrastructure, and a highly regarded school system. In simple 90s jargon, life was good.

Our company, its named changed from *Cavanaugh Weekly* to Utopia Publishing, kept pace with the city and the times as we added two publications in the late 1980s: a glossy, stylish, fashion magazine entitled *Cavanaugh Monthly* and a business and investing magazine entitled *Cavanaugh Business Monthly*. In 1986, motivated by two business needs—more office space and a better location—we moved our headquarters from the warehouse to a four-story marble and glass building in the downtown business district. But, the fundamentals of our business never changed. *Cavanaugh Weekly* continued to thrive and remained the heart and soul of the company and an ever-present force in the city's political landscape. Just as Ben predicted, its format had been proven a winner and copied by other publications.

Championed by Councilman Dale Greenwood, the Cavanaugh Waterfront Towers project was approved by the city council along with concurrent plans to demolish Old Cavanaugh just months before its centennial. In just ten days, cranes, wrecking balls, and bulldozers leveled twenty-seven buildings, and the massive brown dust cloud that floated ominously over the demolition zone made the loss of valuable history and artifacts even more painful for the crowds of protestors. Then, on a bright and sunny spring day in 1983, guest of honor Mayor Dale Greenwood wielded a gold-plated shovel at the groundbreaking for the condominium towers where more than eighty percent of the units had been sold before his shovel even struck the rich, red dirt.

The groundbreaking for the Stanton University student center experienced several lengthy delays caused by the presence of ancient artifacts on the site and did not occur until August of 1983. Ben and I attended that ceremony as well as the grand opening held at the start of the school year in late August of 1985, an evening that was gratifying for both of us. We walked the hallways and felt a great satisfaction from the fact that our vision had become reality. At the end of the fourth floor hallway beside the door to the new office of *The Signal*, we were quite surprised to find a bronze plaque that read:

"On April 10, 1978, the cover article of
The Stanton University Signal,
written by freshmen
Benjamin Matthews and Peter Dalton,
provided the original rationale, recommendation,
and proposal for the construction
of this student center."

From 1982 forward, Tyler worked at KCVN, first as a news intern and later as a field reporter, winning several local media awards for segments she reported. In 1988, she got her big break when she became the six o'clock news anchorwoman and her evening broadcast quickly climbed to highest rated amongst the local news programs. I usually tuned in on the office television around 6:15pm each evening to watch the end of her broadcast and her signature signoff.

"From Cavanaugh to Berlin, those are the events shaping our world tonight. I'm Tyler Danzig and I'll see you again tomorrow."

The second city varied nightly, but it was always a distant location and one mentioned during the broadcast.

Her studio was two blocks from our downtown headquarters so Tyler and I usually met at least once a week for lunch, coffee, or cocktails. Tyler and Ben had remained close platonic friends since their breakup more than a decade ago but had never rekindled their relationship. One day at lunch, just Tyler and me, and after a couple glasses of white wine, Tyler divulged her reason for their break-up.

"Our relationship might have lasted two years, but Ben lost interest much earlier. We didn't actually split up. We just slowly fizzled. I knew his heart wasn't in it. We had sex maybe five or six times in our last six months together."

Lost interest? How was that possible? Tyler was the most beautiful woman I'd ever known, so much so that I'd always been a little intimidated by her, despite our close friendship. How could Ben—or any college kid for that matter—lose interest in Tyler? It was incomprehensible to me.

"Do you think Ben is gay?" I asked.

"No," she answered, "just extraordinarily distracted."

As for me, my own love life was disheartening at best. In 1984, I married a wonderful woman, an elementary schoolteacher named Abigail, but we divorced four short years later. In retrospect, I neglected the most important elements of a fulfilled life, namely heart and home. In my college days, I would've ranked a good marriage as a top priority in my life and yet, while I had it, I took it for granted. As life progressed and I got caught up in the ever-quickening pace of it, I lost sight of what was truly important.

Looking back, my life was out of balance with way too much time and energy focused on our business. It didn't help matters any that my two best friends were career focused people because they made my workaholic ways seem normal. I should've looked to Stan as an example of a healthy life and not Tyler and Ben. Abigail and I rarely saw one another and so she left me. In all fairness, I never blamed Abigail because it was obvious even to me that I wasn't a good husband.

With remarkable ease, Abigail moved on with her life. She married a computer software salesman and gave birth to a beautiful daughter about a year later. I admit that I didn't do nearly as well with my moving on; very quickly, I gave up on the dating scene altogether. For companionship, I adopted a yellow Labrador retriever and named him Scoop. My only consolation was that Scoop didn't drool nearly as much as Abigail.

Most significantly, I kept the promise I made to my mother and myself. In the spring of 1985, I enrolled in Stanton University's professional program; evening classes offered at a satellite campus in the downtown, taking two courses each semester including summer sessions until I completed my college degree. And, in a reversal of our normal operating style, Ben followed my lead for once, progressing at a slower pace due to the demands of his schedule until he graduated one year later. With sheepskins finally adorning our office walls, Ben and I often joked that our bastard child, Utopia Publishing, conceived without the appropriate credentials, was finally legitimate.

In October of 1988, Ben appeared on the cover of *Global Times Magazine*, heralded as an Urban Visionary, and credited in the lengthy article for *Cavanaugh Weekly's* activist role in shaping the city. Quoting from the article, "Ben Matthews is a next generation social reformer, picking up where the hippies of the sixties left off but effecting real change in ways his predecessors only dreamed and sang about. Armed with utopian plans and charismatic leadership qualities, Matthews is a first generation urban visionary and the primary reason that Cavanaugh has become one of the best places in the U.S. to live. He has encouraged citizen involvement in government, championed the strictest zoning ordinances in the nation, and implemented a city council requirement for a twenty year planning horizon pertaining to growth and development."

Needless to say, the article further strained the already adversarial relationship between Ben and Mayor Greenwood when it stated that *Cavanaugh Weekly* had become more influential and more crucial to the city's development than the mayor or the city council. And, making matters worse still, *Global Times* also suggested that Ben would make an outstanding candidate for the mayor's job or even the governor's mansion. Several other national magazines followed suit and Ben Matthews became a name respected locally and recognized nationally.

Since graduation, Danny managed The Bayside Motel in Condor for his friend Robert Cooper. For his efforts, Danny received an efficiency apartment off the back of the motel and a monthly stipend that was barely enough to live on. Still, it was enough for Danny, as he had no greater ambitions. Since the second knee injury, which left him with a noticeable limp, Danny had become a dark, disillusioned character—very different from the lighthearted guy I first met and roomed with at SU. He lived with daily pain in both his lower back and left knee and depended on handfuls of pain pills and shots of alcohol for relief. The combination of the constant pain and his self-medication made Danny difficult to be around. I hadn't made a lot of effort to see him.

One spring afternoon while researching an article in Condor, I dropped in on Danny unannounced and found him behind the motel tossing footballs at a tire he'd hung from an oak tree. The scene reminded me of his stories from his youth and stopped me dead in my tracks. For an hour, I watched him from across the street, tossing perfect spirals through the center of that tire, and then I walked back to my car and left. I couldn't endure the depressing conversation or the emptiness that had replaced the bright light that once shined in his eyes. Since college, Ben stayed in closer contact with Danny than I.

Stan Tilden remained happily married after almost a decade and that was quite an accomplishment considering the rising divorce rates and the demands of our business. He and his wife were the proud parents of twin, seven-year-old boys that made up the backcourt of the *Cavanaugh Monthly* Rockets, a basketball team sponsored by the company and coached by Stan and me. Along with shared coaching duties, Stan and I shared the editorial helm of our three publications under the titles of co-managing editors.

Our managerial style changed from month to month. We'd collaborated on issues in some months and, at other times, focused our energies on different issues. Either way, with two magazines and a newspaper to organize and a staff of more than seventy, there was always enough work to help us avoid any competitive or creative friction. We often joked that the hardest part of our shared duties was keeping the seven year olds focused on a basketball game for forty minutes. Although I must also confess, there were many late nights before deadlines when we wondered whether our writing staff had less focus than our young hoopsters.

All in all, for the four former *Signal* staffers, it had been a very good decade. Our professional successes were undeniable and our personal lives were relatively sane. If I were a religious man, I'd say we were blessed and if I were a gambler, I'd say we were on a roll. Either way, God or luck, I tried not to question it too much. We all lived in nice homes, drove European cars, and couldn't deny that life had given us more than our fair share. Tyler and Ben lived in high-rise, luxury condominiums in the downtown area while Stan and I chose the more conventional lifestyle of homes in the suburbs.

Though I often made jokes about suburbia, I guess, in the end, I gravitated to my comfort zone, and I was the same creature of habit I'd always been, a real suburbanite. In college, I walked the campus each morning. In the new decade, I commuted the same route each morning; first, along the winding tree-lined, country roads of Carlisle Woods where I resided, across Somerset Bridge into east Cavanaugh, through the city's bustling business district until I arrived at Utopia Publishing each morning. If nothing else, I was predictable.

As good as things were, nothing ever stays the same, life always advances, and time moves forward. I didn't realize it at the time, no one ever does, but we were about to face a moment that would change all our lives forever.

* * *

A century ago in the Wild West, men settled their differences with a blaze of gunfire on a dusty street. In those days, Ben would've stood beside the bar at the local saloon and simply declared, "Tell Greenwood I'll be waiting for him on the street in front of the hotel at noon," and followed his challenge with a shot of whiskey. He would've donned a white hat, leather vest, and jangly spurs, strapped on twin, ivory handled six-shooters, and waited for his adversary in the bright sun at high noon. All their past disagreements about zoning, city council policies, and transportation spending would've been resolved by the quicker hand and steadier aim. And I could've offered him encouragement and praise as his feisty and slightly inept sidekick, just like Pancho did for the Cisco Kid.

Resolution of disputes was quick and decisive in those lawless times, but, fortunately or not, our modern justice system didn't allow it. Ben would have to do the next best thing.

At 9am, about one hundred invited guests, mostly prominent business people and the media, were gathered in our lobby beneath the balcony and a podium draped with our company logo. A persistent murmur filled the space as everyone speculated about the subject matter for the press conference, conspicuously absent from invitations sent out three days earlier. As a rule, members of the press, who were inquisitive to the point of snooping by nature, didn't suffer secrets in silence. Grumbling and whining always resulted.

Even Mrs. Matlock, Ben's assistant and the press conference organizer, didn't know the subject matter. She was interrogated many times and always graciously responded, "I honestly don't know."

Only three people knew that Ben was about to announce his candidacy for Mayor of Cavanaugh: Ben, Stan, and myself. It was a carefully guarded secret. Finally, his announcement would end a decade of speculation as to whether or not Ben would seek political office and, if he did, what office? He'd long been considered a potential candidate for several high offices in the state including governor, senator, representative, and Mayor of Cavanaugh. Though many believed Ben's chances for victory were better pursuing the governor's office than taking on this three-term incumbent mayor, I knew his choice was personal and he wanted to unseat this mayor. He wanted to send him packing. As I waited at the podium, I understood how much Ben detested Mayor Greenwood and how much satisfaction he'd get from a showdown with him, whether six shooters were involved or not. He loved this city and he wanted that office. It was as simple at that.

Ben, wearing the requisite blue suit and red striped tie, attire typical of political candidates, appeared at 9:10am and took his place behind the podium. He told me later that he abandoned his signature outfit, a dark blazer, white shirt, and blue jeans, to compensate for his young age. For the first day of his campaign, he wanted to look the part of the candidate. Just as he seemed ready to speak, he stepped away from the podium and whispered to me.

"I've never been more sure of anything in my life," he said. "My life has been a journey that has brought me to this place and this moment."

His words didn't surprise me. Ben believed in fate, pre-ordained destinies, and heavenly intervention. Since her passing almost thirty years ago, Ben has maintained a spiritual relationship with his dead mother and truly believed she watched over him and guided him. Whether real or imagined, it gave him an edge. I always wondered whether great things happened in Ben's life on account of destiny or whether his unwavering beliefs and his resulting confidence had turned his life into a self-fulfilling prophecy. In either case, the outcomes were usually remarkable.

Confirming my suspicions, Ben returned to the microphone, took a deep breath, glanced skyward momentarily, and then looked out at the crowd. With about one hundred people before him, Ben was confident and at ease.

We all have comfort zones. For me, I was always most comfortable on the couch in my living room wearing a sweatshirt and sweatpants while working on the *Weekly*. Time and again, I watched Danny on the sidelines at a football game, and he always looked like he was in his comfort zone, always relaxed and confident. Tyler told me she was most comfortable while relaxing on her bed and listening to music, most particularly the early Beatles songs. One place most people were uncomfortable was in front of large crowds, particularly if public speaking was involved. To the contrary, whenever Ben stood before a crowd to give a speech, he was in his comfort zone.

"Good morning and thank you for coming," Ben said as he greeted all in attendance.

Suspended from the ceiling on thin clear wires behind both of Ben's shoulders were two large banners of the city's skyline in full color. This panoramic image of Ben in the midst of majestic, shining skyscrapers appeared on the front page of *The Dispatch* the next day with the bold headline of "Matthews Announces Bid For Mayor" and made Ben appear formidable and larger-than-life. The image also created a surrealistic, subliminal impression that Ben was an integral part of the cityscape, a flesh-and-blood skyscraper, a skyscraper of a man, as deeply rooted in the bedrock of the region as the towering structures that formed the city's skyline. Many times in the media, it had been written that Ben was the chief architect of the city's progress and that image certainly advanced that legion of thought.

Interestingly enough, when Ben ordered the tall banners, his instructions were to enlarge the photographs so that Optimal Tower, a new downtown skyscraper and the tallest building in the pictures, was six-feet-four-inches tall, Ben's exact height. He had a brilliant sense for staging events, and he wanted his audience to view Optimal Tower and himself as comparable. For his announcement, Ben wanted to be a skyscraper. I'd always said that Ben saw the big picture better than anyone and this undertaking definitely added new meaning to my sentiment. Undeniably, the backdrop was a stroke of political genius.

"'Whenever the people are well informed,' Ben declared, 'they can be trusted with their own government.' These are the words of Thomas Jefferson, one of our Founding Fathers, the author of the Declaration of Independence, and someone who understood the dangers of entrusted power. Jefferson also said, 'Were it left to me to decide whether we should have government without newspapers or newspapers without government, I would prefer the latter.' More than a decade ago, these words inspired the founding of my newspaper, *Cavanaugh Weekly*, and it is these words today that inspire my candidacy for the office of mayor of this great city. Our citizens have made this city great and, as mayor of Cavanaugh, I will continue to work with our citizens—in the same way we worked together while I was publisher of *Cavanaugh Weekly*—to ensure an even greater future in the new millennium."

As part of this panoramic image, Ben announced his mayoral candidacy and then commenced his newly launched campaign with a speech that focused on the future of the city. He touched on all his usual talking points and emphasized that it was time for the city to move ahead on the construction of a light-rail system that would carry Cavanaugh into the millennium. Then, Ben surprised, shocked, and concerned me.

"Our great city needs honest leadership," Ben declared, emphasizing the word honest. "Honest leadership," he repeated once again as my heart plummeted deep into my chest.

Ben continued, "The best interest of the city and its citizens must once again become the focus of our government officials in City Hall. We are at an important crossroad and it is time for the citizens of Cavanaugh to take City Hall back."

Ben had expressed this sentiment privately many times before, but I never expected him to launch his mayoral campaign by attacking the character of the incumbent mayor. This was, indeed, the modern day equivalent of challenging Mayor Greenwood to a gunfight in the street. I expected the campaign would get personal and even ugly in the final, heated days before Election Day, but not now, not this soon. With his character assault on the mayor, Ben had personalized the campaign right from the start, and I was more concerned than ever.

* * *

His hat officially tossed into the political ring, Ben campaigned for the remainder of the day: shaking the hands of well-wishers; schmoozing with local businessmen and women; lunching with contributors; and filming interview footage for the evening and late-night news programs. In a silly nod to political tradition, Ben even kissed several babies at the local mall that afternoon to make his candidacy official. By bedtime that night, most of the voting citizens of Cavanaugh had learned of Ben's mayoral campaign so it was fair to say that Ben had a good first day. It wasn't until after 7pm that evening, when I noticed the light from his office spilling into the darkened hallway, that I was finally able to talk with Ben privately.

"Are you out of you mind?" I asked as I approached his desk.

"What?" he returned. "I thought the day was a great success."

"Your honesty attacks on the mayor," I said shaking my head. "By my calculation you'd been a candidate for all of twenty-three minutes when you first assaulted his character. Don't you think it's a little early in the campaign to take the gloves off?"

"If you think I'm going to act like a politician, then you're missing the whole point. We started *Cavanaugh Weekly* to fill a need our local government and political processes had failed at, getting citizens more involved in governing and thereby creating a stronger sense of community in our city. I am running for mayor, but I have no intention of conforming to the norm. Our city is not working; the norm is not working. I want to make the best interest of the city and the people the priority of our city government. Currently, it is not. I'm not interested in what's politically wise and what isn't."

I didn't see the point of trying to convince Ben that he had just poked Mayor Greenwood in the eye with a pointy stick and started a fight with a brawler. We'd had that conversation many times before and he hadn't been affected by my previous warnings.

"The people of Cavanaugh know me, Pete. I know them. My campaign will be the continuation of an ongoing exchange that has lasted more than a decade."

Ben paused for a moment and looked like he was having a revelation or epiphany of some sort.

"I shouldn't even call it a campaign," he said, correcting his strategy. "It's more of a crusade to reform government."

"That sounds both radical and holy, Ben. I think I'd stay clear of announcing a crusade."

"You're right. But, you get my point, just the same. I'm not hiring political consultants and I'm not interested in how things have been done. We can do better. That's the point."

* * *

"My sources tell me that Mayor Greenwood hurled a stapler at the television when Ben announced his candidacy," Tyler informed me at lunch the following Tuesday. "It struck the screen in the center of Ben's face and put a big crack in it. He hates Ben, you know, always refers to him snidely as Benjamin."

"Well, that feeling is mutual," I replied.

"Ben surprised a lot of people with his announcement, most notably the mayor and his staff at City Hall. But, two hours after the announcement, the mayor and his political advisors held an emergency meeting to discuss Ben's candidacy and developed a strategy to diffuse his momentum. They recognize that Ben is popular amongst the people so they don't want to blatantly attack him. That would backfire. Instead, they're going to focus on his lack of political experience and plant the seeds of doubt in the voters' minds."

"It's going to get negative and ugly," I said.

"I know. I'm concerned about Ben," she responded.

Her facial expression was much more serious than moments earlier when she laughed about the stapler incident.

"Save your breath," I told her and then I brought her up to date on my discussions with Ben.

"He's simply not concerned," I concluded.

"Well, you tell Ben that I expect several exclusive interviews during this campaign," Tyler stipulated, ever the diligent reporter.

It was a beautiful, unseasonably warm, spring-like afternoon as Tyler and I enjoyed a late lunch of croissant sandwiches, pasta salad, and onion soup at a small downtown café called The Parisian. We were seated in a small outdoor patio area, complete with green canvas umbrellas and colorful baskets full of flowers, and we usually dined there whenever the weather was encouraging. Tyler preferred late lunches so she'd be relaxed when her evening broadcast began at 6pm. I enjoyed our lunches so much that I would've eaten anytime.

While waiting for her, I purchased several compact discs at a music store near the restaurant. When Tyler finished her croissant sandwich, she retrieved the shopping bag I'd stashed beneath the table to examine my selections. She flipped through the four compact discs and then returned to one.

"I've heard a few songs off this album," she stated, holding the compact disc in the air so I could see which one she was referring to. "I hear it's one of his best."

"Take it with you," I offered. "Give it a listen."

"I can't. I don't have a CD player."

"You don't have a CD player!" I repeated in astonishment.

As I consumed my final bites of pasta salad, I kidded Tyler that she was a little behind the times, but she remained unruffled and only defended her choice. She told me she preferred the old albums to both tapes and CDs and wasn't concerned that the clarity of the music was better with the newer technologies. Anyway, she had more than two hundred vinyl albums at her condominium.

"The snaps and hisses don't bother me," Tyler said. "To me, they're as much a part of a Beatles song as John's vocals or Ringo's drumming. I particularly like the sound the needle makes when you first put it on the vinyl, before the song starts. It's a vinyl prelude of sorts. When I was in high school, I listened to my albums over and over on my record player in my room. Now, those albums are more than just musical recordings to me; they transport me through time. When that needle touches down on that vinyl, I am sixteen again."

It was rare for Tyler to express her feelings, to let others peek inside her polished and often steely facade. I'd always thought her choice to be a news anchor was fitting, as news anchors do not show their emotions, not even at the most tragic of times. Her profession required her to report on murders, plane crashes, house fires, and child molestation without so much as a hint of sympathy for the victims. Even with close friends, Tyler was staid and professional. Maybe that's why it seemed so special, noteworthy, and heartfelt when she did express her feelings. Even more surprising and entirely out of character, on this beautiful, spring-like afternoon, Tyler started singing a Beatles tune in a whispered, dream-like tone.

"If I fell in love with you/ would you promise to be true/ and help me understand/ cause I've been in love before/ and I found that love was more/ than just holding hands."

Her voice was soft and I felt caressed by the melody. My brain knew she wasn't singing to me, but my heart believed otherwise. She was innocently reminiscing, but the moment had a profound affect

174 | Michael Bowe

on me. I began rethinking complicated thoughts I'd had many times before, thoughts about pursuing a romantic relationship with Tyler.

When it came to Tyler, I'd been a coward. She was the most amazing woman I'd ever known, but I'd used our friendship to absolve my emotional paralysis rather than confront the issues and explore a romantic relationship with her. Once and for all, I promised myself, I'd talk with Ben and ascertain his feelings on the matter. Heck, maybe it won't be an issue at all.

"Pete, Pete?"

Tyler repeated my name, louder each time, until I finally snapped out of my daydream.

"I've got to get back to the studio. Who's turn is it?" she asked, referring to the check.

"I don't know," I replied, still lost in her smooth cover of that Beatles song. "But, I'll take care of it," I added in a strong, assertive tone, signaling, to myself at least, my resolve to change the context of our relationship.

Quickly, I retrieved my wallet from my back pocket and put my credit card at the table's edge.

I've got this, I thought.

"You all right?" she asked as she rose and prepared to depart. "You seem a little distant."

"I have been," I said, "but I'm going to change that."

"Huh?"

"Nothing."

Tyler left while I remained behind and waited for the check.

Now, if I can just stop talking in riddles, I thought.

* * *

It was such a beautiful afternoon that I took the long way back to the office, wandering through the business district and waffling on my resolve. At each street corner, my thoughts about a relationship with Tyler changed. At one street corner, I was determined to talk with Ben, and at the next corner I thought the whole impulse was a bad idea. Was I really willing to risk my two best friendships in this world to pursue a romance with one of them? It seemed highly likely that I'd lose one of them along the way.

As I approached the stately, white fountain in Potter Square, I decided to put this decision into the hands of whichever heavenly spirit handled matters of the heart and toss a coin into the fountain. There were already many coins beneath the glistening, blue water of the fountain, so I rationalized that I wasn't the only desperate soul to ask it for guidance. By the side of the fountain, I reached into my pocket and withdrew all my change so I could select the proper coin for the task. There, amongst the quarters, nickels, and dimes in my palm, was a shiny silver dollar I didn't even know I had. Its shininess and heft struck me as an omen as this was clearly the appropriate coin for the task at hand. Maybe Ben's right about this destiny thing.

Heads I will talk to Ben, tails I will not, I told myself.

I cupped the coin in my hand and blew on it twice. I don't know why. I tossed the coin high into the air, watched it flip end over end, gradually climb to a height of about ten feet, continue its rotation as it dropped downward, break the surface of the water, and come to rest on the bottom.

It was tails. I couldn't believe it.

For a moment, I stared at the shiny coin, easily viewed, as it was larger than any of the other coins. Holding a wreath and arrows in its talons, the eagle was clearly visible beneath the shimmering water. In my mind, I cursed the heavenly asshole that disappointed me.

Where is that damn Cupid when you need him? If he's out of arrows, I know a smug, little eagle that doesn't seem to be doing any good with the ones he's got. Oh, to hell with all them, best two out of three. I will toss the coin again.

I rolled up my right sleeve, reached into the chilly water of the fountain, and retrieved the shiny coin.

* * *

The next couple days were a frenzied blur at the office. Ben's candidacy continued to generate excitement and additional foot traffic throughout Utopia Publishing's corridors, and two of our publications were fast approaching deadline. Ben and I passed several times in the hallway, once long enough to update him on the status of our next editions, but never long enough to consider broaching the sensitive topic of dating his ex-lover. Finally, after several failed attempts to catch Ben in a private moment in his office, I decided that this topic was better deliberated away from the chaos and distractions of the workplace.

After all, I had to be absolutely certain Ben gave the issue thorough consideration before responding. He couldn't change his mind later. It would be too late for all concerned.

At around 4pm that Friday, I walked the hallway to Ben's office to see what his schedule was for the weekend, but I found the door closed and the office already vacant and dark. Approaching from the other direction, buttoning an off-white sweater she'd received as a birthday gift from her daughter, Mrs. Matlock was also preparing to depart for the weekend. I asked about Ben's itinerary.

Mrs. Matlock managed Ben's schedule with both the tenacity and efficiency of a Marine drill sergeant, so much so that Ben often joked that he had to schedule his lavatory breaks. At almost any time, chances were near certainty that she knew his whereabouts, even on the weekend, even outside of work.

"He left about a half hour ago," she told me as she arrived at her desk. Glancing toward her appointment book, she added, "He is having dinner at his father's house tonight. And, he had me pick up flowers at the florist this afternoon so he is probably stopping by the cemetery on the way. He's probably there right now."

For as long as I had known Ben, he had visited his mother's grave at least once a month, and he always took a bouquet of white flowers. While at SU, I accompanied him to the cemetery several times, but he always asked me to wait in the car, as it was a very private moment for Ben. Despite these previous excursions, I had never seen Connie Matthews' grave or headstone and wasn't sure I could find it in the cemetery. I decided to meet him at his father's house. That would be best anyway.

* * *

In the twilight of early evening with a bronze floor lamp shining brightly over his shoulder, Carl sat in the front room of the Matthews' home whittling away at a maple branch as I arrived. He wiggled his wrist and the blade in a slow, deliberate manner causing a wood strand to rise up, peel away from the branch, and drop to the floor. Whittling is the process of removing the unnecessary and leaving the essential, a rural art form that teaches one to envision and then seek the beauty or utility within. Carl had been whittling since he was a boy in the mountains of North Carolina in the 1930s. In his calloused, ink-stained hands, he held four feet of a maple branch with an arched bend near the end and a sharp carving knife. Thin strands of wood, chipped away by the steel blade, lay beside his sandaled feet, as a sturdy walking cane with an elaborate handle was emerging in the remaining wood. Focused on the task at hand, he continued to chisel away at the wounded branch while I leaned in over his right shoulder.

"Is that handsome cane for you or Kirk?" I asked as I admired his handiwork.

"I guess we'll find out in good time," he returned drolly.

Carl had lived with Kirk since Kirk sold The Common Sense Print Shop to real estate developers in 1989. Retirement had been a difficult adjustment for both men, but the developers provided a real sense of closure when they demolished the little shop just three days after the two vacated it. Kirk still grumbled that he hadn't even gotten all the ink stains off his fingertips before the bulldozers flattened his life's work. Whenever Ben or I drove them on errands, we generally avoided Gaines Avenue altogether as the location had a depressing effect on both of them. A strip mall occupied the land where the print shop used to stand.

The reminders of forty years of ink and presses were stored in three boxes in a cedar closet on the second floor of the Matthews' home. In the boxes were the samples from thousands of print jobs that once covered the walls of the shop. On a monthly basis, Kirk retrieved some yellowed documents from the boxes, and he and Carl spent the afternoon reminiscing over it. Each piece triggered many memories, not just about the particular scrap of work, but also about that time in their lives. As a gift, Kirk gave Tyler the menus from Dusenberg's that she'd so appreciated on her first trip to the shop. Several of the older ones were framed in her office.

Carl informed me that Kirk was at the grocery store and he had not seen Ben that afternoon, and then he returned to his whittling. He was typically frugal with contributions to any conversation.

"I've never had much use for talk," Carl would often say.

But his words that afternoon would be the most shocking I had heard in many years.

Ben's trip to the cemetery that afternoon was on my mind so I asked Carl if he was working at the print shop when Ben's mother passed away. Her death was just a few days after President Kennedy was assassinated so it was an unusually trying time for all concerned.

"I started working at the print shop that spring," Carl replied. "Connie died in the winter of that year. She was a troubled woman."

"How so?" I asked.

In all the years I'd known the Matthews family, I'd never heard a sour word about Connie Matthews. Kirk and Ben always peppered their remarks about her with warm praise and adoration. My own impression of Connie was that she had been a loving, maternal, and almost saintly woman. I realized that it was human nature to canonize the dead but just what the hell was Carl talking about?

"You're practically family, Pete," Carl said, "so I'll tell you the truth about Connie's death. But, you can't tell anyone. And, you can't tell Ben or Kirk that you know."

"I won't," I pledged.

My curiosity was roused and I wanted to hear the rest, but I was likewise concerned that we were treading on sacred ground. For all I knew, Ben was kneeling before his mother's headstone as we spoke, deep in reflection and prayer.

"Connie was not a well woman. Sometimes she just wouldn't get out of bed for a whole week. Other times, she couldn't sleep at all. Doctors gave her pills to take, but they didn't seem to do any good. Sometimes, she was a little better and sometimes she was crazy.

"She was mentally ill?" I asked.

"She was a troubled woman," Carl said, only willing to repeat his earlier observation. Immediately, in his facial expression, I saw that he was uncomfortable with my medical diagnosis.

"In the 1960s, the medical profession didn't know a lot about mental illness," I said.

It was obvious that Carl wasn't comfortable revealing personal information about Connie Matthews, a woman he only knew for a very short period of time, a very long time ago.

"Kirk sent me to the house one afternoon to check on Connie and she told me she heard screams coming from within the walls. I didn't know what to tell her. Mostly, everyone made excuses for her and covered up her behavior," Carl told me.

"Then it happened," he declared.

Carl's face saddened. His brow furrowed. He shook his head. Carl was recounting a difficult period for everyone involved; a period he didn't normally like to think about.

"Kirk came home from work one night," Carl continued, still shaking his head, "and found Connie lying on the living room floor. She'd taken a whole bottle of pills. Worst part was that little Ben, all of four years old at the time, was at his mother's side crying, shaking her shoulder, and trying to wake her up. He'd been trying all day."

For me, the image of a young Ben, red-faced and sobbing, squatting beside the corpse of his dead mother, nudging her shoulder for hours, was absolutely heartbreaking. At his young age, Ben didn't know about death or the devastation and finality of that moment, but at some instinctive level within his little being he knew something was horribly wrong, that whatever safety and security he felt in her arms was gone. His feelings must've been primal but no less painful. At some point during that long dreadful day, Ben had to realize he was alone.

"Oh, my God," I blurted. "I had no idea. I always thought she died of heart failure. Many times I've encouraged Ben to have his heart checked because I thought cardiac issues ran in the family."

"The doctor was a friend of the family. Even the death certificate says heart failure."

"Are you sure Ben knows?" I asked. "He was only four years old. Surely, he can't remember that day. Maybe he actually believes it was heart failure."

"He knows."

In typical Carl style, he said nothing more. I didn't press for anything more, and he didn't offer anything more. He returned his attention to the maple branch in his hands, chiseling several more little wood strands away that fell onto the floor beside his feet. I remained silent beside him. I'd already heard more than I could handle at that moment. I needed time to process it.

But, just a few minutes after Carl concluded, the screen door flew open and Ben walked in.

"Hey, I didn't expect to see you here," he said, directed at me. "Are you going to join us for dinner?"

"I was. That's why I'm here, at your house," I responded in choppy sentences, flustered by his appearance. "But I was just telling Carl that I, just this moment, remembered a previous commitment."

I needed to get out of there.

"Oh, that's too bad," Ben said.

I squeezed passed him and headed out the door.

"I'll see you Monday," I mumbled.

10.

At the peak of construction on the Empire State Building, more than 500 loads of materials were delivered daily. On each floor, miniature railroad cars on tracks were used to speed distribution. Deliveries of beams were so precisely coordinated that steel was poured and formed in Pittsburgh, marked according to position in the frame, transported to the site, and hoisted into place, sometimes still warm.

With ominous gray clouds and rain, Monday started drearily, a morning when my mattress and pillow conspired against my efforts to start the day. Though my mood was as foreboding as the low pressure system over the city, I managed to extricate myself from the comfort of 800 thread-count sheets, labor through my morning ritual, and commute to the office. As I drove, the city skyline was cloaked with thin slate-like clouds and looked eerily oppressive in the distance, like a medieval wall to keep out invaders. I wanted to turn around and abandon this day, but I resisted that urge and kept driving toward our building. When I arrived in our lobby, feeling damp and soggy and quite uncomfortable despite an umbrella and full-length raincoat, I noticed a stranger in the corner beneath the gallery of Oscar Rhodes photographs. On a different day, I might not have even noticed him, one hundred feet away, but my mood on this bleak day caused me to take note.

The stranger sat parallel to the wall with his head in one hand and his outstretched fingers pressed against his cheekbone, masking his face. He was conspicuous in his unperceptive manner, like he was doing his darnedest not to look in my direction. His identity was shielded by dark-black sunglasses, which could have no other purpose on this overcast day than to provide cover. As I shook the rain off my umbrella, I finally recognized the visitor, tipped off by the pea coat, and I made my way across the lobby hoping for a genial reunion. But, he never looked up, not even as I stood over him.

"Danny," I said, shocked by his presence. He'd been to the old warehouse many times but never to our downtown offices.

"I didn't come to see you. I'm here to see Ben."

He still hadn't look up. Until that very moment, we hadn't spoken to one another in more than three years, but our lack of contact wasn't the result of a disagreement or fall out—we'd just drifted apart. I never felt comfortable around Danny after college; he'd transitioned from someone with so much promise to someone with so little purpose and that was disheartening to me.

"How are you?" I asked.

"Never better," he replied.

His hand was still resting against the side of his face, keeping me from getting a good look at him. From what I could see, he looked thin, unshaven, and a fragment of his college self.

"I pick up the *Weekly* occasionally," he informed me.

"Yeah," I said, hoping this could mark the start of a more cordial conversation.

"It's free and it makes a good drop cloth when I paint around the motel. I don't read the damn thing."

He still hadn't so much as looked up at me.

"Why don't you come up to my office? We'll get some coffee and a muffin and catch up until Ben arrives."

"I'm just here to see Ben," he said.

At that point, I didn't know what else to say. This wasn't the easygoing Danny I roomed with at SU or even the darker, post-college Danny. This one was just plain rude and ornery. He'd made it clear that he didn't want anything to do with me, and maybe I was a relieved he'd given me this easy way out. After all, we didn't have anything to talk about anyway. Before seeing Danny, I was soggy and uncomfortable. Now, I could add disheartened to the list.

I hate gray, wet Mondays. It felt like all the worst conditions of the universe were pulled together on this dank day to test my will and resolve. And, frankly, I just wasn't up to it.

"Okay," I replied, taking the easy way out.

I didn't question his state of mind or demand an explanation for his behavior. In my mind, I figuratively threw my hands up into the air and gave up on him.

I crossed the marble floor of the lobby, climbed the staircase to the balcony and the second floor, and paused at the top to look back at him. He was still seated in the same position.

This was all perplexing to me and contrary to my lifelong observations about people. I believed most people had the capacity to learn and change with the progression of life but marginally, along the fringes, maybe 10 to 15 percent. Their personalities and character were chiseled into the gray granite of their beings while young and didn't change much over time. They were set in their ways by the end of adolescence. Going forward, change was minimal. Other people, some small minority, can't change at all, stubbornly combatant against all influences and closed off from the world, impenetrable. At an early age, they were formed, set, and hardened.

Danny confounded me. He didn't fit either of my categories and belonged in his own category, and a very rare one at that. He'd changed entirely. He was a totally different person than when I met him fifteen years ago. Not a trace of my college roommate remained in that mean-spirited, son of a bitch in the lobby. How did it happen? What caused such drastic change that made him unrecognizable?

* * *

I passed Mrs. Matlock's desk around 9:15am while Danny was in Ben's office. The door was closed and there was no sound coming from his office, not even muffled conversation. Were they talking? Were they whispering? What did Danny want?

"Did Ben give Danny any money?" I asked as I stood, with a confused look on my face, staring at the nameplate with the Publisher designation on Ben's door.

Danny's visit had provoked a sense of loss in me as I truly missed my old college roommate, but I didn't miss him like I hadn't seen him for a while, I missed him like he was dead. Understanding and accepting these feelings was difficult due to the contradiction in front of me; Danny was on the other side of the door, and yet, my old friend didn't exist anymore. He simply wasn't him anymore. I'd never felt like this before. My morning was shot.

"First thing this morning, Ben requested a check payable to Daniel Granger for five thousand dollars," Mrs. Matlock said, a whiff of concern in her voice. "I'm waiting for accounting to tell me it's ready."

Even Mrs. Matlock, rock solid in her methodical ways, seemed unnerved this morning.

Five thousand dollars! Ben had always been a soft touch for Danny, going back many years, but that was the most money he'd ever given him. What was going on? Was Danny in trouble?

Ben's goodwill checks, or more aptly Danny's welfare checks, started a year or so after we began publishing *Cavanaugh Weekly*. On a sporadic basis, Ben sent relatively small sums of money, usually two hundred dollars per check and never even one thousand dollars in a single year. In the fall of 1983, I first learned of Ben's generosity when I found a cancelled check in the envelope with the monthly bank statement. When I asked him about the payment, Ben made me feel guilty.

"He's our friend, Pete, and he isn't doing very well," Ben answered my inquiry in a judgmental tone.

Instantly, I recoiled.

When we were freshmen roommates at college, Danny had such great potential and such a great work ethic that a substantial life seemed unavoidable. After college, his failures always weighed on me like guilt and I don't truly know why. I can only guess that it was just that I wanted so much better for him.

"He was your college roommate," Ben continued, stating the obvious, with a slant to his words that seemed to suggest, in my mind at least, that I should've been the one sending the checks.

"You've seen him," he added. "He looks like hell. We can certainly help him out on occasion."

After that exchange, I never mentioned the checks again. I felt bad about Danny's lot in life. But, a check for five thousand dollars was worthy of mention and even discussion. I needed an explanation. We had a content review meeting for the next issue of *Cavanaugh Business Monthly* scheduled for 2pm that afternoon, and I knew Ben would attend. I'd talk to him after the meeting.

* * *

Fourteen gathered in the main conference room in the early afternoon of what continued to be a gloomy Monday. At times, it rained so hard that the window, spanning floor to ceiling at the south end of the room, looked like a waterfall. Water cascaded downward in a steady stream like the spring thaw in the mountains. The room itself had a soft blue and gray color scheme with a conference table in the center of the room and framed magazine covers lined the walls—not Utopia Publishing product but rather early editions of *Life, Fortune, Time, Harper's Bazaar, Global Times*, etc.

As the meeting progressed, my day continued to advance in a tone similar to the weather. I was unimpressed, to put it mildly, with the material the *Business Monthly* staffers presented that afternoon, but I was careful, due to my awful Monday mindset, not to pass judgment too quickly. As each of the staffers, one by one, presented their ideas, I wondered: Was their work truly uninspired or was my miserable day shading my opinion?

Ben and I sat at opposite ends of the table. He hated meetings because he considered them unnatural and contrived. While I agreed, I also knew we'd never meet our publishing deadlines without them. Searching for a second opinion about the proposals, I watched Ben's expressions and body language and about midway through the meeting I decided his demeanor confirmed my lackluster opinion. Only Laurie Jeffers, the talented veteran writer who'd contributed the most cover articles on our staff, presented an interesting article about three startup businesses and their obstacles during the first year. But, other than that, these other ideas lacked imagination and substance.

When the writers concluded, Ben confirmed my interpretation of his opinion when he suddenly rose from the table to leave the room, stating his opinion most definitively.

"Pete, your staff is wasting my time. Let me know when you've got some material that is worthy of serious review."

And, just that quickly, Ben was gone. Immediately, the room erupted in quiet rebellion as the staffers halfheartedly defended their proposals, though some conceded during their closing arguments that their work was still in a preliminary state.

"I agree with Ben," I advised them. "I wouldn't plunk down my three bucks to read this fluff. Let's do it again Wednesday at this same time and let me suggest that you all find some more substantive material. Laurie, yours is the single exception. Take it further."

I didn't want Ben to get much of a lead on me so I grabbed the materials I'd brought with me and hustled down the corridor after him. If Ben informed Mrs. Matlock that he had some unanticipated free time, she would fill it. Ben hadn't even reached his chair when I charged into his office behind him.

"What is it?" he asked.

"I want to talk to you about Danny," I replied. "I spoke with him this morning and his attitude concerned me. Is he okay?"

"I don't know," Ben said. "He needed money. He said he was in some trouble."

"What kind of trouble?"

"I don't know, Pete, and I didn't ask."

"You didn't ask!" I blurted.

"I didn't want to know. This is Danny we're talking about. It could be bail or drugs or gambling or loan sharks or, maybe, he's got some girl pregnant. Hell, it could be just about anything. I don't know, and I didn't want to know."

"You didn't want to know?"

At that moment, I noticed dark sunglasses on the right, front corner of Ben's desk, beside his table lamp and phone, incongruous amongst the office materials that surrounded them. Danny must've left them behind. On this miserable day, his sunglasses were a better lapse than his coat or hat so I wasn't concerned by his forgetfulness but by the thought that Danny might have left Ben's office in a hurry. Had their meeting ended abruptly? Everything about his visit that day was disconcerting to me.

"I'm running for mayor," Ben said. "I don't want to be party to any mess that Danny has gotten himself into. I gave him some money. He is going to have to work it out on his own."

"You're right," I responded, now recognizing the prudence of Ben's action. "You're wise to distance yourself from him."

With Danny dismissed, Ben told me about the highlights of the first days of his campaign—from influential commitments of support to plans for upcoming fundraisers—while I wondered whether this was an appropriate time to talk about Tyler. On the one hand, it had been such an incredibly depressing day so far that I questioned whether I wanted to risk disappointment. But, on the other hand, Ben was hard to access anymore so could I afford to let this opportunity get by? I couldn't wait ten months until after the election.

As I weighed my arguments, Ben reached into a cardboard shipping box atop the credenza behind him, its brown tape already cut and side flaps open, withdrew a five-inch wide campaign button, and tossed it my way. Its blue lettering on shiny metal read, "Matthews for Mayor in 1992."

"A political campaign isn't officially launched until you hand out the trinkets," Ben remarked. "I expect you to wear that button until I'm elected."

When Ben reached his arm across the credenza, I noticed the photograph of Ben, Tyler, Danny, and me that graced it. It was taken at the SU graduation ceremony in the spring of 1981 and was, perhaps, my last positive memory of Danny. He was dressed in the traditional cap and gown of the graduating class, Tyler in a yellow business suit, and Ben and me in sport coats. In his right hand above his head, Danny waved his diploma triumphantly, and we all had the look of graduates, so naive and youthful and oblivious of the challenges ahead. It was probably the last photograph taken of the four of us together and, from that point forward, the four of us would usually connote Stan in the place of Danny.

I'd seen that photograph many times before, but it suddenly struck me as prophetic because Ben and I were standing on either side of Tyler, as if she were coming between us, dividing us. Swayed by that image, and yielding to a moment of cowardice, I decided I couldn't jeopardize important, long-term friendships. I got up and started toward the door. But, as I walked away, in the back of my mind, I heard Tyler singing that Beatles harmony again, as softly and sweetly as the other day.

"If I fell in love with you/ would you promise to be true/ and help me understand/ cause I've been in love before/ and I found that love was more/ than just holding hands…"

At that moment, her face and voice were as clear to me as that beautiful afternoon at The Parisian.

"I'll take care of it," I mumbled as I turned back toward Ben, reaffirming the commitment I'd made to myself on that afternoon. All the darkness and gloom that shadowed my every movement all day lifted, and I was back in the patio garden at The Parisian on that beautiful day with Tyler, in spirit at least.

"We need to talk about Tyler," I advised him as I approached Ben's desk again. "I've had something on my mind for a while now."

Just as I finished speaking, Ben's intercom buzzed and Mrs. Matlock summoned, "Ben, it's Steve Todd and he says it's urgent that he speak with you."

"Is Tyler alright?" Ben asked as he extended his arm to the phone to respond to Mrs. Matlock.

"Yeah, fine," I said. "Take your call."

"Put him through, Cheryl," Ben instructed her.

Todd, Williams, Caine, and Duncan was a small, four attorney practice when we first enlisted the services of Steve Todd, a graduate of the Law School at SU, to draft our incorporation paperwork more than a decade ago. Over the years, the law firm's association with Utopia Publishing had produced favorable exposure and lucrative clients. Out of both loyalty and gratitude, Steve always handled the Utopia Publishing account personally, and we've always considered him more than our lawyer. During periods of indecision or conflict, Steve had also been a trusted friend and business advisor and one whose opinion we sought on financial and business matters, not just legal issues. Ben put Steve on speaker, and it didn't take either of us long to detect the cheerless tone of his voice.

"We had a break-in at our law offices over the weekend and we've been busy all day taking inventory to determine exactly what client files were taken. Guys, I don't have a total assessment of what's missing yet, but I can tell you that some of the missing files concern Utopia Publishing. I wanted to give you an immediate but preliminary indication and I will get back to you as soon as we know exactly what's missing. So far, the list of missing materials affects about eight clients, but I don't see any common thread or business connection that might tip us off as to a motivation or reason. We have backup copies of the important documents so the only real damage is that which has been inflicted on your confidence and trust. Pete, Ben, I'm really sorry to call with such news. We'll certainly take actions going forward to ensure that this never happens again."

"I'm sorry to hear this news, Steve, but mostly for your sake," Ben offered as condolence to our obviously distraught lawyer.

"After all," Ben added, "we're not smuggling drugs, fencing stolen property, or laundering illicit monies, so why would anyone want our files? We've got nothing to hide."

"It's very possible that the thieves took extra files to disguise their actual target and intent. It's entirely possible the thieves didn't want the Utopia Publishing files but took them as a decoy," Steve posited.

"I don't buy it," I told Ben after Steve hung up. "I'd be much more inclined to believe that the other files were taken as decoys and the Utopia Publishing files were the real target."

"Why?" Ben asked. "There is nothing in our legal files worth stealing."

"Our legal files are stolen from our law firm shortly after you announce your candidacy for mayor. That's not a coincidence; that's a fishing expedition. It's obvious someone wants to know if there are any skeletons in our closet."

188 | Michael Bowe

"You're just paranoid. I've got a great feeling about this campaign and I know I'm going to win the election."

Ben rarely spoke of his mother so he nearly floored me when he mentioned his visit to her grave.

"Last week when I visited my mother's grave, I could feel her watching over me. She has guided me ever since she left this world. She won't let anything get in the way of my winning this election. But, mayor is only the start. I'm going to make a big difference in this world—I've always believed that. Just have faith, Pete. Don't worry so much."

What could I say? I was dumbfounded and speechless. So what if Mayor Greenwood had a well organized, illegally funded, dangerously corrupt, political machine? We've got Ben's dead mother watching over us. I just needed to have a little faith.

But, I also realized that Ben's theory had a real-world basis in logic, and I was just beginning to better understand his viewpoint.

Mayor Greenwood and his corrupt political machine didn't concern Ben. Quite to the contrary, Ben believed the mayor's legacy of corruption and abuse of office would work to Ben's advantage and create a rallying cry amongst honest business people and community leaders, and Ben already saw signs that this segment of the electorate was forming. In Ben's mind, the mayor's corrupt political machine would prove his undoing and, after more than a decade of illicit activities, Mayor Greenwood would finally have his day of reckoning. By the same line of reasoning, an honest, well meaning, though thoroughly inept mayor would be tougher to defeat than the existing corrupt one. If Ben and his deceased mother were right, this dirty mayor had a definite role to play in Ben's victory and continued ascent into national politics.

It was all as it should be. In the Gospel according to Benjamin Matthews, chapter seven, verse one, immoral people and distressing events often served a grand purpose by leading us all, in the end, to a greater good. And, along those same lines, bad things sometimes happened for good reasons and, again in the end, resulted in a greater good. The big picture was always clearer from the higher plain and not always evident to us here on earth. But, from Ben's viewpoint, everything was falling into place. The fact that Mayor Greenwood was Ben's political adversary made Ben more certain of his destiny and the eventual outcome of the election.

"Did you want to talk about Tyler?" Ben asked, remembering I'd mentioned her before the phone call.

"I do," I answered, a telling choice of words.

"Would you have a problem with me pursuing a romantic relationship with Tyler? I wouldn't," I added quickly, "if it would effect our business or friendship."

Ben responded without hesitation. He said he was certain that a relationship between Tyler and me wouldn't have any effect on our business or friendship. He wasn't as positive about the effect it might have on Tyler and me.

"I can't imagine it working out," Ben said. "You both have such different values and priorities."

"What do you mean?"

"You value character and contribution above all else."

I nodded. His assessment was kind, and I couldn't disagree.

"Tyler," he continued, "is entirely different. She is driven and calculating and most concerned about career and success. Frankly, she is a lot like me and that's probably why our relationship ended."

Well, Ben certainly hadn't focused on her best qualities, but I couldn't dispute that assessment either. Again, I nodded.

In conclusion, Ben summed it up succinctly.

"You'll never rank first with Tyler and I don't think you'll be happy under those circumstances. Her weekly ratings reports will always come before anything that's going on in your relationship. That's just Tyler."

That afternoon, Ben blessed a romantic relationship between Tyler and me if we pursued one, but he also gave me, perhaps more importantly, cautionary words to consider about our compatibility. Undeniably, Ben knew the two of us, Tyler and me, better than anyone and so I was, once again, uncertain of my own heart and intentions.

I had Ben's blessing and thoughts, which were both important to me, and I also had a lot of thinking to do.

* * *

Sebastian Biddle made his first $100 million before he could legally order a mixed drink in most states. At the age of sixteen while a technology prodigy at Stanford University, Sebastian created a software program that enabled large databases to operate faster and more efficiently by employing a methodology he codenamed "Optimal Processing" during development. His software was revolutionary and a game changer for large companies. Within two years of the launch of his company, Optimal, more than 25 percent of Fortune 500 companies had implemented his software to manage their enormous customer databases. By the time he reached the age of thirty, that percentage rose to over 60 percent and Sebastian Biddle became the seventh richest person on the planet with a net worth of $21 billion.

Global Times Magazine heralded his new technology in a lengthy article about Sebastian entitled, "Brilliant Beyond His Years," that included the following excerpt, "Last month, off the radar of everyday working people, in the enigmatic world of computers that few understand, eighteen year old Sebastian Biddle changed the business world with the launch of his new database software that improves the management of enormous catalogs of data. Most of us will not notice the effects of this product launch, but this brilliant, young entrepreneur has single-handedly improved customer service at many corporations, and all our lives will be unknowingly improved in this new, more efficient, hi-tech world."

Sebastian Biddle and Ben Matthews first met in 1982, when Sebastian scouted four large cities, Cavanaugh included, as potential sites for his start-up company. After visiting with many community leaders in Cavanaugh and hearing the name Ben Matthews and his publication, *Cavanaugh Weekly*, mentioned often, Sebastian made an unscheduled visit to our office. Kindred spirits, they bonded immediately. After selecting Cavanaugh, Sebastian was quoted as saying he chose the city for two reasons: the availability of highly skilled technology workers and Ben Matthews. Ben was best man at Sebastian's wedding to his wife, Isabella, in Florence, Italy in 1986 and Godfather to his daughter, Mira, two years later.

A decade later, on First Street in downtown Cavanaugh, Optimal Tower, a project financed by Sebastian, was scheduled to hold its grand opening ceremony on April 13, 1992. Normally, the grand opening of any newly constructed high-rise tower was a widely anticipated event, but this grand opening would be more celebrated than normal, making the city of Cavanaugh the focus of the entire world. Once opened, Optimal Tower would claim the title of World's Tallest skyscraper at one thousand five hundred and thirty-five feet. Joining an already impressive skyline, Optimal Tower would give the city of Cavanaugh its signature landmark, and many also considered the grand opening as marking the arrival of Cavanaugh as a world-class American city.

Even in his early thirties, Sebastian had the appearance of a young software geek who spent many hours each day in a dark room behind a glowing computer screen writing code. Thin and pale with scattered blonde hair, he looked like he checked the mirror every morning to see if it was time for his first shave. Though ridiculously rich, his regular attire consisted of blue jeans, T-shirts, baseball caps, and often sandals. He traveled wherever he wanted without security or an entourage because he wasn't someone anyone noticed. Two days after Ben's announcement, Sebastian, once again, showed up at our offices unscheduled.

"You know you have my full support," Sebastian told Ben as they sipped coffee in Ben's office. "Nothing would make me happier than seeing that mobster in the mayor's office out on the street."

"Your vote is enough," Ben replied, "but this is going to be a very close election so any additional thoughts or ideas you have would be much appreciated."

"That's why I'm here."

Ben knew Sebastian would be an ardent supporter and make an obnoxiously large campaign contribution but his unscheduled appearance in Ben's office signaled that Sebastian had some sort of nonmonetary support in mind, and Ben was brimming with excitement at that prospect.

Sebastian continued. "The grand opening of Optimal Tower will happen in three months, and the event will receive worldwide attention. It'll be the tallest skyscraper in the world. Locals will be enthralled. I want to use the event and the occasion to bolster your campaign."

"How so?"

"You'll be front and center at the event, my friend, by my side during the ribbon-cutting ceremony and the guest of honor with the keynote address after lunch, while I make certain that the mayor's role is embarrassingly insignificant. To all observers, it'll seem like you are already Mayor of Cavanaugh."

"I like it," Ben replied, beaming at the prospect of upstaging the mayor during such a significant event, knowing this plan has the potential to turn the election in his favor.

"I will, however, expect your keynote address to be all about me," Sebastian said, chiding his friend.

"You've got it."

Both men laughed like devious, young boys, gleeful over the hilarious playground prank they just concocted.

*   *   *

For me, the news of my father's passing, more than nine years ago, was devastating and accentuated by the fact that our unpleasant parting two-holiday seasons prior was suddenly our last interaction. Not only did I remember where I was and what I was doing when I heard the news about my father, but my chest still tightened and I still had trouble breathing whenever I thought back to that phone call. In it, my mother's words were frail and dripping sorrow and her message stubbornly refused to fade into the gray area of my mind. On account of our fall out, my father's death could never become a simple milestone marking the progression of life and the passing of the family name through the lineage. Quite to the contrary, I remained haunted by my regret. Though I loved and respected my father all my life, I committed the cardinal sin for a child; I let my father pass while he was angry and disappointed with me. So I lived with that heartache.

Many times I had prayed that I'd never receive another phone call like that one, never again shoulder such regret, and never again carry a casket weighted by more than remains. Most unfortunately for me, it would happen yet again.

* * *

Ten days had passed since Danny's unscheduled appearance in our lobby as well as my conversation with Ben about Tyler. Aside from scanning our lobby for dark, mysterious strangers each morning, I'd pushed Danny's visit out of my mind and dismissed his behavior as typically irresponsible. In a similar act of avoidance, I'd also pushed aside my romantic inclinations concerning Tyler by falling back on the mantra of the terminally lonely, "If it is meant to be, it will be." That way, in both cases, I didn't have to do anything.

In times of personal conflict, I usually responded by throwing myself into my work. So true to form, I turned my focus to the hectic pace required for staying on the profitable side of Utopia Publishing's many weekly deadlines. During the ten day period I avoided thoughts of Tyler and Danny, Stan and I collectively released two *Cavanaugh Weekly's* and, in my opinion, one of the best issues of the *Cavanaugh Business Monthly* ever.

I don't deny my behavior was avoidance. But, I could always count on affirmation and satisfaction from the written word. It was the one thing I truly believed in.

Early one Thursday afternoon, with a flurry of deadlines met and a cyclical ebbing of energy occurring in the hallways, I was not so busily basking in the warm glow of journalistic accomplishment when my office telephone rang and I answered it. It was a familiar voice, raspy and unique, but one I couldn't identify immediately.

"I need to speak with Pete Dalton," the voice said. "Please connect me with Pete Dalton. It's very urgent."

Obviously, the caller wasn't aware that he'd dialed my direct, private line and was expecting an operator to redirect his call. He seemed both distressed and confused.

"This is Pete Dalton," I answered reluctantly, to which the caller responded with a grief stricken wail, "Oh thank God it's you, Pete."

It was Bob Cooper and "Oh God" was right. I hadn't talked to him in more than five years so my immediate premonition was that this call was really bad news. He wasn't calling to suggest we meet for tacos at Maria's.

"Danny is dead," he told me, struggling to speak the words, fighting back his anguish. "He was shot at the motel."

My chest tightened and I struggled for each breath like I was suddenly at high altitude. I recognized the symptoms immediately and braced myself. Losing my father was more devastating than losing my close friend and yet my physical reaction felt the same.

Oh no, not again, I thought.

"I spent the morning at the motel with the police," Coop said. "They don't know much."

Danny's apartment was behind the motel office, away from the motel guests' rooms, so it wasn't necessarily suspect that no one saw or heard anything. But, even if someone had, The Bayside Motel wasn't the kind of place where witnesses volunteered information. Most guests had reasons to avoid the police and remain anonymous, hiding in the shadows, out of sight. Guests came to the motel to "get away" but not in the same sense as vacationers at other establishments.

Coop sounded devastated. I felt worse.

"Will you call his parents?" Coop asked me.

I couldn't think of a more unpleasant task, but I consented. Danny was my college roommate, and I knew his parents better than anyone in Cavanaugh, though I'd only met them in person on two occasions. My call to their home would be the darkest moment of their family history, far surpassing any family crisis that had come before it. It would scar their memories in the same way that my father's death had scarred mine. I could only hope that neither of his sisters answered the phone. I couldn't bear to hear their sweet voices or try to navigate past them to their parents with this terrible news.

* * *

As soon as the first wave of shock subsided, I called Tyler.

"I know," she said, tipped off by the despair in my voice.

She continued. "I saw the story on the wire services just a few minutes ago. I was mustering the courage to call you. I just couldn't find the words."

I told her I hadn't seen Ben all day, but I suggested that we should all get together that night. She agreed and told me she didn't know how she would get through her news program that evening.

"I can't read this story about Danny," she elaborated. "I'll breakdown on live television."

"Maybe it'd be best if you took the evening off," I suggested.

After I hung up, I informed Mrs. Matlock of the death of our friend and she began trying to contact Ben to ask him to call me, though his agenda that afternoon would make it difficult. Ben was scheduled to give the keynote address at a summit of high-tech manufacturers at the convention center later that afternoon and he was probably meeting with organizers and corporate executives in one of the smaller meeting rooms at the center.

"Have him call me after his speech," I told her.

It was after 5pm when Mrs. Matlock finally routed Ben's call to me. After I informed him of Danny's death, the line was silent for several minutes and then he offered an observation.

"It shouldn't come as a surprise," he said. "Danny's associates in Condor are not people of normal life expectancies who die of natural causes. I've never understood why he chose that life. I guess we can assume the five thousand dollars didn't fix his problem."

* * *

Concerned about Tyler, I waited until almost 6pm and then I walked to the lunchroom where a television set was located so I could watch her broadcast.

"Good evening," Tyler said as the program began and I settled into an uncomfortable, molded plastic chair at the lunch table. Based on her determined mindset, I wasn't surprised to see her on the air.

"Our top story tonight," she continued, "Danny Grainger, the former quarterback sensation at Stanton University, was found shot to death in a motel in Condor where he worked as its manager. Wearing only boxer shorts and a T-shirt, Grainger was found lying face down in a pool of blood by a motel guest at 9am this morning. The cause of death was two bullet wounds in the chest. None of the motel guests reported hearing the shots late last night or seeing or hearing anything suspicious between 1am and 3am when police believe the murder occurred. There was no evidence of a break-in, robbery, struggle, or confrontation of any kind, and the police say they have not identified any potential suspects or motive. Captain Tommy Bryant, a twenty-year veteran of the Condor Police Department, told me that the department planned to conduct a thorough investigation of the murder, and he appealed to the public for help."

Captain Bryant, an overweight man with wire-rimmed glasses and a five-dollar haircut, replaced Tyler on the television screen. In a very business-as-usual manner, the captain said, "We ask any citizen who has information about this crime to contact us at Condor Police headquarters. We want the killer swiftly brought to justice."

Tyler returned and spoke extensively about the highlights of Danny's college football career and the records he set, while file footage of his glory days rolled on the monitor behind her. In five similar film clips, Danny threw long, arching passes to wide receivers down field that caught the football without breaking stride on the way to the end zone. Going back to his early days, Tyler recited a long list of accolades including MVP in two state championship games and his selection as a second team all-American. At the conclusion, the monitor switched from action footage to a still frame, head shot of Danny, young, strong, and smiling brightly, on the sidelines of a SU football game, with the caption "Danny Grainger 1959 – 1992."

"Daniel Patrick Grainger, dead at the young age of just thirty-two years old," Tyler said, closing the piece.

*   *   *

Danny was buried in a wooded cemetery in Kimble, PA, just a few miles from the shoebox home where he grew up and the high school he attended. Kimble was a small town north of Pittsburgh that was typical of the rural industrial boroughs that surrounded Steel City. Nothing was freshly painted or gleaming from a recent wash, and everything was covered in grime and soot. Even the rain in Kimble had little cleansing effect. Tall, thin smokestacks and oak and maple trees encircled the town, and its roads were dotted with potholes, some packed with a stony, black mend, others cavernous. Life in Kimble was a hardscrabble existence, but residents were unrelenting in their belief in God, family, and hard work, and unapologetic about the small town they loved like a dirty orphan child.

As I walked the main street of the town, I imagined Danny striding along those same streets as a youngster, determined to excel on the gridiron so he could compete at the college and professional levels and make his way out of that town. Danny was, I speculated, simultaneously driven by his desire for athletic success and the fear of the gray overalls and union cards that awaited locals after high school graduation. Danny's father, Joe Grainger, worked for thirty years as a furnace operator at a small foundry that made metal parts for the auto industry, a blue-collar, industrial job that offered little opportunity or mobility. Seeing his hometown helped me to better understand the determination and grit that compelled Danny to work so hard during his freshman year when he rehabilitated his knee for his comeback.

Along with my deeper understanding of Danny's childhood, I also concocted my own theory as to why Danny moved to Condor after college graduation when his football career was so clearly over and his childhood dreams had been shattered by injuries. In his mind, Danny had failed to fulfill his dream; the dream that got him out of bed on the cold Pennsylvania mornings of his youth and finally out of that gritty town altogether. Returning to Kimble meant accepting a life he'd pledged to overcome, returning meant accepting failure on far too grand a scale. Even Danny would rather flee than return and admit his failure. Ironically, Danny moved to the small town of Condor, a northwestern fishing town not that different from his hometown if you substituted weathered docks and fishing boats for the aged factories and cars. Danny had gone home in the only way he could, until now.

About fifty mourners gathered at the cemetery for Danny's funeral, many in their early thirties with small children at knee and hip level, and I suspected they were childhood friends. They knew Danny during his early glory days as an all-state quarterback, the light and carefree days before the injuries. Waiting for the service to begin, I overheard several conversations with the common theme being that none of them had heard from Danny in a decade. They wondered what had happened to him. And still, everyone came to grieve the loss of the Danny Grainger they once knew, much like me.

One woman remarked that she'd always remember Danny with a broad smile on his face. "He was always cheerful and upbeat," she observed sadly.

Throughout the service, I watched the Grainger family from a distance as they struggled with the painful reality that their only son and older brother was gone forever. I had never witnessed so much grief previously, not at my father's funeral, not at any funeral. In the devastated faces of the Grainger family, I saw how hard it was to accept the death of a loved one at such an early age, long before the gray hair and wrinkles, during the prime of life. Mrs. Grainger, in particular, was the picture of sorrow—her face tearstained, her eyes swollen. When I approached to offer my condolences, she collapsed into my arms, requiring my support to keep her upright. Otherwise, she would've sunk into the same loose dirt as her child. Her body was limp, as her spirit had abandoned it. Holding her, I searched for words that might be a comfort, but there were none. At that moment, and possibly for the first time, words absolutely failed me. In my life, I had never held so much pain in my arms.

"Danny was special to me, Mrs. Grainger," I whispered as I passed her spiritless body to the waiting arms of her husband. Joe Grainger looked equally vacant.

I didn't say it just to be kind. I meant it. The Danny I roomed with at SU was a special person; one I may never fully understand, but also one I will never forget. He may have passed right through my life, but he certainly made his mark.

* * *

With thoughts of Danny's funeral fresh in our minds and no word of progress in his murder investigation, Tyler and I decided to visit Captain Tommy Bryant at the Condor Police Department so we set-off early one morning for the scenic, two-hour drive to the coast.

Along railroad tracks and rural roads, it was still common to come upon pastoral scenes where the sides of barns were painted as advertisements for beer, refrigerators, aspirin, cigarettes, and white bread—American-made products for American families. Expansive, animated, and brightly colored with catchy slogans, the murals blended into the farmlands while subtly delivering their sales pitch. The brands were household names like Kellogg's, Lucky Strike, Coca-Cola, Sunbeam, Schlitz, and Sears. Their heyday was the late 1940s through the late 1960s so what remained was faded by time. Though aged and peeling, they were still beautiful and artistic, and rustic reminders of simpler times.

About a mile outside of Condor on Route 19, the roadside wall of a red barn was painted in a stars and stripes motif with the slogan "Hayes for Mayor in 1976" atop a gently waving flag. Smartly situated beside a sharp bend in the road where cars slowed to twenty miles per hour, I noticed this mural as I passed its field and pulled over to absorb its splendor. Its colors were washed out like blue jeans after 100 cycles in a washer, but the words "Keep Condor a Small Town" were clear enough and apparently indicative of a long-ago campaign against growth and change.

In 1976, Condor was a picturesque town on the bay with three thriving trades, fishing, logging, and tourism, providing employment for its residents and tax revenues for infrastructure and community services. Its downtown area bustled as businesses and families alike enjoyed a quaint, comfortable setting that could have been the subject matter of a Norman Rockwell painting. Streets were clean, parks were green, police and fire were well equipped, and schools were effectual. In a landslide result, Colton Hayes won the mayoral election in 1976 and again in 1980 with the promise to keep Condor unchanged, as it was, a classic tourist town and a great place to live and raise a family.

Unfortunately for Mayor Hayes and the citizens of Condor, the town didn't fare well shielded from the rest of the world. The fishing industry shifted to larger, more modern fleets and moved to the big city where the docks and processing facilities were better suited to the larger ships. The logging industry gradually moved away from the thinned forests that surrounded the town in favor of denser forests further inland. Both industries still existed in Condor but in withered states. Without the tax dollars from fishing and logging, tourism also suffered, and the town slowly wilted from its former idyllic presence. In life, it seems that standing still is just as risky as moving forward—so much passes by.

In the sleepy town of Condor, the 1980s was a decade of decline as the town lost its prosperous, well-maintained aura and slipped into shoddiness and disrepair. Though still surrounded by the stunning, natural beauty that originally lured residents and tourists, the town itself became a worsening eyesore. After employers left the area, residents followed until its population had decreased by almost 40 percent. The section of town now known as "The Deed," the seediest, low life area where Danny lived, worked, and died, emerged as a byproduct of the decay. The reviled Deed was truly the antithesis of the beloved Condor of 1976.

In 1989, at the age of seventy-four, Colton Hayes moved away from Condor, the small town where he was born and raised and once presided as mayor.

*   *   *

Emergency Services—Condor's police department and fire department headquartered together in a two-story building that dated back to the age of flappers—was clearly a bureaucrat's solution to the town's budgetary shortfalls. Further evidence of the financial crunch were two antique fire trucks with expandable, twenty foot ladders mounted on the sides, threadbare firefighting gear, early 1980s era police cruisers, and large, front doors of the fire station that opened and closed by a manual pulley system, all equipment and systems that were outdated and obsolete. As Tyler and I made our way through the building, the aged state of everything around us caused me to wonder whether this town could mount a comprehensive murder investigation. Putting out a house fire would certainly take priority over solving Danny Grainger's murder.

In the cramped confines of the headquarters, fire equipment and personnel occupied the first floor, and law enforcement personnel occupied the attic-like second floor. Near the rear of the building, we found Captain Bryant at his desk with a large basket of French fries in front of him and four junior officers around him.

Speaking in a large, resounding voice, Captain Bryant told the group, "We got him out of his truck, made him take off his pants, and walk home in his boxers. How's that for justice? I can't wait to hear what Sally had to say when her husband arrived home stinking drunk and wearing only boxer shorts."

The group roared with laughter as we approached.

"Can I help you?" Captain Bryant offered as he dipped a handful of fries in ketchup and lifted them to his mouth.

I wondered where he got French fries at 9:30am, but I asked the more pressing question.

"We'd like to talk to you about the Danny Grainger case."

"Tyler Danzig from the TV news," the captain observed as he waved the officers off. "You must be the cameraman," he added, directed at me, revealing more of his sleuthing abilities than I realized at the time.

"No, I was a friend of Danny Grainger," I told him.

"That's going to be a really tough one to solve," Tommy, as he insisted we call him, began once we'd dispensed with introductions. "No weapon, no fingerprints, no witnesses, no physical evidence, and too many motives. We don't have a whole hell of a lot to go on."

Captain Bryant was an experienced police officer, a sincere and kind man, forthcoming about the status of his investigation, but also slow, unmotivated, and distracted, and I didn't get the impression he cracked a lot of cases. It had been said that whether you believed you could or believed you couldn't, you were probably right. It seemed that Captain Bryant believed he couldn't. Many times during our conversation he returned to the difficulties surrounding the case and the reasons why he believed it would be a hard one to solve. Captain Bryant wasn't optimistic, and he spent more time lowering our expectations than talking about the crime or the investigation. We conversed for about an hour at the police station, enough time for the captain to finish his fries and move on to a couple of jelly doughnuts, and then we got in his police cruiser and drove to The Bayside Motel so we could view the crime scene.

The motel was quiet and still that morning. We didn't see any of the motel guests as we made our way along the walkway toward Danny's rear apartment. In the room, on the far side of the bed, there was a bloodstain in the brown carpet, much larger than I had expected, as if every ounce of Danny's blood had spilled from his body, but the remainder of the room was in a normally messy condition, at least for the Danny I knew. I looked for anything that might seem out of place or unusual for Danny. Aside from the bloodstain, his room was as I expected.

"Why did you say too many motives?" I asked.

"Your friend was no Boy Scout," he said as he wiped a dab of jelly filling from his cheekbone, having finally noticed it in the dresser mirror. "I hope that's not news to you, honey?" he directed at Tyler.

The captain continued. "There are plenty of ways to get into trouble in Condor and Danny dabbled in more than a few of them. The word on the street is that Danny was throwing money around like a sweepstakes winner in the days before he was killed. I don't know where he got the money, but getting it or having it was probably what got your friend killed. And, either way, I'm left with about a hundred suspects."

We thanked the captain for spending his morning with us and departed Condor for our return trip to Cavanaugh. In the car, we reviewed what we had learned about the murder itself and the investigation. As we conversed, we realized that Tyler and I had both reached the same unsatisfying conclusion: Captain Bryant wouldn't solve the Daniel Grainger murder case unless the killer walked into the police station with the murder weapon in hand and confessed to the crime. It seemed, at that moment at least, that we would never know what happened to Danny on his last night at the motel.

"I'm hungry," I said as we drove.

"He had the opposite effect on me," Tyler responded.

* * *

For the next few days, I wasn't myself; part of it was the normal mourning anyone would experience after the death of a close friend, but part of it was something entirely different—a gnawing feeling deep inside my gut. Several times a day, I found myself leaving the office to wander the crowded downtown streets, oblivious of the people I passed on the sidewalk, and all the while contemplating Danny's life and death: What did it mean, what was my role, and what could I learn from it? Gradually, I came to interpret the gnawing feeling as my inner voice telling me that I had to find some level of understanding, create some sense of closure, and establish some feeling of peace. Anything would be better than what I currently felt.

I walked. And, the more I walked, the more I felt I was slowly making my way toward understanding. Just as I'd told his mother at his graveside, Danny was special to me. The more I thought about it, the more I realized how lucky I was to have had him as my roommate. Even now, I wouldn't change that. He introduced possibility into my life at a time when I was too young to appreciate it, or even recognize how rare it was. At a young age, Danny had such optimism and talent. As I walked, I noted the similarities between Joe Golden and Danny Grainger, and I concluded that some people were destined for meteoric lives, magnificently bright and awesome for a while until they burned out and faded to black. That initial brilliance was impossible to maintain as it consumed so much.

I walked some more. I thought about Danny's ever-present smile, his sculptured physique, his warm, honest nature, his God-given abilities, his determined work ethic, and his belief in fair play, and I realized that he had the stuff of mythological heroes. Confronted by formidable foes and insurmountable odds, he stood tall, strong, and defiant, confident in his abilities, and always willing to battle. As long as he could stand on his feet, he battled. Wearing pads and a helmet, he battled. Blood spilled, bones broke, knees snapped and, all the while, he battled. On a gridiron in a stadium, he battled. Danny was natural and beautiful until he was tragic and mythic. And, even in the end, his long fall and eventual demise was the stuff of legends.

More than a month had passed since Danny's death and I was finally beginning to understand what was gnawing at me. I was, after all, first and foremost a writer. It was who I was, what I did, and what I loved. And yet, for more than five years, my name hadn't graced a byline in any of our publications. I hadn't done any research, chased any leads, developed any sources, confirmed any hunches, or crafted an article in all that time. In retrospect, I'd spent the better part of the last decade editing other people's handiwork.

The subject of Danny Grainger's life and death was an untold story that needed to be told as only I could tell it. I already knew portions of his story, but there were plenty of details that needed to be mined. I needed to dig into Danny's life in Condor, his daily activities and his associates, and, most particularly, his final days. I needed to understand what happened to Danny after college. When, where, how, and why had Danny gotten so lost? How does an all-American boy like Danny end up broken and disillusioned? What caused him to change so dramatically? I had to tell his story. I owed it to Danny and myself.

But don't get me wrong. It wasn't that I planned to solve the murder, avenge his death, or do anything heroic. I wasn't a superhero, a peace officer, or even a detective. Unlike Danny at his best, I was not mythic. I was a writer. I just wanted to follow the story and tell the tale, wherever it led, whatever the facts. When all was said and done, I'd find my salvation by putting pen to paper and working it out within the 8½ by 11 inch confines of my craft. That's what writers do. It was all so obvious to me now that I couldn't understand why it had taken me so long to figure it out.

Walking some more, I remembered a line from a children's book that my mother had read to me countless times at bedtime in our home, entitled *An Eagle at Sea*. I could still hear my mother's voice recite the words...

"Instinctive feelings always serve as a clue, what comes to one naturally is what he should do."

For me, that meant writing. I would tell Danny's story.

11.

Despite significant precautions, five men died during the construction of the Empire State Building: two fell from heights, one in a blasting accident, and two from impact injuries, struck by a hoist and a truck. When human lives are part of the calculation, the cost of progress can't be measured in simple dollar terms.

The mayor's office at City Hall was a grand round room with state and county flags lining its perimeter and an elaborate seal of the city of Cavanaugh dyed into its carpet. It was an official chamber that demanded decorum, civil discourse, and manners. Though some said the office and its occupant were contradictory, Ben liked to quip that the décor was perfect because the mayor walked all over the city on a regular basis. Having occupied it for eleven years, Mayor Greenwood called it the "almost oval office" and his "second home."

"What's his mood?" Roy Zacharius, the mayor's campaign manager, asked the mayor's secretary as he marched passed her desk toward the office door.

"Same pissed-enough-to-spit-nails mood he has been in since Ben Matthews announced his candidacy," she answered.

Zach, as he was known around City Hall, was a short, thin man in his mid-forties with thinning, flyaway hair that prompted one columnist to brand him the "Albert Einstein of political strategists." He entered the mayor's office, paused to lock the latch behind him, and then took his seat in front of the mayor's massive, dark oak desk.

"We've been busy," he informed his boss. "We've got a lot to talk about."

"I hope so," the mayor returned snippy, like a coffee drinker before his morning fix. "We got zilch from their legal files so I'm more concerned than ever."

While he spoke, the mayor's intercom buzzed.

"Hold my calls," he barked as he slammed the white button on his phone. "No interruptions!"

"Let me put this situation in perspective for you, Zach," the mayor said in a snippy tone. "Each election, a whole new crop of well-intentioned, do-gooders enters political races because they think they can make a difference. Almost without exception, do-gooders don't fare well in politics because they're not willing to do what it takes to succeed. Do you know what it takes to succeed in politics?" the mayor asked in a condescending tone.

"Yes I do," Zach answered, as any campaign manager better, but the mayor continued anyway.

"You've got to raise buckets of money, make unpleasant, personally compromising deals, and kiss a lot of ass. That, my boy, is what it takes to win elections."

"Ben Matthews," Zach interjected, trying to show the mayor he understands his concerns, "is already well-known and popular because he has championed his causes from the safe harbor of his publishing company for a decade. Though most do-gooders don't pose serious political threats, Ben Matthews does."

"He is one dangerous little prick."

"Let me assure you," Zach said, "I understand the importance of neutralizing his campaign early. We have a strategy planned."

Still grumbling, the mayor informed Zach that he'd just read a recent public opinion poll that showed the Matthews campaign ahead by a margin of 13 percent.

"I haven't seen that poll," Zach said, "but it's not unusual for new candidates to enjoy favorable polling results. It's what we call the honeymoon phase," Zach continued. "That'll change shortly."

The mayor grimaced as Zach handed him a black notebook and introduced it by saying, "We need to go on the offensive."

The notebook contained scripts for TV ads and renderings for outdoors ads aimed at discrediting the Matthews campaign before it gained momentum. The ads highlighted the mayor's long tenure in his job and praised his proven track record while subtly questioning Ben's lack of political experience. On the last page, the financial statement for the mayor's reelection campaign showed more than adequate monies to launch their offensive.

"We will plant a seed of doubt in the minds of the voters and the Matthews campaign will falter," Zach stated. "We've got several potent tag phrases like 'Stay the course' and 'The Mayor's Office is No Place for Beginners.'"

"I'm getting more nervous every day," the mayor warned his already nervous strategist, expressing displeasure with the campaign materials and the ideas in general. In reality, it wasn't the campaign strategies that bothered him—it was his opponent. Mayor Greenwood wasn't comfortable with Ben as his opponent in his bid for reelection because he was too popular in the city for his liking. He wanted a way to force him out of the race, something scandalous that would end his challenge.

"I hate that little prick," the mayor shouted. "Dig deeper."

"The Matthews campaign has their first three fund raisers planned for the next two weeks, and Ben Matthews hasn't even hired a campaign manager yet," Zach informed the mayor. "I believe we have an eight week window of opportunity to crush their campaign. These ads will do that."

"We need something more decisive."

"Relax, Dale, we will anticipate and counter every move they make. Ben Matthews is a political novice with absolutely no chance at winning this election."

Though Zach wouldn't know it until the following morning, his credibility was about to be deeply undermined.

* * *

The first fundraiser for the Matthews campaign was held ten hours later in the Platinum Room of the Chancellor Hotel. As a sign of support, our company reserved a table in front of the podium so Ben would look out at familiar faces. Laurie Jeffers, Stan Tilden, Oscar Rhodes, Mrs. Matlock, and me were joined by our invited guests that included Steve Todd, Tyler, and a second anchorwoman from her station.

"It's a good thing we don't have to pay for these seats," Oscar remarked in a whispered comment to Tyler after having noticed the price on the tickets. "I couldn't afford it."

"That's how it works, Oscar," Tyler informed him. "Most of these seats are paid for by corporations who write them off. Very few individuals would pay $500 a seat if it came out of their own pocket. Without the deep-pocketed, many strings-attached, support of major corporations, our political system would grind to a halt."

As I glanced about the ballroom, beneath the brilliant crystal chandeliers that lit the grand hall, I spotted some of the wealthiest and most prominent people in the city and I had two observations. First, a demarcation line was being clearly drawn that evening between the mayor's supporters and Ben's, and second, the bloody war, which would surely follow, was not nearly as lopsided as I would've thought. I knew Ben could count on strong support from the foot soldiers among the voters, but I was pleasantly surprised by the support being shown among the ranks of officers.

As I further surveyed the attendees, many of them having graced the covers and inner pages of our publications, I became less clear about whether Ben's army marched to support Ben or oppose the mayor, a distinction that might or might not have significance as time passed. Either way, echoing Tyler's cynical outlook, there was a lot of money in the room that evening, and I had to believe Ben's campaign was off to a lucrative start.

"I'm going to write an article about Danny," I told Stan and Tyler as the orchestra began playing "Fly Me to the Moon." "I need to find some sense of understanding and closure concerning Danny's life in Condor and his death. I'm troubled by it."

"As a journalist, you're on shaky ground," Stan warned me. "You're too close to the subject matter. Even more importantly," Stan continued, "you might not like what you find."

"I know," I replied. "I'm pretty sure I won't. It will be a dark and seedy tale about one man's wasted potential, ugly descent, and eventual demise."

"But," Stan added, "it's certainly got all the elements of a great article, I'll give you that."

"I want to work with you on the article," Tyler chimed in.

She continued in a serious tone.

"I think it will help me, too. I'm not dealing with his death all that well. I can't come to terms with the idea that I will never see him again."

Tyler wore a sleeveless, sky-blue, sequined dress that evening that complemented her brown tresses and azure blue eyes. Looking stunning, it wasn't an exaggeration to say that she turned every head in the ballroom as she entered. With the sounds of the orchestra behind her voice as she addressed me, all I could think about was how the nickname "Old Blue Eyes" was so horribly wasted on Sinatra.

"I think it would be a good idea for us to work together," I told her, disguising my real thoughts, unless "work" was a euphemism.

Just that quickly, Tyler's blue eyes had erased all notion of journalism from my mind and made me, instead, want to put my arms around her and pull her close. Since that was inappropriate at that moment, I opted for the next best thing—I asked her to dance, though ballroom dancing wasn't exactly in my wheelhouse. I was either moved or desperate; in matters of the heart, it's difficult to tell.

As we stepped onto the dance floor, that heavenly spirit who forsook my cause at the fountain suddenly came to my aid and induced the orchestra to play a sultry version of "The Way You Look Tonight," one of Tyler's favorites.

"Oh, I love this song," she purred as she moved forward and embraced me.

Looking back, I suppose most men and a lot of women had noticed us on the dance floor. It would've been hard not to notice Tyler. She was her own spotlight, shining brightly. And, all things considered, I should've felt awkward and self-conscious, dancing with the most beautiful woman at the fundraiser while a few hundred watched. But, amazingly enough, I wasn't. I was so focused on Tyler that I forgot all about the crown and the circumstances. Granted an interlude with an angel, I was determined to enjoy it.

For four perfect minutes, I floated, caressed by soft strings and gentle piano, warmed by Tyler's radiant smile, adrift in her deep blue eyes, and completely oblivious to any external concerns or attention. We moved all around the dance floor, from the middle to every corner and back again, swaying ever so gently, like palm trees in a light ocean breeze. Though late winter in Cavanaugh, I felt warmed and soothed like a tropical paradise.

On second thought, I'm sure everyone noticed Tyler. They had to! She was the physical embodiment of every man's ideal woman and every woman's aspiration. Who wouldn't notice her? If perchance anyone noticed me, I'd guess they spent the rest of the evening contemplating whether or not they'd ever experienced the bliss surely apparent on my face. It was a moment that would forever shine brighter than the rest in my mind's recollection of the year.

"That was nice," Tyler remarked as the song concluded.

One of the benefits of the written word is the preserving of thoughts, feelings, and events for posterity. My personal history had always remained clearer and truer for me when pen had met paper and the facts recorded in the twenty-six letters of our alphabet. That was why I kept a journal. After our dance, I put felt pen to linen napkin beneath the tablecloth and, unbeknownst to my tablemates, scribbled lines of poetry that captured my elation.

> life can end in a heartbeat
> love can begin with just a smile
> we can lose or find in a single moment
> all that makes our life worthwhile
>
> i believe that in the end
> lifetimes are defined by moments
> and that minutes from a decade
> can provide the real significance
>
> and i believe
> that in my twilight years
> when i have lived long
> and my time remaining
> is merely flickering embers,
> still aglow
> from the burning fire
> that once illuminated
> my passionate youth
>
> the brightest of all moments
> that will define this man's existence
> will be your smile at our first meeting
> and the embrace of our first dance

* * *

After prime rib, baked potatoes, and asparagus spears, Ben graciously accepted the event organizer's invitation to address the crowd. He began rallying the troops as only he could. Most of his speech was boilerplate material about zoning, long-term planning, intelligent growth, quality-of-life investments, the proposed light-rail system, and an overall strategy to prepare the city for the challenges of the new millennium.

Ben was interrupted often by polite applause as the crowd showed their appreciation for his ideas. It wasn't until about midway through his speech that he finally rolled out the heavy artillery.

"When George Washington accepted the presidency in 1787," Ben said, "he was deeply concerned the position not evolve into that of royalty or dictator. When appropriate, George Washington graciously stepped aside so that—in his words—'an election consistent with our constitution can occur of a new citizen to administer the executive department of our government.'"

The crowd hung on his every word.

"George Washington," he continued, "knew that a periodic transfer of power was fundamental to a democracy. In 1951, the Congress of the United States passed the Twenty-second Amendment, which limited all future presidential tenures to two elected terms. Both George Washington and Congress knew that dispersed, limited entrustments of power represented the best protection from tyranny and abuse."

"Oh my God," Tyler whispered in my ear. "He's going to make it a part of his platform to limit the number of terms a person can be mayor. It's brilliant."

"How so?" I asked.

I hadn't been paying attention. I'd heard Ben speak many times before.

Tyler elaborated. "Mayor Greenwood's three terms in office will be seen as negative and undemocratic while Ben's inexperience will be seen as positive and representative of change. It's so subtle and yet effective."

"Dale Greenwood was mayor when I celebrated my twenty-first birthday," Ben said, with a trace of amusement in his voice. "He was mayor when I started my company in 1980, and he was mayor when I first published *Cavanaugh Weekly*."

His amusement heightened.

"He was mayor when I championed zoning reform. He was mayor when I first proposed a light-rail system. He was mayor when I first published *Cavanaugh Monthly* in 1986 and *Cavanaugh Business Monthly* in 1988. As unbelievable as it may seem, Dale Greenwood was still mayor when I celebrated my thirtieth birthday. He has been mayor for all of my adult life."

Ben paused, chuckled, shook his head in disbelief, and then continued.

"Dale Greenwood has been mayor for more than a decade and he is currently serving his third and, if I have anything to say about it, final term in office. If George Washington were here today, I'm quite confident Old George would agree that Dale Greenwood has a very dangerous stranglehold on the office of mayor, this city's future, and the democratic process. Ladies and gentlemen, it is time for change."

This time, Ben was interrupted by applause that only stopped when he motioned for quiet.

"If I am elected," Ben declared boldly, "I plan to ask our city council to limit the number of terms that one person can serve as mayor to two terms. It is not only time for King Dale to end his reign but also time for democracy and the will of the people to be restored in our great city."

The many previous rounds of applause had been polite and restrained, but when Ben finished with his reference to King Dale, the ballroom erupted in a boisterous, almost rowdy ovation. It was an unexpected reaction from an otherwise staid crowd and a sure sign that Ben had found his battle cry.

"You're right," I whispered to Tyler. "It's brilliant."

"If there's one thing I stand for," Ben said later as he began closing his speech, "one thing I believe in, it's three simple words, 'We, the people.' These words are the foundation of our belief system as Americans and the lifeblood of our democracy. Only the people can best decide the course and destiny of this great nation and this great city. It was a revolutionary proclamation at the time because those words placed an unprecedented, extraordinary measure of faith and trust in the people. With three little words, our forefathers created the greatest challenge in human history. They challenged Americans to forever rally, persistently toil, and constantly strive to fulfill the pro- mise embodied in the words, 'We, the people.' Citizenship in this country comes with obligation and demands effort. I will call on all citizens to actively participate in our city's future."

When Ben finished his speech, the orchestra played mellow nightcap music while some savored coffee or final cordials and others departed. As those departing passed behind our table, I overheard comments about the speech and what a great mayor Ben would make. Ben had certainly made a strong impression and secured their votes. Perhaps, for the first time since Ben told Stan and I that he would run for mayor, I felt good about Ben's prospects.

During the first couple songs of the orchestra's final set, most at our table bid farewell and departed, leaving just Tyler, Stan, and me behind. In front of him, Stan had half a cup of coffee, a half-eaten wedge of raspberry tort, and two empty dessert plates, the additional desserts courtesy of the plumper at our table, myself included.

"Do you feel like you're stepping out on a tightrope, Tyler?" Stan asked as he raised his fork, covered with raspberries and yellow cake, to his mouth.

"How so?" she asked.

"Your coverage of this election is going to be a balancing act," Stan elaborated. "Everyone knows that you and Ben are close friends. There will be inevitable accusations of favoritism."

"I always make it a point to be aware of appearances," Tyler said, "but I view this campaign differently. It is a great opportunity and possibly a huge break for me. Ben has already achieved national prominence, and this campaign will only expand his profile. As things heat up, my coverage of Ben and the mayor will get national airtime and I will, with any luck, get a shot at a network job. In my mind, this election is a career-maker for the right newsperson."

Working her way to New York City for an anchor position on the network news had been a career goal for Tyler, dating back almost a decade. In a matter-of-fact manner, she spoke of it often, like it was a matter of time. One year for her birthday, I gave Tyler a New York City guidebook, one of those flimsy, 200-page paperbacks that tourists used to get from the Empire State Building to the Statue of Liberty and then find a good restaurant for dinner. It was my way of telling her, "I know you'll get there." To my surprise, she carried it with her often, highlighted passages in yellow marker, and folded the corners of key pages for quick access. Just like Ben, I never doubted Tyler either.

* * *

At the office the next morning, Ben was euphoric as he briefed me on the results of the fundraiser. He acted like a child who'd gotten everything he wanted on Christmas morning and still had several unwrapped packages. Including ticket sales and donations, proceeds exceeded five hundred thousand dollars, and, since expenses were less than half that amount, the campaign netted almost three hundred thousand dollars. With two similar events scheduled for the following weeks, Ben was confident he'd raise the necessary monies to fund his campaign and give the mayor strong competition in the fall.

"Campaigns are like start-up businesses," Ben said, "more fail from lack of money than anything else. After last night, I know I can raise the necessary money, whatever it takes."

* * *

The mood wasn't so jovial at City Hall. Seated at his desk with his morning coffee positioned at his right, beside the phone, Mayor Greenwood routinely unfolded his morning issue of *The Dispatch* and revealed a bold banner headline that read, "Matthews Proposes Term Limits for Mayors at Fundraiser."

Instantly, steam rose from his brow, mimicking the cup of Joe before him, and his eyes shifted from the provocative headline to the first paragraph of the article. He searched the columnist's account of the event for an explanation of this anti-mayor sentiment, and his normal focus turned into a scowl when he reached the words, "King Dale."

"Goddamn it," the mayor yelled as he threw his newspaper high into the air. "Goddamn that little prick."

* * *

Dark as twilight even at midday, Tyler and I drove the back roads beneath the thick canopy of the forest along Route 19 to Condor three times during the next two weeks with no larger objective than to simply talk to local residents who knew Danny. We dressed casually and comfortably; hoping to fit in, or at the very least, not stand out. In Tyler's case, that was always difficult. Danny's replacement as motel manager was a sixty-five-year old, disabled fisherman with "Helen" tattooed on one bicep and "USS Arizona" on the other. He told us that out of seventy rooms at The Bayside Motel, there were nine residents who paid monthly rates. We started by knocking on their doors.

After two thumps, the door swung wide open and Epiphany Lange, a fiftyish woman with unkempt gray hair, stood before us. In the style of the 1960s, she wore a loose-fitting dress with a flowery pattern and a large silver cross around her neck. She held her hand above her eyes and squinted against the morning glare. No wonder—the only light in her dark cathedral-like room came from red, votive candles glowing in a shrine-like corner of the room before a nearly life-size statue of the Virgin Mary.

"God bless your sweet faces," she said to us.

We didn't ask many questions. We didn't have to—Epiphany loved to talk. As she explained it to us, Epiphany was born Kathy Lange and spent most of her adult life working as a prostitute near the docks in Cavanaugh. More than five years ago, while turning a trick in an alley, Jesus Christ appeared before her and told her to abandon her life and begin a new, righteous one as Epiphany.

"Basically," Epiphany added, "Jesus told me to stop spreading my legs and start spreading his word. Mostly, I help out at the food kitchen and shelter."

When I finally managed to shift the subject matter from her personal salvation to the life and times of Danny Grainger, she was equally vocal and colorful.

"Danny tested me," she proclaimed. "Lord, did he test me! I prayed for Danny, but he remained bitter and angry right up to his death. I couldn't reach him. I couldn't get him to put aside his earthly problems and accept the Lord. He once told me that the Virgin Mary and I were the oddest couple of roommates ever, making Felix Unger and Oscar Madison seem compatible. He was mean."

"Were you here on the night that Danny was shot?" I asked, hiding my amusement. "Did you hear or see anything unusual?"

"I was at the shelter until about midnight, and then I walked back to the motel," she responded. "I noticed a black car parked on the side street beside the motel. Its driver turned on the lights and drove away as I approached the motel. I only noticed it because it wasn't a car you'd see often at this motel."

"A limousine?" Tyler asked.

"No," she replied. "It was smaller and fancier. It looked like it was probably expensive. I don't know cars very well. Jesus doesn't care what kind of car we drive."

"Could you see the driver?" I followed up.

"No, not from there, not at night. I don't even know whether it was a man or a woman."

We thanked Epiphany for talking to us and turned to depart, but she asked us to wait for one minute. We obliged, remaining in her doorway as she crossed the small motel room and dipped her thumb in the cup of water the statue held in its plaster hands. Then returning to us, she pressed her thumb against each our foreheads, one at a time, making the sign of the cross and saying, "May God help you with your search. Amen."

More typical of the residents at the motel was the occupant of Room 44, conspicuously registered under the name John Robert

214 | Michael Bowe

Smith, as if adding a middle name made it more legitimate. He was a gangly, unshaven thirty-something with a fresh scrape across his forehead. Like most we met, he deftly avoided the particulars of his occupation or reason for his stay in Condor, while we introduced ourselves and explained the purpose of our visit.

John, who we'd awoken, spoke freely about his connection to Danny, once he'd extracted twenty bucks for the information, and, as it turned out, connection was the operative word.

"I partied with Danny from time to time," he said, copping to a habit and lifestyle his glossy eyes and track-laden arms had already revealed. "I could always count on Danny to get me some good smack whenever I wanted it."

"Was Danny a dealer?" I asked.

"On and off," he said. "Danny had connections. But the thing about Danny was I don't think he dealt for the money. I think he dealt to fuck with people. He enjoyed it when people came to him dry, desperate, and begging. He was a twisted son of a bitch."

"What was Danny's life like in Condor?" Tyler queried. "Did he have many friends?"

"Friends," John returned with a laugh. "Are you listening to me? He didn't have any friends, except the guy that shot him, if you want to count him. No one liked Danny. If they felt anything for him, they feared him. He didn't want any friends. Danny was a loner who kept mostly to himself."

"What do you mean the guy that shot him?"

"Around here, most people don't have a lot of reason to live. It seemed like Danny had even less reason than most. He had a chip on his shoulder and something eating him out from the inside like a cancer. He never really gave a shit about anybody or whether he lived or died for that matter."

A nervous habit, John paused and surveyed the front of the motel and then continued.

"A couple months ago, some cannery worker found out that Danny was fucking his wife and stormed into Fleck's late one night flashing a gun. This mackerel—that's what Danny called them— wanted the satisfaction of making Danny beg for his miserable life, but Danny fucked him too when he stood up and walked across the bar daring the guy to pull the trigger. But, he didn't. Then, as if that wasn't enough, Danny turned around, gave the guy ample time to shoot him in the back, and then casually strolled back to his seat and his glass of whiskey like nothing happened."

John chuckled, amused by his own story, and looked up and down the motel walkway again. "Like I said, Danny didn't give a shit whether he lived or died. Whoever shot him did him a favor, a big favor. That's the closest thing Danny had to a friend."

Of the motel residents we spoke with, only one saw Danny on the final night of his life, a mechanic who went by the name of Chaw Wilkens. While we talked in his doorway, Chaw held a sawed-open motor oil can for spitting tobacco in his right hand, and I noticed traces of his trade, black grease and oil, on his fingers and under his nails. Chaw had seen Danny at Fleck's that night, between 11pm and midnight, sitting alone in the corner booth he often occupied, knocking back shots of whiskey.

"I was playing pool and never even spoke to him," Chaw told us. "He was in and out in less than an hour."

"Did you see him talk to anyone that night?" Tyler asked.

"No. I didn't notice anyone. But he could've. I didn't pay him much mind."

There were about twenty patrons in the bar that night including a group of cannery workers, but Chaw didn't know any of them by name and didn't know anything about Danny's past conflict with one of the workers.

"Sounds like Danny though," he said with a chuckle, "fucking and fighting."

"Danny had a lot of girlfriends?" I asked.

"No way, man. He fucked a lot of women, but I don't think Danny had any friends, male or female."

It was becoming an oft-repeated theme.

*   *   *

On our next trip to Condor, we met Bob Cooper at Maria's, the spicy dive he introduced me to more than a decade earlier. Coop passed on the greasy fare that he so loved as a younger man, citing a fickle stomach, and opted instead to nibble on tortilla chips and drink tequila. He'd aged a lot since I'd last seen him almost a decade ago, and he looked every second of his seventy years, and then some. I remembered him as wound tightly, but he was more relaxed now in an uncaring, "I don't give a fuck" manner. His wife, Tricia, had passed away a year ago, and I reasoned that her death was partly responsible for the change. From the stories he'd told us years ago, they were very close. She was the purpose in his life; even thugs need love. I figured

Danny's death was weighing on him also, but I hadn't anticipated just how much.

"Danny's death hit me real hard," Coop told us. "I felt very guilty. He was like a son to me."

His eyes welled up as he spoke.

"I gave up on him," Coop continued. "I have to admit it. Hell, he'd given up on himself."

Even more surprising, Coop hadn't seen Danny in almost two years; they'd quarreled and weren't on speaking terms anymore, which seemed like an ongoing pattern in Danny's life. He regularly pushed all that was good and positive in his life away from him, preferring to isolate himself in a solitary state of self-loathing. Danny managed the motel and made the regular weekly deposits of the motel's receipts while Coop stayed away, as unable to stomach Danny as the spicy food on the table before him.

"When Drew Baxter retired from teaching three years ago," Coop said as he explained their fallout, "he left Condor High School without a varsity football coach. Immediately, I sensed an opportunity and it seemed like the perfect place for Danny."

Coop looked for affirmation, so we nodded.

"Sure, the job only paid two thousand dollars per season," he continued, "but it would get him involved in football once again. I don't have to tell either of you that football was Danny's one true love. I thought coaching would surely put that sparkle back into his eyes again. Anyway, I was so excited by the prospect that I called in every marker I had outstanding, every favor I was owed, and, sure enough, I got Danny selected as the new football coach."

Coop was so thrilled by the news that he set out to find Danny, searching all of his usual hangouts. Just before sundown, Coop found him at the dry docks where aged vessels were cleaned and repaired and restored to seaworthy status. Fifteen years ago, workers scrubbed the barnacle-laden hulls of four or five boats at a time, but chances were equal of finding only one boat in progress as finding the docks empty and still now. Larger, modern fishing ships, anchored at the docks in Cavanaugh, had replaced most of the smaller vessels that once sailed from Condor.

With the sun setting in the western sky, Danny sat alone with his legs dangling off the dock. Beside him, the rusting cab of a tall crane; its long arm extended over a single fishing boat, the hull a work in progress, partially scrubbed and restored, partially crusted with sea creatures and plant life. As the day was slowly losing its luster, Coop told Danny the news. Agitated by the conversation, like the topic had reminded him of his injury and caused a flash of pain, Danny rubbed the scars on his knee with his fingers beneath the fringe of his shorts.

"I don't want to coach the team," Danny said. "My football days are over, Coop. I've been banned from the sport."

"What are you talking about, Danny?" Coop returned.

"It's a self-imposed ban," Danny informed him. "My football days are over. It's as simple as that."

"Oh, for God's sake," Coop returned, frustrated with Danny's never-ending retreat from life. "Even old battered fishing boats get mended and returned to action, son. It's time to give your self a second chance. Time to stand up to whatever demons are haunting you and move on. Life is too damn short."

"Don't want it, Coop."

Their heated exchange escalated when Coop informed Danny about the lobbying he'd done on his behalf as well as the fatherly stake he felt in his redemption. But nothing Coop said caused Danny to reconsider. He stubbornly resisted.

"Don't want it, Coop," he repeated several times.

Feeling deflated and defeated, Coop called the principal the very next day and told him that Danny wasn't interested in the job. It was the moment that Coop officially gave up on Danny. It reminded me of my moment in the lobby of our building.

"He'd changed so much, Pete," he said as if he had to justify their breach to me.

I knew his frustration all too well.

* * *

The most surprising revelation about Danny came from an unexpected source: Stan. Late one Thursday afternoon, with yet another *Cavanaugh Weekly* deadline confronted and conquered, I retreated to The Boardroom, a happy-hour locale favored by the downtown financial crowd and the scene of my usual post-deadline ritual, a bacon cheeseburger and fries and a couple of cold beers. Stan knew this routine and entered the restaurant a discrete ten minutes after me.

"What are you doing here?" I asked.

I'd asked him to join me on many occasions, but he'd always declined, opting for home and family, an understandable choice.

"I need to talk to you," he replied, grabbing my forearm so I'd follow him away from the crowded bar area. I suppressed the urge to mention the fact that we spent more than eight hours a day fifteen feet apart—the distance between our office doors—and instead followed him toward the booths that lined the rear wall.

"It's about Danny," he added as we walked.

Sitting opposite him, Stan exhibited the troubled expression of someone needing to unburden himself, so I didn't ask any questions. I listened.

When Stan first started at *The Dispatch*, a veteran writer named Kyle Kennedy covered the local sports scene; included in his beat was high school, college, and the two professional franchises. Kennedy, a brutish Irishman in his late forties, wrote a daily column called "On the Sidelines" and maintained a reputation for drinking and gambling and occasionally waking up in a jail cell at the local precinct. After each arrest for drunk and disorderly conduct, most at the paper figured he'd finally get canned, but it never happened, and Kennedy always resumed his loud, obnoxious ways in the newsroom.

One Monday morning, Kennedy was livid about the outcome of the weekend's SU football game, a tight loss to UWS that had cost him a large wager. Kennedy insisted that Danny Grainger threw the game and bombastically told all present at a staff meeting that he was going to prove it. At the time, the managing editor at *The Dispatch* was a SU alumnus and a fervent Grizzlies fan that didn't think kindly of Kennedy's red-eyed rants.

"Unless you've got some proof," the editor gruffly scolded him, "you keep your big, fat Irish mouth shut. That Grainger kid is going to be the best darn quarterback to ever wear a Grizzly uniform, and this paper isn't going to slander him because you lost a lousy bet."

Despite the stern warning, Kennedy, doubly stubborn, both Irish and a newspaperman, continued his unsavory accusations about Danny, even grumbling on another Monday morning, "Grainger has gone and done it again." Fortunately for all concerned, a short time later, Kennedy left *The Dispatch* to take a job with a newspaper in Portland, and his rumblings about fixed games ceased. Still, rumors never actually died in newsrooms, floating instead like ghosts in the still air above the conversation until relevant again. Newsrooms are as haunted as Louisiana cemeteries.

"Since you decided to do the article, I've struggled with whether I should tell you or not," Stan said. "I don't want to tarnish your memory of your friend. Frankly, I don't know whether these accusations are true or not. In our profession, as you well know, searching for the truth often means sifting through a lot of lies and untruths."

"I'm glad you told me," I replied, never doubting Stan. His integrity was as steadfast as my dog's enthusiastic greeting at my home each evening.

All the while, in the back of my mind, I wondered whether some aspects of Danny's dark, illicit, and forsaken existence were starting to find the light.

* * *

On April 7, 1992, the front-page article for *The Cavanaugh Dispatch* read as follows, "Optimal Tower is a skyscraper unlike its historic predecessors, rising skyward as an artistic endeavor, spirited and soulful, with a steel and glass manifestation reminiscent of Claude Monet's water lilies and instantly dismissive of the gray, steel and mortar structures of the past. The architects and builders have pilfered Monet's color pallet and painted this vertical stretch of the Cavanaugh skyline with the delicate greens and blues and grays and yellows of the flower gardens of Giverny. Somehow, in the structure, the sensibility of an impressionist painting emerges as the muted colors are faded in splotches and sunlit in others, with gradual transitions as subtle as the delicate brush strokes of the master himself. Steel beams crisscross haphazardly throughout the towering façade, which only reinforces its impressionistic essence by emulating the natural randomness of the lily pond. Atop the structure, a simple, fifty-foot spire seems to rein in the freeform work beneath it as it merges the natural splendor into one straight pinnacle skyward. This soaring skyscraper stretches twenty stories higher than its neighbors creating a peaked skyline not unlike the Alps in France that will cause onlookers to gasp and utter, 'C'est magnifique.'

Financier Sebastian Biddle has changed the skyscraper in the same manner he changed business technology in the 1980s; he dared to start with a blank canvas and simply reimagine it. Since the birth of the skyscraper at the close of the nineteenth century, 'World's Tallest' is a distinction that many have sought. In the case of Optimal Tower, World's Tallest is confirmed at 1,535 feet. Whether or not it is also the 'World's Most Beautiful' skyscraper will be the subject of much debate."

220 | Michael Bowe

*   *   *

Four days before the grand opening ceremony, Sebastian Biddle and I waited in Ben's office for him to arrive though neither of us had an appointment with him or any reason to believe he was on his way. In his typical freewheeling style, Sebastian had simply dropped in for an unscheduled visit. In my normally staid style, I needed Ben to discuss our capital budget. An unspoken pact, we both decided to use the opportunity to hang out together. For a guy who'd be front and center on the world's stage in just a few days, Sebastian was as calm and collected as ever. It was early April and he wore only blue jeans, a white T-shirt, and a light-blue V-neck sweater. Through Ben, I'd known Sebastian for a decade and always found him to be fascinating and unassuming—the sharpness of his mind was incomparable, and his wealth was absolutely unimportant to him.

"Did Ben ever tell you that he is the reason I built Optimal Tower?" Sebastian asked me.

He was stretched out on the leather sofa with his hands behind his head.

"How so?" I asked.

"Five or six years ago, Ben and I were in my office at the old Optimal headquarters, and I mentioned to Ben that I was talking with real estate consultants about building a new forty-story headquarters in the downtown business district. He listened quietly while I elaborated on some of the details about the discussions, but I could tell his mind was elsewhere."

"I know that look, Sebastian, and it always means Ben wants to do something impossible."

Sebastian laughed like he understood, and then he continued.

"After a few minutes of silence, Ben blurted, 'Sebastian, don't build another forty-story building—the world is full of forty-story buildings—build the World's Tallest skyscraper. Change our skyline in the same way the Empire State Building changed the New York skyline. Your skyscraper will make Cavanaugh a world class city.'"

"That sounds like Ben," I observed.

"At the time, I scoffed at the idea," Sebastian said. "Like you said, Ben dreams on a ridiculously large scale. It just seemed like typical Ben. I changed the subject back to my ongoing discussions with the consultants and simply dismissed his suggestion."

"So what did he say to convince you?"

"Much later that same evening, Ben asked me what my net worth was and I told him about $17 billion. Then he asked me how much would it cost to build my forty-story office building and I told him about $300 million. He hesitated only briefly and then he asked what I thought it would cost to build the World's Tallest skyscraper and I told him probably $700 or $800 million."

"Those are big numbers," I remarked.

"And then, with one simple statement, Ben convinced me to build a skyscraper," Sebastian stated. "He said, 'Sebastian, if I could build the World's Tallest skyscraper, make an enduring mark on the world, and still have $16 billion left when I was done, I'd do it in a heartbeat. I wouldn't even have to think about it.'"

"You're a man with unlimited resources and options," I said, echoing Ben's argument, "and a man who can make a significant mark on the world if he chooses."

"The more I thought about what Ben had said to me," he told me, "the more I realized he was absolutely right."

"So, in less than fifty words, Ben convinced you to spend almost a billion dollars."

"He is remarkable, isn't he?"

"Four days from the grand opening," I asked, "are you glad you did it?"

"Most definitely," Sebastian replied without any hesitation. "I'm very proud of the project, and Ben constantly reminds me about the positive long-term impact it will have on our city."

"We've included a lot of content about Optimal Tower in our publications over the last year, and I'm curious about one thing: Why are your corporate headquarters on the lower floors instead of higher up on the floors with the breathtaking views?"

"I'm not all that crazy about heights, Pete."

"You're kidding me!" I declared.

"No, I'm not," he said, smiling in a self-deprecating manner. "Believe me, I chuckle whenever I consider the irony."

* * *

As measured by cost, media coverage, and attendance, the grand opening ceremony at Optimal Tower was the largest event in the city's history. All tenant leases for the top fifty floors commenced on April 15th so the upper floors could be open to the public during the grand opening. Both the open-air observation deck on the 115th floor and the enclosed observation deck on the 114th floor were open to the public though the views were equally breathtaking on every floor. Each floor was a stand-alone venue for celebration, with light fare, refreshments, and entertainment. Many different styles of music were represented, ranging from rock bands to strolling Mariachis to solo pianists to jazz quartets to symphony members to a cappella groups. And, each floor was decorated with chandeliers, banners, streamers, balloons, flowers, and large plants to add to the festive mood.

A partial tally of the food and beverages procured for the event included 475 kegs of beer, 12,500 cases of wine, 5,000 gallons of lemonade, 10,000 gallons of soda, 7,000 gallons of coffee, 3,300 blocks of cheese, 3,000 boxes of crackers, 4 miles of sheet cake, 150,000 cupcakes, and 100,000 rolls. Eleven catering companies with 1,200 employees, 550 private event coordinators, 500 police officers, 400 private security personnel, 100 emergency medical technicians, and 120 fire and rescue personnel were present to serve and assist the general public. The planning and coordination of the event started in May of 1991, a full ten months in advance, causing one newspaper columnist to observe that the gestation period for this grand opening was longer than that of a human being. Though never confirmed by Sebastian Biddle, the total cost of the event was speculated to be in the range of $20 to $25 million.

Entrance, food, beverage, and entertainment were all free, but visitors were given time-stamped wristbands that limited their stint in the building to ninety minutes to accommodate the enormous crowds expected.

"My objective for the grand opening," Sebastian told me, "is that people talk about the day Optimal Tower opened for the rest of their lives. I want it to be remarkable and unforgettable."

On the day of the grand opening ceremony, Optimal Tower was open to the public from 11am until 6pm. Cavanaugh Public Schools declared the day a holiday so families with school children could attend the event. In the city's business district, most companies followed the school district's lead and shuttered operations for the day because they knew little work would be accomplished. Even the city's transportation department waived all bus fares for the day, providing free rides for all attending the event. By 10am that morning, the line to enter the building stretched for twenty-seven city blocks. On the day of April 13, 1992, little happened in the city of Cavanaugh that was business as usual.

Two floors required special invitation. The 111th floor was reserved for members of the media, which greatly exceeded local media as teams from the network news programs attended along with reporters and newspaper columnists from 39 states and 51 countries. In all, media credentials were issued to 1,733 attendees and the event was broadcast all over the world, with reports filed in 53 languages. The 113th floor was the site of the official grand opening celebration party hosted by Sebastian Biddle and attended by world dignitaries, business leaders, government officials, professional athletes, movie and television stars, influential and best-selling authors, prominent professionals, and other people of note and significance. Sebastian told me he had more requests for invitations than available, so he had to leave out many people.

"The event planner has a long list of people that I don't even know who are pissed off at me," he stated with bewilderment.

Ben, Tyler, Stan, and I had invitations that allowed us access to both of the restricted floors. The activities on the 113th floor were scheduled to begin at 10am so we arrived at 9am to ensure we didn't miss anything. There were already more than 500 people on the floor and the excitement level felt more like 11:59pm on New Year's Eve than 9am on a Monday morning. As I glanced around the room, I recognized about one out of every twenty faces, and I found that astonishing. People had come from all over the world to simply stand in this building and acknowledge this accomplishment.

"As part of my job, I've covered many major events," Tyler told me as we stood in quiet amazement staring at the extraordinary scene before us, "but this feels far more historic and significant than anything I've covered."

"There are members of Britain's royal family over there," I told her, gawking like a teenager at his favorite pop singer.

With a tall, leafy Bloody Mary in my hand at barely 9:30am, Ben and I spotted an individual we both wanted to meet. Fifteen feet away from us in front of a banquet table, busily selecting ingredients for his omelet, was Stedman Hughes, author of the best-selling book, *The Last Patriot*; the story of a disillusioned Revolutionary War hero who, dissatisfied with the new government, tried to launch a second American Revolution. It was a book that spoke to both of us for very different reasons and one that we'd discussed in great detail. We quickly grabbed some breakfast fare and followed the debonair author to a table, but all Steadman wanted to talk about was skyscrapers.

"I was seven years old," Steadman said, "when my parents took me to the grand opening of the Empire State Building. It is truly one of my fondest memories. The grand opening of Optimal Tower is equally historic. Moments like this one define the era that we live in and our own lifetimes as well."

During my day at Optimal Tower, I talked with some of the most talented and accomplished individuals I'd encountered during my lifetime, and the common sentiment amongst them was that they could not miss this historic event. Several had passed on other noteworthy events or cancelled existing plans altogether and traveled halfway around the world to be there. I was surprised by the importance that each placed on Optimal Tower, as these were individuals who lived extraordinary lives and weren't easily impressed by glitz or glamour or celebrity. Grand openings, state dinners, honorary degrees, awards ceremonies, and celebrity events were regular occurrences for this jet-setting crowd, and still they all wanted to stand atop this building and witness this grand opening.

At 11am, at the First Street entrance to the building, Sebastian, flanked by his beautiful wife and young daughter on one side and Ben on the other, wielded a large, caricature-worthy pair of scissors and enthusiastically snipped the shiny yellow ribbon that cordoned off the doorway, signifying the official grand opening of the tower. As the crowd roared jubilantly, his four-year old daughter snatched the ribbon half that fell near her feet and wrapped it around her waist like a sash as photographers snapped away. When the crowd finally quieted, Sebastian handed the large scissors to Ben and said, "I present these scissors to my longtime friend, Benjamin Matthews, who played a significant role in my decisions to locate my company in Cavanaugh a decade ago and to build Optimal Tower five years ago. At this time next year, I hope to be addressing him as Mr. Mayor."

It was probably that remark that ultimately drove Mayor Dale Greenwood from the festivities that morning. While I had spotted him across the room earlier during breakfast, I didn't see him again after the ribbon-cutting ceremony as he retreated to City Hall when he realized he didn't have a role in any of the ceremonial aspects of the day. At breakfast, in the official program for the day, I'm sure the mayor noticed that the keynote address by Benjamin F. Matthews was scheduled to take place on the 113th floor at 1pm during lunch for the invitees and decided that would be an extremely uncomfortable hour for him. Just as Sebastian intended, this grand opening ceremony also included one of the most public endorsements of a political candidate in the history of American politics, one that had the potential to secure the mayor's office for Ben. Forced into damage control mode, Mayor Greenwood must've recognized there was no upside in his continued presence at the event and left.

"Show someone a photograph of the New York skyline," Ben declared, opening his keynote speech to the most prominent crowd of his career, "and that person will point to the Empire State Building and know it is the New York skyline. Show someone a photograph of the Chicago skyline, and that person will point to the Sears Tower and know it is the Chicago skyline. Show someone a photograph of the San Francisco skyline, and that person will point to the Transamerica Building and know it is the San Francisco skyline. As of today, you can show someone a photograph of the Cavanaugh skyline, and that person will point to Optimal Tower and know it is the Cavanaugh skyline. As of today, the Cavanaugh skyline has its distinguishing landmark, its signature building, and Cavanaugh has joined New York, Chicago, and San Francisco as world class American cities."

Three times that afternoon, I watched Tyler interview both Ben and Sebastian, each man responding in turn to her questions about Optimal Tower as well as Ben's mayoral campaign, as her cameraman dutifully filmed their lengthy conversations. Watching from across the crowded room, I suspected this was Ben's handiwork. Ben understood the value of opportunities and would never let one pass without capitalizing on it, even if he weren't the beneficiary. He knew this event had career enhancing importance for Tyler so he recruited his good friend Sebastian and the two men provided her unrivaled access, much more than any of the other news anchors. In total, Tyler left that evening with more than an hour of interview footage with the two main stars of the event and that access would ensure her share of network airtime.

For more than a year, the hype and anticipation over Optimal Tower was ever-present. Residents of Cavanaugh lived in the constant, ever-growing shadow of the skyscraper, watched its steady upward climb, and eagerly awaited its completion. On the day of the grand opening, more than 500,000 showed up to view the building. My life's work had been the chronicling of humankind, discerning what was relevant and important, and focusing our staff on the significant, what really mattered. More than a decade into my professional career, I thought I had a keen sixth sense as I usually sniffed out significance quicker than an elevator operator asked, "What floor?" But, with the grand opening of Optimal Tower delegated to the history books, I had to admit that until the day of the event, I didn't get it.

I knew the building was tall and dramatic, but what I didn't understand was that skyscrapers are so much more than the physical building, that intangibles like historical reference, societal markers, and universal symbolism are as significant as the structure itself. Describing a skyscraper as a tall building is as inadequate as describing the ocean as a large body of water. Standing before either of those wonders, one immediately recognizes the shortcomings of language and the fact that both skyscrapers and the ocean must be experienced firsthand to fully understand their magnificence. My first indication of the significance of Optimal Tower came when I looked up from street level and then outward from its observation deck. But, I'm not talking about the size of the building or the view—I'm talking about the feeling I experienced within my being.

Human beings have always wanted to exceed previous limits and further expand our horizons and abilities by sailing to the new world, pushing further west, going even faster, or rising ever higher. Skyscrapers are an expression of our endless yearning to conquer our own limitations and create, yet another, new and previously inconceivable triumph. Each successive skyscraper that reaches higher into the sky is a monument to the human spirit and a physical manifestation of unstoppable optimism. In our nation's capitol, there are monuments to the veterans of wars as well as some of our most beloved Presidents, memorials to remind us of our heritage and the past. But, skyscrapers are sacred monuments with a different purpose, signifying the hopes, dreams, and potential of our people and causing us to look inward and forward in the same way other monuments cause us to look back. Analogous to the pyramids of ancient Egypt, in our modern view as opposed to their original intent, a skyscraper is an everlasting monument that stands as homage to best efforts, accomplishments, and enduring spirit.

Beyond the monument aspect, there is a still bigger picture concerning the significance of skyscrapers. Skyscrapers affect us in one way as human beings and an entirely different way as occupants of Earth. Towering over us, skyscrapers fill us with wonder and awe, the very same feeling we get when we stand before the endless ocean or gaze upwards at a billion stars, but the obvious distinction is that we built the skyscrapers. God made the oceans and stars, but we built the skyscrapers to stand as magnificent representations of us as a people— our era, our lifetimes, and our place in this world. In the skyscrapers, we, as a people, are not trying to be God-like, or even compete with the magnificence around us—we know we can't do either—we are simply trying to be worthy of our place in this world and the universe.

Skyscrapers climb toward the heavens above with a simple and unmistakable message: "We are here."

12.

The Empire State Building retained the title of World's Tallest longer than any other, for 41 years. It was the quintessential skyscraper, visited by more than 4 million people each year, and known the world over. Its Art Deco styling, unique history and inspiration, and feature role in more than 700 movies made it special, even in the fabulous New York City skyline.

During our college days, I never would've suspected Danny of illicit activities, most particularly a conspiracy involving football and gambling. After all, football was sacred to him, like religion for most people. It was the thing he was most passionate about. These days, I didn't know anymore.

Without any explanation, I tasked one of our junior writers at *Cavanaugh Weekly* with gathering the betting lines—the listings of favored teams and by how many points for gambling purposes—from the local newspaper for Danny's career at SU. My plan was for Tyler and me to review his performance in each game in relation to the betting line and determine whether his performance could've affected gambling outcomes, thereby determining whether or not he might've conspired to fix games. Our findings wouldn't be conclusive since too much depended on our subjective interpretation of the game film, and still I wanted to judge whether the accusations seemed plausible.

Tyler and I met nightly in an editing booth at the Channel 5 facility. When we signed out footage from the station's archives, we disguised our project as a retrospective of Danny's college football career. In all, we sequestered ourselves in the darkness of that small booth for two weeks, dining on takeout food from nearby restaurants and junk food from the vending machines. Together, we watched more than forty hours of file footage of SU football games, starting with the UWS game, the game that so enraged Kyle Kennedy.

"What's the point spread?" Tyler asked.

"Even," I answered.

An even point spread meant gamblers were betting on either team to win or lose without points to their benefit or detriment.

We vaguely remembered the game as a heartbreaking loss, but neither of us recalled the specifics. Nibbling on Chinese noodles from take-out containers, Tyler and I relived an action-packed first half as two great offensive units were continually responding to the other team's scores by driving the length of the field for scores of their own. Each touchdown was quickly matched by a touchdown for the other team. The quarterbacks' efforts, in particular, were exceptional.

"He was really something special," I remarked, marveling at Danny's coolness under pressure and his remarkable abilities.

But early in the second half, with SU trailing 28-24, the game took a critical turn. Danny guided the Grizzly offense to the twenty-five yard line and, on second down with three yards to go, he underthrew his receiver as he broke toward the sideline. Lacking the necessary velocity, the pass was intercepted by a defensive back and returned eighty yards for a touchdown, producing an insurmountable 35-24 lead for UWS.

Simultaneously, Tyler and I stopped munching our noodles and sat straight up in our chairs, both suspiciously aware of the game changing impact of the play.

"Run it again," I requested, and Tyler immediately reversed the film, causing the defensive player to retrace his steps backward.

"It's not a sharp pass," Tyler said, maneuvering the buttons on the panel before her so that Danny released the pass over and over again. "It seems to float."

"It could've slipped," I offered in Danny's defense. "But, one thing is definite, it isn't typical of Danny's passes. They didn't call him the 'Gun' for nothing."

It was an auspicious start to our project. The very first reel of film produced suspicion. But, most damning for Danny was a similar interception in a later game where he again seemed to take a little off the pass and let it float across the field. If we could have laid the two clips on top of one another and projected them simultaneously, the images and the end result would've been identical. Though SU won the second game, the interception caused the Grizzlies to come up short against the point spread. In that case, it was possible for Danny to win the game and still alter the wagering outcome. Knowing Danny was a dedicated student of the game, it seemed unlikely to me that he'd made the same critical mistake twice, the same poor execution of a sideline pass. Of the twenty-one games that Danny started at quarterback for the Grizzlies, Tyler and I decided his play was suspect in three of the games. And though we couldn't be certain, I also surmised that Danny's betrayal and subsequent guilt might explain his spiritless state in later years as well as his "banned from the game" comment.

"Danny was the classic all-American boy," Tyler insisted. "There's got to be a lot more to his sellout than we know. He didn't suddenly decide to fix football games on his own. Either someone made him do it or someone conspired with him."

"And, why did he stop?" I asked. "His senior year was not suspect at all. All his game efforts in his final year for the Grizzlies were legitimate. We've got to talk to Coop again."

"Oh, shit!" Tyler declared. "I'm getting sick of that drive."

* * *

When we arrived at his home at 10am the next morning, we found Bob Cooper seated in a threadbare recliner in the front living area, wearing boxer shorts and a robe, and blankly staring at a game show on the television before him.

"Come in," he said, awakened and obviously surprised to see us at the screen door. He asked us to wait in the living room while he retreated to the bedroom to put on some clothes and comb his hair.

"We should've called ahead, Coop," I remarked as he clumsily made his way to the bedroom.

"That's okay," he replied.

In the living room, newspapers, magazines, dirty dishes, junk mail, and even clothing were scattered about the carpet and undusted surfaces. Even the upright piano in the corner of the room, which had surely seen better days, its wood dingy and its strings out of tune, had stacks of yellowed papers and hardback books piled upon it, likewise for the bench. In contrast to its surroundings, the clean, uncluttered mantle stood out like a glimmering oasis and drew our attention, the focal point of an otherwise unkempt room. On the mantle above the fireplace, a dozen picture frames were displayed, every one a photo of Coop, Tricia, Danny, or some combination. Though there wasn't any common blood in their veins, the photos looked like family portraits, and the images, in my mind at least, made Coop's fatherly concern, Tricia's motherly devotion, and Danny's embittered solitude that much more tragic.

During his years in Condor, Coop's business activities often sidestepped both the law and legitimacy so we knew we could be direct with our questions. He wouldn't be offended. In fact, selling stolen merchandise out of his motel had always been a profitable sideline for him. For a man who had spent most of his life in a small town, Coop knew how the world worked.

Coop emerged from the bedroom.

"Do you know if Danny participated in any gambling schemes that involved Stanton University football games?" I asked, a little leery to hear his response.

"I know he considered it," Coop answered. "I don't know if he went through with it."

As he passed the TV set, Coop turned the volume down. Then, he returned to his recliner. Tyler and I moved some debris from the sofa to a nearby coffee table and sat opposite him. I braced myself for disappointment.

"One real foggy night, Danny came to visit us just after dinner as Tricia was washing the dishes. I remember it well because Tricia scolded Danny harshly for driving in such conditions, with such limited visibility, but Danny calmed her by saying the fog was only thick near the coast, that the rest of the drive had been better. Right away, I knew he had something on his mind because it was a weekday and, in those days, we saw Danny on weekends, either at games or when he'd come for a visit. When Tricia returned to the kitchen, he told me he had a chance to make a lot of money if he kept the Grizzlies' margin of victory under the betting line in an upcoming game. He wanted to know if I thought he should do it."

"What did you tell him?" Tyler asked.

"I told him a man has to look out for himself in this world. If Danny had a chance to make some money, he should go for it, right?"

Neither Tyler nor I responded to his question, preferring to treat it as rhetorical. Instead, we exchanged quick, subtle glances that expressed our disbelief over his mistaken logic, without faulting Coop. We both knew that, in his own streetwise way, Coop had Danny's best interests in mind. Coop loved Danny like a son, and he only wanted what he thought was best for him. He simply lived by a different code than us.

"It's not like Stanton University paid Danny for filling those seats every Saturday afternoon," Coop continued his rationalization, "and his football career was only going to last so long. A professional career was a long shot at best so he had to look out for himself."

There truly was honor among thieves. Coop, knowing small conspiracies were always better, didn't ask any questions about the plan. He didn't want to know the details. On the tough backstreets of Condor or any crook's road to easy street, when it came to felonious plans, shady schemes, and dirty deals, what you knew could most definitely hurt you. I remembered Coop once telling us jokingly at a meal at Maria's that, "the only way you can be sure someone will keep your secret is if that person is dead." He was a tough, no-nonsense character (without any character) when it came to business.

Coop suppressed his natural curiosity, his con man's urge to participate and his protective instincts. Instead, he offered Danny the single best piece of advice he knew as Danny departed that night.

"If you do it, Danny," Coop advised him, "make sure you're smart and don't get caught."

Danny only nodded and didn't indicate his likelihood of participating in the scheme. And, at that point in time, more than a decade later, Coop said he couldn't even guess whether Danny had participated. His only observation was that Danny was conflicted about the offer and the opportunity.

"I could see it weighed heavily on his mind," Coop added.

Through the screen door, Coop watched as Danny ominously faded into the dark shadows, light mist, and thick fog of that Condor night, a precursor of the years to come. As events would unfold, his exit that night was the beginning of his long, slow fade in Condor.

"We never spoke of it again," Coop told us.

* * *

Whenever we uncovered information that was pertinent to the investigation, I phoned Captain Bryant and briefed him on our findings. He always responded promptly to my calls and acted quite interested in the information, often repeating pieces of what I said like he was jotting notes on a pad. I appreciated his readiness and enthusiasm, but I also wondered why he never knew any of my information in advance. Why hadn't their investigation uncovered it?

I would've given up on their investigation altogether, but Captain Bryant called me one afternoon with a follow-up on one of my leads.

"We located the cannery worker that Danny argued with in Fleck's," Captain Bryant said. "His name is Luis Silva, and he was in Fleck's again on the night of Danny's death, just as you suspected."

"Does he have an alibi for the time of the shooting?"

"He does but not a good one. He left Fleck's at 11:00pm and he says he went straight home. His wife is his alibi, but I make it a rule to never trust spouses as alibi witnesses. Obviously spouses have a lot of reason to be less than truthful."

The captain paused. "Although in this case, she would be better off if Luis was in jail. We send a squad car to their apartment at least twice a month to break up a brawl and, though she's always bruised and bloodied, she never presses charges. It's a bad situation."

"Did anyone else hear him or see him around the apartment building that night?" I asked.

"Not that we found," he replied, which I interpreted as meaning that no one from the apartment building came to the police station on their own to report seeing Luis that night.

"Where's the ketchup?" the captain demanded, apparently distracted by a fast food delivery. "We'll keep digging," he said when he returned to our conversation.

"Good," I told him, though I knew that mine was depleted.

*　*　*

My article became an ongoing joke between Stan and me. Or, more correctly, I should say Stan got a weekly chuckle out of it.

More than two months had passed since I first told Stan I planned to write an article about Danny, with much of that time spent in Condor, and Stan seemed to derive pleasure from reminding me of that fact. Granted, under normal circumstances, two months was more than enough time to research, compile, and compose more than ninety percent of the articles that we published in either of our magazines or the *Weekly*. So, what was different about this article? Why was it taking so long? Our writers lived with deadlines. Why shouldn't I?

I didn't have an answer.

On a weekly basis, more for his amusement than anything else, Stan asked me whether he should allocate space for the article in the next issue.

"Soon," I'd always answered without elaboration.

I was making progress. I'd learned a lot about Danny's life in Condor, mostly unpleasant, about his angry days, philandering nights, and his bloody death. I'd written many pages of the article. And still, I couldn't evade a nagging feeling that I needed more. Regardless of the time passing, I couldn't wrap it up and publish it like it was just another article. This was different; there was no denying it. I didn't know whether that feeling came from the personal or journalistic part of me, but I knew I couldn't declare the article finished yet.

Basically, in my heart, I knew the article would be complete when I realized a sense of peace and closure from the material, simple as that. And, that hadn't happened yet. And, that might still be quite a ways off. After all, at this point in my investigation, Danny was the first murder victim in the history of criminal enterprise where just about every traditional motive applied as a possible scenario for his death, including a drunken argument, revenge for a slight, an angry husband, a jealous lover, a soured drug deal, pissed-off associates, a botched robbery, and a gambling conspiracy. I simply had to narrow it further.

"Soon," I continued telling Stan. "Soon."

Stan chuckled.

* * *

I'd met plenty of people that disliked Danny Grainger, some probably enough to murder him, but I only knew of one individual who'd actually pointed a gun at him, so visiting Luis Silva was the most logical next step. But, when I told Tyler that we needed to have a conversation with Luis, she suggested I continue without her.

"I've got other responsibilities," she said. "I can't dedicate my career to one story. I've got to get on with my other work."

I understood completely. Over the last three months, we had spent a lot of time away from our respective duties and, at this point, Tyler's other obligations must've beckoned. Her boss questioned her many days in Condor the same way Stan taunted me about mine. And, I couldn't fault either of them. Their journalistic instincts told them it was all a big waste of time and maybe they were right. But, I couldn't stop. I couldn't leave it unresolved.

Fortunately for me, Stan wasn't my boss.

I told Tyler I'd keep her posted on my progress, and I made the next trip to Condor on my own.

* * *

My first stop in Condor was the police station to pick up a mug shot of Luis Silva.

"Take your pick," Captain Bryant said as he placed Luis Silva's criminal file in front of me, including a selection of eight mug shots clipped to the front of the folder.

"We've used a roll of film on that guy," the captain continued. "He's a real piece of work."

I hesitated. The mug shots of Luis Silva were intimidating and Stan and Tyler's comments echoed in my mind. In all eight mug shots, he looked really pissed off. His face was a cross between a bulldog and a German shepherd. He was so scary that he could've supplemented his cannery income by working part-time as a junkyard dog, and I could only imagine how scary he'd be in real life, face to muzzle. Worse yet, I knew Luis wouldn't find me intimidating at all. Anyway, the real question was more basic: What the hell was I doing? Maybe they were right. Maybe I was wasting a lot of time.

If I needed another reason to simply pack up and go home, one was blatantly obvious, especially to me—I was out of my league. I'd never been involved in a criminal investigation, never even covered one. Hell, the last article I actually researched and wrote was about an eighty year old woman who came west on the railroad when she was eleven, a human interest piece for Christ's sake. And, beyond my lack of experience, I couldn't continue in this half-in, half-out manner, always accepting consolation from the fact that I had no official role in this matter. With Luis Silva glaring up at me, I had serious second thoughts about the article entirely. What the hell was I doing?

In my mind, I drew the proverbial line in the sand. I had to decide. Either commit or walk away. From this point forward, it was all or nothing. If I opened that file, I was officially joining the investigation and would pursue the whole truth as never before. Otherwise, I should walk away right now and get on with my life—just like Tyler. In simple rebuttal of my fears and concerns, I thought about my old roommate and that large bloodstain on his carpet and, when my ten minutes of soul-searching was over, I opened the file.

One at a time, I flipped through the loose pages in the file, making mental notes as I proceeded. Luis Silva, his wife, and two young children moved to Condor less than two years ago and, in the short time that followed, Luis had been arrested eight times for a variety of minor offenses including drunk and disorderly, disrupting the peace, and domestic battery. In the middle of the folder, there were several photographs of Luis' wife, Yolanda, both eyes blackened, her face swollen, her bottom lip split, taken several months ago as supporting evidence for battery charges that she later dropped, as was often the case.

Luis Silva was no model citizen, but he'd been worse. In his twenties, he served three stints in prisons for armed robbery, two liquor stores and, interestingly enough, a small motel. These days, according to his police file at least, Luis limited his illegal activities to drunken fistfights and disturbances, both around town and at home.

"Don't let his recent petty offenses fool you," Captain Bryant advised me. "Luis Silva is a violent and dangerous man, and there's no telling what he'll do. I feel for his wife, but we can't convince her to press charges. She's afraid of him. Be careful if you talk to him."

At the motel, Epiphany recognized Luis the moment I placed the photo in front of her.

"That's Luis Silva," she told me. "Sure, I know him. His wife used to work at the motel. She is as sweet and kind as that son of a bitch is evil."

Epiphany said she saw Luis regularly about town, at the motel, Fleck's, or at the soup kitchen. When I asked, she also said she remembered seeing Luis on the night Danny was shot. Turns out, she practically bumped into him near her motel room.

"I passed Luis as I arrived home that night," Epiphany said. "Right there on the walkway," she stated, pointing fifteen feet up the sidewalk to the corner of the motel. "I didn't think anything of it. I figured he was drinking with some of the cannery workers who were staying at the motel. There's always a couple of rooms of them."

After talking with Epiphany and several other motel residents, I proceeded to the White Brothers Cannery to talk with Luis Silva himself, and lastly to their apartment to talk with his wife, Yolanda. It wasn't deliberate on my part, but it was fortunate that I spoke to the two of them separately. Using facts I'd gotten from motel residents, I was able to get both Yolanda and Luis to reveal information that their spouse didn't know. I wouldn't have gotten the information otherwise. Based on several days of canvassing, I pieced together a sordid tale of deceit, abuse, and manipulation that culminated with a murder plot to kill Danny at the motel.

When I met Yolanda, she had sad brown eyes, a markedly bruised cheekbone, a determined will, and one obvious character flaw that cursed her existence: Yolanda couldn't pick a decent man to save her life. And, as it turned out, her predicament had become a matter of life and death.

For almost a year, Yolanda worked as a maid at The Bayside Motel, cleaning bathrooms, changing sheets, making beds, replacing towels, and doing laundry. Six months into her employment and under undetermined circumstances, she began having sex with Danny on an almost daily basis in whichever room happened to be unoccupied. When he finished, Danny promptly returned to his managerial duties, leaving Yolanda with little more than a quick peck on the cheek and one additional room to clean. Still, from her viewpoint, Danny didn't beat her or demean her so he was as close to a real gentleman as she'd ever encountered. Yolanda knew no better.

One morning before their romp, Yolanda informed Danny that she thought she might be pregnant with his child. Danny was furious and hurled a lamp against the wall. He told her he wanted nothing more to do with her or her bastard child.

"It's not my problem," Danny yelled, so loud that the whole motel could hear his declaration. "Do I look like a daddy to you? Just get the hell out of here, you bitch."

Danny fired Yolanda that morning and told her to never return to the motel again. Desperate, she contrived a plan to rid herself of the miserable, good-for-nothing, men in her life. When her husband, Luis, returned home that night, Yolanda hysterically recounted an elaborate story she'd spent the afternoon rehearsing, infusing her performance with the dramatic license of an actress in a telenovela. She told Luis that Danny had entered a room she was cleaning and violently raped her. Through tears and streaked mascara, she said she wasn't going to work at the motel anymore.

"I can't go back there, Luis," she said. "Please don't make me go back."

Just as she hoped, a furious Luis retrieved his gun from the top drawer of the dresser and raced off into the night in search of Danny. An hour later, Luis found him at Fleck's and confronted him. But, it was at that moment that Yolanda's plan disintegrated. Danny didn't cower or even deny the sexual encounters. Quite remarkably, he challenged his accuser to shoot him. Luis, suddenly aware of the room full of witnesses and the prison cell that awaited him, didn't pull the trigger. Instead, he stormed out of Fleck's, shouting words in Spanish of threats and revenge. He returned home to their apartment, even angrier, and beat his wife as he'd done so many times before.

"He had such anger in his eyes," Yolanda said, "I was sure he'd kill me."

Luckily for Yolanda, at around 2am that morning, a Condor Police officer, summoned by 911 calls from neighbors, pulled Luis off his bruised and bloodied wife. But, even a dazed Yolanda knew the police couldn't protect her. She welcomed the reprieve, sought comfort from ice cubes from the freezer, but knew it was just a break in the beatings. Luis wouldn't stop until he killed her.

Luis was released from jail late the following afternoon after Yolanda refused to press charges. She didn't dare cross him. If she did, she knew things would only get worse, and the end result would be two motherless children. Yolanda said she wasn't as concerned about her life, but she would never allow her children to be harmed in that manner. That afternoon, when Luis returned, she promised herself she would get rid of him, once and for all, before it was too late. She devised a new plan and coolly bided her time, while waiting for her moment. She was desperate but smart. She liked her new plan. She just had to make sure it played out this time. If it did, Danny would be dead, Luis would be serving a life sentence or worse, and she would be a free woman.

Each night, when Luis hustled off to the bars to rendezvous with his demons, Yolanda anonymously called The Bayside Motel to determine Danny's whereabouts. On a few occasions, she even crept passed his motel room in the darkness to see if he was there. In order for her plan to work, she needed her small universe to align properly: Luis must be stinking drunk and fighting mad, and Danny must be alone in his room. Finally, her planets found their proper orbits and she tearfully informed Luis that she was pregnant with Danny's child. Just as she hoped, Luis' reaction was a more furious replay of the first incident. He threw her across the small apartment, her head struck the wall, breaking a hole in the stucco, and once again he stormed into the bedroom for his pistol. From the next room, she heard the dresser drawer smash against the bedroom door after Luis had retrieved his weapon.

"Lord, he's going to kill somebody tonight," she prayed as she cowered in the corner. "Please make it Danny and not me."

Luis dashed out of the bedroom with gun in hand. He paused and momentarily pointed the weapon at Yolanda's forehead.

"No, Luis, no," she begged. "Think of your children."

"I should kill you, whore," he told her, his finger pressed to the trigger. "But first, I'm going to kill that violador," he shouted, referring to Danny as a rapist.

Twenty minutes later, as Luis stumbled through the shadowy alley behind the motel, he heard two gunshots and saw a tall man with black hair exit Danny's room. The stranger walked calmly to a black car parked on the side street and made his getaway. Luis didn't hesitate. He never considered checking on Danny's condition or calling the police. He rushed away from the scene as quickly as he normally rushed to the local bars. The gunshots had a sobering effect on him.

"I got the hell out of there, man," Luis told me, his breath heavy with alcohol from the night before, still not aware that his wife had been playing him for a fool. "I had my pistol with me," he said in broken English. "The police would lock me up."

Either Epiphany and Luis collaborated on their story about the lone figure and a black car, or Luis was telling the truth. To me, the two seemed like an unlikely alliance.

At their apartment, I asked Yolanda if I could see Luis' gun, and she produced a loaded forty-four-caliber pistol from the splintered drawer of their dresser. Over the years, we'd published articles about gun safety so I was familiar with different handguns. Since the murder weapon was a thirty-eight-caliber handgun, I believed Luis' account of that night though my instincts told me never to believe anything he said. I'd uncovered a complicated plot to murder Danny, but it wasn't the one that produced his death. Someone else got there first.

Obviously, I couldn't condone Yolanda's deadly intentions, but after listening to her heart-wrenching tale for an hour, I also couldn't ignore her desperation. As she spoke, her eyes were glazed with an ever-present sheen of fear. In my mind, her predicament was comparable to a terminal illness with no known treatments—she was biding time, simply waiting for matters to go from bleak to worse. If she weren't a human being, the humane thing to do would be to shoot her and put her out of her misery. It was all very tragic.

For a brief moment, I even thought about relaying some of the juicier tidbits of this sordid triangle to Captain Bryant and let him reach whatever conclusions he might. Though I knew Luis Silva didn't murder Danny, he'd probably be starting a life sentence in the state penitentiary by the end of the year. And, while that seemed an appropriate punishment for the horrible way he treated his wife and children, I couldn't do it. It was wrong.

* * *

By this time, my expectations of the Condor Police and their investigation were so low that the only way they could disappointment me would be if it turned out they murdered Danny Grainger.

At their headquarters, Captain Bryant and his band of officers finally confirmed what I suspected all along: There wasn't an actual, active, on-going investigation into the murder of Danny Grainger. The reality was that Danny was just another lowlife who'd been killed on the seedy, forgotten side of town, and his case file had been closed as soon as his corpse was shipped to Pennsylvania. Drug overdoses and murders were commonplace where Danny was shot—an area known as The Deed where society's castaways lived on the margins. No one in Condor, except for Coop, cared how Danny died. It was evident when I saw the file.

It started with a hunch. If Danny had a late night visitor, as Epiphany and Luis suggested, there might be something in his room that would tell me the reason for the visit. So, I interrupted his second breakfast one morning and asked Captain Bryant if I could see the crime scene photos. Unlike the police, I knew Danny. I might spot something that had been overlooked. Captain Bryant had always been obliging but, much to my surprise, he handed me the whole file.

"Here it is," he said, turning from the file cabinet. "That's the whole enchilada: crime scene photos, interviews, reports, everything. Have at it."

I was shocked. Weren't murder investigations confidential? Was I getting special treatment, or were police files now open to the media and general public? Was the case closed? I was confused and Captain Bryant sensed my bewilderment.

"Is something wrong?" he asked.

"No, everything's fine," I stammered. After all, I wanted to see the file.

The file was thin and incomplete. I sat at a large table in the corner of the station with it open before me, suffering quiet horror and disbelief over its contents, with Captain Bryant's words still echoing in my mind, "Everything." It was safe to say the police hadn't turned the town upside down or left no stone unturned in their efforts to solve this crime. Nor had they rounded up the usual suspects. They'd done little more than file the mandatory paperwork. Everything was, in reality, very little.

There was a police report, written on the morning of Danny's death, with statements from three motel residents, and four follow-up field reports from subsequent interviews, including Yolanda and Luis Silva. In her report, Yolanda lied by saying Luis was home with her that night. Additionally, there was the coroner's report, three tickets for items in the evidence room, and fifteen photographs from the crime scene. From what I saw in that file, the Condor Police Department hadn't spent twenty man-hours investigating the murder of Danny Grainger. Even Tyler and I had worked a lot harder than that, and we weren't getting paid to do it.

To me, it was painfully obvious that they never had any intention of finding the killer. They didn't care. I was furious, but I quashed my urge to castigate Captain Bryant. It would've served no purpose. As useless as he was, he was my ally on the police force.

Once I regained my composure, I turned my attention back to the folder. In the police report, Officer Darrell Lawson reported that a motel resident, Gus Bailey, one I had not met, saw Danny return to the motel alone at approximately 11:45pm and walk directly to his room. By all indications, he was the last person to see Danny alive, except his killer.

With no signs of forced entry or struggle, Lawson speculated that Danny knew his killer. Other aspects of the crime scene supported his theory. Danny had allowed his killer to enter his room and close the door behind him. At that hour of the night, Danny wouldn't have acted that way if the killer were a stranger. Also, Danny was shot next to his bed, on the opposite side of the room from the doorway, again indicating admittance of the killer. And finally, because no one at the motel heard the shots, the door was closed when the shots were fired.

On the red evidence tickets was a description of the item or items held in the evidence room. Evidence ticket B10289 was issued for two thirty-eight-caliber slugs, each removed from Danny's chest by the coroner. As part of their review of the crime scene, two officers conducted a search of the motel grounds and nearby dumpsters, but the murder weapon was never located. If the gun had been disposed of in the nearby vicinity, it was most likely in the mud at the bottom of the bay.

Evidence ticket B10271 was issued for two fibers found on the carpet near the doorway that seemed foreign and without match in his room. There was no indication on the ticket concerning the suspected source of the fibers or whether the fibers had been sent to a lab for testing. The last evidence ticket, B10272, was issued for a pair of sunglasses found under Danny's body, which struck me as very odd. Why would Danny wear sunglasses in his own room after midnight? Then again, maybe the sunglasses were already on the floor and Danny fell on top of them after he was shot?

The entryway and doorframe of the room were dusted for fingerprints, but the state forensics team wasn't any more successful in their search than the two dumpster-diving officers had been. Seven prints were lifted at the crime scene; wholes and partials, and all were conclusive matches to one Daniel Grainger.

Only one noteworthy statement was contained in the follow-up interviews that were conducted. Doug Taylor, another motel guest, had returned to the motel just before midnight. After he'd parked his car in the motel's lot, he noticed a black sports car, alone on the road at the time, drive past the motel, turn onto Manning Road, and park beside the motel. Doug Taylor made three people who had seen the black car that night, but no one identified its make or model.

It was hard for me to look at the crime scene photos that included Danny. Five of the fifteen showed him lying chest down on that large bloodstain I'd seen firsthand, his arms at his side, an image so vivid in my memory that, on some nights, it disturbed my sleep. I didn't want to reinforce that image so I glanced at those photos and moved on. On my worst days, I never imagined that someone close to me would meet that type of end.

Snapped as the photographer pointed the camera lens around the perimeter of the room, the remainder of the photos showed the state and contents of the room. It wasn't much different from his side of our dorm room at college. There was trash and clothes everywhere but, unlike our dorm, only two posters adorned the walls, one of Joe Namath and one of his beloved Pittsburgh Steelers; otherwise only a few newspaper clippings hung on the walls.

With the naked eye, I couldn't read the newspaper clippings so I borrowed a magnifying glass from one of the officers. There were four in all, three yellowed by age and one newer clipping. The oldest was an article from *The Signal* that appeared shortly after Danny's debut in 1978 entitled "QB Grainger Gives Grizzly Fans Hope." Next chronologically was the top half of the front page of the first issue of *Cavanaugh Weekly* dated May 5, 1980. The last of the older clippings was an article from *The Condor Bugle*, dated March 10, 1982, entitled "Former SU Football Star Settles in Condor." And finally, the newest clipping was the front-page headline and accompanying photograph of

Ben and towering skyscrapers from *The Cavanaugh Dispatch* earlier in the year that read "Matthews Announces Bid for Mayor."

One photograph reminded me of the sunglasses. Taken after Danny's body had been removed from the crime scene, it showed the sunglasses, mangled by his body weight, on the bloody carpet.

"Can I see this item?" I requested as I presented the evidence ticket to a junior officer seated near the evidence room.

"Sure," he answered, pulling his keys from his pocket, never inquiring about my part or purpose. Then, I noticed his name on his breastplate, Yost, a name I recognized from the police report I had just finished reading. Officer Yost had assisted Officer Lawson at The Bayside Motel on the morning of the murder.

"That was my first murder," he stated proudly.

Yost had short blond hair, big, green eyes, and light freckles on his youthful cheeks. He wasn't my idea of a cop.

"Are you close to solving it?" I asked.

I knew the answer, but I wanted to hear his response. I hoped he'd negate my suspicions about the lack of an investigation.

"It's your first case, after all," I added.

"We don't solve many cases in The Deed," the young officer said. "Witnesses rarely come forward in that area so cases are harder to solve. The captain told us not to waste our time."

It was just as I suspected.

The Deed was an eight-block area of seedy streets with bars, massage parlors, strip joints, tattoo shops, and liquor stores. After sunset, a brisk marketplace emerged where everything had a price but little legitimate commerce occurred. On the westernmost edge of The Deed, The Bayside Motel was home to many of its residents. Condor Police had never tried to clean up The Deed, but strived instead for containment so it didn't intrude on respectable Condor.

"So this case is closed?"

"Not officially."

Yost handed me a large plastic evidence bag with B10272 written across it in bold, black marker containing the sunglasses, still caked with dry brown blood. As I examined them, I flashed back to the last time I saw Danny alive, seated in the Utopia Publishing lobby near the Oscar Rhodes gallery. Unless he had a second pair, which I didn't think likely because he lived on a limited income and couldn't afford a reserve pair, these were the same sunglasses he wore that day, the same sunglasses he'd left in Ben's office. My mental picture of the sunglasses on the corner of Ben's desk was still clear in my mind.

244 | Michael Bowe

I had hoped the crime scene photos would reveal something unusual, something that might provide a new investigative tract, but the sunglasses presented an unthinkable scenario. Ben's car was a metallic black, 1990 Saab, sporty in profile, and thereby consistent with the description of the vehicle seen parked alongside the motel that night. And, Ben was six-feet-four-inches tall, so his general description matched the tall, dark figure seen leaving the motel and getting into the car. Was it Ben's Saab? Did Ben visit Danny that night? If not, how did those sunglasses make their way back to Condor? Did Ben have a reason to kill Danny? Was Ben capable of murder? Did more transpire in Ben's office than he had told me?

I had more questions than I'd ever imagined the crime scene photo session could produce, but the biggest question was the one that was most troubling: Did I really want to know the answers? After all, Ben was my best friend and my business partner; our personal fortunes and professional lives were intertwined. In this case, maybe ignorance was bliss. I could count on ignorance from the Condor Police. But could I live with it?

* * *

"I don't believe it," Tyler said defiantly after I briefed her on my findings in Condor, including my suspicions about the tall figure seen walking away, the black car parked alongside the motel, and the sunglasses underneath the body.

She continued, "Ben is the most driven and ambitious person I've ever known, but he's not capable of murder. I think you've let your imagination get away from you."

It was 2:15pm on a Thursday afternoon. We both felt guilty about our conversation, as we'd put Ben's name in the same sentence as murderer, and that felt like a serious betrayal. After all, we both admired and respected him. He was our friend. He was also the most astounding person we'd ever met, and we traveled in accomplished circles. In the back of The Boardroom, we were hunkered down in a booth, all as part of an investigative scheme I'd concocted so I could ask my best friend and business partner one innocent, little question: When was the last time he saw Danny?

I arranged the whole affair, everything from arrival times to booth selection, and even scripted the mealtime conversation, every detail except our lunch orders, though I recommended the fried chicken salad. I asked Tyler to meet me at 2pm so I could brief her on the details of my plan and enlist her help. As was true of most dishonest activities, I needed an accomplice. Earlier that morning, I'd left a message with Mrs. Matlock asking Ben to join us for lunch at 2:30pm. I knew his schedule was light that afternoon and, since the three of us hadn't had a meal together in two months, I was confident he'd come.

My plan was simple. I would casually steer the conversation to Danny, tell my story about my interaction with him in the lobby on that gloomy day, and then ask each of them when they saw him last. As part of a casual conversation among friends, I hoped I could avoid alerting Ben to the fact that he'd become a suspect in my mind. I didn't want to hurt him.

"I won't do it," Tyler protested, more defiantly than before. "We are his friends, Pete. If you suspect Ben, just ask him the damn question. Let him explain himself."

Before I could persuade her, Ben strolled in the front door of the restaurant. His walk was light and bouncy like the frontrunner in a mayoral election. Though always positive, Ben had been more upbeat than ever since the grand opening of Optimal Tower and the more than five-point bump that he received in the polls.

"He's here," I said, unclear of the status of my plan. "Just follow my lead."

"Have you been waiting long?" Ben asked as he approached.

"No," I answered.

I'd never lied to Ben—not that I could recall anyway—and certainly not about anything significant. Heck, we were journalists so honesty was fundamental to our belief systems. In our world, the truth mattered. And, on top of that, our professional lives and personal fortunes were so intertwined that we had to be able to trust each other. Our friendship had always been rooted in honest communication.

At that moment, I realized I was fidgeting with the knife from my place setting. The scenario was too symbolic for me—a knife in hand for a stab in the back—too much of a physical Freudian slip, so, guilt-ridden, I quickly returned the flatware to its place on my napkin.

Tyler was right, no doubt about it. I should have been direct. It was the right thing to do. After all, we'd been best friends for a lot of years. Still, I couldn't do it. Several times during lunch, I tried to ask Ben candidly, but my mouth refused to provide the words. I just couldn't tell my friend that I suspected him of murder. I couldn't do it, but I still had to know.

It was Plan A. When the chips were down, Tyler would come through, or so I hoped.

Throughout my story about Danny, Tyler had a firm grin on her face. From her expression and body language, I couldn't guess whether she planned to back me up, but it was too late to change the plan. Much like Yolanda Silva, I had a good plan, and I had to see it through.

"Then Danny responded, 'I'm here to see Ben, not you,'" I told them, replaying my encounter on that bleak February morning. "He was so rude. Hell, I offered him a cup of coffee and a muffin."

"At least he talked to you," Tyler volunteered when I finished, causing me to breathe a deep, silent sigh of relief. It must have been her reporter's curiosity that got the best of her. "Danny walked away from me without saying a word the last time I saw him."

Seven years earlier, while still a field reporter, Tyler was in Condor to cover a major drug seizure at the docks, some two million dollars worth of cocaine and a customized speedboat. She had just finished filming her segment when she noticed Danny amongst a small crowd of onlookers across the street. But when she called out to Danny, he didn't answer, wave, or even acknowledge her presence. He put his head down, turned away from her, and walked briskly up the street; his distinct limp evident with each hurried step.

"I couldn't believe it," she said, scowling. "It was Danny."

"When was the last time that you saw Danny, Ben?" I asked, mustering my most causal, nonchalant voice.

"The same morning you did, Pete, in my office," Ben stated.

"You never saw him after that?"

"Nope, I gave him money, and that was the last I saw of him."

* * *

Two days later, I learned the reason for Tyler's change of heart and complicity at The Boardroom. While I rambled through my lengthy story about the last time I'd seen Danny, Tyler remembered a loan that she'd made to Ben during college. At that moment, in the booth at lunch, she didn't remember the circumstances but, when interwoven with our subject matter, the loan was suddenly suspicious. Her recollection of this long-forgotten transaction roused her curiosity enough that she wanted to hear Ben's response to my question. Then, further roused by Ben's apparent lie, Tyler used her free time at the station to peruse old planners, journals, and bank statements searching for a notation concerning the loan. Eventually, Tyler found the $7,000 loan on a bank statement and confirmation in her planner.

"It doesn't look good," she said on the phone one evening, "Help!" by the Beatles playing ironically in the background. "He borrowed the money four days before the UWS game and gave it back five weeks later."

"So he put together a bankroll for a wager on the game?"

"It looks that way. I can't remember why Ben said he needed the money, but I think it might've been that the print shop needed a new machine. I don't recall. I trusted him."

13.

Completed in 1973, at a cost of $800 million, more than twice the original projection, the World Trade Center became World's Tallest at 1,368 feet, 118 feet taller than the Empire State Building. On September 11, 2001, the WTC was the target of the most horrific terrorist act in U.S. history when it was struck by hijacked aircraft and destroyed. Standing prominently above the rest has its risks and downside also.

In early June, Ben hired a campaign manager. Kitt Blanchard was a no-nonsense, forty-seven-year-old political strategist with shocking auburn hair and emerald green eyes from the "Great State of Texas," her words. To me at least, her personal style seemed better suited to a freeway truck stop than a political campaign, but she came highly recommended as her clients always won their elections. Kitt talked trashy, but she lived and worked hi-tech, relying on research and data to win elections. Her methodology for unseating incumbents and beating the deeply-entrenched, good old boys was a simple two-pronged approach: Know the voters better than they know themselves and tell the voters what they want to hear.

After meeting Kitt, I wondered if Ben understood the nature of his selection. Fundamentally, he wanted to make a difference and make politics work for the people, and yet he partnered with a political maven, a crafty strategist who manipulated the electorate and managed campaigns like warfare, with a win-at-any-cost mentality. Kitt didn't impress me as the right choice for Ben unless, of course, status quo was the new tactic and simply winning was the new priority.

"I love it," Kitt boasted in her Texas drawl, standing in my office doorway after our introduction. "Used to be men opened doors for women, and now, men come to me to open doors for them."

In attire consistent with her home state, Kitt wore blue jeans, a white shirt with silver studs, and gray snakeskin boots. When it came to her attire and personal style, she wore her rebellious home state like a badge of honor.

"Kitt managed the senate campaign of Linda Converse in her victory over incumbent Reed Madison," Ben said. "On the national level, it was the biggest upset of the last election."

"Did the country a service," Kitt added. "Reed Madison was one mangy varmint who never should have been seated in the senate. Our paths crossed a day before the election and Reed was as nervous and twitchy as a whore in church. He knew his day was at hand."

Ben's lead in the polls had evaporated as quickly as summer rain on a Houston highway. The most recent results gave him a two-point advantage but, with a three-point margin of error, it was, for all practical purposes, a dead heat. There hadn't been any dramatic moments that had turned voter sentiment and tightened the race, nothing like Ben's "King Dale" speech or the grand opening of Optimal Tower. The gap had tightened for two reasons: Ben's honeymoon period was over and the mayor's constant barrage of assaults on Ben's lack of political experience via billboards, bus displays, and local television spots were working.

In one TV commercial, Mayor Greenwood, wearing a beige sweater with brown elbow patches, relaxed before a fireplace in the mayor's office while reflecting on the 1980s and the progress made during his time in office. A deliberate response to Ben's use of the skyline in his announcement speech, the mayor exhibited two skyline photographs, one from 1980, when he was first elected and a second of the more developed skyline of the present day with Optimal Tower in the center of the image.

"We've come a long way," the mayor said. "Together, we've accomplished a lot. But the job isn't done, and we shouldn't turn our work over to the unskilled and unprepared."

No one—not experts, media, or pundits—expected Ben to win easily, many not at all. In any race, at any level of government, under any circumstances, a three-term incumbent was a formidable political foe. Better than anyone, Kitt knew what she was up against and what it would take to win. This election would be decided November 3rd and not a day sooner. In her mind, the key to winning was to run like a marathoner and save something for the end because the candidate with momentum in late October would squeak out a victory. Kitt was determined to make sure that was Ben.

"I've done my research," Kitt remarked, "and I can guarantee one thing—Greenwood won't make any mistakes. He's a veteran politician, and he's not going to open the door for us. We're going to have to kick the damn door open for ourselves."

* * *

Kitt never "waited for cow pies to dry on her boots," whatever the hell that meant. It wasn't something I wanted to ponder. Two hours after our introduction, Kitt reappeared in my office doorway with a yellow legal pad and pen in hand. She requested an hour of my time to go over background information.

"If you want to get the lay of the land, you've got to walk the fences," Kitt offered as a rationale for our time together.

Professionally, Kitt was determined, diligent, and smart, and I'd always respected those qualities in people. Personally, she was a colorful character and quite different from anyone I'd ever known. Instantly, she both intrigued and entertained me, so I couldn't help but enjoy our time together.

I liked Kitt, I respected her, but I didn't always understand her. When she spoke, she often quoted her mama, daddy, grandpa, grandma, and preacher and always peppered every exchange with folksy anecdotes, some I understood, some I didn't. Often, I was left behind, distracted from our conversation because I was trying to figure out something she said, searching every English course I'd ever taken for a translation.

At one moment, referring to a campaign swing through Boise years ago, Kitt remarked, "We went through that town like Epsom salts through a widow woman."

For the next five minutes, I missed everything she said; I stared blankly and watched her lips move while repeating over and over in my mind, *Epsom salts through a widow woman? What the hell does that mean?*

I had my doubts about Kitt, but I was determined to help the campaign in every way I could. For fifty minutes, I dutifully provided Kitt the information she needed for crafting a strategy. I recounted our years together, Ben and I, including meeting at SU, our connection, our freshman article, our early days at *The Signal,* the student center announcement, Ben's concept for a weekly newspaper, dropping out, starting the newspaper, refurbishing the old warehouse, starting-up our business, Ben's column in the *Weekly,* his contributions to the city council's policies, Ben's national acclaim as an urban visionary, our business expansion as Utopia Publishing, the addition of two monthly publications, and finally, Ben's decision to run for political office.

As I told our story, I experienced something unusual. My own words affected me deeply on both an emotional and spiritual level. Like some kind of out of body experience, I felt like I was listening to the details of my own history for the first time, and I was very aware of just how remarkable Ben's and my shared journey had been. Most particularly for me, an unremarkable boy from suburbia with modest dreams and simple ambitions, the last decade had been absolutely incredible, way beyond anything I dreamed as a young boy. My real life had clearly exceeded my dreams and that was unusual.

Kitt listened intently and took many notes, but it wasn't until I concluded that I learned her real purpose for our time together. This was politics, after all.

"I need to be prepared," Kitt said, clicking her pen closed and placing it in her studded breast pocket, as if to signal that we were now officially off the record.

"Politics is a dirty game," she continued, "and nothing shuts down a campaign quicker than a juicy scandal. A little preemptive spin and damage control can go a long way to avoiding disaster, but I've got to be prepared. Are there any issues in Ben's professional or personal life that could derail his campaign? If so, let's get them on the table right now."

It was ironic timing. Two days ago, without hesitation or doubt, I would've answered "nothing," no secrets or scandalous issues, no way. Unequivocally, Ben was the most honest and forthright person I knew, and ethics would not be an issue in his campaign. He was squeaky clean. I would've said that I trusted Ben with my life or my children's lives, if I had any. Two days ago, I would have said that.

Now, however, I suspected that Ben was involved in the death of our friend and, as never before, I found myself questioning his actions, like hiring Kitt for instance. Would Ben kill Danny if his mayoral campaign were in jeopardy? I didn't know the answer to that question anymore. That's right, I didn't know.

"No," I answered Kitt. "Nothing that I know of."

I almost added that Ben was squeaky clean, but I stopped myself short. I'd answered her question, and I didn't feel the need to elaborate. Two days ago, I would've elaborated, not today.

"How about a drink?" Kitt asked, noticing the late hour on her watch, a blue "Lone Star" on its face. "I always like a very dry martini about this time each day."

Did she say martini? Just when I thought I was starting to figure Kitt out, she confounded me again. I would've guessed her drink of choice to be whiskey shots or beer or even tequila—not martinis. One thing about Kitt was clear: expect the unexpected.

It was just after 5pm. Ben and Kitt planned to walk to the Matthews for Mayor Campaign Headquarters in Whitehall Tower and stop for a drink on the way. Kitt would office at the headquarters and assume responsibility for the mostly volunteer staff of eleven. In the four months since Ben rented the space, the campaign staff had limped along, lacking experience, structure, and direction. Ben was confident Kitt would remedy that quickly.

We adjourned to a booth at The Boardroom and ordered a first round of refreshments, a couple pints of beer for Ben and myself and a chilled martini with three olives for Kitt.

"I'm surprised you ordered a martini," Ben remarked as the waiter placed the round of drinks on the table, echoing my earlier thought.

"Oh, I'll drink just about anything," she replied, "but I like to start with a martini."

With that said, Kitt raised her glass and declared, "There is nothing like a martini when it's time for making a toast, but always two at most; three and I'm under the table; four and I'm under my host."

We all laughed. Kitt's face creased near the eyes and the corners of her mouth, revealing character lines that another woman might've covered up or surgically altered, but not her. Kitt wore little makeup and never said or did anything phony. She was as real as they came. In her own words, she was as real as her grandma's biscuits. And, character lines or not, Kitt was still an attractive woman, with chiseled cheekbones and a figure that defied time. I couldn't help but envision a younger Kitt turning every head from Dallas to Houston, with more buck and kick than any rodeo bronco.

"My first job as a campaign manager," Kitt informed us, "was in 1970 when Jack Banks ran for Mayor of Austin. One week after I accepted the job, at a locally televised debate, his opponent, Tommy Piper, approached me offstage and began whispering his best pickup lines in my ear, some really vulgar stuff. He had no idea who I was."

Kitt paused as the waiter placed another martini on the table.

"A shot of whiskey next round," she instructed the waiter. "Anything for either of you boys?"

Neither of us had even consumed half our pint yet so we both shook our heads from side to side.

Kitt continued. "You have to realize that, in those days, there weren't many women in politics, least of all, Texas politics. So, I let this crude bastard, who had coincidentally made his fortune in crude oil, ramble on and on, and I even feigned some interest until, finally, when the stage manager called for the candidates, I introduced myself. Tommy Piper turned white as a ghost and never recovered that night."

Kitt laughed loudly.

"He didn't know what to say. He was totally off balance throughout the whole debate. Banks slaughtered him and won that election by fifteen points."

*   *   *

At the end of June, Kitt confirmed my fears about her methods when she summoned Ben and me to campaign headquarters to review new polling results. As part of the rationale for the meeting, she said we needed to realign our strategy with this new data because it revealed weaknesses in the current strategy, which sounded to me like political lingo for we need to change the message and "tell the voters what they want to hear." Though I wasn't clear why Kitt included me, my morning had been slow so, for curiosity sake, I accompanied Ben.

On arrival, it was quite obvious that Kitt had transformed the fledgling staff into a formidable political force, as there was a new buzz in the office and a new energy in the air. Instead of the usual milling about, half of the staffers purposefully typed labels and stuffed mailing envelopes while the other half busily worked the telephones to solicit support. In the midst of it all, an enthusiastic Kitt, armed with a clipboard and a street map, gave last-minute instructions to two college students on bicycles who were going to distribute campaign posters to local merchants for display.

"Wait in my office," Kitt directed us as we entered, making it clear we were on her turf now.

Four weeks ago, on arrival in Cavanaugh, Kitt's first official act as campaign manager was to commission a polling company to survey voters and formulate a snapshot of sentiment regarding the candidates and the issues. Two days ago, the polling company couriered a thick, burgundy binder with "Warshaw, Reading and Kite, Political Polling Results, Client: Benjamin Matthews," imprinted on the cover. As I entered her office and noticed the bulky binder on her desk, I got a sinking feeling in the pit of my stomach, though I never imagined its full significance. That document, I would soon learn, would serve as Kitt's bible for the next five months and provide the basis for Ben's platform as well as every public appearance he'd make. Kitt believed in giving the public what they wanted.

"You don't win elections by arguing with the voters."

According to extensive polling results, Ben was perceived as a charismatic visionary with an aggressive style while the mayor was perceived as a wise and cautious patriarch. Voters, according to Kitt's interpretation of the report, preferred to associate themselves with Ben but were likely to vote for the more conservative mayor in November. With that warp in mind, Kitt believed the polling results were wrongly skewed in Ben's favor and she further believed he'd lose by at least five points if the election were held on that day. In a prosperous place like Cavanaugh, voters opt for status quo instead of change. When times are good, change is viewed as for the worse so voters tend to move toward the conservative end of the spectrum. Everything Kitt said made sense, but the new strategy she advocated would be hard for Ben to accept.

"We've got to soften our approach," Kitt advised her client, "move to the middle of the road. If voters think that a vote for Ben Matthews is a risky proposition, they won't flip that handle in your favor."

"What do you mean by soften our approach?" Ben asked.

At that moment, I flashed back to Ben's pledge to launch a campaign focused on preparing the city for the new millennium and I knew he'd never stand for political posturing. According to Ben, most politicians betray the voters because they're unwilling to address the difficult issues that might cost them the election. His campaign was going to address the hard issues and the difficult choices. He wanted to talk about the future in a way that readied his city for the challenges ahead. Reflecting on his philosophy, I braced myself for the heated words and shouting that seemed inevitable.

But true to form, Kitt was prepared. She quickly flipped to a section near the back of the binder that measured voter sentiment on key issues and told us that her biggest concern centered on the light-rail system. She explained it this way.

When voters think about government projects, they never think about positive end results or future benefits but, instead, think of higher taxes and governmental waste. In their minds, it is the typical and expected outcome. In his campaigning, whenever Ben mentions the light-rail system in a speech, voters think about higher taxes and governmental waste, not about the modernization of the transportation system and the positive effect it will have on the city. And, it is never wise to run for office with a platform that includes higher taxes and governmental waste. Quite to the contrary, it's political suicide.

"It's like telling Texans you're going to outlaw horses," Kitt said. "You ain't gonna win the election and, to make matters worse, they'll probably run you out of the state."

I will miss Kitt, I thought.

Ben would never compromise and adopt Kitt's new platform. His visionary ideas and the light-rail system were the centerpiece of his campaign. How could he soften it? Kitt might as well have told him that he was too tall and had to shrink three inches. It just couldn't be done.

"The light-rail system is critical for Cavanaugh in the new millennium," Ben protested. "Its construction is as critical as clean air and water."

"Ben," Kitt interrupted, "I'm not saying that the city shouldn't build the light-rail system. I'm telling you that you shouldn't make it the central issue of your campaign. It'll hurt your chances of getting elected. I can assure you of that."

"It's the very heart and soul of my campaign," Ben insisted. "It's the single largest reason I'm running for the office."

"First, you've got to get elected," Kitt said. "Then, you can build the light rail system. It's just a question of sequence."

After ten more minutes of debate, Ben finally conceded.

"Alright, Kitt," Ben allowed, "I want to win this election so I guess I've got to trust my expert."

The meeting only got worse from there.

Often, campaign managers hired private investigators to do "opposition research" that really meant finding the dirty little secrets of their opponents, basically anything embarrassing or scandalous that could derail a campaign. Kitt once told me that, without exception, every candidate has dirt, and it was just a matter of which of the competing campaigns found it first. These investigators, most with extensive law enforcement experience, performed background checks on candidates that were far more rigorous than the business sector, going back to birth and really deep into their private and professional lives. Kitt also told me that these investigators numbered around a baker's dozen but that the absolute best was a former secret service agent based in Houston named Xavier Willis. His nickname was "the Gravedigger" because he uncovered secrets that eventually buried the secret keeper.

In a large white envelope, containing no other markings than Xavier P. Willis embossed in fancy script in the upper left corner, the gravedigger's eleven-page investigative research on Dale Greenwood was in front of Kitt on her desk. Under the guise of, "we need to know what we are up against," Kitt opened the envelope and began to read select findings from the pages of the report.

"Ben," I pleaded, interrupting Kitt as she gave us a preview of the contents of the scurrilous report, "please tell me you're not going to resort to this kind of mudslinging to win this election."

"Pete is right," he responded. "I don't want to hear anything more about what's in that report. You should file that away because we're not going to use it."

"Your call," Kitt conceded. "But, I think you should hear one more item. It concerns you."

"Read it," Ben instructed her.

"After the Restore Old Cavanaugh Rally in November 1978, organized by then college student Ben Matthews, then Councilman Dale Greenwood conspired with the dockworkers union to graffiti and damage the visitor center at Cavanaugh Waterfront Towers so that the supporters at the rally would be blamed. The damage shifted public support from the restoration of Old Cavanaugh to the construction of the CWT and helped Greenwood win the mayor's office."

"How could Xavier find that information?" I asked.

"I already told you," Kitt responded. "He's the best."

"I've known that Councilman Greenwood was involved," Ben remarked. "It's one of the reasons I want his office."

I was thankful I accompanied Ben to that meeting because I never would've believed what happened otherwise. At most, it took Kitt thirty minutes to rewrite Ben's entire platform and strategy. Right in front of me, my principled friend had faded to gray, disappeared altogether, then reappeared as some sort of deal-making, political animal, not all that different from his adversary, the mayor. He was suddenly dumbing down his platform and avoiding the hard issues to get elected. He was now willing to parrot any scripted message put in front of him and say whatever the voters wanted to hear. The things that were most important to Ben, the very reasons he was running for the office, were suddenly off the table. Though Ben had taken a firm stance against mudslinging, I suspected that could change if the race was close in the final days. After all, Kitt Blanchard won elections. Despite a refreshing start to the campaign, we were clearly moving towards politics as usual.

Though a newcomer to the political scene, I also suspected that my friend was boarding a well-traveled campaign bus that had far too many miles on it and far too little maintenance in it, one that was sure to break down along the way. Politicians, it seemed to me, often made the mistake of thinking they could ride the political process to their destination, then retrieve their character and integrity later, like a package left in a bus station locker, never realizing that they had a one-way ticket and there was no going back. One could pull the cord, sound the little tinkling bell, and get off the bus, but no one could go back. Some things are not retrievable.

Danny once told me that if you put a price on something truly priceless, you lose, simple as that. "Once you participate in that kind of transaction," he said prophetically, "you're never the same person again. You've sold a part of yourself."

Coincidentally, I finally began to understand what Danny was talking about all this time. From my research into his life in Condor, I thought I understood his downfall. Danny had sold the one thing that was most important to him, and there was no coming back from that, no way to redeem his self. Similarly, there wasn't anything I could say to dissuade Ben from making the same mistake; the same type of sellout and betrayal but, more importantly, I was beginning to believe Ben had bigger problems anyway.

* * *

When it came to investigative techniques, I was winging it, relying mostly on insights gleamed from detective shows in my youth. Who would've thought that my many hours on the couch in front of *Ironsides, MacMillan and Wife, Dragnet, Columbo*, and *Streets of San Francisco*, would finally pay off? Stealing a page right out of *The Rockford Files*, I put together a photographic lineup of three black,

European cars, a BMW, a Mercedes Benz, and a Saab, so I could show them to Luis Silva and Epiphany Lange. Neither was familiar with automobile makes and models, particularly not foreign luxury cars, but maybe they'd identify the car seen at the motel. As further proof I watched too much television, I also consulted the *Farmer's Almanac* under phases of the moon to gauge the visibility on the night of the murder and discovered, much to my chagrin, that it had been a moonless night, horrible conditions for identifying a black car.

During my drive to Condor, the information from the almanac weighed on my mind, and I wondered if I was on a fool's errand. How could Epiphany and Luis identify the black car when they saw it on a moonless night? But, on arrival at The Bayside Motel, I noticed something I hadn't on previous visits. On Manning Road, just a half block north of the location where the black car was parked on that fateful night, stood a streetlight that illuminated much of the block. Maybe, it wasn't a fool's errand after all.

I knocked on Epiphany's door at a little past noon, but there wasn't any response so I walked three blocks to The Wayfarer Shelter where I knew she spent a lot of her time. From past conversations, I'd learned that Danny visited the shelter for the free lunches on occasion, so I also wanted to see the shelter and its clientele. Anytime I could experience what Danny's life was like in Condor, I tried to put myself in his place. Unfortunately, it was never a pleasant experience.

Little had been done to restore the old cannery that housed the shelter as several of the windows were broken, floor tiles were chipped or missing altogether, and a large, gaping hole in a corner of the roof was patched with plywood. A tall white bucket caught the drips of water that fell steadily from the ceiling like sand into an hourglass, as if time was running out on both the building and its clientele. Aside from a commercial stove and a serving area, the building looked more suited for demolition than occupancy. There were no beds, cots, or even chairs, as I would've expected and only sleeping bags marked the areas for each of the shelter's residents.

While serving hot soup and stale sandwiches to a couple of regular patrons, Epiphany spotted me the moment I stepped in the door. From behind the serving station, she waved for me to come over.

"How about some lunch?" she offered me as I approached the food line. "It's not fancy, but it is nutritious," she added.

"Thank you," I said as I accepted the bowl. But I declined the baloney and cheese sandwich she offered next.

Epiphany promised to join me once she finished serving the lunch crowd, so I found a spot against the wall, next to an old man with a scraggily gray beard and worn clothing, where I could quietly enjoy my soup. It was piping hot, full of noodles, and better than I expected. Sitting there, I thought about how hard it must've been for Danny to swallow the soup at the shelter, a charity meal for the hopeless and needy and how his days in Condor had few high points. With so much promise in his youth, he had to be absolutely beaten down and demoralized by the reality of his existence to stand in line for a free bowl of soup. As I slurped the broth from my spoon, the old man next to me ripped his sandwich into little pieces and dropped them into his bowl, producing a broth and mustard mixture that almost caused me to lose my already shelter-tested appetite. A few minutes later, when the old man smiled in my direction, I saw that he had only two teeth, and I understood.

"Walter," the old man said as he extended his hand.

"What's the best meal they make here?" I asked awkwardly.

"Best meal?" he answered with a weary laugh. "It's chicken soup and a baloney sandwich every day."

I felt like such a jerk, but I had no idea how these shelters worked or how anyone ended up here. It was hard for me to imagine falling so far as life on the streets or prison for that matter. No one ever imagines that life could take such a harsh turn. But, it happens all the time.

Aside from the toll the years and streets had inflicted, Walter looked like an average man, probably even handsome and strapping in his twenties and thirties, facing a life full of promise and possibilities. Mindfully, I avoided any details about Walter's predicament, as I didn't want the unthinkable to suddenly seem possible in my own life. By the time Epiphany joined us, I felt depressed. With each passing day, I learned more about Danny's life in Condor, and it was always heartbreaking. I had all but forgotten the three photos in my pocket that brought me to the shelter in the first place. Between spoonfuls of soup, Epiphany reminded me.

"Pete, if you don't stop visiting so often I'm going to think you've got a thing for me. What brings you here today?"

I was too embarrassed to retrieve the photos from my pocket but, in my mind, I couldn't help but acknowledge the irony. I'd come to this dreary hovel, this refuge for the abused and downtrodden, overflowing with suffering and heartache, awash in poverty and misfortune, to discuss expensive foreign luxury cars. What had become of my compassion? Had the profession of journalism or the process of getting older toughened my sensitivities to the point that I was unaffected by another person's plight? I couldn't bring myself to produce the photos, not in front of Walter anyway.

"Can we take a walk when you finish your soup?" I proposed.

"Okay, but I better warn you, young man," she responded, "before you go getting yourself all let down and hurt. The lord is my only suitor anymore."

"I understand."

On the quiet street corner in front of The Wayfarer Shelter, Epiphany studied the photos intently, flipped back and forth between the snapshots several times, and made me think she couldn't decide.

"Mmmm, Mmmm," she finally said, "those are pretty cars."

Not the response I was after.

"Do you recognize the car you saw that night?" I pressed.

"How much do cars like that cost?" As was true of our prior conversations, Epiphany was easily distracted.

"Do you see it there?" I asked again.

"You know," she replied, drifting again, "in my previous profession we had a saying—you better make sure you're working your side of the street or else there will be trouble. Are you working your side of the street, honey?"

"I am, Epiphany. I am," I replied exasperated, not wanting to acknowledge the insightful nature of her streetwise inquiry. "Do you see it there?"

"Should I be worrying about you, honey?"

"No, there is nothing to worry about," I said. "Do you see the car in those photos?"

"Yeah, that's the one," she declared and handed me the photo of the Saab.

"Are you sure?"

"What do you mean, am I sure?" Epiphany blurted. "I don't know what kind of car that is, but I ain't blind or stupid. That's the car, alright!"

* * *

An hour later, at the employee entrance of the White Bros. Cannery, I waited for Luis Silva to exit the building for his afternoon break. At the bayside plant, on the cool, moist sea air was the strong stench of raw fish, which made my short ten-minute wait seem as long as a typical wait at the Department of Motor Vehicles. At 2:01pm exactly, the gray, metal door flung wide open and a parade of workers in white overalls streamed out. Instantly, I was knocked two feet backward by the rush of seafood odor, but I tried to act unaffected. Seafood workers were immune to it. After about a dozen had exited, Luis emerged with a group of workers from the salmon line.

"What the hell do you want?" he blared. "I've got fifteen minutes to piss and smoke a cigarette. Leave me alone."

But, after some coaxing and the promise of a twenty-dollar bill if he picked the right car, Luis reluctantly took the photos from my hand, quickly glanced at each car, placed the photo of the black Saab on top, and handed them back to me.

"That's the car," he said, as he snatched the portrait of Andrew Jackson from my fingers and then walked away.

Two for two, I thought to myself. I had confirmation.

Swearing off seafood forever, I left Condor a little dazed by the afternoon's testimony. All things considered, it seemed the case against Ben was more than circumstantial now, and I could no longer dismiss the gambling connection or the sunglasses as coincidental. Two witnesses saw a black Saab at the motel at the time of the murder. Sure, it could have been another coincidence, someone other than Ben in a black Saab, but even a best friend and longtime business partner had cause for suspicion. Still, I needed more.

*   *   *

Over the next few days, I bounced around Condor with no real direction or purpose, unsure of how to proceed, hoping to stumble onto something, anything. I needed a new lead, a fresh angle, another suspect, or some additional evidence concerning Ben. I talked with a lot of people and revisited the police file, but I got nowhere. As evidence of my frustration, I even requested a list of owners of black Saabs in the greater metropolitan area from the DMV, but none of the names on the list had any connection to Danny. I was stuck. And, since I couldn't exactly flash Ben's photo on the streets of Condor or at the motel, I had no idea how to proceed. I was truly at an impasse.

On my return to Cavanaugh late one afternoon, I miraculously stumbled onto something, a new investigative tract to follow. About an hour from the bay, while still navigating along the rural farmlands on Route 19, I realized I forgot to fill the gas tank. My car was low on fuel, the needle straddled the red line by the E, and the indicator light was illuminated and flashing. Each flash seemed like a message.

"You idiot, you idiot," it seemed to repeat over and over.

Reduced to ounces and not gallons, I didn't know if I'd make it to the next gas station, an Exxon before the entrance ramp to the Cavanaugh Freeway, probably eight or nine miles at least from my current location. Instantly, a little moisture appeared on my forehead, shoulders, and underarms—those nervous sweats that you get when you're suddenly anxious and you know you're in trouble. How could I have been so forgetful?

"No," I screamed several minutes later as the car began to sputter and shake, clearly running out of juice. When my progress was reduced to a fast coast, I guided my car to the side of the road.

In my circumstance, my only comfort was the fact that I'd managed to stop my car in the cool shade beneath a large maple tree. Briefly, I considered walking to the gas station, but I'd never hiked in the great outdoors and didn't think this was the right time for me to start. Had I set out for that gas station on foot, I knew a search and rescue team would be looking for me at first light the very next day. In the shade on the quiet roadside, I waited for a passerby to offer assistance.

After a short while, a deliveryman in a white, refrigerated truck with "Ocean Fresh Seafood" on the side in red pulled alongside my car and asked, "You out of gas, mister?"

Though a handful of sarcastic replies popped into my mind, I smiled and politely responded, "Yes." Bobby, from the red stitching on his white coat, was kind enough to pour the remainder of a five-gallon gas can into my tank and, as he did, he told me that he drove Route 19 daily and usually found someone stranded on the roadside at least once a week.

"Always city folk," he added, as he looked me up and down. "People from Condor know better."

On my previous trips, I'd been more conscientious, always refueling at one end, in Cavanaugh or Condor, knowing that the round trip required almost an entire tank of gas. Since I left Cavanaugh that morning with a less than three-quarters of a tank, I knew I'd have to refuel in Condor that afternoon, but I'd just plain forgot.

Driving the remaining miles of winding roadway to the Exxon station with my mind still focused on fuel, I thought about how high my gas credit card bills had been the last few months as a result of my trips to the coast, and something else occurred to me: If Ben drove his

Saab to Condor on the night of the murder, he would've filled his gas tank in the city before leaving because he wouldn't want to refuel after murdering his college friend. Though Ben had never planned a murder before (that I knew of), he was smart enough to know not to risk being seen in Condor that night. And then, after the nearly 250-mile round trip, Ben would need to fill his tank again the next day in the city. If it was, indeed, Ben's black Saab in Condor on the night of the murder, his credit card receipts might confirm it.

* * *

"We've got a game tonight," Stan reminded me as we passed in the hallway, him on his way out, me just arriving. "You're going to make this one, right?"

Stan was referring to the Utopia Publishing Angels; the little league baseball team Stan and I coached each spring that, once again, featured his twin sons and children of other employees who also played on our basketball team. My attendance had been pretty erratic at both practices and games this season, due to Danny's death and the research on my article, but I knew I could count on Stan to cover my frequent lapses, much the same way he did at work.

"I can't make it," I responded, feeling as guilty as I had at the shelter that day.

"The kids really miss you when you're not there," Stan replied as he continued to backpedal down the hallway.

Then, Stan turned the corner into the lobby and was gone. A moment later, I collapsed into my chair. Sitting there, I realized how different I was now than six months ago. Before Danny's death, I was a very organized, productive editor who enjoyed a myriad of activities and a group of good friends in my spare time. Since his death, I've become so obsessed with Danny's story that it's been at the expense of everything else in my life. These days, I had no spare time or other interests. For good or for bad, I had to get this stuff behind me. My old life beckoned.

Quite fortunately, Tyler called on the phone and took my mind off my guilt.

"Where have you been?" she asked, like an anxious mother who'd searched for her missing child all afternoon. "Wait, let me guess, Condor," she said, answering her own question. "I've been calling you all day. Make sure you watch the network news program tonight."

"I watch your show every night," I said, a slight exaggeration but acceptable between friends. In my distracted state, I'd missed the network distinction and only heard news.

"Not my show," she returned, "the network news program."

It seemed like an important announcement, but Tyler didn't give me an opportunity to ask, "Why?"

With one final blurt, she was gone.

"I gotta go. I'm on in five."

It was 5:45pm so I had forty-five minutes until the start of the network news program, enough time to take a quick peek at Ben's calendar and expense reports, all maintained in Mrs. Matlock's area, but not late enough in the workday that I could be certain the building was empty. The prudent approach would've been to wait until after the program concluded, but my curiosity was stirred and getting the best of me. Besides, on many occasions in the past, there had been legitimate reasons for me to retrieve information from those files. If someone came by while I was rummaging in the files, I'd simply act casual, grumble about having to work late, and disguise my snooping as a work-related endeavor.

Listening for voices, typing, coughing, sneezing, or any other sounds of a human presence, I walked down the hallway to the vacant reception area just outside of Ben's office where Mrs. Matlock's desk and file cabinets were located. Nonchalantly, I ducked into the small, secluded kitchen area just passed her file cabinets so I could grab a soda and continue my reconnaissance.

As I flipped the pop-top on the soda can, the popping, fizzing sound echoed through the corridors like a coyote howl through a desert canyon at night, providing me with a newfound sense of security. Surely, I'd hear anyone approach. The building wasn't empty, but it was empty enough that sound carried for a long distance.

Mrs. Matlock's area was orderly and immaculate. She was a marvel of efficiency, and as her employer I wished we had ten more just like her. She performed her duties with the discipline of a marine drill sergeant and was equally scary if you dared cross her systematic ways. "Everything in its place and a place for everything"—that was her motto. Ask her for a file or expense report and she would produce it instantly, never fumbling through stacks of unfiled papers or cabinet drawers like the rest of us. Personally, I doubted whether hospital operating rooms could match her methodical placement of equipment and supplies or her cleanliness for that matter. There was never any dust or dirt anywhere, even deep into the awkward crevices between the file cabinets or computer keys.

On occasion, we had needed access to Mrs. Matlock's desk or file cabinets after she'd gone home for the evening, so she kept a key ring behind a philodendron plant on a file cabinet near the window, an arrangement only Ben, Stan, and I knew about. And, you can bet we never dared leave anything out of place when we finished.

After a quick glance in all directions, I retrieved the key ring and opened her top right drawer where she kept Ben's appointment book, her most sacred resource. It was a black book, bound in leather, with 1992 imprinted in gold on the cover and similar in appearance to many bibles. I flipped through the pages to March 9th and 10th and, just as I thought I remembered, Ben spent the day of Danny's murder as well as the following day at a conference for hi-tech manufacturers at the convention center. Mrs. Matlock's notations indicated that Ben attended the afternoon session on March 9th, from 1 until 6pm and then both sessions on March 10th, 8am to noon and 1 to 6pm.

On the second day, I remembered waiting anxiously until Ben finished his speech so I could tell him the news about Danny's murder. Those types of memories have a way of remaining clear and vivid in your mind, no matter how hard you wish for them to fade. Could it be that Ben already knew?

I carefully returned the appointment book to its exact position in Mrs. Matlock's drawer, and then I closed and relocked it. Turning away from her desk, our expense account drawers, Ben's and mine, were located one above the other in the first of Mrs. Matlock's three file cabinets. Still wary that others might be working late, I took the precaution of unlocking both file drawers so, if anyone approached, I could act like I was retrieving something from my own file drawer.

Ben's expense information was neatly arranged in hanging folders by month, so I flipped through March 1992 until I found his credit card billing statement. Each of the eight transactions on the statement for a purchase of gas ranged from 10 to 13 gallons, leading me to conclude that Ben's tank probably held 15 gallons, and he generally refueled near the one-quarter slash on his fuel indicator. On March 9th at 9:17pm at the Texaco station near Ben's condo, he purchased 12 gallons of gas, and then he returned to the same station on March 10th at 7:15pm to purchase another 11 gallons. Since the convention center was less than a mile from his condo, Ben had 12 gallons of gas not accounted for in his daily planner.

My mission almost complete, I heard rustling on the other side of Ben's office door and I froze in place. Too early for the cleaning crew and too late for Mrs. Matlock, I realized I hadn't checked to see if Ben was in his office. Sure enough, as I stood still as a statue, the door opened and Ben emerged, engaged and fumbling, his briefcase open in his right hand, his car keys and a few loose sheets of paper in his left. Like someone juggling drinks and hors d'ouvres at a cocktail party, he struggled to put the papers into his briefcase and take his car keys out, at the same time. I felt as off-balance as he looked.

Ben was surprised by my presence.

"Hey," he said. "What are you looking for?"

"I, I just needed to check an expense report I submitted last month," I answered, my arm still elbow deep in the proverbial till.

In my startled state, I hadn't opened my file drawer or closed Ben's drawer as I'd planned. His credit card statement was in my hand, and his file drawer was fully extended in front of me. My position was precarious at best. Once again, a little moisture appeared on my forehead, shoulders, and underarms—those nervous sweats that you get when you're instantly anxious and know you're in trouble. Previously, I didn't want Ben to think I suspected him because I didn't want to hurt him, but now my concern was quite different; I was afraid he might hurt me if he found out I suspected him. Though I'd never been good at playing it cool, I went deep within my being to summons whatever little bit of calmness was in there.

"Padding your expenses again?" he cajoled.

"Exactly," I responded nervously.

I hoped Ben would rush by me—late for whatever, wherever, I didn't care. He was always rushing off somewhere.

Oh, God, make him late for something.

I didn't think I could bluff through a casual conversation.

But, instead of rushing off, Ben rested his briefcase on the back of Mrs. Matlock's chair, extended his arm in my direction, and offered me one of the loose pages he'd been trying to put away.

"Take a look," he stated. "Tell me what you think."

As nonchalantly as I could, I placed his credit card statement face down on top of the file cabinet and received the single page from Ben, a campaign letter being readied for mass mailing. Trying to appear interested, I moved my eyes back and forth across the page, while never actually reading any of it, except for the greeting, "Dear Citizens of Cavanaugh." I mumbled, "Uh huh" and "Mmmm" several times during my feigned review and determined the right moment to hand the letter back.

"It's good," I said. "Nicely constructed and not too political in tone. I'd vote for you if I got that in my mail."

"Feel like a drink?" he offered.

He told me he was meeting Kitt for one, or several in her case.

"No thanks."

What a lie!

14.

From 1974 to 1996, World's Tallest returned to the birthplace of the skyscraper: Chicago, Illinois. But, with projects climbing higher in foreign skylines, it was clear that the title was equally prestigious abroad. Inevitably, in 1996, the Petronas Towers in Malaysia became the first skyscraper outside the U.S. to claim World's Tallest when it reached 1,483 feet, 33 feet taller than the Sears Tower.

Frustrating for Tyler, only two of her segments had been picked up by the network news program, a four-minute segment about Ben Matthews and the city of Cavanaugh that coincided with his cover article in *Global Times Magazine*, and a three-minute segment about the grand opening of the World's Tallest skyscraper, Optimal Tower. While she'd received a lot of praise from network executives, the exposure didn't produce the promotion to national news anchorwoman that she wanted. Undaunted, Tyler continued to believe she was one juicy segment away from getting the call to New York.

For her first national segment, her portrait of Ben was similar to the portrayal in *Global Times*, that of a young, charismatic publisher who championed well-planned growth in his hometown. Tyler quoted the article as having labeled Ben an "urban visionary" and the founder of a revitalization movement that was re-sculpting other U.S. cities as well. The *Global Times* article, Tyler's segment, and other exposure served as the first sightings of Ben's rising star on the national scene, heralding him as an up-and-coming leader, one who'd be influential in national issues and elections in the future.

As flattering and significant as her segment was for Ben, Tyler did more for Cavanaugh tourism in four minutes than the chamber of commerce accomplished in four years. Though not quantifiable, some meaningful percentage of Cavanaugh's visitation, as well as its rapid population growth during the 1980s, was surely attributable to that segment. At the time, Tyler believed the national exposure would be the first of many network segments as well as her ticket to New York. Little did she know, five years would elapse before her next.

For her second network news segment, Tyler interviewed Ben and Sebastian Biddle during the grand opening ceremony for Optimal Tower. In actuality, she had almost an hour worth of footage with the two high-profile entrepreneurs but managed to trim it down to a very insightful three-minute segment. After talking in great detail about the new tower, Tyler deftly switched the topic of their conversation to the mayoral race.

"Sebastian," Tyler asked the young billionaire, "you've been widely quoted for the two reasons you selected Cavanaugh as the location for your company more than a decade ago. One of those reasons was Ben Matthews who is standing right here beside us. Can you tell me two reasons you're supporting Ben Matthews in his campaign for mayor?"

"I'll give you one really big reason," Sebastian replied, "and one really small reason. The really big reason is Optimal Tower. That building cost almost $1 billion and that makes it the single largest investment I've ever made. I believe the future of my investment and the future of this city is better if Ben Matthews is mayor. My really small reason is my four-year-old daughter, Mira, who will grow up and attend schools in Cavanaugh, and I believe her future will also be better if Ben is elected."

"That seems like a lot of pressure, Ben," Tyler said, turning to the mayoral candidate, "Sebastian is willing to entrust you with his two most precious assets."

"Well, Tyler," Ben replied, placing his arm on Sebastian's shoulder, "I was best man at Sebastian's wedding, and I am Godfather to little Mira so I'm very familiar with this man's most precious assets. I can tell you he is rich beyond his wealth. Sebastian has been a very good friend of mine for more than a decade, and I really appreciate his endorsement of my campaign."

"You talked about the Cavanaugh skyline in your keynote address and you referred to Optimal Tower as the signature landmark. How important is this skyscraper to the future of this city?"

"It's a game changer," Ben declared. "Having the World's Tallest skyscraper as part of our skyline will make the world take note of all the great things happening in our city."

Fortunately for Tyler, she didn't have to wait another five years between network segments like her first one. Just two months after the Optimal Tower segment, Tyler was back on the national airwaves.

With the title of the segment, "A Showdown in Cavanaugh," displayed on the large screen behind him, network news anchor, Charles Waterman, introduced Tyler to the network audience by saying, "We go now to Cavanaugh and correspondent Tyler Danzig from our affiliate station, KCVN."

In front of City Hall, with eight, tall white colonial columns as a backdrop and about fifty people milling in the town square behind her, Tyler took the hand-off from New York in a poised, confident manner, demonstrating the seasoned newsperson she'd become in her more than five years as anchorwoman of the local news program and more than ten years in the news business altogether.

"Thank you, Charles," she said, and then she smoothly transitioned into her report. "Of all the political races that will be decided November 3rd, none will be more closely watched than that of rising star Ben Matthews' contemptuous challenge for the office currently held by three-term incumbent Mayor Dale Greenwood in this stately building behind me, Cavanaugh City Hall."

When Tyler signed off that evening, I thought her segment was one of the best of her career. It was nationally relevant, journalistically balanced, and shrewdly presented, in an appetite whetting and melodramatically teasing manner. She described the upcoming campaign as a sensational spectacle and an irresistible horserace, one that would pit youth against maturity and new ideas against convention, with the future of a vibrant and thriving metropolis dangling in the balance. Each candidate's profile was carefully constructed to ensure there wasn't a whiff of bias on her part. She talked about Ben's youthful charisma as well as the mayor's role as elder statesman. She talked about Ben's plans for a light-rail system and the mayor's plans to modernize the busy seaport. Describing the race as a contentious brawl, Tyler even suggested that the two candidates shared only one thing in common: complete disdain for their opponent. She said the citizens of Cavanaugh were faced with a divergent choice and one that would truly determine the fate of their city in the new millennium.

"It will be a skirmish, a generational battle, and an 'Election Day for the ages,'" she promised as she closed her report.

True to television's tradition of cliffhangers, this first segment about the mayoral election was designed to create ongoing interest that would surely command follow-up segments by the network. From my perspective, it was obvious Tyler planned to turn these two campaigns and the results of the election into a network news miniseries. It had been a long time coming, but this was finally her career-making story.

Within ten minutes of her signoff, my phone rang, and I knew that it was Tyler calling.

"It was great, Tyler," I stated when I picked up the receiver. "I think it was your best work to date."

"Don't patronize me, Pete," she shot back. "This is way too important to me."

"I really mean it."

"I'm so excited," she exclaimed. "It's finally going to happen. I can feel it. New York City, here I come."

I was excited for Tyler, but my mind was still focused on Ben's American Express statement and its revelation, which created one more task that still had to be accomplished that evening.

"I'm going to the Angels game," I told her when she asked me to join her for a drink and, though I needed one even more now than forty minutes ago when Ben had offered, I declined again.

"I need to talk to Stan."

* * *

Red Rain Field, named for its rusty runoff during spring downpours, was a magical place; a Little League baseball diamond carved out of the old growth forest to create a fairy-tale setting where youngsters were transformed into major leaguers. It had crisp white lines that marked the base paths on four sides of a red dirt infield, an outfield as lush and green as an Irish meadow, and towers of brilliant white lights beside redwoods that provided illumination. Heightening the experience, the massive trees that surrounded the field fashioned a natural amphitheater with amazing acoustics so that when ball met bat the resulting "crack!" echoed through the ballpark. Far and away, it was the best venue the Angels played at all season and maybe the best Little League baseball field west of Williamsport.

When I arrived at the field, the game was in the fifth inning with the Angels at bat and trailing 4 to 3, but I didn't take my usual seat on their bench, opting instead for the top row of the bleachers on the third base side. After all, I hadn't rushed out of the office or driven like a maniac to help with the coaching effort or even watch the game. The Little Leaguers weren't my focus at that moment. I only wanted to talk with Stan.

I was so lost in my thoughts that I didn't notice the outcome. All of a sudden, the diamond was empty, and the lights dimmed in the outfield, slowly returning the forest to its natural state. The players, now gathered beside the dugouts, hooted and hollered, tossed their mitts and hats high into the air, and then dispersed into the throng of waiting parents. When the dust settled, Stan, who was busy placing baseballs and bats into an old duffel bag, noticed me sitting alone atop the bleachers and sent his twin boys scampering toward the parking lot to ride home with their mother.

"What's the matter?" Stan asked as he scaled the aluminum benches.

"Ben killed Danny," I blurted.

He was shocked; all color and expression emptied from his face, making it obvious that he'd never seriously considered the possibility. And, why would he?

"No way," Stan responded, vehemently defending his friend and employer. "You've let this tragedy get the best of you. You're obsessed with it and you're not thinking clearly. Let it go."

"He did it. I wanted you to hear it from me first."

Stan didn't want to hear my theory, but I told him anyway. I summed it as follows.

In the fall of 1979, I believed Ben conspired with Danny to fix at least three SU football games, by shaving points or losing the games altogether, and profit from wagers on the games. Ben was motivated by his need to raise money to start our company, and Danny went along because he was angry and disillusioned by the unfairness of his first college football season. When Danny learned about Ben's campaign, he threatened to expose their illegal activities, to publicly confess their misdeeds. Obviously, Ben couldn't allow that revelation because it would've destroyed his business and his campaign so silencing his accomplice became the only way to ensure his political star would continue rising.

Three witnesses saw Ben's black Saab parked outside The Bayside Motel around the time of the murder and Ben's credit card receipts showed that he drove about two hundred fifty miles on the night of the murder. On Danny's last visit to Ben's office, he had mistakenly left a pair of dark sunglasses behind, and that same pair of sunglasses was found at the murder scene beneath Danny's lifeless body. Why Ben returned them is unclear, but the sunglasses might've been the excuse for his visit that night. Stealing once again from the hokey detective shows of my youth, I said, "Ben had the requisite motive, means, and opportunity to kill Danny and as far as I can determine, all the evidence points at him."

Would Ben murder his friend to protect his prominent position in the community and his mayoral campaign? As difficult as this conclusion was for me to accept, I now believed he would.

"I don't buy it, Pete," Stan protested. "There is just no way Ben killed Danny. They were friends. We were all friends. We went to school together."

I understood Stan's loyalty and his refusal to look objectively at the facts. He had a wife, two kids, and a mortgage, and he didn't want to see his family's security undermined. I couldn't blame him for that. If Ben was arrested, the fallout would be detrimental to our business and there'd be collateral damage as well. We'd all suffer.

It wasn't my intent to hold a trial or persuade Stan of Ben's guilt, like a two-man jury of his peers in deliberations under stadium light. In the coming days, I planned to confront Ben, and I knew that nothing would be the same after that; our personal and professional lives would be forever changed. I didn't know what would happen, but I knew I had to warn Stan that it was coming, just as surely as the red rain that rechristened the ballpark every spring.

* * *

For almost a week, my thoughts of a confrontation with Ben consumed me in an obsessive manner. Frankly, I was out of control. Sometimes, I played a game with myself to see how long I could go without traveling this well-worn mental byway, trying instead to concentrate on work, watch television or focus on something trivial. When I inevitably lost, I told myself that it was a good thing because my obsession with Danny's murder was reaching a natural zenith and would subside soon, allowing my life to return to normal. Either that or I was going insane. I really wasn't sure.

Though it's not comparable, I was reminded of the incident in college when I had too much to drink and broke the water pipe in our dormitory restroom early sophomore year, causing the entire floor to flood. When the hall manager knocked on his door, Ben covered for me by saying we'd worked in his room all night. And, even more remarkable to me, Ben never even mentioned that incident again, never chided me, and never made jokes about it. He knew I harbored a lot of guilt over the incident, and so he let it go. He covered for me, forgave my incredible stupidity and moved on—just like a true friend would. I so wished this incident was one we could put behind us and move on. But, it wasn't. Property damage could be overlooked, but murder had to be dealt with.

During much contemplation, I searched my heart and mind for a strategy and the right words, ones that would cause Ben to confess if guilty and allow us to remain friends if innocent. I wavered between innocent inquiry and intense interrogation, but I wasn't sure that either would work. The more I analyzed it, the more I believed Ben would simply deny any involvement, and I couldn't accept an unsubstantiated denial. In that case, we couldn't remain friends or business partners, and so, for Danny's sake and my own, I needed a means to make him address the charges. I couldn't allow him to dismiss the evidence as circumstantial. One way or the other, I had to get to the truth and no other outcome would be acceptable.

But how?

My interactions with Stan were a little tense around the office as he maintained his belief in Ben's innocence and refused to consider any other possibility. But, out of respect for our longtime friendship, Stan only raised the topic on two occasions. He restated his opinion on the matter simply and eloquently with four little words, "Let it go, Pete."

* * *

It was early August, three months from Election Day, and I'd come to the considered conclusion that the only way I was going to learn the truth about Danny's death was to use Ben's mayoral campaign as leverage; nothing carried more sway with him. So, after considering the circumstantial nature of the case, the fact that justice and punishment weren't my jurisdiction or concern, the good citizens of Cavanaugh, Stan, the other employees at Utopia Publishing, and the publications themselves, I concocted a plan. But before proceeding, I needed to put some protective measures in place before confronting Ben. I needed to take some precautions. While it was hard for me to imagine that Ben would kill me; three months ago, I would've said the same thing about Ben killing Danny.

Late one afternoon, I documented the whole investigation, deposited the evidence in two yellow mailing envelopes, and hand-carried the materials to Tyler's television studio, arriving just after she began her broadcast. Many times before, I'd watched her deliver her daily summation from the comfort of the production booth. I knew the crewmembers, their roles and responsibilities, and even the functions of some of the knobs and switches on the control panel before them. Often, I'd stood beneath the red "On Air" light and marveled at their modern, electrified world of journalism. It was always a fascinating production.

But, that night was different. I wasn't myself. I'd spent the last two hours safeguarding my life, and that was an uncustomary role for me, one that put me on tilt. I'd never been a thrill-seeker, always preferring comfort and safety to adventure and risk any day, a mindset developed in the security of the suburbs. With each day that passed, it was that much clearer to me that I wasn't cut out for this line of work. While I watched the program that evening, I clutched the mailing envelopes tightly against my sport coat at chest level and swayed in place, unaware of my anxious demeanor and the effect it was having on people around me. Ten minutes into the broadcast, the production manager asked me to wait for Tyler in her dressing room.

I've got to pull it together, I told myself.

Tyler arrived twenty minutes later.

"What the hell is the matter with you?" she asked.

As she did, I fumbled with the door and tried unsuccessfully to lock it. Tyler moved me aside and secured it herself. It was clear her frustration with me was increasing.

Only slightly relieved by the locked door, I briefed Tyler on my plan and asked her to safeguard the two mailing envelopes as my insurance policy, so Ben wouldn't harm me.

"Hypothetically," Tyler proposed, trying to act like the voice of reason, "let's assume Ben killed Danny. "What exactly do you plan to accomplish by going forward with your plan? Danny's not coming back and you're going to hurt a lot of people."

It wasn't the response I expected. All along, I thought Tyler supported my quest for the truth, regardless of the outcome, or whether friendships or livelihood or anything else was jeopardized. After all, it was our quest for the truth. We'd launched this investigation together six months ago, made many trips to Condor, met with the police, stood beside the large bloodstain, uncovered key evidence, and questioned some unsavory characters. On my way to her studio that night, I had wrongly assumed Tyler wanted to see it through.

"He's this close to the mayor's office," Tyler observed with her hand extended, her thumb and index finger spaced about an inch apart. "You'll ruin everything, Pete."

That gesture and her desperate look made it all suddenly clear to me. Tyler had an interest in this political campaign and election, and she didn't want to see anything get in the way of her ticket to New York. Her plan was in jeopardy; it seemed my plan didn't fit her plan. Ben and Danny were her friends, but her resistance had nothing to do with her loyalty to either of them. It was all simply defense of ambition. It was all about Tyler.

"Just put those envelopes in a safe place," I said as I unlocked the door and prepared to depart. "I won't ask for anything more."

* * *

My nights were torture. At 5am in mid-August, I welcomed the end of another excruciatingly long one. For the past week or so, my daily struggle with my single-minded thoughts had spilled over into the darkness, making it impossible for me to clear my mind and sleep. Hourly, I checked the illuminated clock face on the nightstand beside me like a beacon directing my futile journey, wishfully hoping that I had either dozed off or that morning was near and my misery would soon end. Like Ben, I'd become an insomniac, and I could only hope my condition was temporary.

Without sleep, my appearance and mental capacities reflected an unhealthy and overly worn condition. I wasn't thinking clearly and I knew it. Though I couldn't turn my mind off, I couldn't focus on anything either. On the positive side, all this extra time had allowed me to work out the final details of my plan and I was now ready to proceed, irrationally perhaps, but proceed just the same.

At 6am, I called Ben at his condominium and asked him to meet me on the service road behind the Utopia Building at 8:30am, before he went up to the office.

"Just be there," I told him when his tone wavered.

The service road was two heavily tarred, unmarked lanes of blacktop that separated our headquarters and its neighbor to the rear, the Continental Bank Building, the second tallest building in the downtown, twenty stories below Optimal Tower. In my overwrought and somewhat irrational state, I'd decided that its windowed offices would ensure hundreds of witnesses to our conversation, and their presence would prevent Ben from retaliation. Our conversation would be witnessed but unheard—the perfect arrangement for this meeting. I would be safe.

Unfortunately for both of us, I hadn't considered the noisy, smelly diesel trucks that frequented the service road.

"You look like hell," Ben observed as he approached me.

I couldn't argue with him. I was unshowered and unshaven, with large, dark circles under my eyes, and I hadn't sent any clothes to the dry cleaners in three weeks. What little vanity remained since my early twenties had vanished several weeks ago as I struggled with more important issues. In so many ways, I was at a low point in my life.

To those office workers above the thirtieth floor, I'm sure we looked like two ants standing at the base of two towering redwoods and, looking up in their direction, only a sliver of blue sky and a few wispy clouds were visible from our position. While the offices were just beginning to stir above us, we stood alone in the alleyway, seventy yards west of the loading dock for the Continental Bank Building where a food service delivery truck was slowly backing into its mooring. As the driver inched the massive truck ever closer, the engine noise and warning sound made it difficult for us to hear one another, and the alley slowly filled with diesel exhaust, producing a noxious blend when combined with the ever-present smell of sour milk from the dumpsters. Ben was understandably perplexed by my choice of venue.

"What is this all about?" Ben shouted. "Are we here in this noisy, filthy alley for a reason?"

"We're here because I believe you shot Danny!"

"What?" he returned.

I couldn't tell whether he'd used the word in a "What are you talking about?" sense or an "I can't hear you!" sense so I repeated it, much louder this time.

"I believe you shot Danny."

"Are you out of you're mind?"

Without doubt, I expected strong denial from Ben, but his particular choice of words rattled me. He didn't have to question my sanity—God knows I'd done that for days. As I detailed the evidence, Ben appeared cool. In turn, he asserted his innocence, denied any involvement, and insisted it was coincidence. It was a steely denial.

278 | Michael Bowe

"There's absolutely no way Danny conspired to fix football games for my benefit or anyone else," Ben said at one point. "I went for a drive after the conference," he said later, in an attempt to dismiss the fuel purchases.

Mostly, Ben returned to the heart of his defense and the oft-repeated refrain of his denial, "Danny was our friend," he insisted.

"It's a lot of coincidences," I shouted while a second delivery truck pulled into the alley from the opposite end, adding noise and exhaust as it did.

"Coincidences—that's exactly what they are," Ben returned. "There isn't one piece of real evidence, and still you're convinced I killed our friend. Does any one else know about this crackpot theory?"

"I'm not convinced, but you need to know two things: I'm determined to learn the truth and I've taken precautions," I informed him. "If anything happens to me, my information will be forwarded to the police."

Ben laughed. "Oh what, you think I'm going to kill you now?

Ben forced a second laugh, but obviously wasn't in a laughing mood. Angrily, he kicked an empty beer can on the ground and his entire body spun around in a circle.

"Shit," he screamed.

Ben continued. "I'm only concerned that this malicious tale will destroy my campaign quicker than you can say 'Goodbye Utopia Publishing.' You'll ruin it all if you go to the police."

"You've got a choice," I informed him, and then I told him the rest of my plan.

It was up to Ben. I gave him two options. He would choose.

If Ben was guilty and wanted to prevent my findings from resulting in an official investigation, a murder conviction, and life in a state penitentiary then all he had to do was drop out of the mayor's race and distance himself from Utopia Publishing. Like the Condor Police Department, I would close my investigation of Danny's murder, and that would be the end of it. Stan and I would run our company as if nothing happened, and the collateral damage would be minimal. Whether it was justice or not, Ben would simply give up his life of prominence and withdraw from public life.

If Ben was innocent, he had nothing to fear from an official investigation. In that case, Ben should decide to continue with his campaign, and once the electorate spoke, win or lose, I would turn my findings over to the Cavanaugh Police Department and he would be cleared by a thorough investigation. Additionally, if he was elected, the investigation could be conducted with discretion, as he would be mayor.

My plan wasn't a perfect plan, but it accomplished enough as it prevented the two most unacceptable outcomes. First, if I contacted the Cavanaugh Police Department, and, after an official investigation, Ben was innocent, I would've undermined his campaign, damaged our publications, and hurt a lot of people. That was clearly unacceptable. Secondly, and conversely, if Ben was guilty, we couldn't continue as business partners, and I couldn't stand by while he won the mayor's office, a job in which the public placed so much trust. That was also unacceptable. As I said, my plan was imperfect, but it accomplished enough. I was too tired to engineer a perfect plan.

"Goddamn it, Danny," Ben blurted, a slip, "reconsider this craziness. You're not going to accomplish anything and you're going to hurt a lot of people. You can't bring him back, you know."

"You know," I said, "the only thing I've learned with certainty is that aside from Bob Cooper, me, and the Grainger family, nobody cares what happened to Danny at The Bayside Motel that night. But, that doesn't make the truth less important. Your life of significance isn't more important and more deserving than Danny's wasted one. It doesn't work that way."

"You don't understand, Pete."

At that moment, we were interrupted and physically separated. An eighteen wheeler pulled out of the loading dock and crept up the alley toward us, its gears grinding, engine straining, and black diesel smoke puffing from dual exhaust pipes above the roof. Ben stepped backward to the north in the direction of the Utopia Publishing Building and I moved backward in the opposite direction. The large truck, with Casey Brothers Trucking on the door of the cab and a large religious mural on the cargo box of the gates of heaven, St. Peter graciously greeting new arrivals, and the words, "Don't Wait Till The Gate To Review Your Life," passed surrealistically between us.

Was I imagining it? Admittedly, I was tired. I stared up at the image—a line of angelic persons waiting in a blue and white, sky and clouds panorama, and, for one brief moment, when the truck was positioned just right, I felt like I was standing at the end of the line. If that mural was a sign or missive I wasn't getting it. I was way too tired. Do the right thing, maybe; that's all I could come up with at that moment. And oh, how frustrating that was! God communicated with me, but all I got from it was how shoddy I looked at the end of the line. I wasn't angelic at all. On the other hand, maybe it was meant for Ben and the mural was on both sides of the truck's cargo box. I didn't know.

When the truck cleared us, Ben had vanished, presumably into our building. I assumed Ben got so many heavenly communiqués that he didn't feel the need to remain. Regardless, my task was complete, and I knew I'd sleep through the night. I felt it immediately. I was relieved. A huge burden was lifted off my shoulders, and I even felt like I was standing straighter and taller now. Most appropriately, it was Ben's burden now.

Amen.

* * *

For a week, Ben avoided our offices, but maintained his high profile otherwise. On one typical day, Ben snipped a yellow ribbon to open a soccer park in the morning, visited a retirement community in the afternoon, and then addressed a group of women business owners at dinner. Via television and *The Dispatch*, I followed his appearances, wondering if his busy schedule was a sign that he'd considered the ultimatum and decided to complete the campaign, win or lose the election, and undergo a police investigation down the road. Thus far, he hadn't shown any signs of exiting the race.

With two months until the election, Kitt, using her marathon analogy, sensed the finish line ahead and accelerated the pace for the final kick. For the people of Cavanaugh, Ben was everywhere, showing up nightly on their television sets during events and photo opportunities as he continued to be an unavoidable part of their daily lives. Ben's public presence had never been higher, but as the days clicked off, I sensed that he was suffering a private, inner turmoil.

Normally, Ben thrived in these conditions, ones that involved personal challenge and professional limelight, and yet, in a couple of the recent film clips, I detected unease. One morning, my observation was confirmed when I received an express package at my desk with a note from Tyler attached that read, "What the hell is going on?"

Enclosed was a film clip from his speech the prior evening where Ben, speaking to a group of city workers, suddenly transgressed from polished to frazzled by drifting into an imagined childhood story that included his deceased mother. Most in attendance, including the film crew from KCVN, didn't give his childhood reminiscing a second thought, thinking it merely scripted, political theater. Only those who knew Ben personally, outside of his public life, would recognize the personal unraveling in process. Ben rarely spoke about his mother in private and never in public.

"My mother always told me," he said uncharacteristically and almost nonsensically, "that our world is flawed and full of fat, greedy, uncaring politicians who unfairly deprive hard working people of the decent lives they deserve and their fair share of prosperity. 'You can change that, Ben,' she told me. 'You can make a difference.'"

During close-ups, Ben's eyes glistened with tears, which probably caused many to wonder if his mother had died recently, or during his twenties, not when he was four years old, not thirty years prior. Previously, I'd never seen him out of control. Wherever he went, whatever the circumstance, Ben always looked like he owned the place. But he looked troubled that evening, even dazed.

"I won't disappoint my mother," Ben proclaimed defiantly. "I will make a difference."

* * *

The very next day, Ben yielded. He was unable to hold off the inevitable any longer. It appeared spontaneous but I knew better. Ben had reached an unavoidable conclusion that, I was sure, had hounded him since that morning in the alleyway. He couldn't go to prison and live a confined life. In truth, Ben would have enough difficulty accepting private, insignificant reclusion, much less imprisonment. If Ben was guilty, if he did indeed kill our friend, Danny Grainger, option one, relinquishing his mayoral campaign and leaving Utopia Publishing was his only choice. He'd finally accepted it.

Following an awards breakfast honoring city firefighters at the Pierpont Hotel, Ben stopped abruptly, at the bottom of a red carpet that adorned the hotel's front steps, before a small throng of reporters and cameramen, and spoke words that would quickly echo throughout all Cavanaugh, like a cry for help through the cavernous streets of the city beneath its towering skyscrapers.

"It saddens me deeply," Ben said, "but, for personal reasons, I'm withdrawing my name from the ballot, and I will not seek nor accept office on November 3rd. I ask that the members of the press respect my privacy and allow me time and space during this personally challenging time. God bless the city of Cavanaugh."

He left quickly, with no further elaboration of his decision, visibly anxious and unsettled.

I doubt that ten minutes elapsed before I'd learned the news. It was everywhere. Most of the local stations, both television and radio alike, interrupted their morning programming to cover the fast breaking news story. After hearing a news report on her portable radio at her desk, Mrs. Matlock, acting both distraught and concerned, stood in my office doorway and relayed the transmission.

"Should I try to reach him?" she offered, knowing we usually conferred in times of crisis.

"No," I responded, not fully prepared for the news, with no words of comfort ready for her. She left looking even more concerned than when she arrived.

There was no reason for me to talk with Ben. As I expected, Ben accepted my offer without communicating with me first, knowing that the terms and conditions we'd discussed were both nonnegotiable and binding, and he trusted that I would wholly honor my portion of our arrangement. And I would. Somewhere in searing solitude, Ben was accepting a harsh reality. He was realizing that when he pulled the trigger that night at the motel, sending those bullets into Danny's chest, he forsook friendships, Utopia Publishing, public life, and, to an extent, his own life. Danny warned Ben. He couldn't deny it. There were lines that, once crossed, could never be undone.

Sitting at my desk, I considered the possibility that I might never see Ben again and that was hard for me to accept. The most significant person in my adult life, the person I loved and respected most, my business partner and closest friend, was instantly gone from my life, disappearing from the stage like a volunteer from the audience in a magic show. Though there was no mystical poof of white smoke or special utterance of magic words, he was just as gone.

Many questions rushed into my mind. How would Ben move forward from this point? What could he do next? How would he live with himself? I couldn't imagine the answer to any of those questions.

Alone with my thoughts at an unexpected moment in my life, feeling muddled by passed events, recent events, and the prospects ahead, only one thing was clear to me: My longtime, collaborative venture with Ben Matthews was over.

That much was certain.

That much I knew.

15.

Skyscrapers are larger than life, defy convention, expand the imagination, grant unrivaled views, and, as part of a skyline, form astonishing concrete mountain ranges. In the universal scheme of things, skyscrapers are mankind's best attempt at creating something equal to the wonders in the natural world. Only God can make a tree, so men build skyscrapers.

It would've been wise for me to follow Ben's lead one last time and hunker down in seclusion away from the madness. Though Ben cited "personal reasons" as his reason for abandoning his mayoral campaign, the word "personal" didn't cause any restraint among members of the media. Quite to the contrary, personal reasons were alluring code—a harbinger for a salacious tale that only piqued their collective interests. By early afternoon, our lobby was crammed with reporters and cameramen, camped out like Boy Scouts at a spring jamboree, and my sources told me the scene was the same outside Ben's condo and the Matthews' home. In the cramped confines of our lobby, members of the media smoked cigarettes, drank coffee, played cards, exchanged war stories and jokes, but mostly waited. Lobbies are normally places for waiting, but on this day, ours was abnormally saturated by smoke and impatience. The scene was indicative of one of the more unpleasant aspects of modern journalism. Sometime during the twentieth century, an unsavory sensationalism had crept into the journalistic mainstream and tainted the profession, much to the disdain of more traditional journalists like myself.

284 | Michael Bowe

Coming from an appointment, Stan arrived during the vigil, setting off a firestorm as he wove his way through the campers. Most knew Stan and his position at Utopia Publishing so cameras rolled and questions flew as he struggled to make his way to the stairs.

"I only know what I've heard on the radio," Stan announced.

"Is Ben ill?" one reporter shouted above the rest.

"Was Ben photographed with a prostitute?" another cried out.

A saying amongst reporters was that nothing ended a man's political career quicker than being found in bed with a dead woman or a young boy. These reporters were determined to learn which applied.

Stan arrived at my office. Aware of the accusatory nature of his questions, he deliberately closed and locked the door behind him before sitting in the chair before me. He sat quietly for more than a minute.

"What does this mean?" Stan asked, bewildered. In all our years together, I'd never seen Stan bewildered.

"It means what you think it means," I responded, unwilling to speak the words myself, preferring to consider the matter resolved, past history, and forgotten. After all, that was the terms of my arrangement with Ben.

"We won't see much of Ben," I said, "but we'll keep his name in place as publisher and he'll retain his ownership in our company."

"He killed Danny," Stan whispered, leaning toward my desk, shaking his head in disbelief. Until that very moment, it was as if Stan hadn't allowed himself to seriously consider that possibility.

I didn't respond.

"I'm sure we've got a morale issue here," I said, concerned for the rest of our employees. "Our version of this whole mess is that Ben simply decided the job of mayor wasn't for him."

Stan didn't respond. This was a belly punch for him and he looked as if the wind had been knocked out of him. I knew exactly how he felt because I'd been in the same shape previously. The only difference was that I'd had time to accept it, and my breathing had returned to normal. Ben wasn't just our friend and business partner; it was far more complicated than that.

For both of us, Ben was someone who made a difference. We believed in Ben. In truth, we idolized him. He was extraordinary. A whole city would be hurt by Ben's ruin. We were lessened, too.

And, worse still, at the heart of it all, it wasn't just about Ben. It was even more than that. It was about believing in someone. In light of recent developments, believing in someone was suddenly a precarious position and accepting that cynical a view of life was as painful as losing our friend. Neither Stan nor I wanted to live cynical lives.

* * *

Later that afternoon, I received an unscheduled lesson in meteorology as I experienced firsthand what it was like to be a small, coastal town when a category five hurricane made landfall. Absent the candidate, Kitt was hounded and hassled by reporters—all morning long, all afternoon long—and was, quite understandably, one pissed-off, unemployed, former Matthews for Mayor campaign manager when she slammed my office door. Unlike most coastal cities, I had no warning at all, no chance to evacuate or even batten down my belongings. It was too late. Hurricane Kitt was about to blow my office off the proverbial weather screen.

"Goddamn it," she yelled.

Her face scowled, her brow V'd.

I winced.

"Where is he, Pete?" she demanded. "I'm going to kill him."

Ben didn't forewarn her. Kitt learned about Ben's sudden exit from the mayor's race the same way most of us did and she was as angered by that as the announcement itself.

"I don't know," I said, in a fearful tone, ready to dodge any objects that blew my way. "I don't expect any of us will hear from Ben for quite a while."

As the words left my mouth, I knew my observation was a mistake, but I couldn't get them back. And, Kitt picked up on it right away. With that one little sentence, I'd disclosed a lot more than necessary; I'd told Kitt that I had knowledge of Ben's motivations and state of mind. I should've kept my observation to myself.

"What's this about, Pete?" she shouted. "I want to know. I have a right to know."

I didn't want to part with Kitt on unpleasant terms, but I knew she'd never let me wriggle out of this one. She looked as frustrated as the reporters in the lobby.

"You need to leave, Kitt," I instructed her, trying to end this standoff quickly.

Kitt glared, her fury increased.

"Mrs. Matlock," I beckoned with my intercom button pressed. "Call security. I've got a trespasser in my office."

Kitt deserved better, much better, but it wasn't my debt to be paid. I liked her and didn't feel good about treating her in this manner, but I had no other option.

Fortunately, Kitt departed before security arrived, mumbling, "You son of a bitch," as she slammed my door behind her.

* * *

Most outside observers would have concluded that this had to be one of the worst days in my life, and yet it wasn't. It was a matter of perspective. From my perspective, this day marked the end of a difficult period, and, hopefully, the start of a new and better one. The truly significant issues concerning betrayal, murder, and death were behind me, having been confronted and resolved. Already, my life was flashing positive signs that a more normal state was returning. I was sleeping more soundly at night, I felt refreshed, stronger and wiser from the experience, and ready to begin a new chapter in my life.

At the time, I didn't know there were several pages remaining unturned in the current chapter.

* * *

That evening, I left the office and walked to the KCVN studio, tailed by several reporters chasing some misguided notion that I might duck into a dark alley and rendezvous with Ben. In reality, my plans were intentionally mundane. I was going to watch Tyler's broadcast from the production booth and then grab a late dinner. I was thinking Italian, a plate of saucy lasagna, some warm garlic bread, and an expensive bottle of red wine. Hopefully, Tyler would join me.

I arrived ten minutes before air, and, as expected, the activity level in the booth was at a frenzied pace as crewmembers readied film clips from what had been one of the biggest news days in recent years. On a monitor above me, Mayor Greenwood, with a noticeably relieved Roy Zacharius beside him, commented on Ben's announcement.

"I won't speculate about Ben Matthews' reasons for dropping out of the race," the mayor said. "I will only say that Ben has always acted with the best interests of the city in mind, and I wish him well in whatever his next endeavor might be."

"Cut it there," a woman frantically instructed the technician at the panel. "That's fifteen seconds, and it will fit perfectly."

When I arrived, no one shouted, "Hi, Pete," like they usually did. It was crunch time. Time waits for no one and journalists know better than most the inflexible quality of deadlines. I settled into my little corner beneath the "On Air" light and tried to stay out of the way. Only Tyler acknowledged my presence with a subtle, little wave and smile, as she underwent final makeup seated at the anchor desk.

"Thirty seconds until air," a voice on the loudspeaker alerted the crowded studio.

People scrambled in every direction, clearing center stage and taking up positions at their stations in the wings. "Five, four, three, two, one," the voice added moments later, and the red light illuminated above my head. As if choreographed, all eyes turned to Tyler. She read the words on the teleprompter before her, flowing passed like fallen leaves in a gentle stream.

"Our top story tonight is one that has created a firestorm of speculation in this city like few before it. Benjamin Matthews, owner of Utopia Publishing, publisher of *Cavanaugh Weekly, Cavanaugh Monthly*, and *Cavanaugh Business Monthly* sent shockwaves through the city this morning by announcing that he was withdrawing his name from the ballot and wouldn't seek the office of mayor come Election Day, November 3rd. Matthews made the announcement while leaving the Pierpont Hotel after a breakfast honoring city firefighters."

On the monitor, Tyler's face was replaced by a film clip of Ben recorded that morning. Lasting only forty seconds, it was the first time I had seen his statement, and, to outsiders, it might have appeared spontaneous, but the presence of a limousine told me otherwise. As soon as he finished, Ben climbed into the back of the black car and was whisked away from the scene. Ben seldom rode in limousines.

Tyler returned to the monitor.

"Though Matthews cited personal reasons for his decision to exit the race, this reporter has learned that Ben Matthews is currently a suspect in a Cavanaugh Police investigation of the death of former Stanton University football star and longtime Matthews' friend, Danny Grainger, found shot to death in a motel room in the sleepy bayside town of Condor last spring. At this very moment, police are executing two search warrants obtained late this afternoon for Ben Matthews' downtown condominium and the family home in South Cavanaugh. Matthews' alleged motive for the crime is believed to be related to a gambling conspiracy involving SU football games and carried out by Matthews and Grainger in the fall of 1979."

288 | Michael Bowe

I was shocked. My heart sank. One way or the other, it seemed Tyler was determined to get the national exposure the campaign promised. All I could figure was that she had decided to add new life to her cancelled election race by enlisting the police and adding a new twist. The murder investigation and trial would be bigger and more sensational than the campaign and election. Could the police have found out in some other way? Had they cracked the case? I doubted that. Only five people knew this scurrilous tale— Ben, Danny, Tyler, Stan, and me. And, in my mind at least, there was more chance that Danny spoke from his grave than Stan, Ben, or me. So, that left only Tyler. And, I'd given her the evidence.

A few minutes later, my suspicions were confirmed when a longtime friend of Tyler's and her regular contact on the police force appeared on the monitor. Apparently, Tyler had turned over my two mailing envelopes of evidence to the detective and, in return, he started the investigation and, additionally, must've promised exclusive access going forward.

"We're currently searching the two Matthews' residences," the detective began, "for evidence that might connect Ben Matthews to the murder of Danny Grainger. This is an ongoing investigation so I have no further comment at this time."

As he concluded, it was painfully obvious to me that a deal was struck. Clearly, the lights of Broadway beckoned.

What was the value of a longtime friendship? Tyler, Ben and I had been friends for fifteen years, the entirety of our adult lives, and she'd brokered those friendships for network airtime. But, I wasn't angry and I wasn't surprised. I was only stunned.

I wasn't interested in her explanation. I didn't wait for the show to conclude. I'd seen enough. With Ben's face above me on the monitor, I left the studio. If I'd learned one thing over the past six months, it was that retribution for sins of betrayal, whether against one's self or others, came hardest from within. We were—each of us—our own hanging judge. Tyler would have her reckoning, as certainly as Danny and Ben did.

As I walked to my car and drove to the suburbs, my sadness had many layers, and I tried to consider each before I arrived home. In my analysis, Tyler had convinced herself that airing this major news story was her responsibility and she couldn't let friendship keep her from her professional duty. My issue with her rationalization was that I didn't believe her motivation was pure, and I suspected that many years would pass before she'd acknowledge that truth. In truth, her motivation was her career, and her duty as a journalist had little to do with it. Tyler was, however, right about one thing: Friendship shouldn't be used to hide criminal activity or immoral actions.

It was never my place to act as judge and jury and pronounce Ben's sentence. Wrongly, I had designed a deal, brokered an outcome, declared it justice, and salved my conscience. After this evening's turn of events, Ben would most likely end up in the state penitentiary serving a life sentence, and, all things considered, that was the truly just result. After all, he killed a man. He had killed our friend. In my heart, I still preferred my outcome to the now unavoidable drama and inevitable trial that would surely unfold over the next few days and coming years, but that didn't make it right. My deal with Ben was not justice—it just suited me better.

As I pulled into my driveway that night, I had a strong feeling that I had reached an end, like that sudden jolt at the end of a roller-coaster ride at an amusement park. In an instant, your body moves forward, then back, and you are shaken, but your body comes to a rest, and the ride is over. I felt that finality. Our long ride together, Ben and I, most likely ending with Ben's arrest and incarceration, was clearly over, but I could take comfort in the fact that it had been one hell of a ride, definitely an A ticket, one of great triumph and tragedy. For my two bits, I'd certainly gotten my money's worth.

* * *

The loud ring of an antique phone on her nightstand awakened Tyler at 7am. It was a call she'd long anticipated.

"Tyler Danzig?" the female caller inquired.

"Yes, this is Tyler," she said, still groggy.

"Please hold for Charles Waterman."

"Good morning, Tyler," the network news anchorman said in his highly compensated baritone when he joined the call. "I want to congratulate you and thank you for that excellent segment about Ben Matthews last night. Your segment ran on the national news program and seven hundred local affiliates. It was an excellent report."

"Thank you, Charles," Tyler returned. "There is no one whose opinion I value more."

"I'm sure I don't have to tell you," he observed, "that if Ben Matthews is arrested, this will be the next 'Trial of the Century.' I find it amusing, Tyler," he added chuckling, "that there are, in reality, three or four 'Trials of the Century' each century but this one will

290 | Michael Bowe

certainly qualify as the latest. If he is arrested, his story and trial will lead the network news every night. What do you know about the chances of an arrest?"

"My sources tell me that they expect an arrest warrant to be issued by midday. He will be in custody by nightfall."

"If that happens, Tyler, we'll need your segment in time for the national broadcast on the East Coast every night. Coordinate your efforts with our producer. She will be expecting your calls. We're going to be working together on this one. Keep up the great work."

* * *

The next morning, Mrs. Matlock appeared in my doorway again with another recounting of a radio broadcast she'd heard just moments before. She looked as anguished as the previous day, multiplied by a factor of ten. Her eyes were sad; her shoulders hunched. She wasn't a young woman, and she looked like she couldn't take much more.

"An arrest warrant has been issued for Ben," she said.

I had a hunch I might know where to find Ben so I left the office immediately and went in search of him. Normally, in times of conflict or trouble, Ben would seek out his father, Kirk. They were very close. Ben would normally go home. But, in this instance, Ben was cutoff from his father, as he knew the police were at both of the family's residences. Unable to reach Kirk, in my estimation, Ben would do the next best thing; he would seek comfort and solitude at his mother's gravesite, a place he visited often. So, I went in search of Connie Matthews' headstone.

While driving my car, the rain fell obnoxiously against my windshield—too lightly for the rapid setting on the intermittent wipers, but too heavily for the unhurried one. First, the wiper blades loudly scraped the dry windshield and then they waited so long that I couldn't see the road ahead. Impatiently, I switched the setting back and forth, more anxious over Ben's state of mind with each swipe, concerned he might do something drastic. I didn't want to bury a second friend.

It is an undisputable law of physics that water always finds the lowest level in an incredibly efficient manner. No matter how tiny or tight, it penetrates any crevice that will facilitate its downward flow, steadily descending in search of lower planes. Facilitated by fluidity and gravity, it rolls and spills—lower and lower—seeping into any pathway until it finds the bottom. In our physical world, water is as efficient as gravity is unforgiving.

Human beings are mostly water. The body is made of more than 70 percent water and it is always tragic when human beings, true to their chemical composition, emulate water during difficult periods in their lives and allow a transgression or misstep to lead to lower descent. Like water, they gain momentum as they slide. Water can be beautiful to watch as it cascades downward in its transparent and fluid simplicity, but some human beings also have a tendency to fall and sink, like water without the beauty.

In the last decade of his life, Danny was living proof of this steadfast law of nature. Aided by addictions, he found one lower level after another, sinking deeper and deeper, descending in ways I never would've imagined. Like the spring runoff in the mountains, his descent was steady and efficient. Danny had sure found rock bottom, his lowest, most miserable level—that was undeniable. Somehow, I hoped to stop or slow Ben's descent. I had to find him.

When I finally reached my destination, I drove through the tall, black gates at the entrance to Crossroads Cemetery and, shortly thereafter, I spotted a lone, solitary figure amongst the stones and crosses in the grassy field. It was Ben all right. He was seated on the ground, his back against his mother's headstone, his hair soaked and face wet, wearing a gray full-length raincoat, only partially buttoned in the front. I exited my car and approached slowly, extending my black umbrella to shield us both from the steady drizzle, reminding me of the efficiency of water.

Ben had stoically watched my approach and then shamefully lowered his head when I arrived. In silence, I gathered my thoughts as I stood over him.

"A warrant has been issued for your arrest," I advised him, figuring that to be the most important detail at that moment.

"I suspected as much," he replied.

Rain and tears streaked his face.

"Why did you do it, Ben?" I finally blurted, breaking what had been a long silence. "What happened in your office that day?"

Ben wiped the moisture from his weary face with an upward swipe of his hands and, as part of the same motion, combed his damp black locks backward away from his face. I'd never seen Ben looking so tired and worn, as if twenty-five years of insomnia had caught up with him on this day.

"Danny was going to ruin everything," Ben said.

He shook his head. He didn't seem remorseful. Ben seemed more distressed over what was happening to him than what he'd done to Danny.

"Everything," he repeated, his voice trailing off.

* * *

"Good morning, Mayor Matthews," Danny said as he greeted Ben that morning in his office. Ben was as surprised by Danny's presence in his office as I'd been earlier in the lobby. It wasn't a pleasant surprise.

"I've got to tell you," Danny continued, "I find it troublesome that you're running for an office often addressed as 'Honorable.' Seems a little hypocritical, doesn't it?"

"What do you want, Danny?" Ben demanded as he closed his office door. "Money?"

Unlike his earlier encounter with me, Danny looked Ben in the eyes. In fact, he glared at him.

"Money won't heal me," Danny replied, angrily. "You see, my transgression was the worst type, a sin against my very being, a betrayal of all that I held sacred, an action that will scar my soul for eternity. Unfortunately for both us, you can't buy redemption."

"Cut the theatrics," Ben suggested as he picked up his phone. "Mrs. Matlock," he barked into its receiver, "have accounting prepare a check payable to Daniel Grainger for five thousand dollars."

"I don't have time for your bullshit," Ben added, directed at Danny after he hung up the phone.

"I don't want your goddamn money," Danny stated. Instead, he informed Ben that he was planning to confess their misdeeds before the rolling cameras of the media at a press conference on the football field at Stanton University.

"You ruined my life," Danny added, "and I am going to return the favor. It's time you joined me in my little corner of Hell."

Sure enough, during our junior year, Ben had recruited Danny as his helmeted accomplice so he could raise start-up capital by wagering on football games, outcomes easily facilitated from Danny's position at quarterback. At the time, Ben was desperate for money because he'd struck out with so many venture capital companies that his vision for *Cavanaugh Weekly* was fading. As always, Ben's sense of the inner workings of people and his timing was perfect. At the time, Danny was disillusioned and vulnerable. From the sidelines, he'd watched a player of lesser abilities occupy his spot at quarterback. Then later, his frustration was compounded when he learned that his coach had been sexually involved with his rival. For Danny, football had been trivialized and dishonored. His dedication to the sport, previously at religious intensities, had sunk to an unprecedented low. So what if he held back a little to help a friend? For the first time in his life, football was merely a game.

"So those payments to Danny were extortion?" I asked, trying to piece it all together.

"No," Ben said as he rose to his feet. "It was never about money for Danny. He got his cut from my wagers, but he never asked for money again. I sent him money when I realized Danny was going to be a problem, to keep him silent. He was struggling after college. He lived with constant pain from his football injuries. He took any pills he could get his hands on to ease the pain. He drank a lot. He was fast becoming a bitter, angry asshole. But, I knew loyalty was still central to Danny. I tried to trade on it."

It rained harder than ever. I remained beside the stone beneath my umbrella as Ben paced around it, soaked from the downpour.

"He acted like we'd sold our country's nuclear secrets to the Russians," Ben ranted. "I couldn't get Danny to put our wagering behind him."

While circling the marker with Constance Marilyn Matthews chiseled in gray granite, Ben abruptly dropped to his knees and looked skyward. With tears and rain streaming down his face, he screamed at the heavens, "He wanted me to kill him. He dared me."

In exactly two months, Danny told Ben he planned to reveal their little secret, their wagering conspiracy, at a press conference on the football field at SU, as if he was challenging him to use the interim to stop him. He didn't come right out and say it, not in so many words at least, but the implication was clear.

The revelation would ruin Ben, discrediting and dismantling everything he'd worked for, personally, professionally, and politically. And, stopping it would also ruin him because killing Danny, whether he got away with it or not, would leave Ben with guilt comparable to Danny's. Plus, Danny's death, in Danny's own mind, was an added bonus since Ben would end his daily suffering. It was definitely the mad, twisted scheme of a tormented and suicidal soul, someone who had clearly found his own rock bottom.

On the night of the murder, Ben took a handgun from his father's house and drove to Condor, arriving at a little after midnight.

He parked alongside The Bayside Motel and walked to Danny's room. On arrival, Ben turned the knob before knocking, and it was unlocked. In one movement, he opened the door, stepped inside, and closed it behind him. Inside the room, there weren't any lights on, only the bright glow from the television set. Danny was in a reclined position on the bed. He barely stirred.

Unfazed by his unscheduled but somewhat expected caller, Danny slowly rose from the bed and faced Ben. The two men stood just fifteen feet apart, and Ben tossed the sunglasses in the air toward Danny. He caught them. Their exchange was almost as brief.

"Are you surprised to see me?" Ben inquired, holding the gun in his unsteady, gloved hand, trying to determine whether there was any bluff in Danny's bravado.

"I'm not surprised," Danny replied coolly, uncommon for someone staring at the business end of a gun barrel.

"I was expecting you," he added.

"I will shoot you, Danny. Don't doubt it."

"I know. You have to do it. There's no limit to what you'd do to save your career or campaign."

"Any chance you'll reconsider?" Ben asked.

"About as much chance as you and me traveling back in time and undoing what we did."

Ben felt obligated to offer Danny a reprieve from his self-imposed death sentence but never expected he'd accept the offer and back down. Danny had been disillusioned, bitter, and angry for more than a decade, living a vacant and purposeless life. He had peaked at a young age. All that remained for him was constant descent, like water. Forcing Ben to shoot him would be his last spiteful act, his last known ambition.

Ben fired the handgun twice. Despite his lifelong interest in the colonial period and the Revolutionary War, this was the first time he'd fired a gun. As a small whiff of smoke rose from the weapon, Danny grasped his chest, dropped to his knees, then face down on the floor, and it was over just that quickly.

"My hand was shaking so much, it was amazing I even hit him," Ben told me, with a first, slight trace of remorse in his voice.

"Why did you take the sunglasses?" I asked, something I had wondered about since the crime scene photos.

"I don't know," Ben returned. "The sunglasses seemed like an excuse for the visit, a way to gain access to the room. If Danny didn't open the door or if he questioned the purpose of my visit, I'd tell him I was returning his sunglasses. It didn't make a lot of sense. He knew exactly why I was there. He wanted me to do it."

* * *

Ben returned to the position I'd originally found him, seated on the ground, his back resting against his mother's stone. I moved to the other side of the headstone and sat beside him, duplicating his position, like a couple of gargoyles on opposite corners of a tall building. Already soaked, I retracted the umbrella and tossed it onto the ground beside me.

The rain continued. We sat quietly.

"We have to call Steve Todd," I finally suggested. "He'll coordinate your surrender to the authorities."

Ben nodded.

Reluctantly, I left Ben at the cemetery. From a nearby pay phone, I called the law office, and the receptionist summoned Steve from a settlement meeting to answer my call. He'd heard about the arrest warrant and was expecting our call.

"Where are you? Where is Ben?"

"We're at Crossroads Cemetery."

"Ben knows he's got to turn himself in, right?"

"He's ready, Steve."

"I'll be there in fifteen minutes."

* * *

Steve arrived unceremoniously in an unmarked police car with a homicide detective from the Cavanaugh Police Department acting as his chauffeur. Alone, he approached to confer with his client while the detective waited patiently in the car, all in accordance with the terms for Ben's surrender. In the time it took Steve to walk from the curb to Constance Matthews' gravesite, two minutes at most, he was almost as soaked as Ben and me, having arrived as the downpour accelerated.

Steve and I looked at one another other, rain pouring off our chins, foregoing any pleasantries or greeting under the circumstances.

"I've arranged for your surrender, Ben," Steve informed him. "From this moment forward, don't speak to anyone but me."

Ready to execute the arrest warrant, the homicide detective approached us. He'd allowed Steve two minutes alone with his client as promised. Now, it was time to place Ben under arrest for murder.

Ben's eyes were vacant. He looked up toward Steve and right passed him to the city's skyline in the distance, as it seemed to lure his attention, not Steve, not the detective. Viewed through the downpour, the buildings were gray and stark, even forlorn, but Ben's gaze contained affection and longing, like he was standing in the door of a bedroom, watching his lover sleep within the sheets of the mussed bed, preparing to leave her forever, never to see her or touch her soft skin again. In many ways, over the last decade or so, the city of Cavanaugh had become Ben's mistress and muse, as well as the uncontested love of his life.

At that moment, a blue and red news van with KCVN in blue across its cargo area screeched to a halt behind the unmarked police car parked at the curb. The KCVN logo slid quickly toward the back of the van as the sliding side door opened and Tyler and a cameraman leapt to the curb. The two approached rapidly, hustling through the heavy rain to the gravesite, while Tyler shouted questions at Ben from a distance, drowning out the detective who was reading Ben his rights.

"Would you like to make a statement, Mr. Matthews?" she called out at Ben. "Did you kill Danny Grainger?" she followed up.

As I watched the detective slap the handcuffs on Ben's wrists, the man in the cuffs was suddenly unrecognizable to me. It wasn't Ben anymore and that person could never again be the Ben Matthews I knew. He'd fallen too far. People don't recover from something like that. Danny couldn't do it, and Ben wouldn't either. No one could. That kind of fall caused irreparable harm.

*   *   *

On the last day of August, after filling a cardboard box with photographs, clippings, and a handful of awards from thirteen years in the publishing business, I departed my office for what might be the last time. I wasn't sure. All I knew for sure was that my heart wasn't in it anymore, and I had to get out for a while at least. I also knew I was leaving our company in Stan's capable hands though our magazine's futures were about as uncertain as mine. Circulation had fallen steadily since Ben's arrest and would probably decline further after his conviction.

Yes, Ben's conviction was inevitable, just a matter of time. When the police searched the Matthews' home they only found one of two handguns registered to Kirk Matthews. Many years back, Kirk had purchased two thirty-eight caliber Smith and Wesson handguns and, while the printing presses still operated, he kept one at the home and one at the shop. In 1989, when Kirk closed The Common Sense Print Shop, he brought the second gun home. Unfortunately for Ben, on the night of the murder, when he grabbed a gun, he choose the very gun that Kirk had fired one year earlier to scare off a burglar who'd broken into their home late one night.

Kirk reported the incident to the police but never told Ben, for fear of worrying him unnecessarily. With a quick dab of plaster and a little swipe of white paint, Kirk mended the bullet hole, but the slug remained in the attic insulation until the police dug it out, just a day after Ben's surrender. Not coincidentally, it was a perfect match with the two slugs taken from the chest of Daniel Grainger. After shooting Danny, Ben threw the handgun into the choppy waters of the bay, but the matching slug foiled Ben's attempt to distance himself from the murder weapon. The police didn't have the gun, but they had Ben.

Whether the district attorney had the evidence to convict Ben without the ballistics evidence was debatable, much was circumstantial and key testimony came from an ex-hooker and a convicted felon. And all things considered, Ben had money on his side and money often confounded the justice system by presenting testimony that blurred the line between real evidence and opinion. A high-priced lawyer might've produced reasonable doubt and Ben might've walked, fated to live the rest of his life as a social outcast, but a free man nonetheless. But now, with the murder weapon connected to him, Ben was going to jail and no barrister with a $350 hourly rate was going to save him.

"I'll be going now," I told Stan, standing in his doorway with the box in my hands.

"You keep in touch," he returned, though we both knew that was a given. In reality, neither of us knew what to say.

I walked the hallway to the door of the lobby where I paused and rearranged my grip so I could open it.

"Hey," Stan called out to me, his head popping out of his doorway. "When am I going to get that article?" he asked, looking to land one last jibe before I departed.

"Actually Stan," I said, smiling because I finally had an answer for him, "after all that I've been through, I think it's a book."

Epilogue

In the autumn of 1929, the American stock market suffered a major crash. October 28th and 29th were notable dates and thought of as the crash, but the truth was that it was part of a much larger decline that continued for several years, wiping out much American wealth as well as all sense of normalcy. When the stock market finally bottomed in July of 1932, in the midst of the Great Depression, the Dow Jones Industrial Average had lost almost 90 percent of its value. For most Americans, many of whom had immigrated to this country in pursuit of their American dream, their daily existence had become a nightmarish and futile search for meals, shelter, and employment.

Simultaneous to the financial upheaval, a handful of architects and builders in New York City looked over sketches, drawings, and plans for the most amazingly spectacular building that had ever been considered, one that would climb 102 stories in beautiful Art Deco splendor, become an instant, incomparable design, engineering, and construction marvel, and claim the illustrious distinction of World's Tallest. Despite the ongoing adversity in the nation, with its epicenter only blocks away, all involved in the project were determined that the building would be built because it was simply too significant, too magnificent, and too beautiful not to be built.

In January of 1930, despite the crash, the looming depression, and an office glut in New York City, the excavation of the building's foundation commenced. In the following months, the building rose into the city's skyline at a rate of four-and-one-half stories per week, a production pace never seen before or matched since. On opening day, May 1, 1931, the Empire State Building achieved an occupancy rate of only 23 percent, despite promotions and reasonable rates, leaving most floors tenantless and vacant, causing some at N.Y. newspapers to label the new skyscraper, the "Empty State Building." At the time, many considered the building to be a failure.

But, oh, what a glorious failure it was.

About the Author

Michael Bowe is a graduate of Georgetown University and recipient of a Masters in Business Administration (MBA). He is an accomplished businessman, entrepreneur, investor, novelist, and poet, and a resident of Vashon Island, WA, a short ferry ride from Seattle. The San Francisco Book Review heralded his first novel, *Skyscraper of a Man*, as "a stunning and inimitable debut with Silver Screen potential."

If you enjoyed this novel, please suggest it to your friends and family, post a review on Goodreads and Amazon, or mention it on your social media sites. As an independent author, I really appreciate your kind words and recommendations.

Made in the USA
San Bernardino, CA
02 March 2020